SWEET DISTRACTION

Julien had been grateful for that promise of enforced silence. It could have been the opera, he had told himself, where he would have been trapped for an entire evening in a box visible to hundreds of spectators while he conversed with Miss Allen in front of her aunt—or worse, in front of Mrs. Childe. Ten minutes in the concert rooms at Hanover Square had revealed his mistake. Conversation, in the campaign he was conducting, was a shield. It permitted deflections, sidesteps, counterattacks. It was amusing. It was distracting. And now, sitting next to Serena Allen, there were no distractions.

He was achingly aware of her, of the tension in her shoulders and her fierce grip on the program in her lap. She was pretending to read it, and beneath her swept-up hair the back of her neck curved downwards, delicate and vulnerable. Even when he forced himself to look straight ahead he could see the pale, graceful arc out of the corner of his eye. Looking at his own program was no better. He could not stop thinking about her.

BOOK YOUR PLACE ON OUR WEBSITE AND MAKE THE READING CONNECTION!

We've created a customized website just for our very special readers, where you can get the inside scoop on everything that's going on with Zebra, Pinnacle and Kensington books.

When you come online, you'll have the exciting opportunity to:

- View covers of upcoming books
- Read sample chapters
- Learn about our future publishing schedule (listed by publication month *and author*)
- Find out when your favorite authors will be visiting a city near you
- Search for and order backlist books from our online catalog
- Check out author bios and background information
- Send e-mail to your favorite authors
- Meet the Kensington staff online
- Join us in weekly chats with authors, readers and other guests
- Get writing guidelines
- AND MUCH MORE!

**Visit our website at
http://www.kensingtonbooks.com**

THE SPY'S KISS

NITA ABRAMS

ZEBRA BOOKS
Kensington Publishing Corp.

www.kensingtonbooks.com

ZEBRA BOOKS are published by

Kensington Publishing Corp.
850 Third Avenue
New York, NY 10022

All Kensington titles, imprints, and distributed lines are available at special quantity discounts for bulk purchases for sales
promotion, premiums, fund-raising, educational, or institu-
tional use.

Special book excerpts or customized printings can also be created to fit specific needs. For details, write or phone the office
of the Kensington Special Sales Manager: Attn. Special Sales
Department. Kensington Publishing Corp., 850 Third Avenue,
New York, NY 10022. Phone: 1-800-221-2647.

Zebra and the Z logo Reg. U.S. Pat. & TM Off.

First Printing: March 2005
10 9 8 7 6 5 4 3 2 1

Printed in the United States of America

As always, many thanks to my research assistants and travel companions: MKM, Mom, Dad, and the indefatigable Rachel.

1

Julien Clermont rode over to call on the Earl of Bassington two days after receiving the earl's note. The delay was, in his opinion, a remarkable feat of self-restraint. Kicking his heels in the village for forty-eight hours with his quarry less than six miles away had not been easy, but Vernon had persuaded him. According to the valet's unerring sense of propriety, an interval of several days was required for persons of Clermont's consequence before taking up such an invitation.

"Ah, yes, my consequence," Clermont had said. "We mustn't forget that."

"It would not do to appear too eager," his servant reminded him, "under the circumstances."

That argument had silenced him. He had sent off a civil reply thanking the earl and vaguely promising to call at his earliest convenience. But when the designated morning proved wet and blustery, he refused to listen to Vernon's warnings about muddy boots and colds in the chest and other disasters which might result from riding over to Boulton Park in the rain.

"I've never taken a chill in my life. As for the mud, Bassington has an army of servants, you told me so yourself. They can mop the front hall if I track in a bit of dirt."

"It is not customary in England to pay the first call in inclement weather unless one has the use of a carriage," said Vernon stiffly. "Only regular visitors will be expected on a morning like this."

"I most certainly intend to be a regular visitor." Clermont picked up his leather notebook and stuffed it into a small satchel along with the case for his magnifying glass. "And," he added, looking out the window of his parlor on the upper floor of the Burford Arms, "it has stopped raining."

"Not for long," was the valet's parting shot as his master headed out the door.

Vernon was right, as usual. Julien had barely passed the junction at the outskirts of Burford when the sky began to darken. By the time he came up to the stone wall, which protected Bassington's park from the traffic on the Bath road, tiny drops were beginning to brush the side of his face.

He drew rein and thoughtfully eyed the rusted iron gate in the wall. If he kept to the road he still had three miles to go. The gate, he knew, led to the wood which adjoined the lower end of the garden west of Boulton Park. He had explored this part of the earl's land several times now, and had even ventured into the gardens late one night. If he cut through the trees and went over the hill, he could be at the house in ten minutes. What was worse—to arrive soaked, or to trespass yet again, this time in daylight?

He knew what Vernon would advise: retreat to the inn and wait until tomorrow. Or hire the hideous carriage which sat, slightly tilted to one side, in the stable of the Burford Arms. Waiting until tomorrow was out of the question. And picturing the state of the upholstery in the inn's ancient vehicle, Clermont decided that even a very damp visitor would make a better impression than a visitor who was picking tufts of decaying mustard-colored velvet off his garments as he climbed the front steps. All in all, it made sense to take his chances on the shortcut. There was not much risk that he would be spotted approaching through the park. No gardener was likely to be out in this weather, and he had never seen a soul on his forays into the wood during the past week. He dismounted and led his horse up to the gate. It was unlocked. He had pried open the padlock himself on his first expedition into the enemy's territory.

The gate gave its customary screech as he pushed it open, and a clump of blackbirds darted up from the branches above him. His horse sidled and stamped at the sound, sending more birds into the air. Closing the gate behind him produced yet another eruption. He swung back into the saddle and turned his horse onto the narrow path which threaded its way east from the road. There was a long, muddy ascent, which he remembered, and several gullies full of melting ice, which he had not remembered. The gelding, slipping once or twice, grew nervous and Clermont judged it safer to proceed at a walk. The wind had picked up, and drops were showering down on him from the leafless branches. Still, he thought, he would emerge from the woods in a minute or two and, if he were lucky, could cut down to the front drive before the rain began in earnest.

He was not lucky. At the bottom of the hill, just as he was riding up out of yet another mud-filled ditch, the bushes ahead of him shifted suddenly. A short, slight figure leaped out onto the path in front of him, wearing a shapeless wool hat pulled down over the eyes and a large red muffler, which concealed the lower part of his face. One gloved hand was clenched at his side. The other was holding a pistol, pointed straight at Clermont.

Clermont's first thought was that some gamekeeper was about to shoot him as a poacher, and while he fought to get his startled horse back under control he was trying to remember which of his six pockets held the earl's letter. But as the chestnut subsided, it dawned on him that keepers rarely lay in wait for poachers at ten in the morning. Moreover, the person in front of him was rather small to be a keeper—not to mention oddly dressed, in a short jacket and breeches which clashed oddly with the shapeless hat. The hand holding the pistol was trembling violently. Above the muffler, blue eyes were bright with a feverish combination of terror and exhilaration.

It was a boy, he realized. He took in for the first time the fine leather boots, the silver buttons on the jacket. He would give good odds that this was Bassington's son. The eleven-year-old viscount, according to the groom at the Burford Arms, was "a rare handful," an assessment which appeared to be, if anything, an understatement. And the gun was a deadly one, a long-barreled dueling pistol, with a trigger made to go off at the lightest touch. Clermont thought that on balance he would have been safer with an angry gamekeeper.

"Stand and deliver," the boy croaked in what was meant to be a gruff bass. The effect was somewhat spoiled by the layers of wool over his mouth.

"Is your pistol loaded?" demanded Clermont, hoping the answer was no.

"Yes, of course," said the boy indignantly in his normal voice. The muffler slipped and Clermont caught a glimpse of a fine-boned face and fair hair before the would-be highwayman hastily pulled it up again.

Keeping his tone casual, Clermont said, "Are you certain? Did you keep the powder dry?"

The boy looked down involuntarily at his damp jacket.

"Let me have a look." Clermont nudged his horse forward and reached for the gun. "I'll return it," he promised, as he saw the boy hesitate.

Grudgingly the gun was released.

"A Manton," Clermont said matter-of-factly as he examined it. "One of the new ones, with a water-proof pan. If you loaded it correctly, the powder should be fine." He held it out at arm's length, pointed it over the trees, and pulled the trigger. A sharp report set his horse dancing and produced a veritable explosion of agitated blackbirds. "Is that how you knew I was coming?" he asked, gesturing towards the clouds of birds. "From seeing the birds fly up near the gate?"

"You liar!" The boy was furious. "You said you would give it back!"

Julien extended the pistol. "Here it is."

"But now it isn't loaded!"

"Otherwise, I assure you, it would be very irresponsible of me to keep my promise." He added in severe tones, "This thing can fire if you even twitch a finger, let alone wave it up and down as you were doing. You could have killed my horse just now playing your little game of highwayman."

The boy looked taken aback. "That's only Budge's chestnut," he muttered sulkily after a moment. "He can't be worth much; he shies at everything and stumbles if you try to make him trot when he doesn't want to. I'll wager my father wouldn't have to pay more than five pounds for him."

"You could have killed *me*, then," Clermont pointed out.

"You're a trespasser. For all I know you're—you're a robber. Or a smuggler."

The wind dropped for a moment, and in the lull, Clermont caught the sound of voices shouting. They faded away and then grew closer. He heard hoofbeats and an agitated cry: "Master Simon! Master Simon, are you here?" Then another, breathless voice, calling out that there were footprints on the path.

"This is your fault," hissed the boy, glaring. "They would never have found me if you hadn't fired the gun."

"Who is 'they'?" asked Clermont, holding out his hand imperatively for the pistol.

"My tutor and Bates." Sullenly the boy relinquished

it for the second time. "You're not going to keep it, are you?" he asked, looking anxious. "It's my father's."

For answer, Clermont leaned over and flipped the telltale slouch hat into the bushes. "Unwind that muffler," he advised. "And don't say anything foolish."

The next minute an elderly groom had cantered up, followed by a blond man in his twenties with one of the worst seats Clermont had ever seen. The groom simply eyed the boy in grim silence, but the younger man slid clumsily off his horse, scolding before his feet even touched the ground.

"Simon, have you no consideration for your mother? She is nearly in hysterics! We've been searching for half an hour, and when we heard the gunshot I assure you the countess was not the only one to feel anxiety on your behalf." He surveyed his pupil with displeasure. "What she will say when she learns you have been out in the wet without your cap I do not know. You promised faithfully, you may recall, to wear both your cap and your muffler and to return at the first sign of rain or snow."

"I beg your pardon, Mr. . . . .?" Clermont interposed.

"Royce," said the tutor stiffly.

"Mr. Royce, then. Your pupil saw me struggling with my horse and came to assist me. I am sure you would have done the same." Having successfully diverted attention from Simon, he anticipated the tutor's next question. "I was riding along the road south of the park and saw a suspicious-looking fellow in a frieze coat prying open the gate. I shouted and he ran into the woods; I followed him in, of course, and when he heard me behind him he fired at me. My horse took exception to the noise, and if this young man had not run up and seized the bridle I believe I should have taken a nasty fall."

"Is this true?" demanded the tutor, frowning at the boy.

"Are you calling me a liar?" Clermont's tone was

mild, but the groom, who had been examining the torn branches of the shrubs near the path, suddenly lifted his head.

Royce drew himself up. "Who might you be?" he asked, still suspicious. "You do realize that you are trespassing? I've a good mind to summon the constable and see what he thinks of your story about a man in a frieze coat."

Sighing, Clermont fished in his pockets until he found the envelope. "This will no doubt be a disappointment to you," he said, holding it up so that the crest was clearly visible, "but the earl is expecting me. He has kindly offered to let me examine his father's butterfly collection. My name is Clermont."

There was a stunned silence. Simon was the first to break it. "*You* are the old man who is coming to look at the butterflies?"

"Simon!" said the tutor sharply.

"Well, they always are," Simon said. "Old, that is. And they hunch, and smell of cheap snuff, and wear spectacles. I wish I could see Serena's face when she discovers you are her latest charge!"

"That's quite enough." The tutor had Simon's arm in an iron grip, but he smiled thinly at Julien. "The earl is indeed expecting you, Mr. Clermont. I have been serving as his secretary lately and recall your correspondence perfectly." He added, in the most natural tone Clermont had heard him use, "I fear I am better suited to secretarial duties than to pedagogical ones. I must ask you to forgive the viscount's lack of conduct." He added in a low voice to Simon, "After you have changed into dry things and had your tonic perhaps you will write your father's guest a note of apology."

"No, no, that won't be necessary," said Clermont hastily. But the tutor was pushing the errant viscount onto his horse and leading the animal off with a sketch of a bow in farewell.

"If you'll follow me, I'll show you around to the stables, Mr. Clermont," said the groom. He scrupulously avoided looking at the slight bulge in Clermont's coat pocket.

After studying the older man for a moment, Julien took out the pistol and handed it to him. "Make sure you clean it before you put it back," he said. "And you might advise the earl to lock his weapons away from now on."

The groom snorted. "Much good that would do. Master Simon can open any lock in the house. Why, he's taken his mother's jewelry out of the safe just to plague her."

"Why isn't he off at school?" asked Julien bluntly.

"He has a delicate constitution," the man explained, his face expressionless.

Julien raised one eyebrow. "Indeed. How very convenient."

"Just so, sir," said the groom with feeling, pocketing the pistol and the coin which accompanied it. "I'll see this is returned, and no one the wiser."

2

Knowledge of herbs and simples, now, alas, thought suitable only for rustics, was once the province of every well-bred woman.
— Miss Cowell's Moral Reflections
for Young Ladies

Serena was in the still-room, scowling at a jar filled with a pale, viscous liquid, when the maidservant came to fetch her.

"Begging your pardon, miss," said the girl breathlessly. "Your aunt sent me to tell you that a gentleman is here to see the butterflies, and would you be at liberty to show him upstairs and explain how the trays are labeled."

"Is Mr. Royce not available?" she asked, looking up briefly.

"He is with Master Simon, miss. And in any case the countess asked for you particularly. Apparently this gentleman will be working with the specimens in the locked cabinets, and Mr. Royce is not familiar with them."

"No, he isn't." With a sigh, Serena untied her apron and hung it on a hook. "I might have known one of the scientists would arrive just now," she muttered, giving the jar a black look. "Five crowns this wretched thing cost me, not to mention the knife I ruined cutting it open, and it *still* hasn't separated."

The maid peered curiously at the jar o

dowsill and then at the fibrous shards piled on the table. "What is it?"

"Coco-nut oil. Or it would be, if it would only separate." Serena frowned. "Perhaps I did not dry the meat long enough before I pressed it. Or I should have opened the window sooner when I was chilling it." She began to ruffle impatiently through the untidy pile of recipe cards on the table, until an embarrassed cough from the maid reminded her that a visitor was waiting.

"It does smell rather nice, miss," offered the maid timidly as she held open the door.

Serena, after three hours of struggling with her extraction, was heartily sick of the cloying odor. But she knew the maid was offering an apology for interrupting her, so she smiled wryly over her shoulder as she went over to the basin and rinsed her hands. "I hope my aunt agrees with you, since I suspect I will reek of Coco-nut for the rest of the day." She looked around for a towel, remembered that both of them were now sitting under the disemboweled fruit, and wiped her fingers surreptitiously on her skirts as she ducked into the back hallway. "Could you return this to Mrs. Fletcher?" she asked, locking the door and holding out the key. "I'll go straight up to the library."

"Certainly, miss." The maid tucked the key into one of her apron pockets. "But the gentleman is in the drawing room, with your aunt." She added diffidently, "The countess hoped it would not take you too long to change and join them."

"The drawing room?" Serena looked at the maid in astonishment. The butterfly-men, as Simon called them, were usually received by Royce and taken to the library, which adjoined the cabinet-rooms. Occasionally the earl would stop in and greet an especially learned visitor. The countess, however, paid little attention to the scientists and certainly had never admitted one to her drawing room. Frowning, Serena considered what prompted her aunt to this unusual hospitality. Out of the corner of her eye she spotted two servants hurrying down the kitchen stairs. Something was odd. Breakfast was long over; luncheon two hours away. And now the maid was sidling away, avoiding her gaze.

"Lucy," said Serena. There was an edge in her voice. The maid stopped, looking wary.

"This gentleman isn't by any chance a *young* gentleman, is he? An unmarried young gentleman?"

The maid hesitated. "I'm sure I couldn't say, miss."

Serena raised her eyebrows.

"Whether he might be married, that is," the maid said hastily, conceding the question of age.

"Well-dressed?"

"Yes, miss."

"I will wager," said Serena between her teeth, "that he has no more interest in butterflies than you do."

"Oh, no," said the maid earnestly. "I think they are lovely—that is, Mrs. Fletcher permits me to help Hubert dust the trays every so often, only in the first two cabinets, of course, the ones all the visitors can look at. . . ." She turned pink and started again. "It's a very polite young man, and he has a magnifying glass in a case, and a notebook, and a pincushion, and a little ivory rule, just like all the other gentlemen." The tone of her voice made it clear that in all other ways he was most unlike the usual denizens of the library.

"If he were just like all the others, he would not be in the drawing room," Serena pointed out. "And no one would have thought I needed to change my gown." Her eyes narrowed thoughtfully. "Am I presentable?" she asked abruptly, holding out her skirts and pivoting slightly.

"With all due respect, miss, no," said Lucy, surveying the frayed cuffs of Serena's wool gown and the still visible patches of damp at the hips.

"Good," said Serena with a cold smile. A

headed purposefully for the stair which led up to the drawing room.

The Countess of Bassington surveyed her preparations with satisfaction. Fresh flowers had been brought in from the greenhouse and set on the side table. The Sheraton chairs and the small table were now behind a screen. A chaise and wing chair huddled awkwardly in the corner by the pianoforte. There remained in the center of the room only three pieces of furniture: a low-backed armchair (her own headquarters for this first stage of the campaign); a walnut and ivory tea table, which would soon hold some light refreshments; and her latest acquisition, an elegant scroll-backed sofa covered in Chinese silk. How very fortunate that she had been walking by the library when Pritchett had brought the young man in. How fortunate, as well, that the visitor's damp, untidy clothing had not misled her for an instant. Her trained eye had noted the ruby stick-pin hanging slightly askew in his cravat, the fine cut of his jacket, and then, incredulously, the gold signet ring. The startled butler, who had expected to leave the visitor to await Royce's convenience, found himself hurrying off with orders for two of the upstairs maids, a footman, the housekeeper, the earl's valet, and even Bassington himself.

The aforesaid footman, still slightly out of breath from a rapid bout of furniture moving, now reappeared, holding the door for the earl.

"Go away," said the countess to her husband. "You were not to come up until I sent for you."

The earl took in the flowers, the little island of furniture, and the hovering servant. "May I be excused from whatever is afoot?" he asked. "I am rather occupied at the moment."

"You most certainly may not be excused! I need you."

"What is it today? Comforter of the bereaved Sir Reginald? Patron of Lady Orset's hospital? Surely Serena could assist you? I thought you were not at home today; you told me at breakfast it was too wet for callers."

She looked at his rumpled jacket and the telltale inkstains on his cuff. "You've been working." It came out as an accusation.

"My love, it is sometimes necessary," he said mildly. "There is a war on, you know."

"I hoped Royce would be able to do more for you," she muttered. "He certainly isn't a very good tutor; I only kept him on because he seemed as though he could be useful as a secretary." She had had other reasons for encouraging Jasper Royce to remain at Boulton Park, but she had kept them to herself.

"He is useful. But he is also, my dear, a bit of an ass—if you will excuse my blunt language. I daren't trust him with this. And if Sir Reginald and Lady Orset and the Derrings and all our other neighbors will be offended to find me shut up in my study when they call, I shall have to go back to London."

She doubted he would execute this threat; he did not like London at this time of year. But she knew that any sign of irritation in her husband required careful management. Normally she would have sent him back to his reports with her blessing. He was already turning to go, believing he had won the battle.

"George!" she said, pleading.

He looked exasperated.

"I know what you are thinking, but it is *not* Sir Reginald," she added hastily. Their elderly neighbor, a wealthy and childless widower, required frequent consolation for the perfidy of his younger relations, who unfailingly proved to have no sense of duty or affection but merely to be waiting for his demise. His visits usually lasted far longer than the conventional morning call and involved detailed explanations of the latest changes in his will.

"That young man who wrote to inquire about the butterfly collection. Mr. Clermont. He has just arrived. And," she said with unusual emphasis, "he is wearing a very remarkable signet ring."

"What's his ring to do with anything? Clara, I wish you would not talk in riddles. If you insist, of course I shall come up. Briefly." He grimaced. "He did have a letter of introduction from young Derring; they were at school together. I suppose I should make an appearance."

"He's in one of the spare bedrooms at the moment; the storm caught him and I sent Tuckett up to help him with his wet things. He will be down at any moment." She glanced at her husband's stained cuff and debated asking him to change his shirt, then thought better of it and waved him away. "Off with you; I don't want you here yet. But be sure to come up the minute I send for you."

The earl was used to his wife's stage-managed social events; he bowed ironically and moved to the door.

"Oh," said the countess, as though remembering. "Bates says we had an intruder in the park. Mr. Clermont tried to pursue him and was shot at for his pains."

"The devil you say!" Shocked, the earl swung around. "I beg your pardon, Clara. But why did Bates not tell me at once?"

No need to worry now that her husband would not come up when she sent for him in half an hour, she thought, very pleased with herself. He might not care, as she did, about presentable young men, but he would certainly want to hear about a stranger prowling through the park. Two days ago he had become so obsessed with the notion that robbers were in the neighborhood that he had even hired guards to patrol the gardens at night.

"You told Pritchett you were not to be disturbed," she reminded him. She herself, of course, routinely ignored these orders.

Snorting in disgust, Bassington stalked through the door, which the impassive footman was still holding open.

"Good morning, Uncle." At the sound of Serena's voice in the hall the countess gave a silent sigh. There was a crisp bite to the consonants which was all too familiar. And indeed, here was her niece, striding into the room in a manner very reminiscent of the earl's irritated departure a moment earlier. She was not precisely frowning, but her expression was wary and hostile, and, of course, she had not changed her gown.

The countess surveyed Serena cautiously. Her hair was still in its braided coronet, and the smooth brown surface gave off little glints of red as the light struck it. Her dress was wrinkled, true, but the color—a deep green—was flattering. Serena's gray eyes tended to take on the hues of her clothing, so that just now they held a faint hint of emerald at the edges. And her posture, which was sometimes lamentable, was always at its best when she was angry. All in all, the countess decided, it could have been worse, and she surprised her niece by greeting her with a warm smile.

"You sent for me, Aunt Clara?" the girl asked. Her voice was softer than it had been in the hall. She had expected a scolding for her appearance, the countess realized, and was flustered by the omission.

"Yes, dear. It seems we have a very distinguished visitor who would like to look at the butterflies, and after I receive him I would like you to take him up to the library yourself. I hope you do not mind."

"Would—would you wish me to change? I was in the still-room," she added, flushing slightly.

A peace offering, thought the countess. Ever since her sister's only surviving child had come to live with them eight years earlier, she had taken innumerable vows to be more patient with the girl, to respect her preferences, and to refrain from giving her advice. She made another silent pledge now. "No, no," she said airily. "I had thought of it, but perhaps it is just as well; I understand Mr. Clermont wishes to work with the late earl's diaries, and some of the volumes are in a sad state."

"You mean that they smear flecks of red leather on everything they touch," said Serena with a trace of a smile. She started to say something else, but the door opened again.

The footman reappeared, flanked by Pritchett, who announced impressively, "Mr. Clermont, milady." He stepped aside and made way for her guest, whose appearance, unlike that of her niece, was now quite acceptable. His neckcloth and jacket had been pressed, his boots had been cleaned, and his hair, which had been falling over his forehead earlier, was now neatly combed. For the first time she got a good look at his face, and especially his eyes. They were very dark, with dark lashes, in curious contrast to the fair hair, which was growing lighter as it dried.

"Ah, Mr. Clermont," she said, holding out her hand. "I do hope Tuckett has made you more comfortable." Her eye searched automatically for the fascinating ring. It was now gone. A thin indentation across the base of his finger reassured her that she had not been hallucinating. Why had he removed it?

"Less disreputable, at any rate," he said smiling and bending over her hand with practiced grace. "I had not meant to put you to so much trouble, Lady Bassington. I should have postponed my call until the weather was less threatening."

"Nonsense," said the countess briskly. "At this time of year in Oxfordshire, you might spend weeks waiting for a fair morning." She gestured Serena forward. "Mr. Clermont, allow me to present my niece, Miss Allen."

Serena's eyes widened slightly, but she nodded gravely as the visitor bowed. Clermont, the countess noted with satisfaction, did not seem at all surprised by the wording of her introduction. And, as she had suspected, he was distinctly taller than Serena, something few men could claim.

"A pleasure," said Clermont formally. "I understand that you are the guardian of the Bassington cabinets, Miss Allen. I hope it will not be inconvenient for you to assist me for a few moments this morning. Once I have seen the labeling system I usually do quite well on my own, so you need not fear I shall plague you further."

"And what is your particular interest in butterflies, Mr. Clermont?" Serena asked, in a tone of voice which the countess could not help but label "skeptical."

"I am, in fact, more interested in moths. Particularly the new lunar moths described by Hübner." He gave a slight shrug. "But those are primarily Asian, and your collection is more noted for its African and South American specimens, if I am not mistaken."

Now what has he said to make her frown so? thought the countess in exasperation. There was a light knock at the door, and she turned in relief, expecting to see the maidservant bringing in the tea tray.

It was Pritchett, however. He was frowning as well. "Mr. Googe is with his lordship, my lady," he announced lugubriously. "And he would like to speak to Mr. Clermont at his earliest convenience."

"The constable is here?" Lady Bassington was aghast. "Whatever for? And what would he want with Mr. Clermont?" Then she recollected the intruder in the park. "Oh," she said, turning to Clermont in relief. "It is only about the man who fired at you. It is very tiresome, but I suppose you will have to go and be interviewed."

Serena found herself studying Clermont surreptitiously while the constable went through the laborious process of recording five pages of notes on the incident in the park. She had surprised herself by volunteering to escort him to her uncle, and surprised herself even more by remaining, seating herself inconspicuously at one side of the room in case Googe should notice her and decide that she had no business there. Which, in truth, she did not. But she was curious. Her aunt's reception of the visitor suggested strongly that he was yet another suitor, attempting to court her under the guise of examining butterfly specimens. And if he was indeed intending to woo her among the trays in the cabinet-room, she wanted to know why.

Her circle of admirers, up until now, had not included handsome young men. It had consisted almost entirely of middle-aged widowers who were prepared to overlook her small dowry and her chequered past. Was Clermont under the hatches, as Simon would say? Would even her modest portion do? Was he a Cit who had decided to marry into the peerage? Or an ambitious young politician, hoping for her uncle's patronage? True, he had responded promptly and knowledgeably to her question about his researches. That had surprised her but had not changed her initial impression that his interest in Boulton Park had nothing to do with butterflies.

His appearance, she had to admit, was unexceptionable. Quiet, expensive, well-cut jacket. Boots which must have cost even more than the jacket—and whose polish could never have been restored so quickly after his muddy ride unless they had been meticulously maintained by an experienced manservant. Fine, narrow hands. No inkstains on the fingers. She looked again at his face. Narrow, like his hands. Reserved. In the half-shadows of the study the high forehead and finely cut features took on an otherworldly purity, especially when a stray beam of light from the tiny window caught the gold highlights in his hair. She recalled his graceful bow over her aunt's hand in the drawing room. No, this was no Cit.

She had stared too long. He raised his head suddenly as Googe's rumbling voice paused—she realized that she had been unaware of who was speaking or what was being said for several minutes—and she was caught, pinned, frozen, by those unexpectedly dark eyes. Embarrassed, she glared, refusing to look away. He regarded her gravely for an instant, then turned back to the constable.

"If we might conclude our business, then, Mr. Clermont?" asked Googe, with an anxious eye on the increasingly impatient Bassington. "I'll just be asking you to confirm the following items." He cleared his throat importantly. "One young gentleman, by name Clermont, normally residing in London, presently lodging at Burford Arms, Josiah Budge, innkeeper. Riding on saddle horse hired from said inn was adjacent to forest gate of park land belonging to the earl of Bassington and observed burly man in frieze coat prying open said gate. Pursued individual, but lost sight of him in trees. Individual then fired at gentleman—what sort of gun did you say it was, sir?"

"Blunderbuss, I thought," said Clermont.

Serena, who had heard the shot clearly through the open window of the still-room, frowned but said nothing.

"Blunderbuss, yes," said Googe, looking back at his notes. "Gentleman cannot give more detailed description of intruder." He stopped, looking pleased with himself, and waited for Clermont to nod assent. Then he said in his normal voice, "I'll be off then, my lord? I fancy I'll pay a visit to Purvis and his son. They've been grumbling about your gamekeeper since last winter, claiming he took up traps from their side of the hedge. I reckon they mistook Mr. Clermont here for Jackson and decided to give him a scare."

Bassington rose and acknowledged Googe's bow as he left the room. But he did not immediately dismiss his guest. "So, you are a friend of young Derring?" he inquired casually.

"We were at school together, yes."

"Do you mean to call on Mrs. Derring while you are here?" The earl's gaze narrowed slightly; he was watching Clermont's face.

"Not unless I stay longer than I have planned. I saw Philip in London, and he told me his mother was presently with his sister in Lincolnshire. I gather Maria is to be confined any day now."

Bassington relaxed and nodded genially. "Just so; I had forgot."

"It may be just as well," said Clermont. "Were she and Mr. Derring in residence they would be pressing me to stay with them, and I would eventually have to yield and would find myself arriving at your library every day at half past two."

Serena smiled to herself. The Derring household was notorious for keeping London hours even in the country. Mrs. Derring often stayed abed until noon, and breakfast was not even served until ten.

There was a tap on the door and Pritchett came in, with a martyred air. "Mr. Googe's compliments, and could the gentleman assist him in identifying the place where the shot was fired, Bates being unable to recall precisely."

Clermont gave an oddly rueful half smile but then rose obediently and followed the butler.

"Pritchett will bring you straight up to the library when you return," Bassington called after him. "And Serena," he said, turning to her as she rose, "you should go at once and get the keys to the cabinets. The poor young man! Soaked, fired upon, and now prosed at by the worthy Googe. He has been here for nearly an hour and has yet to see a single specimen."

She waited until she was certain the servants were out of earshot. "Uncle, I know perfectly well you did not forget about Maria's confinement. You went across to say good-bye to Mrs. Derring with Aunt Clara just last week. And I heard you say yesterday that it was lucky the babe had not decided to arrive during the snow-storms last month."

The earl grunted, picked up a small pile of papers, and began to hunt through them.

"You were *testing* Mr. Clermont," she persisted.

"Nonsense."

She folded her arms. "He's a suitor, isn't he? You were trying to find out how well he knows the Derrings."

"Serena, I would not agree to receive any young man, no matter how well-connected, who proposed to woo you underhandedly by pretending an interest in the collection. You know that perfectly well."

"What if he didn't propose it? What if my aunt did?"

"I cannot imagine that she would do anything of the sort." His tone was not as firm as she would have liked. He set down the papers and cleared his throat. "It is true, however, that your aunt was hoping to greet our guest more formally."

"That is to say, I should be prepared for an elaborate luncheon now that her plan to display me in the drawing room was foiled." She pictured herself next to Clermont on the Chinese sofa in her still-damp gown, giving off Coco-nut vapors, and offered a prayer of thanks to whatever god had brought Googe so quickly from the village. But she had no illusions: the ordeal was only postponed. Her aunt was probably rearranging the small dining room at this very moment. At least now they would be at table, and she would have food to pretend to eat, and her own chair. She sighed. "I suppose I should change my gown."

He gave her a grateful smile. "Your aunt would be very pleased."

"And I suppose *you* will be forced to join us for luncheon."

The smile disappeared. "By damn, you're right," he muttered. "So much for my memorandum."

3

In one wall of the anteroom which led to her uncle's study was a small door, set into the paneled wall. It led to a back hall, and thence to the kitchen stairs and the domain of Mrs. Fletcher. Usually Serena enjoyed ducking into the servant's passages, where she could walk quickly without being reproved for unladylike deportment ("ladies must appear to glide serenely," Mrs. Childe had reminded her on numerous occasions). Now, however, she was moving in a slow, hesitant fashion very unlike her normal brisk stride. The unusual interest shown in Clermont by her aunt and uncle was suspicious, and Clermont's own story even more suspicious. She would wager everything she owned that Simon had fired that shot, and she could not see why Clermont would protect her cousin unless he wished to ingratiate himself with the family.

She paused for the third time at the head of the stairs. It would be very embarrassing to be caught. But if she went right now—if they had stopped to put on their coats, which they would surely do in this weather . . . She turned around and hurried to the conservatory. There was no one there, to her relief. She would have to hope that Lucy had already been in to water the plants. Otherwise the maid would find her lurking behind an orange tree and spying (to give the thing its true, ugly name) on her uncle's guest. It was a choice location for spying, at least. From her position at this end of the glass-enclosed terrace she had an excellent view of the gardens, and, more importantly, of the side door in the opposite wing.

A minute went by; two minutes; three. She was beginning to wonder if she had missed them, but then two figures emerged. Googe was trying hard to keep up with Clermont's long strides, and she smiled slightly, watching the short, round body bobbing in Clermont's wake. A third figure appeared now, hurrying after them. Bates? No, it was Pritchett, holding an umbrella and walking very, very fast. In fact, if she had not known Pritchett for eight years she would have said that he was nearly jogging. She leaned forward, as though the three men would be easier to see through the wet glass from an inch closer. In the fogged tableau, Clermont turned back and waved the umbrella away.

"What on earth?" she muttered. Her aunt maintained decorum in her household. A footman seen running in any Bassington home would be sacked instantly. And until now, she would have sworn that Pritchett would slit his wrists sooner than trot after a guest. Especially with an umbrella. Pritchett held by the customs of his youth, which decreed that umbrellas were for females.

"Well, well." She stared out the window a moment longer, then walked quickly out the other end of the gallery and made her way downstairs to the housekeeper's office to requisition the keys. Since an unfortunate incident with Simon, these were kept on Mrs. Fletcher's person at all times and released only to Serena or the earl.

Mrs. Fletcher was waiting for her impatiently. "High time you were here, Miss Serena," she said, unhooking the tiny silver keys from a ring at her waist. "I sent Hubert to find you; I'm needed upstairs."

"Luncheon?" guessed Serena as she slipped them into her pocket.

The housekeeper sniffed. "More like a royal banquet, if you ask me." Her sour gaze swept the kitchen, where the cook and two helpers were frantically assembling dishes. "And I'll wager that greedy Googe will have the effrontery to come right back in and smear mud all over the floor and hang his wet jacket in front of my kitchen hearth and demand another tankard of ale."

Since Googe had been pursuing the housekeeper since the day she had put off mourning for her husband six years ago, this seemed a safe wager.

Pritchett, looking strained, tapped perfunctorily at the half-open door.

"Yes, in a moment," snapped Mrs. Fletcher, seizing another, larger ring of keys from the top of her desk. She eyed Serena up and down, and Serena, knowing what was coming next, fled.

"You're to change your gown!" bellowed the housekeeper after her, so loudly that Serena was sure Clermont could hear it at the other end of the park.

"I will, I will," she promised under her breath as she ran up the stairs and dodged through another service corridor into the library. "I'll open the cabinets, and show him how to find everything, and then I'll have time while he is looking through the trays. But right now I want to see what's in his satchel." The moralists were right: one crime led to another. Spying begat more spying. After Pritchett's obsequious pursuit with the umbrella, she was more determined than ever to find out whether Mr. Clermont was in fact interested in butterflies, or whether his main interest was *Serena Alleniana*.

When she had surveyed the contents of his bag, however, she was forced to admit that Lucy had been correct. He had brought all the usual paraphernalia of the serious naturalist. Pincushion, in case any specimens were dislodged, with three sizes of pin. Rule. Magnifying glass—a very fine one, mounted in silver and ebony. Two pens, and several colors of ink. Note-book, mostly blank. That, at least, was evidence against him. Normally collectors brought extensive notes about their own specimens with them, to compare against Boulton Park's holdings. Still, the abbreviated list which filled the first three pages told her Clermont was famil-iar with the rarer items in the cabinets. And some did use a fresh book for each collection. The last item was a small sketchbook. This, too, was blank, but tucked into the back, folded carefully in half, was an exquisite watercolor of a deep purple butterfly. She recognized it after a minute as a blue diadem. There were two in the Bassington collection.

"I see you have started unpacking my things." The mild voice came from right over her shoulder.

She hadn't heard any footsteps; it was much too soon for him to have returned from the park. Yet there he was, looking gravely courteous rather than outraged.

As always, when put on the defensive Serena's instinct was to attack first. "Did you do this?" she demanded, holding up the watercolor.

"It's very fine, isn't it? No, alas."

"Your sketchbook is empty," she said pointedly. "Save for the blue diadem here." She gave it to him.

"It's usually empty." He folded the painting back up and tucked it away. "My intentions are good. But the ex-ecution falls so far short of the intention that I give up and razor the pages out." He showed her the inside cover of the book, and now she could see a little line of page stubs. "If ever I produce anything one-tenth as good as this"—he tapped the folded watercolor—"I shall en-gage to keep it in the book."

"Who did paint it, then?"

He smiled. It was a perfectly polite smile, but some-thing in his eyes suggested that he was well aware of her hostility and found it amusing. "A lady of my acquaintance." After a pause just long enough to be suggestive, he added, "A granddaughter of Mendes daCosta."

"Oh," she said in a small voice. DaCosta had been one of the founding members of the Aurelians, and a Fellow of the Royal Society. Then she rallied. "I had thought perhaps your wife might be assisting you in your researches."

Now he was definitely amused. "I am not married, Miss Allen."

It was her turn to smile, a smile which showed all her teeth. "I had a narrow escape once myself," she said sweetly. "As I'm sure you will agree, it is not always easy to preserve one's independence in the face of well-meaning relatives." *Don't think me ready to fall in with my aunt's schemes, you coxcomb.*

He was not dull-witted; she had to give him that. He took her point at once. But instead of changing the subject, as she had expected, he guided it into less dangerous territory. "Surely even unmarried folk have duties and responsibilities. Are you, for example, a dedicated student of butterflies, or is your guardianship of this collection more in the nature of a filial obligation to your uncle?"

"I am an amateur," she admitted. His dark eyes were studying her face carefully, and, flustered, she busied herself with the keys, turning them in her hands as though deciding which was which. "But in comparison to anyone else here at Boulton Park, I suppose I must be reckoned the nearest thing to a naturalist we possess." She picked up the volumes she had laid out on the table and moved over to the door of the cabinet-room. "Well," she corrected herself, "there is Simon. My cousin. He will suddenly decide that he must learn all there is to know about, say, black beetles, and poor Mr. Royce will be compelled to read through everything in the library about insects for weeks, and send to London for pamphlets, and go on expeditions to the cellars hunting for live ones. It usually is something rather revolting, like black beetles," she added reflectively. "Sometimes I fancy Simon does it solely to annoy my aunt."

He held open the door to the smaller room for her, and as she walked through ahead of him, she suddenly remembered something else Simon might have done to annoy his mother.

"Did Simon fire that shot?" she asked, wheeling around to face him. "It didn't sound like a blunderbuss."

For the first time since she had met him he looked unsure of himself. Before answering, he hesitated.

"Will you keep what I tell you in confidence?"

"I knew it," she muttered. "Drat the boy. That means yes, I take it."

He shook his head. The slightly amused smile was back. "I fired it."

"*You* did?"

"Your instincts were correct, however. Simon had, er, borrowed one of your uncle's dueling pistols. I managed to remove it from him for a moment and decided to discharge it before he could point it at me again."

"I see." She did see. She shuddered at the picture of Simon with a loaded dueling pistol and wondered briefly how on earth Clermont had persuaded her cousin to hand it over. "Where is it now?"

"I gave it to the groom—Bates, is it?—to be discreetly restored to its place."

"Why?"

He shrugged, an odd, careless gesture which seemed to belong to another person. "Might I ask you a question in return?" he said after a moment. "What does this man Purvis look like? The one the constable mentioned?"

Serena frowned. "Stout, square-faced, dark hair."

"I would be very grateful, then, if you could let me know how Mr. Googe's investigations are proceeding. Unfortunately I described the fellow as burly, since that is the usual description of villains in the penny papers.

I was hoping Purvis might prove to be thin and weasel-faced."

She smiled at that, a real smile this time. "Very well," she promised. "I shall keep you informed." She turned back towards the cabinets. "How long will you be in the neighborhood?" she asked over her shoulder.

"Three or four days," he replied absently. He was looking around, now that they were fully inside the octagon which held the Bassington collection. Against each of the eight walls stood tall mahogany cabinets—wide ones against the six side walls; narrow ones on each side of the window, which faced north, and the door, which led back into the library.

"All the cabinets but two are unlocked," Serena explained, moving to the other side of the room. "These two, by the windows." She unlocked them, then pocketed the keys. "I'm afraid I will need to lock them again before you go down to luncheon; they can never be left open."

"They contain the specimens purchased from the Drury estate?"

"Yes." She moved briskly around the room, pointing at the numbers etched in brass on the top corners of the other cabinets. "The other cabinets are numbered, and the trays inside are lettered. This register"—she held up the smaller of the two volumes she had carried in—"lists specimens by cabinet and tray number; the other is by date of acquisition. Unfortunately the late earl fell ill before he could catalogue the specimens in the Drury cabinets; they were his last purchase."

"Might I also see his journals, perhaps?"

She had forgotten that he had written to request access to the diaries as well. Stepping out into the library, she rang for a footman. "They don't mention the items in the locked cabinets," she warned him while they waited for the servant to appear.

"So I was told. But Lord Bassington did know Drury

personally, and I hope to find some reminiscences." He
looked intently at the door, as if willing a footman to appear. Even after the man had been dispatched on his
errand, Clermont lingered in the outer room for a moment, staring after him. Then he turned to her, urbane as
ever. "I am very grateful for your assistance, Miss
Allen."

It was a dismissal, unmistakably. He was already
moving towards the cabinet-room.

"Please ring if you need anything," she said, trying to
match his cool tone. "I am afraid my aunt is planning a
formal luncheon, but you should have a few hours to
work before it is ready." With the barest of nods, she
withdrew, uncertain whether his obvious lack of interest in her was a ruse, an insult, or a relief.

By the end of the day, her uncertainties had only mul-
tiplied. If Julien Clermont was pursuing her, he was
concealing it admirably. When she had returned with
the keys nearly two hours later, he was totally absorbed
in the diaries and only rose to greet her several seconds
after she had come into the room. A tray was out on the
table, with the ruler set down next to a particularly fine
South American skipper; a quick glance showed that his
notebook had several new pages of scribbles in what
looked like Latin. He made no excuses to detain her
when she unlocked the Drury shelves again after luncheon, and he took his leave politely at five after
refusing an invitation from her aunt to stay for dinner.

Nor did he seem to be cultivating her uncle. His table
manners were impeccable, and while the party consumed
the countess's elaborate midday meal he conversed ami-
ably, but he did not display any special interest in politics.
In fact, when Sir Charles Barrett—another last minute
guest, who had stopped on his way north from Bath to
consult her uncle—made some caustic observations about

the current disarray in Parliament and solicited Clermont's views, Clermont shook his head and expressed an utter inability to understand the workings of government. "Insects are much more straightforward," he had said, smiling.

"Especially dead ones," Barrett had retorted.

Clermont had laughed.

And yet her aunt, for some reason, clearly believed this visitor was very important. She had seated him at her right. This was not only a flagrant violation of protocol, once Sir Charles had appeared, but a poor tactical choice if her aim was to interest him in Serena, who was necessarily relegated to her uncle's end of the table. The countess had hovered over Clermont, urging him to try every dish and solicitously changing the topic of conversation if it did not seem to engage him. When the invitation to dinner was declined, she had then asked if perhaps the following evening might be convenient. Pressed so hard, Clermont could not refuse, but even Serena could see that the impetus was all her aunt's and none of his.

Most curious of all was Sir Charles's behavior. Before continuing on towards London he had come to find her in the still-room, where she was struggling once again with her extraction. He was an old family friend—the Barretts' town house in London adjoined the Bassingtons', and Sir Charles and the earl often worked together on projects for the Foreign Office—but she had been surprised to see him.

"I beg your pardon," he had said. "Lady Barrett asked me most particularly to see if you might have a recipe for elderberry syrup."

She stared incredulously. Elderberry syrup was so simple that a child could make it. But she went over to her recipe box, pulled out the card, and began to copy it. It took less than one minute, since the recipe said: "Boil one pt. fresh elderberries, crushed and strained, for 1 hr.

Add 1/4 cup honey, ginger, and juice of one lemon. Strain twice; top with three fingers brandy and seal."

Without comment she handed the card to Sir Charles.

He sighed. "Miss Allen, you do not make things easy, do you?"

"I prefer honesty," she said shortly.

"Very well, I shall honor your preference. What can you tell me of Mr. Clermont?"

"Almost nothing. He arrived today, and is working with the Drury collection."

"Your uncle mentioned that he is a friend of young Derring."

"Yes, he seems to know the family well." It was disturbing, in fact, that her uncle and now Barrett would question a personal reference from Philip. After a mercifully brief period when he had fancied himself in love with her, Philip had become one of her most trusted friends.

"Do you think he is, in truth, interested in butterflies?"

She hedged. "He is certainly knowledgeable." How could she put her suspicions into words? She had no evidence, none, only a vague feeling that Clermont was somehow alien to the world of the lepidopterists.

To her surprise, Barrett seemed to understand. "It looks right and feels wrong," he suggested.

"Yes." After a minute, she added reluctantly, "My aunt might have arranged for him to visit here to—to make my acquaintance."

"I had not thought of that possibility," he had admitted. "Still . . . if anything suspicious occurs, I would urge you most strongly to tell your uncle immediately. I shall make some inquiries of my own in London."

She had promised, and he had taken his leave, pocketing the recipe card as scrupulously as if Sara Barrett had really requested it.

All in all, it had made for an unsettling and confusing

day, and in a moment of panic she had made it even worse by excusing herself from dinner, pleading a headache.

Now she was sitting up in bed with a book, but she had not read more than a few pages. She was furious with herself. She hated deceiving her aunt and uncle; she hated females who conjured up headaches to escape obligations; she hated cowardice. And it was all for nothing, because her aunt would of course stop by to check on her, and the interrogation about Clermont which she had been dreading would be conducted in private—where it would be direct and thorough—instead of via arch innuendoes at the dinner table. She was hungry, as well.

There was a tap at the door, and she braced herself to confront the countess, but it was Lucy, with a tray.

"Would you be feeling well enough to eat something now, miss?" the maid asked. "Your aunt will be up shortly; they have just left the table." She set the tray down; there were rolls, cold chicken, a fruit custard, and some port, as well as a cup of bouillon. As a form of penance, Serena sent back everything but the broth. She sipped it slowly, deriving a morbid enjoyment from her stomach's protests at being fobbed off with flavored hot water.

"How are you, my dear?" The countess came in, drew up a chair, and sat down by the bed, peering anxiously at Serena. "Do you think it is something catching? Simon is not feeling well, either, poor boy."

Serena had momentarily forgotten her aunt's obsession with Simon's health. His illness, she was certain, was no more real than her own. Simon was lying low to avoid questions about the shooting incident in the park. Perhaps she could blame her current moral lapse on him: Simon was certainly a proficient liar, and feigning illness was one of his specialties. But it was unfair to blame an eleven-year-old boy for her own misbehavior, especially since his shams would have been discovered long ago if Serena had not been his willing coconspirator.

"It is nothing," she reassured her aunt. "I am already much better."

The countess eyed her anxiously. "Are you quite sure? You are so seldom ill, you know. And certain diseases can be very deceptive. Tertian fever, for example, recedes quickly after the first attack but then returns two days later with devastating force."

"Aunt Clara," said Serena, exasperated, "how on earth would I have contracted a tertian fever? I have never been out of England, and it is a disease of the tropics!"

"One of the butterflies, perhaps?" her aunt suggested doubtfully.

"Nonsense," said Serena firmly. "Those butterflies have been dead for years. Decades, in most cases. And have been fumigated with sulfur, to boot."

Her aunt brightened; she was a great believer in the sanitary properties of fumigation. "That's so; I had forgot." She rose as if to leave, then hesitated. "Perhaps as a precaution, though, you should keep to your bed tomorrow?"

For a moment Serena was tempted. She had succeeded beyond her wildest dreams in distracting her aunt from Clermont. If she wished, she could stay in bed for the next three days and never see the man again. Then she gave herself a mental shake. "Certainly not. I should be bored to distraction. And what of poor Mr. Clermont?"

The countess sat back down. "Ah, yes, Mr. Clermont. Tell me, Serena—"

A sudden loud noise from overhead silenced her. Both women looked up, startled.

"That was from Simon's room," said Serena, trying to conceal her relief at the interruption. He had probably slipped climbing up the passage behind the chimney, but the countess would go up and find him weary and chilled—a plausible invalid.

"He must have had one of his nightmares." The countess was on her feet again, headed for the door. "I'm sure the disturbance in the park this morning has upset him; he is such a sensitive child." And she hurried off—but not, Serena knew, fast enough to catch Simon before he could get back into his nightclothes.

She picked up her broth again. It was cold. And then, thinking idly about Simon and his mischief and the events of the day, something suddenly struck her. If there had been no intruder breaking in through the west gate—if Clermont (as he had all but admitted) had concocted him to protect Simon—*then why had Clermont slipped into the back side of the park through a private, locked entrance?*

4

A gentleman strives to appear to advantage on horseback.

—Precepts of Mlle. de Condé

Clermont did not return immediately to the inn when he left Boulton Park. Tension and anxiety had taken their toll, especially combined with a day spent sitting deciphering the late earl's handwriting and fetching out new butterfly trays every so often to allay suspicion. It was dusk, it was still drizzling, and the road was not familiar, but his first impulse was to set his horse to a brisk canter and take a long loop back to the inn. He was desperate for physical activity. The chestnut, however, was not. Even the encouraging words *dinner* and *stable* failed to produce more than a shambling trot.

When all his attempts to spur the horse to a reasonable pace (or, from the equine point of view, an unreasonable one, given the poor light and the half-frozen road) were unsuccessful, Clermont determined on a different solution to his frustration. He would set himself a concrete, practical task and carry it out. This would furnish the illusion that he had accomplished something in the last three days. And what more urgent, more practical task could he imagine than to find himself a decent mount? He rode on past the inn, therefore, and headed south for several miles until he reached the Bath road, where there was a substantial posting house. Here he acquired a bay mare with the ominous name of Tempest, who proved her suitability for his purposes by tossing her head furiously, shying at his hat, and attempting to bite him. There was a very satisfactory wrestling match most of the way back to the inn, and he arrived at the Burford Arms bruised, disheveled, and feeling much better.

"Well, I'll be, it's Tempest!" Jeb, the innkeeper's grandson and part-time ostler, stared open-mouthed at the mare as Clermont and he rode up. "Where's my granda's horse, then? Sir," he added belatedly.

"He'll be sent back tomorrow from the Queen's Rest. I fancied a bit of a challenge." Clermont swung down from the saddle and attempted to hand the boy Tempest's reins.

Jeb backed away instinctively. "She bites, sir," he offered by way of apology.

Sighing, Clermont fished a coin out of his pocket and handed it over.

"And she kicks, as well," Jeb added hopefully.

A *douceur* was one thing, extortion was another. Clermont tried the same cold stare he had given the viscount in the woods when demanding the pistol. It worked. Jeb grudgingly took the reins and led the horse away, muttering under his breath about fools who would exchange a well-behaved horse like Satin for a she-devil infamous in three counties.

Inside the inn, Clermont got a cheerful welcome from Budge, who promised to send a bottle of wine up straightway. Upstairs, however, his welcome was less cordial. Vernon was waiting with folded arms in the parlor of their small suite.

"Well?" he demanded as soon as the door closed behind his master. Recollecting his duties, he took Clermont's coat and hat and hung them up.

"Well, what?" Clermont dropped into a chair by the hearth with an exhausted sigh and stretched his legs out. "I'm afraid my Hessians will require all your skill; they've been soaked three times today."

The valet came over and tugged off the boots. Then, standing up again: "Was he in residence? Did you see him?"

Moodily, Clermont stared down at his stockinged feet. "Yes."

"And?"

"And what?" snapped Clermont. "Do you imagine I declared myself immediately? I am not such a fool."

"What of the girl?"

"The niece? She suspects something, I think. A bit of a shrew." He thought for a moment, remembering her tall, slender figure, the gleaming coil of hair, the gray-green eyes. "A very personable shrew," he amended.

"Then you intend to continue your visits."

There was a long silence. "Yes. Yes, I suppose so. I've gone too far to turn back now."

"I still don't like this scheme," grumbled the servant, picking up the boots and examining them. His sour face might have been due to the sad state of their tops, or it might have betokened general moral disapproval.

"Your suggestion, as I recall, was that I should write the earl a polite letter demanding that he reveal confidential and very delicate matters to a man he had never met." Clermont's tone was decidedly sarcastic.

"That would have been the course a gentleman would have followed," said Vernon stiffly.

"There is some question as to my claim to that title."

Vernon raised his eyebrows. "*I* am a gentleman's gentleman. I have been with you for more than ten years. Therefore, sir, *you* are a gentleman." And with great dignity he bowed and withdrew, holding a mud-spattered boot in each hand.

"I don't think Aristotle would have approved of that syllogism," Julien muttered.

* * *

Clermont set out well before nine the next morning for Boulton Park and discovered that Jeb's description of Tempest was all too accurate. This second battle was much more difficult than their first. The horse was fresh; he, on the other hand, was sore from their contest yesterday. Moreover, he was impatient to reach Boulton Park and the animal sensed it. She tried to scrape him off against a stone wall, came to several sudden stops calculated to pitch him over her head, and reared at the sight of a hedgehog uncurling. This last episode, unfortunately, proved to have a witness. He was inside the park, following his route of the previous morning, and when he finally forced the mare back onto all four feet, he discovered Serena Allen standing about ten yards away.

"Good morning, Mr. Clermont," she said politely. There was a hint of amusement in her tone. "I did not expect you so early. Nor did I expect to see Tempest with you."

He dismounted and led the horse up to her. Unlike Jeb, she did not back away, but she did step neatly to one side, keeping Clermont between her and the mare. He lifted his hat slowly, keeping a firm hand on the horse's bridle. "Good morning. I take it you and my new mount are acquainted?"

"Oh, most folk hereabouts know Tempest. Our neighbor, Sir Reginald, fancies himself a judge of horses and bought her several years ago. When he realized his mistake, he searched desperately for a buyer. He even proposed that my uncle should purchase her for me—a quiet lady's saddle horse, he called her. Luckily Bates had already heard the gossip. In the end, the Queen's Rest took her and now they hire her out to obstreperous London sprigs who ask for a 'lively one.'"

"An apt description of me, I collect."

She studied him carefully, and he saw a faint smile. "I would not call you a sprig. You are too tall, and your clothing too sober. But I presume you did ask for a lively one."

"To my sorrow, yes," said Clermont dryly. "Still, my folly has provided you with some morning entertainment." He thought ruefully of the ridiculous picture he and Tempest must have made, attacking a hedgehog with the *levade*.

"Not at all. You handled her quite well."

Was that condescension? Clermont was not vain, but he knew himself to be a fair horseman, and he bristled.

"I would say, rather," she continued, "that you have provided me with the answer to the question which guided my walk today."

"Oh? And what question was that?"

"Whether the west gate had been locked again. My uncle meant to ask Bates to see to it, but he must not have done so yet." Her gray eyes met his, and there was an unmistakable challenge there.

He cursed his thoughtless decision to use his shortcut again. He had been eager to make up the time he had lost arguing with the mare. "It is still unlocked," he said calmly. "I'm afraid I took advantage of that fact to shorten my route. I hope you—and your uncle—will pardon the liberty."

She gave some vague reassurance, but he could see that she was still suspicious, as well she might be. Not, he thought, someone who took much trouble to conceal what she was thinking. Her face was an open book: wary, scornful.

"Do attractive young ladies walk unescorted in the wilds of Oxfordshire frequently?" he drawled, hoping that gallantry would fluster her. Or at least distract her. "Perhaps I should spend more time here."

She did not seem flustered, but she did not seem gratified, either. "My aunt would prefer that I have someone with me," she said coldly. "Since I try to go out most mornings and did not wish to keep a servant from other chores—or waste my breath trying to persuade Simon to come out for some fresh air—she agreed that I might walk alone so long as I remain within the park. *Ordinarily* it is quite safe here."

He ignored the provocative emphasis on "ordinarily." "If I should come this way tomorrow, would I have the pleasure of meeting you again?"

"Tomorrow," she pointed out, "the gate will be locked." There was the faint smile again. It was not a friendly smile.

He was forced to curtail his work with the diaries early that afternoon. No matter how often Lady Bassington assured him dinner would be a small family affair and there was no need for an eight-mile round trip back to the village, he knew it was safest to return to the inn and change. Having prevailed at least on this point, he let the countess persuade him to accept an offer of transportation in the Bassington carriage and found himself, at the sophisticated hour of eight, being shown into an imposing salon by Pritchett.

"An intimate family meal, ha!" he muttered, taking in the men's knee breeches, the women's jewels, and the squadron of hovering footmen in powdered wigs. In addition to the earl and the countess there were at least a dozen strange faces turning expectantly towards him. But he had been bred to this, and he murmured suitable courtesies as various guests were presented. The Reverend Bertram Asquey with his sister, spouse, and freckle-faced son; an elderly couple whom he vaguely remembered meeting long ago at the Derrings; Lord and Lady Orset and their two older daughters; and a pair of nearly identical-looking young dandies who seemed to be connections of Lady Orset. The numbers were completed by a distant cousin of the countess, a widow named Mrs. Childe.

The last two diners to make an appearance were Serena and Royce. They had evidently been quarreling, for he heard her hiss, "Enough; I will speak with Simon later," just as she came in the door, and her color was high. Anger certainly became her—a fortunate circumstance, he thought, seeing how often she seemed to be angry. Her eyes sparkled, her mouth was set in that enigmatic half smile, and there was a defiant tilt to her head. She measured him with her gaze, and he felt her animosity transfer itself effortlessly from Royce to himself.

"Excellent, we are all here now," said Lady Bassington briskly. She nodded to a footman, who disappeared, and in a few minutes the doors to the dining room were thrown open. "Mr. Clermont?" she said, looking up at him. He realized that he was meant to take her in to dinner.

When Lady Bassington had introduced Serena to him yesterday, he had not really noticed the manner of it. Now, however, it was becoming unmistakably clear that the countess must somehow have surmised his rank. She had presented Lord Orset to him, rather than the reverse. He was seated at her right again and offered every dish first. The other guests were obviously well aware of the apparent irregularity and stared at him covertly all through the meal. In his head the interminable debate began: what should he do if someone addressed him by his title? Ignore it? Explain? It had taken him two months to teach Vernon not to use it, something he forced himself to recall when he was annoyed with the valet. Servants were naturally inclined to snobbery on behalf of their masters. It might well take him twice that long to train Vernon's replacement.

It was more comfortable during the brief interval allowed the gentlemen for port and cigars. With fewer guests and more general conversation, Clermont was able to sort his male companions into three groups: those who had been told something (Bassington and Orset), those who were mildly curious (the rector and the elderly neighbor), and those who were oblivious (the younger men). The women, however, were more aware of social nuances, and when the men entered the drawing room Clermont felt nine pairs of female eyes boring into him. It was almost a relief to see that the countess had contrived to leave a place empty next to her niece. Better the hawk than the vultures, he thought, and made his way over to the sofa. The elderly cousin was seated in an adjacent chair, and to his dismay she rose and made a deep curtsey as he approached.

"My lord," she murmured. The jet beads on the brooch pinned to her turban nearly touched her skirts, she had dipped so low.

"Mr. Clermont," he corrected.

"Of course, if that is your preference." She gave him a peculiar smile, her lips pressed tightly together, and then curtseyed again and backed away.

If she had been his worst enemy she could not have angered and humiliated him more thoroughly. He had to physically restrain himself from looking around to see who had noticed.

"What was that about?" Serena was staring in bewilderment after her cousin's retreating form.

"I believe she is under some sort of misapprehension. Perhaps she is a bit hard of hearing?"

"Mrs. Childe? Far from it." She shook her head. "How odd. Normally she takes care to be very well-informed about all my mother's guests. She was asking Aunt Clara about you just a few minutes ago."

It was time to change the subject. "You are looking very elegant tonight, Miss Allen," he said.

"So are you, Mr. Clermont." She glanced pointedly at his conservative black breeches and white waistcoat, which matched those of every other male in the room. "I had meant to warn you that Aunt Clara's notion of an informal potluck is nearly twenty for dinner with eight courses, but I see you deduced that for yourself."

"The luncheon yesterday was fair warning. May I?" He didn't wait for an answer but seated himself beside her. "How did your aunt gather such impressive numbers on one day's notice?"

Serena smiled cynically. "She told them there was a distinguished visitor, of course, and dropped coy hints about the real purpose of your visit." The smile vanished suddenly; she leaned towards him and asked fiercely, "What is the real purpose of your visit?"

Two days' worth of encounters with Miss Allen had prepared him for something of the sort. "To consult the late earl's journals and examine some of the specimens he acquired from Drury's estate," he answered at once. "What leads you to think otherwise?"

She sat back and looked at him calmly. "First," she said, "you do not behave like a collector. You had no sketches in your sketchbook, for example. And the diaries you have been reading are from the 1780s, a decade before my uncle's father began corresponding with Dru Drury. Second, Aunt Clara is behaving very oddly towards you. One would think you were a royal duke from the way she has received you. And third, you have not explained why you were in the park yesterday morning or what induced you to lie to protect my cousin."

She had not lowered her voice, and Clermont looked around instinctively to see if anyone was paying attention. The countess was glancing their way, but she was at the other end of the room, and their nearest neighbors, the two dandies, were ogling one of the Orset girls, who had bent forward to listen to something her sister was saying, revealing a considerable expanse of bosom. Somewhat reassured, he sat back in his turn and smiled politely in case her aunt was still watching. "Miss Allen," he said through his teeth, "allow me to remind you of the nature of drawing-room conversation. Its most salient characteristic is that it might be overheard by others in the drawing room. It is therefore usual to confine oneself to remarks about the weather (for ladies) or to compliments on the appearance of one's female companions (for gentlemen). On further acquaintance it is permissible to discuss books, music, and theater. Politics and religion are frowned upon. Inquisitions are beyond the pale. I have done my part—and, I might add, my compliment was sincerely meant. In return you suggest that I am some sort of criminal."

"And you have not answered my questions."

"Very well." He glanced around once more to make certain no one was listening and steered a course as close to the truth as he dared. "I explained why I have no sketches. You may believe me or not, as you choose. The journals: I have consulted a number of different volumes, and some of the later ones referred back to earlier voyages of Lord Bassington which caught my interest. Your aunt, I am afraid, has apparently overestimated the significance of some of my family connections. I came in through the back gate of the park yesterday—it was already open, by the way—because I wished to arrive at the house before it began to pour. As for your cousin, let me ask *you* a question. If you caught an eleven-year-old—a child, unknown to you, but obviously well-bred and meaning no real harm—in a similar situation, would you have exposed him in front of his tutor and a groom?"

Her eyes fell. "No," she acknowledged, "in your place I would likely have done the same. Although if you had known Simon better you might not have been so certain he meant no real harm."

"That boy should be at school," he muttered, remembering.

"He should," Serena admitted, "but my aunt will not hear of it. And to tell the truth, I would miss him." Her face softened for a moment and he blinked, astonished at the transformation.

Well, he thought, *so that's what Miss Allen looks like with her guard down.* He stored it away for future reference.

"In any case," he said briskly, "you need not concern yourself with my nefarious purposes, since tomorrow will be my last day at Boulton Park."

"It will?" she was clearly surprised.

"I am afraid so. I have engagements in town."

"I will not be here tomorrow," she said. There was even a tinge of regret in her voice. The announcement of his departure had, as he had hoped, allayed her suspicions. "I am promised to Fanny Orset for the day."

"In that case, might I ride over on Thursday morning and say farewell? I am truly very grateful for your help these past two days."

Her guard was back in place, but her tone was almost courteous. "You needn't trouble yourself."

"It would be my pleasure," he assured her. "After all, Tempest deserves a final chance to unseat me."

Philip Derring looked puzzled when Sir Charles Barrett hailed him just outside Hatchard's. The two men barely knew each other. Barrett's urgent invitation to join him for a drink at his club was clearly even more unexpected. Catholics were not normally made welcome at White's.

"I believe I've just met a friend of yours at Boulton Park," Barrett explained after the servant had brought them a small bowl of punch. He ladled out a cup for Derring and passed it across. "An intriguing young man,

name of Clermont. I was hoping you could tell me more
about him. It looked to me as though he might be pursuing Miss Allen, and I have always had a great regard
for her."

The younger man looked shocked for a moment.
"Julien? Courting Serena?" Then his face cleared. "Ah,
no, now I remember! He has gone to look at the butterflies! He asked me for a letter weeks ago."

"Is he a scientist, then?"

"No, no." Derring sampled the punch. "More of a
gentleman adventurer, I would say, although he is very
well read and can talk about nearly anything so plausi-
bly you'd swear he had taken his degree in it."

This answer confirmed Barrett's worst fears. His
heart sank. "How long have you known him?" he asked
casually.

"Fifteen years. More. We were at school together,
then spent a year sharing lodgings in Bologna—
couldn't attend university in England, of course. He
studied medicine. We came back here, and Julien had
some sort of dustup with his family, went off to Canada
for several years. I still have the letters he sent me. He
had some remarkable experiences. Shot a bear, as I recall, which might not seem all that unusual, but the
creature was in his bedroom!" He reflected a moment,
then added, "I suppose he is a bit of an amateur naturalist, at that. He wrote me that he had dissected the
bear, as well as a number of other animals. And I know
he has been calling on someone here in London who
was connected with that butterfly-hunter's club Bassington's father patronized."

"The Aurelians."

"Yes, that's it." He took another drink. "I hope he has
been made welcome at Boulton Park? I was the one
who urged him to stop in there when he told me he had
become interested in butterflies."

"Lady Bassington certainly seems taken with him."

Derring grinned. "He's very charming, is Julien! Particularly to the ladies. With that face, and those odd dark eyes and gilded hair."

"You looked taken aback when I mentioned that he might be paying court to Miss Allen," probed Barrett. "How much of an adventurer is he? Ought I to warn Bassington?"

Derring's grin vanished. "Julien Clermont is one of my oldest friends," he said stiffly. "I would vouch for him under any circumstances, to anyone. If I looked taken aback, it was because he has told me repeatedly that he will never marry."

"Many young men make such promises."

"No, he means it. He's very proud, in his own quiet fashion, and his situation is—unusual."

Barrett refilled his guest's cup and waited. "In what way?" he said at last, after Derring had been sipping reflectively for a minute.

"He's illegitimate," said Derring bluntly. "His grandparents have treated him quite well, all things considered, but the stubborn fool believes he has no right to accept the position they have conferred on him, still less the right to ask a well-born girl to share it. And unfortunately, his family is very, very highly placed. Too highly placed for Julien to be content with some tradesman's daughter."

"How high?" asked Barrett, leaning forward.

"You'll keep this to yourself? Julien would have my head if he knew I had said anything."

Sir Charles Barrett's fabled ability to elicit confidences from near strangers was based largely on his reputation as a man who could keep a secret. "You have my word on it."

Derring drained his cup and looked defiantly at his host. "Royalty."

5

The tender and compassionate nature of Woman makes her especially well-suited for the task of nursing.

— Miss Cowell's *Moral Reflections for Young Ladies*

Vernon was clearly delighted that they were leaving. He bustled about, whistling cheerfully as he packed.

"Have you settled with the landlord?" asked Clermont, shrugging out of his greatcoat. He had gone for a quick early-morning ride.

"Yes, sir. Did the mare give you any trouble?"

"Nothing I couldn't handle," he said absently. "She gets one more chance, when I ride over to Boulton Park after breakfast."

"Can't fathom why you would want two outings on that she-devil in one morning," muttered Vernon.

"I'm celebrating our first dry day in Burford," Clermont said. "And since I shall be spending the afternoon and evening in a post chaise, I can use the fresh air." Vernon was traveling on ahead with the luggage, which was already piling up near the door. It was a mystery to Julien why he should need so many boxes and trunks for a one-week excursion, but Vernon was always horrified when his master suggested taking fewer changes of linen or only two jackets. Even during their expeditions into the Canadian forests he had insisted that Julien bring items which had gone unworn for months: a dressing gown, evening wear, silk waistcoats.

A serving maid edged into the room carrying a large tray and looked around for a place to set it down.

"Ah, very good," said Vernon, sweeping a pile of shirts off the table by the fireplace to make room for the tray. "Your breakfast, sir." He nodded to the maid in dismissal and pulled out the room's lone chair with a flourish.

"The coffee-room is suddenly beneath me?" said Julien sardonically, seating himself.

"There were Uncouth Persons there earlier, sir, and I deemed it advisable to ask for a tray to be brought up."

The Uncouth Persons were presumably the two farmers he had seen talking to Budge when he had gone through on his way to the stables an hour ago. He suddenly wished he could have breakfasted with them. Perhaps they could have told him something more about Boulton Park and its inhabitants. The late earl's journals had been frustratingly vague on all matters not connected with insects or tropical plants. But the thought of trying to interrogate two rustics was repugnant, almost as repugnant as the charade in the cabinet-room. Nor, he suspected, would he make a very good job of it. "Here, my good fellows! A tankard of ale for you, with my compliments, and would you happen to know where Lord Bassington was on such and such a day, in such and such a year? Or whether he has received correspondence from a certain foreign country? Sent monies abroad secretly?" The chances of a pair of farmers possessing the information he needed were vanishingly small, and even if they did, the close-mouthed folk of rural Oxfordshire would never pass on anything they knew of their noble landlord to a stranger.

He stared at the tray. Food at the Burford Arms was plain but well-prepared, and there was a substantial platter next to the coffeepot with boiled meat, spiced plums,

two coddled eggs, and some rolls. He couldn't eat any
of it, he realized. Perhaps his stomach was being prudent, given the strenuous schedule he had laid out for
the day. He contented himself with sipping coffee and
looking over his notes until a reasonable amount of time
had passed, crumbling one of the rolls to stave off inquiries about his appetite.

"I'm off again," he said abruptly, shoving his chair
away from the table. "What time is the post chaise
coming?"

"Noon." Vernon was struggling with a recalcitrant
strap on one of the larger bags.

"Tell Budge to have the boy wait if I am not back by
then."

The valet looked up, startled. "It's just gone nine now.
Are you planning a long stay?" He had tried yesterday
to persuade Clermont that there was no need to ride over
for a farewell visit this morning, that it would delay
them considerably on their trip back to town. Julien did
not want to start that argument again.

"If Lady Bassington invites me to stay for luncheon, I
promise to decline," he said. He grabbed his coat, waving
off Vernon's attempt to help him on with it, and slung it
over his shoulder. "Don't wait up for me when you reach
London," he added. "If I start out late, I may stop for the
night in Twyford." Ignoring a final protest from the valet,
he clattered down the stairs.

The price for clear skies at this time of year was frigid
temperatures. He stamped up and down in the yard to
keep warm while Jeb led Tempest back out. No mud this
morning; the ground was frozen. The mare picked her
way unerringly through the stiff ruts as he headed east
from the village. He would miss her, he thought. She really wasn't a bad animal if you were willing to let her
work off some of her excess energy before you asked
her to behave.

He turned onto the road which ran along Bassington's

land. He was warmer now and enjoying the brilliant purity of the sky. The tree branches looked like fine lace, and tiny crystals in the stones of the park wall glinted in the sun. When he reached the iron gate he swung off Tempest's back with no hesitation. It was still unlocked, in spite of Serena Allen's warning, because he had slipped Bates a sovereign and asked him to delay repairing the bolt for a few days. Tempest didn't like the noise the gate made, but she was getting accustomed to it and only sidled a bit as they went through.

"Well, girl," he said softly, mounting up again. "Shall we have a last run up to see the view? Perhaps we'll meet Miss Allen on her morning walk and give her another excuse to glare at us." He guided the mare onto the path which ran up the hill. The bottom part was steep, and he held her to a walk, but the slope leveled out near the top, and he urged her to a trot as they neared the summit. Then a canter—a bit fast for this terrain, he knew, but he had ridden this way half a dozen times now. The path was broad here and ran across a clearing and then up between widely spaced trees. He was rounding a curve just below the crest of the hill when it happened. He heard Tempest snort, felt something whip across his cheek, and then he was hurled from the saddle and deposited into a painful, splintered darkness.

Simon was the one who found Clermont, although he generously gave his spaniel most of the credit afterwards, pointing out that he would never have gone up to the top of the hill if Bandit had not wandered off. It was a lucky chance that boy and dog had gone out that morning at all; Serena did not conceal her surprise when he met her at the bottom of the garden. Like most eleven-year-olds, Simon did not care for aimless walks. A goal was required, a goal beyond tramping along sedately for a certain distance, admiring the view, and turning back. Today's goal was to test his new field glass—escaping his geography lesson in the process. And like most eleven-year-olds, Simon did not walk at a steady pace. On the lower part of the hill he had lagged behind, feeling sulky and tired. Serena had been far ahead when he had spied the falcon. At once he was full of energy, and charged up the path, calling urgently to the dog to follow. The falcon, wheeling lazily overhead in the clear winter sky, paid no attention to Simon's cries or Bandit's barking. It banked gradually over to the left, and Simon veered off the main track, trying to keep it in focus. This proved to be impossible, at least while he was trying to walk at the same time.

Impatiently he flung himself down on the brown turf and peered around through the eyepiece as he waited for his pet to catch up with him. In the dim light of a tangled bramble patch he fancied he could see a few small, huddled shapes—birds, hiding from the falcon. They would explode out of the brush in a feathery cloud when the dog arrived. He wondered if he could train his glass quickly enough to see what one of the birds would look like magnified while it was flying. He was practicing this maneuver when his cousin came up next to him.

"Lovely, isn't it?" she said. Her cheeks were rosy with the cold, and she was panting slightly. Simon looked down towards the great house in the valley for one moment, then turned back to the birds.

"Looks the same as always to me," he said. "I don't know why girls sigh over nature." He switched to an affected falsetto. "Oh, my dear, you must see the valley from here! An enchanting prospect!"

"I have never sounded like that in my life," objected Serena, eyes flashing.

"Well, perhaps you are not quite that bad," he admitted grudgingly. "But Fanny Orset is. And you did write a poem about the gardens once."

"Simon! I was sixteen!" She looked at him suspiciously. "That reminds me—my old copybook has gone missing. Have you seen it?"

"No," he lied. In fact, it was under the sofa in the old nursery, where Serena had thrown it at him a month ago. He had just seen it a few days earlier when he was searching for a gear which had rolled across the floor and had taken the opportunity to refresh his memory of Serena's literary indiscretions before sliding it more securely out of sight. One never knew when one might need ammunition against Serena.

"It's beautiful out, but Aunt Clara will think it too cold for you," she said regretfully. "Shall we go back down?"

Simon frowned. "I'll catch you up; I must find Bandit." He looked around, annoyed. The falcon was long gone, the tiny birds had hopped or flown away, and the spaniel was probably lost again. He had a gift for falling into disused fire pits, or getting trapped under logs, or chasing cows who then turned around and terrified him so that he fled to the nearest hedge and cowered until Simon rescued him. A few shouts produced no response; grumbling, he shoved the glass in his pocket and started up towards the trees at the top of the hill, calling as he went. At the edge of the grove, he called once more, debating whether to continue on or trust the dog to find his way home. A faint sound reached him. He shouted more loudly, and this time he was sure that he heard Bandit's whine in reply.

The wind freshened, and he noted it with a grimace. If the wind started howling around the house, his mother would never let him hear the end of it; he had promised to turn back at the first sign of a change in the weather. As if the thought had been an evil omen, a gust roared across the top of the hill and nearly knocked him over. He realized suddenly that he had lost his hat back by the bird thicket. With an increasing sense of gloom he climbed on, through a stand of ash. The wind was louder, but he could hear Bandit clearly now, whining and yelping sporadically. Just where the path leveled out, there were two larger trees. Under the nearer tree was Bandit. And he was sitting on what appeared to be a dead body.

"Good Lord, it's a corpse!" said Simon, with a mixture of horror and enthusiasm. He peered more closely at the man's body. "Wait, he's only injured, I think. Move, Bandit, you're smothering him." The dog was sitting right on the poor fellow's head. "Get *off* him, you blasted mongrel!" Simon commanded crossly, heaving the old spaniel aside. The injured man lay unmoving, eyes closed, but Simon could see the slight rise and fall of his chest, and the pulse at his temple. He's lost his hat, just like me, thought Simon. There was blood and dirt on the man's face, and his lips were beginning to turn blue with cold. That was why it took Simon a minute to recognize him.

He scrambled up. His initial excitement was evaporating rapidly, replaced by panic. "Serena!" he screamed. He tore back down the path, yelling as loudly as he could. "Serena!" She was already a good distance away, but the wind must have carried his voice to her. She turned and looked back. He flailed his arms helplessly to show distress, then beckoned urgently and pointed back to the trees.

She hesitated, and Simon knew what she was thinking. He had played far too many pranks recently. She knew about the pistol, for example, and had given him an unusually stern lecture about the difference between boyish fun and downright idiocy. But she turned and began trudging back up the hill.

"It's the butterfly-man!" he yelled. "He's dead! Or not dead, but hurt, very badly." He could see Serena's eyes widen; she shouted something in reply, but he did not wait, suddenly afraid Clermont was expiring at that very moment. He ran back into the trees and pushed his way through the brush, not even bothering with the trail. Clermont was still there, and still breathing. Simon knelt down and tried to ascertain where he was hurt. Several places, it appeared. There was a shallow cut across his cheek, which was still bleeding a bit. It looked almost like the mark of a whip. Another graze on the side of his head. More blood on his neckcloth, mixed with leaves and dirt. And he was lying hunched over, as though protecting his left arm, which was cradled on his chest.

Simon heard a scrambling sound, and Serena appeared, breathless. "There you are!" He had never been so glad to see her in his life. "He's just over here, under the trees. He's all over blood." His voice trembled slightly. "Do you think he's dying?"

His cousin bent over the injured man, peered at his face and lifted his wrist. "No," she said after a moment. "He's just taken a bad knock on the head. He'll come round soon, I should think. But we must get him inside quickly; his hands are like ice. Here, give me your coat." She tucked it clumsily around Clermont's shoulders. "Can you run down to the stables and get some men up here with a litter?"

Immensely relieved to turn over responsibility to someone else, he pelted back over the top of the hill, then stopped.

"Serena!" he called, turning back, "I see Bates on his way here already."

She emerged from the copse after a minute and looked down towards the valley. The head groom was riding up the path at a slow trot, leading another horse. "Aunt Clara must have decided it was too windy and sent after you," she said. She sounded relieved as well. She waved vigorously until Bates spotted her and waved in return, then she hurried back into the trees, trailed by an anxious Simon.

"Are you sure he isn't dead?" Simon asked doubtfully

as she knelt again by her patient. "That's quite a bit of blood."

"Dr. Wall says head wounds always bleed a lot," she replied absently. She took out her handkerchief and dabbed at the cut on Clermont's cheek.

Bates appeared at the top of the path and, taking the situation in at a glance, dismounted in one leap and tethered both horses to a small tree.

"What's this, then?" he asked, looking from the unconscious man to Simon and then to Serena.

"I would say that Mr. Clermont finally lost a round against Tempest," answered Serena, brushing off her skirt and standing up.

Simon was staring over her head. He tugged at her sleeve, pointing. "It wasn't Tempest," he whispered. "Look." A thin length of brown rope about ten inches long was dangling from a branch of the tree, almost invisible against the trunk. A matching fragment, considerably longer, hung from a smaller tree on the other side of the path. Bates swung into the saddle of the nearer horse, his face grim, and rode up to the second tree, retrieving the rope end and holding it straight out from the branch over the path.

"Rider's shoulder height," he said succinctly. "Clear the horse's head. Knock off the man on his back. An old horse-thieves' trick. After we get this gentleman down the hill I'd best send for Googe again, Miss Allen."

"And Dr. Wall," she said, looking down at Clermont. "At once."

"Well, he's a bit battered, but I don't think it's anything serious. Crack in the wrist bone, or perhaps a severe sprain, a few cuts, and a nasty blow to the head. Should recover, with proper care. Unless, of course, he develops a fever." Doctor Wall tugged at a frayed pocket and extracted his pipe, then, recollecting where he was, hastily replaced it. Serena saw the habitual gesture and hid a smile. She and the doctor were old friends. Lately, in fact, there had been an unspoken conspiracy between them to wean the countess from her fixation on Simon's constitution. Dr. Wall had been recommending more and more exercise, and his tonics now tasted suspiciously like ginger water, with an occasional decoction of lovage—equally harmless—for variety. If they had been up in the old nursery, where they had spent many hours together when Simon really had been ill, several years ago, she would have let him light the pipe. But here in one of the guest rooms, it was impossible.

The physician tapped his fingers on the bedpost. Clermont was asleep now, thanks to a stiff tot of laudanum, but his color was poor, and he tossed a bit even under the restraint of the drug. "Fits of shivering, abdomen cold to the touch," Dr. Wall mused. "Consistent with chill, especially in this weather. Enlarged pupils, bruises on head and neck, confusion, dizziness—consistent with a blow to the head. A rather serious one, I am afraid. And his pulse, Miss Allen! His pulse!" He took up the unbandaged hand lying on the counterpane and held it out to her, as though it had been detached from the sleeping body. "Feel that," he commanded.

Puzzled, Serena leaned over and laid two fingers gently on the inside of the wrist. At first she felt nothing unusual, but when she made as though to withdraw her hand, the doctor gestured at her to wait. After a few moments she realized that the beat, though reasonably strong, was very slow. She compared it to her own, and even allowing for her present state of agitation, the difference was marked. "Most interesting," she said feebly. She had no idea what such a disorder of the vessels might mean. But she did have a vague impression that patients who were chilled, and those who had been given laudanum, had slower pulses. Was a slow pulse in itself dangerous?

"Exactly," said the doctor triumphantly, as though he had read her thoughts. "The cerebral bruising, the effect of the cold, and above all, the sedative—a mistake, a most lamentable mistake, but of course you were not present, my dear Miss Allen, you would never have allowed it!—so that now we are at some risk for congestion of the lungs."

"Mrs. Digby did not know," Serena objected, forgetting about medical reasoning in her need to defend the old nurse who had dosed their visitor. "He was trying to get up, insisting he was perfectly fine. She thought it was for his own good."

"It would be for Simon's good if the earl pensioned off Mrs. Digby," grumbled the doctor. "Boy should be at school, not malingering at home with a nursemaid and a tutor. No wonder he looks peaked, hounded by a pack of old women every time he gets mud on his breeches or brings in a frog from the pond." His attention went back to the young man. "He seems otherwise quite healthy," he said, frowning down at his patient. Lifting a corner of the counterpane, he pulled aside Pritchett's old flannel dressing gown (the only warm garment which came near to fitting their guest) and poked gently at the bruises on the torso, completely unconcerned with Serena's potential embarrassment. Before she looked hastily away she saw a slender chain around his neck with a gold ring at the end of it. "You say someone rigged a trap at the top of Clark's Hill?"

"Yes, they strung a rope; it caught him on the neck, evidently. Bates has sent a message to my uncle and gone into the village for the constable. He thinks it is some poachers, trying to frighten old Mr. Jackson."

"Frighten! Kill, more likely. This gentleman would be dead now had Simon not found him."

"Well—" Serena floundered for a moment. "If it *had*

been Jackson—he is rather short—I think it would only
have knocked his hat off. But," nodding down towards
the bed, "he is quite tall—perhaps you did not notice—
he was already in bed when you arrived." To her
chagrin, she could feel her face grow pink.

"Taller than you, hey?" The doctor looked up at her
with a smile. "Well, your uncle's gamekeeper is certainly not a large man." Jackson was, in fact, so short
and round that he was nearly spherical. "Perhaps you
are right, and they merely meant to give Jackson a scare.
But I hope that they can convince a magistrate of their
intentions. Because it looks to me like a case of attempted murder, and this young man appears to be of a
station in life where such matters will not be brushed
aside easily."

"You may be right about that," she said slowly. "He is
a friend of the Derrings who was here looking at the
collection, and my aunt seems to know his family. She
has gone into a frenzy making arrangements to nurse
him; you would think he was a prince of the blood.
When he told her he could easily be cared for at the
Burford Arms she snapped that no one of his lineage
would be tended by tavern wenches while she was mistress of Boulton Park."

"That is just as well," said Dr. Wall dryly, picking up
his bag and moving towards the door. "He should not be
moved for at least three days and must not be allowed to
walk more than a dozen yards at a time for several days
after that."

"Oh." Serena digested this for a minute. Her aunt had
believed that they would only need to keep him here for
a day or so. But Dr. Wall was not an over-cautious
physician. If he prescribed rest, there must be a good
reason. With a sigh she followed the doctor towards the
anteroom. His hand was on his pocket flap again, and
Serena knew he was itching to be out of the house. "I'll
ring for Pritchett and have him show you out. My aunt

is conferring with Mrs. Fletcher and it is probably best if you do not take your leave of her. She will trust me to pass on your instructions."

"No need," he said gruffly. "I can show myself out, been here often enough." He was headed towards the foyer before she could even reach the bellpull but paused momentarily. "Ah, Miss Allen, one more thing." He handed her a small paper twist. "If he develops a fever, give him some of this powder dissolved in hot water or tea and feel free to send for me again." The pipe was out of his pocket already, and he tamped it absentmindedly on his boot, leaving a small pile of tarry ash just inside the anteroom doors.

An elderly manservant on his way in paused and discreetly swept up the pile into his own handkerchief. He looked harassed.

"Bates has returned from the village, Miss Allen. Constable was gone out to the weir, but they've sent a boy to notify him. And the boy stopped at the inn, as you requested, to see if they could send on the sick gentleman's effects, and to summon his servant."

"Well?" she said impatiently.

"Mr. Clermont's man packed up his gear and left this morning; said his master was following him to town."

"Drat," said Serena under her breath. She had hoped that most of the nursing could be done by Clermont's own valet. According to Bates, the manservant had been regaling everyone at the inn with tales of his heroic devotion to his master in the wilds of Canada. Here, in her opinion, was an ideal opportunity for devotion. She had tended Simon after a blow to the head once, and it had involved quite a bit of holding basins while he retched. Now it would have to be Mrs. Digby and herself. She looked down at the pale, aristocratic face. His brows were drawn together slightly. Probably even in his drugged sleep he was dimly aware of what she was sure must be a ferocious headache.

In the anteroom, Simon was waiting, nearly bouncing in his excitement. "May I see him?" her cousin said, trying to look around her as she emerged. "Will he recover?"

"No, you may not, and yes, he will recover. *If* you do not plague him. I thought you were meant to be in bed yourself. You were soaked by the time we got back."

There was a timid knock at the outer door.

"If that's Nurse, I'm not here," said Simon, retreating to a shadowed corner and preparing to slip behind a tall chair.

The door inched open, and Mrs. Childe peered around it, then tiptoed into the room. "I came as soon as I heard the dreadful news," she said in a whisper. "I will take the first turn to watch at his bedside. Poor dear Serena, you must be quite worn out with everything." She patted Serena's arm. "Go and rest; Mrs. Digby and I will be here."

Serena repressed the urge to ask the older woman where she had been on all the nights years ago, when Serena and the nurse and the countess between them could barely keep Simon quiet and dosed. She knew perfectly well that the widow had no skills in the sickroom. And while something about Clermont made Serena uneasy, it seemed excessively cruel to subject him to an incompetent harpy when he was injured and helpless. She glanced over at Simon in an instinctive appeal.

"Oh, no," he said, coming forward. "I believe it will be just you and Serena. Nurse has just been telling me that she cannot tend Mr. Clermont, because she has never been exposed to it. Nor can we have any of the servants in, because of the danger of infection. It is very fortunate that you and Serena are immune."

"Infection?" Mrs. Childe looked at the three of them in alarm. "Exposed to what, pray? I thought he had fallen from his horse? Has he some sort of *disease*?"

"Oh, if you have already had it, you cannot catch it again," Simon assured her. "But it is a common complication of head injuries, you know."

"It is?"

"Yes, Nurse said that the blotches are already appearing." He turned to Serena. "He has blue marks on his chest, does he not?"

As always when Simon embarked on one of his elaborate schemes, she was feeling a bit stunned. She managed to nod, though, and, remembering the bruises beneath the wide, smooth neck, reflected that her answer was not technically a lie.

The other woman gave a faint shriek and backed away. "There seems to have been a misunderstanding," she said, breathless. "I—I don't believe I have been exposed. Perhaps I can be of assistance when he has recovered a bit."

"Say nothing to the servants," Simon warned her as she sidled towards the door. "It would cause a dreadful panic."

"Of course not," said Mrs. Childe as she backed out of the room and disappeared.

Simon leaned against the door and grinned.

"And what would you have done," Serena demanded, "if she had asked you what the name of this illness was?"

"Oh, I would have thought of something. 'Occipital fever,' perhaps, or 'Cerebellan ague.' Better yet, a Latin name. *Pestis equicadensis. Pox Childeae.*"

"You are horrid," she said. But she was laughing.

"Are you sure I cannot just peek in? Just for a moment? You're in my debt, you know, for saving you from Mrs. Childe."

She was in his debt. Sometimes she felt guilty about how much she enjoyed watching Simon make fools of adults she disliked. Putting her finger to her lips, she opened the inner door and beckoned. They stood for a moment, side by side in the doorway, looking at the unconscious man.

"Isn't it exciting?" Simon whispered to her. "Who do you suppose tried to kill him?"

6

George Oliver Clement Piers, fifth Earl of Bassington, believed in *noblesse oblige*. After a short but spectacular career as a rake in his twenties, he had come round to the idealistic notion that peers had a duty to serve their country, and for many years now he had been fulfilling not only his own obligations but also those of at least a dozen other men. A cautious and intelligent politician, he wielded considerable influence in Parliament, in spite of occasional displays of obstinacy more suitable to a Whig than a Tory. His appearance contributed to his reputation: he was squarely built, with a high forehead and a mantle of salt-and-pepper hair which flew about his head when he gestured during speeches in a most satisfyingly philosophical fashion. He was a member of several learned societies, as his father had been before him, and corresponded with scholars in five countries. All in all, he was someone whose judgment and discretion were highly regarded. The urgent summons from his wife had not shaken him; the news which greeted him, upon his arrival home, that a mantrap on his lands had nearly killed an innocent visitor, surprised and dismayed him, but did not fluster him.

Now, however, he was on the verge of losing his temper, and his secretary was desperately trying to placate him. Once angered, the earl was a difficult man to appease.

"My lord, perhaps you are mistaken. I sifted through

every paper on both desks, and found nothing, and there is no record in my logbook of any such letter."

"Of course there is no record!" The earl's face was beginning to flush. "A messenger delivered it to me personally, and I took good care to secrete it in a safe place yesterday. At least, I thought I did. The instructions from the ministry were quite explicit; no one else was authorized to read it, not even you." Misinterpreting the look of apprehension on his secretary's face, he added, "Royce, you must know that there is no question of any fault on your part. It is clear what must have happened: I did not lock it away, and the staff once again ignored my instructions and tidied my study."

The younger man grimaced; six days earlier, a confidential memo had disappeared from the earl's desk and after a frantic search had been located in the nursery grate, on the verge of being used as fuel for toasted cheese by Nurse Digby and Simon. Then, shortly afterwards, a letter written by the earl which he could have sworn he had sealed and handed over to a courier had also gone missing. It, too, had surfaced—unsealed, in a pile of the countess's correspondence awaiting her husband's frank. That was when the earl had hired the guards.

"Should I question the maids, my lord? Or would you prefer me to look about quietly first?"

Bassington rubbed his left temple wearily. "Hunt through these rooms yourself before we involve Mrs. Fletcher. It has the same wrapper as the other. Start here in my desk; perhaps I have misremembered where I put it." He took a small key from his waistcoat and unlocked the two drawers tucked under the surface of the cherry writing table. "Try my father's bookshelves next; I was looking through them yesterday and it is possible that I might have absentmindedly set the packet down while hunting through his journals."

"If I have no luck here or in the cabinets, how should I proceed, sir?"

"Call in Mrs. Fletcher, I suppose." The earl frowned. "I should have taken your advice and purchased one of those new strongboxes, Royce. Although frankly I thought they would simply be an irresistible challenge to Simon, and he has already broken the locks on two of his mother's jewel cases. Nor did I wish to call attention to these papers by suddenly ordering special furnishings for my study."

Royce carefully avoided looking at his employer. "And the nursery? Would it be worth searching in there before consulting Mrs. Fletcher?"

"I'll look myself," growled the earl. "And if I find the least hint that Simon has been sneaking in here, I'll cane him black and blue, weak chest or no." He started to leave, then checked. "Did you say anything to Googe about the missing letters when he was here a few days ago?"

"Certainly not!" Royce looked horrified. Then, more doubtfully, "Should I have?"

Bassington shook his head. "No, your judgment was quite right, my boy. This is no matter for a parish constable. He wished to come out at once, of course, when he heard of this morning's news, but I put him off for a bit. Don't mention this business to him unless I give express instructions." He picked up a sealed packet from the desk. "Get this off to Barrett right away. It should have gone first thing this morning, but her ladyship wanted to put in a note of her own for Barrett's wife."

"Very good, my lord." The packet was carefully set aside.

"Mind that you check the seal personally and *watch* the man put it in his confounded bag."

"I will do so, my lord."

"And Royce—"

The blond head, already bent over the drawers, looked up.

"Try to restrain your longing to reorganize my desk," said the earl mildly. "I realize that it appears disorderly to someone of your fastidious temperament, but I am the one who needs to be able to find my personal papers, not you."

Royce's apprehensive frown relaxed slightly as the earl's footsteps faded away towards the main staircase, but he looked more thoughtful than relieved. The storm, he suspected, was not averted—merely postponed. When he was sure Bassington was out of earshot, he gave a sharp tug on the bellrope and waited impatiently for someone to appear. His expression softened further when he saw the familiar figure of Coughlin in the doorway.

"Thank God it's you," he said, dragging the ancient servant all the way into the office and closing the door. "Is his lordship with the countess?"

"Yes, sir."

"Is he likely to be engaged for some time?"

Coughlin observed cautiously that the countess was very concerned about the mishap which had befallen Mr. Clermont.

"Do you think you can find Simon and help him straighten up his workshop before his father comes up there?"

"His lordship is planning to visit the nursery?" gasped Coughlin, appalled.

"He is," said Royce. "And he said that if he saw any evidence that Simon had been in this suite, he would beat him." There was a moment's silence as both men visualized the normal state of Simon's kingdom, strewn with clock gears, padlocks, necklace clasps, and innumerable other dismembered items. The chaos alone would enrage the earl, who, like many untidy parents, detested his own habits when they appeared in his son.

And amongst the dozens of half-assembled contraptions on the nursery table, there would surely be something that had originally been located in the earl's study.

"I'll find him at once," promised the old servant. "And if I come across any papers, I'll bring them straight to you."

Well, thought Royce, Coughlin had not missed the implication of the unlocked drawers and the earl's threats. Not surprising, since most of the upper servants had been involved in the earlier searches for the missing memoranda. "Yes, that would be best," he said quietly. He stood staring down at the cluttered drawers for several minutes after the servant had left. Then, with a sigh, he began sorting letters into piles atop the gleaming rose-colored lid of the writing table.

Mrs. Digby was snoring lightly in a chair next to the four-poster when Serena peeked in late that afternoon, accompanied by a maid carrying a small pot of chamomile tea. The patient was apparently asleep as well. But after Serena had gently shaken the nurse awake and sent her off to get some supper, she saw that the dark eyes were open, looking at her blankly, as though he were trying to remember who she was.

Then he frowned. "Miss Allen," he said slowly, as if responding to a difficult question from a schoolmaster.

He was speaking more to himself than to her, but she answered him. "Yes?"

"Where am I? And what happened?"

"You do not remember being knocked off your horse? We found you at the top of Clark's Hill. You are at Boulton Park."

Another frown, a moment of puzzlement, and then suddenly he closed his eyes and fell back onto the pillow with a soft groan. His mouth tightened and he pushed himself up again, swinging his legs over the side of the bed.

"Where is my shirt?" he said, wobbling a bit as he sat up and then staring in dismay as his unclad legs emerged from the bedclothes. Serena hastily averted her eyes as he took in the patched dressing gown, the splint on his wrist, and the poultice strapped to his ankle. "Where are my clothes?" He propped himself up against the bedpost, looking around as though expecting to find garments hanging down from the tester.

"Your clothes were filthy; we had to remove them. And you must lie back down. The doctor said that you are not even to get up for three days and will need nursing for some time beyond that—perhaps a week. We sent over to the Burford Arms for your luggage, but there has been some misunderstanding." She judged that he was still too disoriented to be asked about his servant's departure at the moment.

"A week?" he repeated in a daze, ignoring the rest of her speech. "No, no, impossible." He turned to her, steadying himself with his good hand. "If you please, Miss Allen, I must get dressed. What time is it? Could you fetch me my shirt and breeches? I can have them cleaned at the inn."

"Dr. Wall's orders were most explicit. It is out of the question for you to return to the inn. Now, or in the morning." His eyes went to the leafless trees visible through the window, as though he were contemplating climbing out, and she tried a more persuasive tone of voice. "Consider the situation for a moment from my uncle's point of view. You have been injured on our land, and the villain who set the trap is most likely one of our tenants. Should you insist on leaving, my uncle will be held responsible if you fail to recover properly."

He nodded wearily and allowed her to pull the covers back up over his legs.

"How are you feeling? Any fever?"

"No, I don't believe so."

She reached out and felt his forehead. It was not burning hot, but far warmer than her hand. Judging from her long experience with Simon, the fever was just settling in and would come into its own the following day.

"I must contradict you; you do have a slight fever, and I suspect it will grow worse. Dr. Wall left some medicine for you." She poured out a half cup of tea.

He ignored her. "Perhaps one of the grooms could go to the inn and inquire if my servant could come here to fetch me? He is very conscientious; you could relinquish me to his care, surely?" He saw that she was about to object and added in an exasperated tone, "If you insist, I will take the medicine with me. And summon Dr. Wall to the inn tomorrow."

"Your servant," said Serena, "appears to believe that you are headed to London and has gone off to Town with all your luggage. I am afraid you are obliged to remain here for the present." She was hunting in her petticoat pocket for the little packet Dr. Wall had given her and did not see his expression at this piece of news, but she did hear him sigh again. After a brief struggle with the side seam of her dress, she pulled the paper out and poured a small portion of it into the tea. "And I am also afraid that you will have to drink all of this now that I have added the powder to it."

"What kind of powder?" he demanded, wary.

"It isn't a sedative, if that is what you are thinking." She stirred the mixture vigorously. "Although it does have a very strong taste; I believe it has horehound in it." To her relief, he did not object further and drank the concoction down.

"We will, of course, send for your servant if that would make you more comfortable. I suppose he could be here by the day after next."

"It won't make me more comfortable," he said

gloomily. "But it will make him more comfortable. Even if you send no message at all, he will return here on his own. The moment I fail to arrive in London he will be certain I have been kidnapped or murdered or lured into some gaming hell."

"Gaming hell?" Serena raised her eyebrows. "In rural Oxfordshire?"

That brought a brief smile, but almost immediately the gloomy scowl returned. "Vernon is a pessimist, especially where I am concerned."

"Well," she pointed out, "you *are* injured. Think how gratified he will be to have his fears confirmed for once."

Clermont spent the next twenty-four hours in a state of dull misery. His head was throbbing viciously, with his wrist offering a counterpoint in a minor key. One ankle was swaddled in bandages and occasionally sent little stabs of pain up his leg. Overlaying all of it was a haze of nausea and dizziness, which made it impossible to fall asleep properly; most of the first evening the best he could do was to doze off for ten minutes at a time. He hated feeling queasy, hated it with a passion. He would rather slice open his face than suffer an hour's indigestion. At present, of course, he had both a gashed face and nausea.

In addition to his physical tribulations, a constant series of disquieting images presented themselves to him as he lay, half awake. Vernon in London, realizing what had likely happened. Vernon spending the entire journey back down to Burford composing a scathing lecture on his imprudent folly. Vernon delivering the lecture— that part was not so bad—but then fussing over him and treating him, as he always did in the presence of strangers, with a deference which bordered on idolatry. Clermont strongly preferred Serena Allen's brand of nursing, unsympathetic and brusque though it might be. His hostess, on the other hand, who came in several times and fluttered over him—literally fluttered, waving her hands like a distressed bird—had obviously seen his signet ring before he had remembered to take it off, and she looked likely to rival Vernon in deferential display. And the most disquieting image of all, the memory of the brown rope across the trail, the memory of the terrifying realization that there was nothing he could do to avoid it.

On the evening of the second day, he began to feel markedly better. Dr. Wall visited briefly and warned him this state might be temporary, but Clermont was so delighted to be rid of the nausea that he disregarded this warning and persuaded Mrs. Digby (a far less severe guardian than Bassington's niece) to forego another dose of Dr. Wall's powder and fetch him instead some watered wine and a plate of toasts. His clothing had been returned, to his great relief, although he had not been permitted to get dressed yet. Perhaps, he thought, he would confound the pessimists and recover sufficiently by morning to escape Boulton Park before Vernon's return. Feeling very satisfied, and, for once, properly sleepy, he dropped off.

A loud noise in the middle of the night startled him awake. Later, he realized it had come from the fireplace; when he first woke, however, he was only conscious of acute misery. His head was on fire; his entire arm was aching; his stomach was in turmoil. He tried to sit up and could not, but when he collapsed back onto the bed he found the sheets soaked with sweat. He began to shiver uncontrollably. The covers seemed to be winding around him, damp and threatening, and he tried to throw them off, then remembered how cold he was and pulled them back over his chest.

A strange old woman appeared and tried to pull off the covers and he shouted furiously that he was cold, damn it, and forcibly wrested the sheets out of her hand.

Then he noticed that the bandages on his wrist were too tight; the skin felt swollen and hot. He tore the wrappings off and burrowed under the quilts, still shivering. He reached mechanically for reassurance in back of the pillow as he did so and was hit by a fresh wave of anxiety. His gun! Where was his gun?

He demanded its return, at once, in his most imperative tones. There were more noises, doors opening, alarmed voices. He lay still, with his racing pulse thudding in his ears, and as it slowed sanity returned. The strange old woman was Mrs. Digby. She had been trying to straighten the bed, not steal the quilts. His bandage had been wound on tightly to hold the splint in place on his wrist. His gun was in his saddlebags, which were, of course, somewhere in Oxfordshire on the back of that accursed mare.

He pushed back the covers and said, embarrassed, "Mrs. Digby?"

The old nurse hurried over from the doorway.

"I do apologize," he said. "I was—I believe I must have had a nightmare."

She surveyed the tangled sheets, the damp spots on the pillow, and peered into his eyes. "What you had, young man, was a bout of fever; that's clear enough," she said with asperity. "Likely you'll have another spell before morning, and it's my own fault for letting you get round me with your pleading that you fancied a piece of toast and wouldn't it be dry and hard to digest without a bit of wine. Miss Serena will be very cross with the both of us." She nodded significantly towards the hall, and he heard hasty footsteps.

His chief nurse burst into the room, anxious and disheveled. She was in her nightgown, with a dressing gown thrown over it but not tied. Her hair was tumbling down her back, and her feet were bare. When she saw her patient sitting up in bed, looking rather shamefaced, she stopped abruptly. A slow flush rose up her neck. She

was angry, he realized, and embarrassed. She was also
the most glorious thing he had seen in years. The thin
lawn nightrail flowed down her like the drapery on a
classical statue, and as the pink rose into her face he
thought momentarily of Galatea, of cold marble brought
to life.

"Hold still, do," the old nurse said to him, scolding.
She was binding the splint back onto his wrist. To Serena she said, turning sideways for a moment, "He's
himself again, Miss Allen, and now I'm sorry to have
fetched you out of bed at this hour, but he gave me quite
a turn. Tossing, and pulling at his splint, and swearing,
and the sheets soaked."

Serena stalked over to the bed and examined the
sheets and pillows. She pointedly avoided looking at the
occupant of the bed. "These bed linens will have to be
changed," she said. She disappeared for a moment, and
Clermont heard her speaking to someone in the hall.

"Emily said something about a loud noise," she said
to the nurse as she came back in, trailed by a sleepy-
looking maid.

"There might have been something—" Mrs. Digby
began cautiously.

"Yes, from the chimney," he interrupted, happy that it
had not been a hallucination. "It sounded like a door
closing, or a lid banging down."

Serena and the nurse looked at each other.

"That young devil," muttered Mrs. Digby. "I
declare—" She was silenced by a warning glare
from Serena, and vanished, murmuring something
about tending to Master Simon. Clermont's bed
was speedily remade and a fresh warming pan provided. Serena's last act before she vanished back
down the hall was to stand and watch him while he
drank a double dose of Dr. Wall's powder. She
must have put something else in it as well, because
he found himself shortly overcome by drowsiness.

He slept again off and on, dimly aware that someone was sitting in a chair next to the bed but never summoning up enough energy to look and see who it was. Finally a change in the light prompted him to open his eyes. He saw Serena, now fully dressed, standing by the window and holding the curtains slightly aside. The sun was just coming up.

She turned at the rustle of the sheets. Her face was in shadow, but he fancied there was an almost wistful quality to her expression.

"Go back to sleep," she said softly.

He was suddenly, perversely, wide awake. "What are my other options?" He reviewed them mentally: flee Boulton Park clad only in a nightshirt and dressing gown or lie in bed contemplating all the reasons why his presence here was dangerous, unethical, and probably futile.

"I could read to you," she offered, to his surprise. "If you like."

He blinked. "If it is not too much trouble—"

She was already moving towards the door. "History? A novel? Poetry? Sermons? What do you prefer?"

"Anything but sermons," he said, before he could stop himself.

She laughed and disappeared, returning a few minutes later with a slim octavo volume.

"What is it?"

"You must guess." She cleared her throat. " 'What dire offense from amorous causes springs—' "

"Pope. 'Rape of the Lock,' " was the instant response. Curious, he asked, "Do you like him? I thought he was rather out of fashion these days."

"I find him very restful after a dose of Mr. Coleridge," she said tartly.

"Well, then, fire away," he said, settling back to enjoy himself. Pope was not his favorite English poet, but he suspected Miss Allen might be able to persuade him differently, at least in her present amiable mood.

She read very well, and he found himself annoyed by the inevitable interruptions: a maid building up the fire and opening the rest of the curtains; Mrs. Digby with fresh bandages; another maid with some broth; occasional pauses by Serena to comment on what she saw from her seat by the window. It must have been well past nine o'clock when she suddenly froze, looked out the window for a long moment, and then swore under her breath. Not a maidenly oath like "Confound it" or "Drat," either. He had distinctly heard the word "Damnation."

"What is it?"

"Never mind," she said, jumping up. "I'm afraid I'll have to leave you for a bit. I'll send you Mrs. Digby again."

" 'Two handmaids tend the sick, alike in place, but differing far in figure and in face,' " he offered, after a moment for rapid calculation of the meter.

"That is *very* unkind to Mrs. Digby." Her tone was frosty, but he had seen the telltale twitch at the corner of her mouth.

"Pope," he said gravely, "is not kind."

7

Warned by Pritchett that there was "a bit of a situation" upstairs, Bassington approached the hallway leading to the sickroom with caution. Googe, after waiting patiently for two days, had finally been summoned by the earl. Unfortunately, Bassington had neglected to consult the nursing staff about his decision, and the constable was apparently having some difficulty persuading them to let him see their patient. Sure enough, as the earl rounded the corner to the east wing he spied his niece standing with her arms folded in front of the door to the guest suite.

"Do step aside, miss," pleaded the exasperated Googe. " 'Twill be only a few questions. Mrs. Digby says the gentleman sat up and ate some breakfast. If he can eat porridge then surely he can speak with me for a minute. I'll take care not to tire him, I promise."

"It was not porridge," said Serena sternly. "He cannot tolerate solid food yet. He had broth. And he only sat up briefly while we changed the bandage on his head. I'll not have him disturbed for no good reason; he was very poorly last night." She looked bone-tired, and the earl deduced correctly that the patient was not the only one who had had a difficult night. There were hollows under her eyes, and her movements looked stiff and weary. Unlikely, he decided gloomily, that she would take the scolding he was about to give her in good part.

Serena spied the earl approaching, and her face

brightened. "Uncle, do help me," she said. "Mr. Googe insists on interviewing Mr. Clermont, but he is still far from well. I cannot see why it is so urgent."

"Your lordship!" Googe had also taken heart at Bassington's appearance. "I'm sure you understand my position, my lord. Following on the incident last week this is a very suspicious matter." His voice took on a plaintive note. "Just a brief conversation. To ascertain the basic facts. So as to be able to set an inquiry in motion, as is my duty."

"I'm afraid he is right, Serena," said Bassington. "I confess to some alarm myself, although I trust you will not repeat that remark in your aunt's hearing. And I allowed Mr. Clermont a full day to recover before I summoned Mr. Googe."

"You may have half an hour," was her grudging concession. She rapped on the door, held a low-voiced conference with Mrs. Digby, and ushered them into the sickroom.

Clermont was propped partway up and sipping a steaming mug of something whose odor made the earl wince in sympathy. At the sight of the two men he tried to sit up properly and began a long, courtly period about inconvenience and regrettable foolhardiness, but Bassington waved him to silence.

"No, no, Mr. Clermont, I should be apologizing to you. I am mortified that a guest of mine should suffer such an outrage on my land. We will, of course, do our utmost to discover the criminals. Mr. Googe"—he indicated the constable with a gesture—"would like to speak with you for a few moments, if you feel able."

"The constable? Criminals?" Clermont frowned. "But it was a prank, surely? Some boys playing a game, perhaps, who ran off and left the rope, not realizing what might happen?"

"Beg pardon, sir, my lord," interposed the constable, "but Bates and I have already been up and inspected the ropes. No boy tied those. A grown man, on horseback, and a large man at that."

"Poachers, most likely," added the earl.

"I do not wish to press charges," said Clermont, with an unconscious arrogance that Bassington noted and filed away. "You need not trouble yourself further, Mr. Googe."

"I am afraid the matter cannot rest there," said Bassington. "You see, Mr. Clermont, I shall press charges. Because the trap was in all likelihood not intended for you. It was either intended for my gamekeeper or for me."

"Good God," muttered Clermont, obviously startled and dismayed. In another moment he had composed himself. "I did not think of that, sir. In that case I would be glad to assist Mr. Googe now, if that is convenient."

The first part of the interview was a meticulous repetition of the information he had given four days ago. It was established once again that Mr. Clermont, a resident of London, had been staying at the Burford Arms. Whilst riding a hired horse (Googe did forget himself here so far as to observe that he had never heard of Tempest needing human assistance to jettison her rider before) Mr. Clermont had come upon an unexpected obstacle in the form of a rope tied across the path across Clark's Hill. No, the gentleman had no enemies in these parts. No, he had seen nothing suspicious after his initial encounter with the man in the frieze coat: no traps, no other evidence of poaching. In general, he had found the paths unfrequented. Occasionally he had seen Miss Allen walking on the hillside.

"Yes, my niece usually walks in the mornings," the earl confirmed, abstracted. "My son is supposed to accompany her on fine days, but he often lies abed."

"He was out yesterday morning, Uncle," interposed Serena. "For which we are all very grateful."

Googe cleared his throat, reminding them of his

mission. "And last, if I might have a full description of your injuries, sir?"

Serena answered for him: "Sprained or possibly broken wrist, blow to head, cuts, twisted ankle, chills, fever."

There was silence as the constable faithfully recorded every item. "I believe I'll spend a few hours at the Burford Arms," said Googe to the earl, closing up his notebook and heaving himself to his feet. "See if I hear anything useful. I've spoken with Purvis about that earlier matter, and he swore up and down 'twaren't him, but I'll be curious to discover where he might have been yesterday morning."

Bassington acknowledged Googe's bow as he left the room. But the earl did not leave, in spite of a warning glare from Serena. Something was nagging at him, something to do with Clermont's response to one of the questions. When Googe had inquired whether Clermont had enemies, the man had clearly hesitated. How had he phrased it? That he knew of no one in England who held any brief against him?

"I noticed that you hedged a bit when Mr. Googe asked you about enemies," he said slowly. "Is there anyone who might have intended that trap for you?"

"I doubt it." Clermont stared thoughtfully down at the bandages on his hand. "There is my cousin," he acknowledged finally. "My grandfather gave me an estate which should have been part of his portion."

"Is he in England?"

Clermont shook his head. "I thought he was in Italy. But when my servant returns from London, I will have him make inquiries." He frowned. "In fact—now that I think of it, he did once hire someone to challenge me to a duel. Perhaps it would be best to ask Mr. Googe to wait, until Vernon can ascertain his whereabouts?"

"I think Purvis a far more likely culprit," said the earl.

"Googe will probably have a confession from him this evening, and we can dismiss your mysterious cousin."

"That is what I am afraid of," muttered Clermont.

"In the meantime," continued Bassington, who had not really taken in this last remark, "I beg you to consider Boulton Park your home. We will endeavor to make your stay as comfortable as possible."

"Time is up, Uncle," announced Serena, rising.

Reluctantly, the earl got to his feet. "What happened, by the way? At this duel your cousin contrived?"

"Oh, I disarmed the fellow without much trouble." Clermont gave a twisted smile. "My family had made sure that I had all the requisite skills to take my place in an extinct aristocracy. Fencing, shooting, dancing—you know the sort of thing."

Serena accompanied her uncle to the door and stepped out into the hall with him. Laying her hand on his arm, she began, "I beg your pardon, Uncle, but could you tell me whether—"

As he noted her drawn face and hastily dressed hair he remembered his wife's instructions. "Did you sit up with that young man last night?" he interrupted.

"Mrs. Digby and I took it in turns, yes," she admitted. "The night before as well."

"Your aunt was right, then; she told me you had been there alone for several hours."

"And what is wrong with that, may I ask?" she responded, on the defensive. "Or do you think some poor maidservant should lose a night's sleep to play propriety? I would not have trusted anyone save Mrs. Digby to watch him in my place; he was quite ill. And Dr. Wall prescribed some powders which would be dangerous if the dose were mismeasured."

"Don't try to cozen me with measures and doses, Serena," said her uncle sternly, "or remind me that you have nursed Simon many times, or describe the sensible practices of the Ursuline nuns. This sort of thing simply will not do here in modern-day England. If you must remain with Mr. Clermont, one of the maids will be assigned to stay in the room with you."

"For mercy's sake, Uncle, he can barely sit up! And tonight I will only be stopping in once or twice; he is coming along very nicely. Or would be, if you and Googe had not plagued him just now."

"Even so," said the earl implacably, "the servants will talk—or, more to the point, Mrs. Childe will talk, and your aunt will be mortified. You may ask Mrs. Fletcher to relieve the maid of duties for the rest of the day, if that will salve your conscience about keeping a servant awake. This is quite a different affair from your vigils with Simon." He saw her fuming and neatly forestalled further objections by saying, "You had something you were going to ask me?"

Serena bit her lip. "Yes. I—I wondered if it was usual for gentlemen to have firearms with them in bed."

"What?" He was startled. "No, it most certainly is not! Why do you ask?"

"Well—" she hesitated, then said in a rush, "apparently Mr. Clermont normally sleeps with a gun under his pillow."

"How very odd. But then, Philip wrote that he lived in Canada for several years. He may have acquired the habit there."

His lack of concern must have at least partially reassured her, because she headed off towards her own room without pursuing the issue further. But Bassington stood frowning for a moment. Something was bothering him; something connected with Clermont, and it slid away from him whenever he tried to think about it. Something about the young man's appearance, perhaps? Or something he had said? Or something he *hadn't* said when Googe had questioned him about the attacks? With an exasperated snort he gave up and headed back down to his study.

* * *

"I have some good news for you," Serena announced when she visited her patient later that day. He looked worn out, which was not surprising, since he had just endured a visit from her aunt. Having been present at several of the earlier visits, Serena could predict the course of this one: renewed apologies for the accident, deftly passing on to a suggestion that he might require a long stay at Boulton Park, and, from there, moving to coy hints about why such a stay might be a desirable thing for all parties. She wondered if the countess had been less coy and more direct in her absence. The thought made her shudder. But certainly Clermont had exhibited no signs of embarrassment or self-consciousness on seeing her just now.

"You are releasing me from durance vile?" he said promptly.

She shook her head. "Not quite yet."

"Tempest has reappeared unharmed?" He had been asking after the missing animal every day.

"As a matter of fact, yes, she has. And your saddlebags have been sent over." She beckoned to a tow-headed footman, who came in and deposited the bags on a table by the armoire. "That will be all, Hubert." As the footman withdrew she moved purposefully over to the table.

Clermont looked alarmed. "There is no need to unpack the bags—my servant—"

She was rummaging through one of the pouches. "That is the second piece of good news," she said over her shoulder. "Your servant should be here tomorrow morning. With your luggage. I'm sure you will be very glad to have your own clothing again. As well as this." She turned, holding out a small pistol.

He was silent for a moment, then reached out and took it. "I made quite a fool of myself last night, didn't I? I was hoping only Mrs. Digby had heard me bellowing that I needed my gun." But she noticed that he checked it carefully to see if it was loaded and tucked it firmly down between the mattress and the side of the bed.

"Worried about men in frieze coats?" she asked dryly.

He grimaced. "I've been meaning to consult with you on that topic. I'm afraid that your uncle and Googe have put the two incidents together and come up with something much more serious than is warranted."

"I consider the second incident fairly serious," she said coldly. "You were almost killed. But I take your point. You feel that someone—presumably me—should enlighten my uncle about the real source of that shot on Tuesday last."

"Well, yes and no. Yes, he should be told. But no, I don't think you should do it."

"You?" She was astonished.

"Certainly not!" he said, clearly very offended.

"Well then, who? I think Bates suspects, but it is hardly his place—"

He interrupted her impatiently. "Simon, of course."

She sat down slowly in the chair, which had been drawn up next to his bed. After a long moment, she said quietly, "What a sad commentary on how badly spoilt Simon has become these past few years. That solution did not even occur to me, and of everyone in the household I am closest to him."

"Is he—dishonest?" He said it as though he were holding up a toad.

She shook her head. "Not in the way I think you mean. He tells raspers, as he calls them, by the bushel. He feigns illness. He opens locked cupboards in Mrs. Fletcher's office and switches all the plate from one to the other. But most of that, in my opinion, is simply pent-up energy."

Clermont repeated what was becoming his refrain to

the ballad of Viscount Ogbourne: "That boy should be in school."

"My aunt thinks him sickly. And he was, when he was younger. He was quite ill, off and on, for two years." She stared off into space. "He was only four when the first bout of pleurisy hit, and he was so patient, and brave! I nursed him; I had just arrived and barely knew my aunt and uncle; it was a relief to have something worthwhile to do. We became, in effect, brother and sister. And then he recovered, gradually, but my aunt never believed it. So now he takes advantage of her fears, and I stand by and permit it."

"What of your uncle?"

"He defers to my aunt on all domestic matters."

"The doctor?"

She smiled suddenly, a mischievous smile. "Dr. Wall and I have in fact been mounting a campaign to promote Simon from an invalid to a healthy boy with a slight tendency to colds in the chest. It is a delicate operation; a year ago Dr. Wall told my aunt straight out that Simon was not really ill and she nearly dismissed him on the spot."

He changed the subject suddenly. "Speaking of Dr. Wall, he told me that if Vernon returned he would authorize my removal to the inn the day after next."

"Did he?" she said in her blandest tones. The old doctor had conferred with her, of course. "Congratulations."

"Your aunt is pressing me to stay on, however, as a guest rather than a patient." His dark eyes studied her carefully as he spoke.

"Why do you tell me this?"

"Because I will decline if it will make you uncomfortable," he said bluntly.

"I thought you were eager to be gone," she said, equally blunt. "The phrase 'durance vile' was used, not completely in jest, only a few moments ago."

"There is a difference between being confined to bed

on a diet of broth and medicinal teas and being a guest
of the Earl and Countess of Bassington," he pointed out.

"Not much of a difference," she warned him. "At least
if I have anything to say about it. You will still need to
rest frequently and eat a light diet for several more
days."

"A light diet!" He groaned. "Do you know, I would
kill for a piece of bread. Or cheese. A big, square hunk
of cheese. Apples. Grapes." His face brightened. "Wait,
don't invalids eat grapes?"

"They do," she conceded, "when their host's succes-
sion houses contain grapes. Which ours, alas, do not."

"Oh," he said, disappointed.

"If I procure grapes, will you stay?"

He looked at her curiously. "Do you want me to
stay?"

She wasn't sure of the answer. For that matter, she
wasn't sure where she could find grapes at this time of
year.

"I think you might be good for Simon," she said at
last.

"If he doesn't kill me, or disable me, or steal all my
worldly goods."

"And do you have any worldly goods, Mr. Clermont?"

His brows shot up. "My, what an inquisitive young
lady you are, Miss Allen. Yes, I do. A very ample sup-
ply, in fact. Is there any particular reason you wished
to know about my finances?"

She lowered her head, mortified. This time she really had gone too far. "I don't want you to—to take
advantage of my aunt," she said in a low voice. "Perhaps
she seems foolish to you, but she is very good-natured
and I owe her a great deal."

"Miss Allen, look at me."

She did. His eyes held hers, imperious.

"I am not here to fleece your aunt. I am not here to

steal the Bassington rubies, if there are any Bassington rubies. I am not here—let us put our cards on the table—to court you. Believe it or not, I am here to read about the travels and researches of the late earl." He smiled suddenly, a speculative smile which made her very uneasy. "Although come to think of it, a discreet flirtation would be a charming way to distract me from the trials of my convalescence."

She glared at him. "I am *not* interested in a discreet flirtation," she hissed.

"Well," he conceded, "it is true that discretion is not your strong point."

"I think I liked you better when you were ill," she informed him crossly. Turning, she swept towards the door using her best glide. But she paused at the last minute and turned around. "You may stay if you wish."

He inclined his head gravely. He did not smile, which was wise. If he had she would have told him that, on second thought, he made her very nervous and perhaps it would be best if he did leave.

When she looked in again before going down to dinner, half hoping he might have changed his mind on his own, he was asleep. With the dark eyes closed and his gold and brown hair falling across his face, he looked from across the room remarkably like an older version of Simon. No wonder she didn't trust him.

8

Somewhere a clock chimed midnight. His door was open a crack—the old nurse had not closed it properly when she had left an hour ago—and the strokes could be heard distinctly in the silent house. He had slept for several hours earlier in the evening; now he was lying awake, enjoying life without Vernon. It was not pleasant to have a continual headache, or to worry about whether his wrist was broken instead of sprained, or to be confined to bed and half starved. But it *was* pleasant to have a respite from his servant's well-meant, solicitous, endless hovering. Miss Allen, with her efficient hostility, was in some ways a breath of fresh air.

He was being unjust, of course. Vernon could not help a touch of paternalism; Clermont's aunt had engaged him to wait on Julien years ago. To Vernon, his master was still a boy, and all Clermont's actions were judged as though he were sixteen. The sojourn in Canada was, in the servant's view, a three-year fit of pique. The decision to conceal his title and be known as plain Mr. Clermont: foolish pride. The visit to Boulton Park—no, he decided, he didn't want to revisit Vernon's blistering denunciations of his current enterprise.

Their last quarrel, which had taken place just after their arrival in Burford, had ended with Clermont threatening to dismiss the valet if he said one more word to him on the subject. Since then Vernon had confined himself to the occasional enigmatic quotation from the

Bible, addressed in a loud voice to inanimate objects. The washbasin, for example, had been told that "a fool uttereth all his mind," while Julien's greatcoat (or perhaps the clothes brush) was the recipient of "can a man take fire in his bosom, and his clothes be not burned?" Clermont wondered what Vernon would come up with in response to the news that his master now intended a stay of ten days as Bassington's guest.

Well, tomorrow he would find out. In the meantime he would make the most of his solitude. He tucked his good arm behind his head and contemplated the dull glow of the banked embers in the grate. At some point, he knew, one of his nurses would come in again and check on him. Should he wish for the shapely shrew, or the kind but dull Mrs. Digby? In his present optimistic mood, he could see advantages either way. Mrs. Digby could probably be cajoled into bringing him something to eat. And Miss Allen, besides being undeniably attractive, maintained a guarded distance which appealed to his sense of mischief.

He heard a noise like a door closing and pushed up onto his elbow, expecting to hear footsteps coming down the hall towards his room. He could tell by now, from the pace of the steps, which of his nurses would appear. But he heard nothing more, except a faint series of thumps behind the chimney. It was still gusty outside—there had been a rainstorm earlier in the evening—and after another minute without any activity in the hall he concluded that the wind had torn open a shutter and was now banging it occasionally against the wall of the house.

Conscious of a slight feeling of disappointment, he sank back down onto the pillows. The bed gave a disgruntled creak, the wind flung a belated spatter of raindrops against the window, and there was another thump from the fireplace, accompanied by an odd odor of wet wool. Then silence. And a full minute later, barely audible over the noise of the wind, a soft footstep.

Clermont's eyes, well-adjusted now to the near darkness, made out a faint movement on the other side of the room. His good hand shot down between the mattress and the bed frame and found his pistol. It made an audible click as he cocked it, and he heard a startled exclamation from somewhere near the window.

"Stop right there," he ordered curtly. "Don't move; I've a gun and I hear very well. If I sense motion I will fire at it. Who are you? What are you doing here?"

No answer, just a cough, quickly smothered.

Clermont added two plus two and came up with four. He sighed and lowered his weapon. "Viscount Ogden, I believe? Or is it Ogbourne? My apologies, I took you for a thief. I'm setting down the pistol." He released the hammer very slowly and audibly. "Might I ask you to come over to the nightstand—two or three paces ahead, slightly to your left—and light the candle?" There was still no reply, but he knew he had guessed right. The boy stepped over to the little table, moving with an assurance which told Clermont that he was an old hand at navigating in the dark. After only a brief fumble, he saw a spark, and the candlewick guttered slightly in the boy's trembling hand and then caught. The widening arc of light showed him Simon's face, very pale, mouth clamped shut, eyes wide with apprehension.

"Well, which is it?" Clermont prompted. "Ogden, or Ogbourne?"

"Ogbourne," whispered his visitor mechanically. Then he recovered his powers of speech in a rush. "You won't tell, will you? I'd no notion of disturbing you, I was just trying to get back upstairs without being seen."

"That was you the other night as well, wasn't it? The bang from the chimney?"

"Yes. Sorry," said the boy in a small voice. "I didn't mean to make such a noise, but I don't often go this way, and I had forgotten how the handle worked. I was tugging at the wrong end for the longest time, and I pulled too hard, and it just flew back suddenly and clanged right into the wall."

"What handle?"

"To the little iron door in the chimney wall. Lots of the fireplaces in this house have them—a little door, and you can get into a space between the fireplace and the outer wall of the house and climb down to the next floor. That is, I can. You wouldn't fit."

Now Clermont could see that there were, in fact, a few flecks of soot in the fair hair and more soot smeared across one shoulder of the jacket. "The stairs, of course, are to be avoided?"

"Well, if I don't want Nurse to catch me, they are. She comes some nights to see if I'm asleep, and when she finds my bed empty she lurks about at the top of the staircase trying to ambush me. But if I can get back to my room without her seeing me, I can convince her that I was hiding somewhere in the attic the whole time." Simon said this last with considerable satisfaction.

"The whole time . . . when you were, in fact, where?" asked Clermont, moving slightly to one side in the bed so that Simon could sit down. Now he knew where the wet wool smell had come from; the boy's jacket and nankeens were wet, and a slimy brown clump of leaves left a smear on the quilt as Simon settled himself.

"Oh, out." Simon waved his hand vaguely. "I have a weak chest, you know, and Nurse and my mother are always saying I look unwell, and dosing me, and making me lie down, and I *hate* lying in bed when I'm not sleepy. So I found some other ways to get in and out of my room, and when I'm restless I can take a—a— constitutional."

"A constitutional? At midnight? In February?"

"A gentle walk is good for the health and can be beneficial in cases of insomnia," recited Simon in a sing-song voice.

"You," Clermont retorted, "should be at school."

"My mother says schools are dreadful places, especially for boys who are delicate." Simon looked prim. "You sleep in a damp, unheated garret with dozens of other students, and there isn't enough to eat, and they tell you where to go every minute of the day and flog you if you are tardy."

"It's true that the school day is rather regimented," admitted Clermont. "But the rest is nonsense. I was at Old Hall in Hertfordshire for nine years. No garrets. No floggings. And I had my own study the last two years I was there."

Simon digested this in silence for a moment. Then his eye fell on the pistol, a small model covered with silver inlay and elaborate scrollwork. "Not much of a gun," he said scornfully, picking it up without waiting for permission and hefting it. "Wish I'd known you were threatening me with this little toy. Couldn't hurt anything much bigger than a rabbit with this, I'd wager."

"Wrong again," said Clermont, smoothly recapturing the weapon. "I killed a very large bear with that gun some years ago. You have to hit between the eyes, of course. The gauge is too small to be sure of killing a large animal if you aim for the body."

Simon was looking sullen. Ashamed of his earlier fright, Clermont guessed.

"You should get back to your room," he said, giving the boy a gentle shove. "Don't worry, I won't tell anyone I saw you." The boy, still scowling, had nearly reached the door when some unaccountable impulse led Clermont to add, "You know, this gun can be unloaded without firing it. Would have come in handy last week in the park."

In an instant Simon was back by the bed. "You're gammoning me," he said.

"No, watch." With three neat twists, Clermont unscrewed the barrel from the stock and removed the bullet from its chamber.

Simon's mouth was wide open.

"I'll show you how to fire it, once your cousin lets me out of bed," he offered as he replaced the barrel. "It's Dutch, spiral bore, very moderate recoil and wonderfully accurate."

"And to think I said you would be a good influence on him." Her voice came from the doorway and did not sound amused. This time her hair was neatly braided, and she was wearing a shawl over her wrap. But she looked just as irritated as she had that first night when she had burst half undressed into what she thought was a crisis in the sickroom and found Clermont gaping at her while Mrs. Digby rewound his bandages.

Simon and Clermont both froze in place. She stepped into the room, closed the door quietly but firmly behind her, and stood, arms folded, glaring at them. Her cousin scuttled quickly from his position by the night table to the relative safety of the other side of the bed.

"Where on *earth* have you been?" she asked Simon in a low, furious voice. "You are lucky I heard Mr. Clermont talking and realized you might be in here; Mrs. Digby is hunting for you everywhere!" She caught sight of his bedraggled nankeens, with the telltale fragments of muddy leaves clinging to the sides of his legs, and groaned. "Not the secret forest?" Simon nodded sheepishly. "Take off your wet things, and wrap yourself up in this for the moment," she ordered, handing him her shawl. "I'll go distract her and fetch your nightshirt. Leave your clothes here; I'll collect them later and smuggle them upstairs."

She turned to Clermont and raked him with a withering glance. "As for you, you are meant to be convalescing, not entertaining midnight visitors. You should be ashamed of yourself, encouraging him like this! And"—as her eye fell on the muddied coverlet—"I see that your bedding is wet *again*. Do you think the servants have nothing to do but change your bed linens every night?" The injustice of these accusations left him speechless, and before he could point out that she was far more guilty of corrupting Simon than he was, she had disappeared in an angry flutter of braids and nightclothes. Clermont thought he heard her mutter some imprecation containing the words "ungrateful" and "odious" as she went through the door.

Simon was hastily stripping off his boots and stockings and kicking them under the bed. "I shan't take off my shirt and breeches until I have something to put on, no matter what she says," he grumbled, wrapping the shawl around his legs. "It's not decent. I'm not a child anymore."

"What is the secret forest?" Clermont asked, intrigued.

"A tunnel from the cellar; it comes up under the woods in the park. Everyone always makes a fuss because I have to crawl a bit at the end and I get muddy."

When Serena reappeared with a nightshirt he wriggled into it and out of the rest of his clothes with the ease of long practice.

"Hurry!" she told him, giving him a push. "She's looking in the kitchen now; you've time to get upstairs and open the attic door before you get back in bed."

He skittered towards the door but turned at the last minute.

"Sir? Did you mean it?"

"Yes, I promise you a shooting lesson."

Grinning, Simon grabbed the door frame and swung himself exuberantly out the door.

"Now you have just rewarded him for misbehaving," she said disapprovingly as she gathered up Simon's scattered clothing.

"*I* did not send Mrs. Digby to the kitchen."

She sighed. "You're right, of course. And I haven't yet dared suggest to him that he tell my uncle about the pistol." Absentmindedly, she sat down on the edge of the bed and stared at the muddy bundle in her lap. "That task requires more eloquence than I possess, I'm afraid."

It was tempting to lead her on, to encourage her in what he suspected might be a lengthy conversation about the wayward viscount. He might be able to pry some information about Bassington out of her in the process. And she was very pretty, in her white night-gown, with the candlelight reflecting off the smooth curves of her braids. But it was even more tempting to take revenge for the insults she had heaped on him a few minutes earlier.

"Why, Miss Allen," he murmured, moving closer and taking her hand, "when you told me you were not inter-ested in a discreet flirtation I had no notion you might in fact be more partial to an *indiscreet* flirtation." He bent over and pressed a light kiss on the palm. Then on the wrist. One more, just behind the wrist.

It occurred to him that she should be resisting. He lifted his head and looked into her eyes. They were wide with shock, deep gray mirrors edged in lamplight. With a great effort, as though he were moving through water, he lowered her arm and laid it gently on the bed. His gaze slid down to her mouth. He wasn't thinking about revenge any longer. He drew in his breath, very qui-etly.

She sat, paralyzed, for one more moment. He saw her take it all in—that she was in her nightdress, seated on the bed of a strange man, about to be kissed. Then she jumped up and fled, scarlet-faced.

Sir Charles Barrett was leafing idly through a small stack of letters at the breakfast table, setting half aside unopened, glancing quickly at most of the rest, and reading through the few items which seemed urgent. His wife, long inured to silence at breakfast, was placidly sipping her chocolate and perusing the latest communication from Masters Edward and James Barrett, penned in haste from school and pleading for an immediate advance on their quarterly allowance. Sir Charles had handed it to her with the recommendation to let the rascals stew in their own juices.

"What do you think it is now?" she asked.

"Same as last time, they've placed some absurd wager and lost all their money."

"Last time they were here in London, consorting with that limb of Satan, Simon Viscount Ogbourne. I didn't realize this sort of thing went on at school as well."

He lifted his head from his own correspondence. "My dear," he said mildly, "much as I would like to blame Simon for the failings of my sons, I am afraid it is not quite so one-sided. Who took Simon down into the crypt under St. Paul's, for example? And who showed him how to pick locks?"

"Ned and James would not have been able to teach Simon lock-picking if *you* had not allowed your friend Colonel White to instruct the two of them first," she pointed out acerbically. "For an entire afternoon, using our own house as a testing ground. What were you thinking?"

"God knows." In fact, he had been thinking that when he was a schoolboy he had always longed to acquire a few practical skills, like lock-picking, in addition to Latin and geometry. He went back to his letters and separated one sheet out of a thick packet. "Here, this is for you. It's from Clara Bassington; she enclosed it with Bassington's to me."

"They're coming up to town later this month," she said, peering at the spidery handwriting.

"Yes, so Bassington says. And a good thing, too, with this Russian business unresolved." He continued skimming the earl's letter. Negotiations with the Tsar's minister continued; Royce had finally located the misplaced file; had Barrett heard anything more of the Austrian position;

there had been a curious incident. . . . Barrett frowned, sat up, read more carefully. In his last letter, Bassington had mentioned that their mysterious visitor was leaving the next day, and Barrett had breathed a sigh of relief and suspended his inquiries into Clermont's background. Now it appeared the man was still there—and was actually staying in the house, after a very suspicious accident.

He got up, swearing under his breath, and rang the bell.

"Yes, sir?" A footman materialized instantly. Sara Barrett ran a very well-ordered house.

"Is Crosswell here yet?" This was his secretary.

"I believe so, sir. Shall I ask him to step over this way?"

"If you please." The man vanished, and Barrett gave his wife an apologetic look. "Do you mind, my dear? I would like to finish my breakfast, but this may involve rather tedious matters."

"Oh, I was done eating ages ago," said his wife. "I was simply keeping you company. I'll leave you to Crosswell's tender mercies."

The secretary, a pleasant-faced young man of twenty-two, appeared almost as quickly as the footman had and held the door for Lady Barrett on her way out.

Dispensing with the courtesies, Barrett held up the letter. "This is from Bassington," he said. "Remember his visitor? Mr. Clermont? I had asked you to look into him, and then I told you to drop it? I need you to pick it up again. There's been some sort of riding accident, and Clermont is now ensconced in Boulton Park being waited on hand and foot by Miss Allen and Lady Bassington. The whole thing smells to high heaven."

"Er," said Crosswell, blushing slightly. He was very shy, too shy, Barrett thought regretfully, to realize his ambition to serve in parliament. But he would make some minister an excellent secretary.

"Yes?" Barrett said encouragingly.

"Er, didn't quite drop it." The thin face turned even redder. "Got curious. Knew someone who had been at Derring's school. Younger, of course, my age. But thought I would ask. Bastard from noble line, odd name. Schoolboys fond of that sort of gossip. Thought my, er, acquaintance might remember something. And he did."

"What?" Barrett was accustomed to his secretary's condensed style of speaking.

"Clermont not English. French."

"You believe Clermont is *French*?"

"My friend will swear to it, sir. Many émigré students at Old Hall after the Revolution. Catholic schools in France closed for years during the Terror, you know."

"You are telling me there is a Frenchman at Boulton Park right now, a Frenchman who speaks perfect English and has told no one of his origins?"

"Er," said Crosswell, "yes. Very likely."

"Hell," said Barrett with feeling. He rang again and ordered the footman to institute an immediate search for one Philip Derring, a young man from Oxfordshire lodging somewhere near Mount Street. "It's urgent," he called, as the footman withdrew. "And if you do find him, bring him here at once."

"What if you can't locate Derring?" Crosswell asked after the footman had disappeared once more.

"Then we call in the dragoons." Barrett picked up his coffee cup. "And in this case, that is not a figure of speech."

9

A gentleman does not announce his rank when introducing himself.

—Precepts of Mlle. de Condé

Clermont's brief respite from Vernon's supervision came to an end at half past ten in the morning of his fourth day at Boulton Park. There was a familiar knock on the door and an equally familiar failure to wait for permission to enter. The valet marched in, followed by two cowed underlings with an enormous trunk which they deposited, under his supervision, next to the armoire. They returned a few moments later with a crate of books, Julien's equipment case, and a cloth-covered basket. On their final trip they brought in two armchairs and a Persian wool coverlet. Only after dismissing them did the valet finally deign to greet his master, who had been watching the proceedings in horrified fascination.

"I trust, sir," said Vernon in arctic tones, "that you will see fit to inform me next time before you nearly kill yourself."

Clermont started to protest that it had been an accident but thought better of it. It had not, in fact, been an accident, and in any case, the best strategy with Vernon was to remind him who was master. "What is *that*?" he demanded, pointing at the trunk.

"Your new trunk." Vernon opened it. It was full. "I took the liberty of purchasing a larger one."

Julien hadn't imagined he owned enough clothing to take up that much space, even if Vernon had brought everything in his wardrobe. He was wrong; Vernon had brought everything in his wardrobe, and it did fill the trunk. Spare riding gear. Evening clothes. Two dressing gowns. A variety of jackets and pantaloons for day wear. Dozens of neckcloths. Stockings. Pumps. Slippers. His evening cloak and silk hat, for heaven's sake, as though an opera house might suddenly materialize in the middle of the earl's garden. Sixteen shirts. As they emerged, neatly folded, his jaw dropped. "Did you bring *all* of my shirts?" he asked, incredulous.

"Yes, sir. Not being certain of the competence of the earl's laundress. Nor of how long you might be planning to stay." This last came with a very pointed look, which Julien pretended not to see.

"And are those books? Why on earth would I need books at Boulton Park? The library here is one of the best in England!"

Vernon sniffed. "I have it on good authority that invalids often prefer familiar volumes, as less taxing to their faculties during convalescence."

"I am *not* an invalid," said Clermont between his teeth. "I am nearly recovered, in fact."

"Miss Allen tells me otherwise." He added, significantly, "I have already spoken with her and assured her that I will do my utmost to carry out her instructions for your care."

He should have known the two of them would form an alliance. His hopes of solid food, centered on the mysterious basket, withered and died. He lay back and watched Vernon finish unpacking, eyes half-closed. Clothing was stowed in the armoire; the books set out; furniture rearranged; curtains twitched open to admit more light. The basket proved to contain four jars of pale brown jelly, which Clermont recognized immediately as belonging to the class of foodstuffs consumed only by those who could not leave their beds and find something more appetizing. He let it all pass without comment until Vernon removed two silver and ivory brushes from the bottom of the trunk and laid them on the table by the armoire.

"Put those away," he said sharply. They were the only items with his crest he owned besides the ring. He couldn't take a chance, especially after Lady Bassington's reaction to one glimpse of the signet.

"But, mi—" The valet cut himself off before the forbidden title could emerge.

"Exactly." He gave Vernon a quelling stare.

"But, *sir*, we have no other brushes. And your hair, if I may say so, requires more than a comb to maintain its proper appearance."

"Be sure to put them away every time after they are used, then."

"Yes, sir." There was a long pause. "I take it, then, you have not had an opportunity to, er, discuss your concerns with Lord Bassington?"

"Not a conversation I would choose to have while lying flat on my back with a dent in my head," he pointed out dryly. "I thought I might wait a bit."

Vernon coughed. "If I might venture to suggest—"

Another quelling stare, and the valet subsided. Julien had heard it all before. A proper gentleman would write a letter. A slightly less proper (and less patient) gentleman would call upon the earl in private and pose the question straight out. A gentleman would *not* snoop through family diaries under the pretext of conducting scientific researches. Nor would he accept the hospitality of a man he considered an enemy.

For years he had been a proper gentleman. He had followed his aunt's rules, which covered everything from how much to eat at formal dinners (less than your host, especially if he outranks you) to when it was appropriate to attempt to kill an opponent in a duel (if he has called you a coward; otherwise, you must only wound him). When he was young, she delivered her injunctions in person, daily, beginning on the day his grandfather formally acknowledged Julien and conferred one of the family titles on him. Once Julien had gone away to school she turned to moral epistles, each with its own subject heading ("On the class of females permitted as mistresses to young men of questionable birth"). Vernon was her master-stroke. Handpicked for his knowledge of the aristocratic code of conduct, he was her means of making a vicarious return to the daily lectures—lectures which, she constantly reminded Julien, he could not afford to ignore.

"Mistakes which in others would go unnoticed will be seen as evidence that your birth has tainted you," she had told him on the occasion of the first lecture ("Gentlemen conceal pain, even when they are being caned for misbehavior," delivered during the caning, which she administered herself when the new marquis defiantly refused to thank his grandfather for his generosity). "You must prove yourself fitted for the position your grandfather has given you. At any moment, no matter how well you have done up until then, you may ruin yourself with one careless word or gesture." He had been five years old.

Now, twenty-four years later, he had finally decided it was time to act like a bastard.

Serena poked her head cautiously into the sickroom after several gentle taps on the door went unanswered. She expected to see her patient in bed, dozing. Instead, for one disoriented moment she thought she had opened the door of the wrong room. Fresh flowers were on the mantelpiece and the nightstand, two new armchairs had been arranged to form a small circle near the bed, and the fire was burning brightly (without smoking, as it usually did). Tucked partially behind one side of the massive armoire at the other end of the room she glimpsed a very large trunk. On the other side stood a clotheshorse, with a jacket and inexpressibles hanging neatly over the rods. A paisley rug had been tossed over the bedclothes and extra pillows in starched cases were plumped against the headboard.

Her patient had been transformed as well. His bandages had been adjusted and partially covered with a black silk bandeau. The bright hair had been trimmed, he had been shaved, and instead of Pritchett's faded dressing gown, he now sported one of claret-colored silk. He was seated at a small table with Simon, both of them peering intently at a metal and wooden contraption which Clermont was adjusting with some brass screws along one side.

"Goodness," she said faintly, more to herself than to either of the occupants of the room. Her eyes moved around the room, finding more additions—a candelabra, a small oval mirror, a stack of leather-bound books on the lower shelf of the nightstand. A volume lay open on the bed; she recognized it as one of the late earl's journals and, curious, stepped over and looked at the passage Clermont had been reading.

15th July. Caracas. Weather continues fair tho quite warm, but the Capt. evinces much impatience to be gone before storms begin. Geo. and Chas. inclined to turn for home as well, neither yet being, in truth, of an age to dedicate themselves to scientific inquiry. Chas. has proved in all a poor traveler, but Geo. professes himself much pleased by the Sights of the New World and has engaged himself to accompany me again nxt. yr. to Russia.

There followed a list, with crude drawings, of some half-dozen specimens collected that day, none of which were moths or butterflies. She turned to the front of the volume. It was dated 1783. George must be her uncle, then, and Charles his cousin. They would have both been in their early twenties. Perhaps the late earl ended by regretting his decision to introduce his son to the joys of travel. Her uncle had spent more time abroad than at home after that first expedition to the Caribbean, and several times he had been given up for dead, only to resurface just when his hopeful cousin had borrowed large sums of money on the expectation that he would now be the heir to the title. Then, fifteen years ago, George Piers had married the daughter of a family friend, produced Simon, and settled down to exploit his now-numerous and very valuable foreign connections as an unofficial consultant to the government.

A harsh, grating sound from the other side of the room called her attention back to Clermont. He was hunched over the table, rotating a handle set into the frame. Simon was staring, fascinated, at a round metal plate which flashed and whirled and sent off tiny sparks. The noise made her wince. After what seemed like a small eternity, it stopped. Clermont straightened and said to Simon, "You can see now—look along this edge—it's already distinctly rounded—"

But Simon had caught sight of her, and, warned by his change of expression, Clermont turned. His dark eyes were glittering with excitement, and in his crimson robe and black headband he bore a disconcerting resemblance to the swashbuckling villain of some lurid novel.

"May I ask what you are doing?" she said.

Her tone was mild, and she had in fact meant her question for Clermont, but Simon's uneasy conscience translated her query into an accusation. "Mr. Clermont invited me," he said defensively. "He sent Hubert to find me, and I came in properly, through the anteroom."

"Did you truly invite him?" she demanded, looking at the alleged host.

"Yes." Clermont frowned, twisted one of the screws slightly, then looked up again. "It wasn't precisely my idea. Hubert—if that is his name—helped my servant to unpack this and mentioned that it might interest the viscount."

"How very—odd," she said. "I am surprised Hubert would forget himself so far as to hint that one of our guests should share a valuable piece of machinery with an eleven-year-old boy."

Clermont grinned. "His exact words, if you must know, were: 'Take care Master Simon don't catch sight of this, sir, or you'll never see it in working order again.'"

Laughing, she said, "Now, *that* sounds more plausible! But you chose to ignore his warning, I take it? Perhaps I should tell you about my clock, which has not chimed since Simon 'repaired' it. Or about the waterless fortnight in the kitchen while the pump was being replaced. Or about my aunt's jewels, which had to be entirely remounted after Simon took the stones out of three different pieces and switched them."

"No need," he assured her. "Hubert enlightened me. I believe he also mentioned a model ship, a distilling apparatus, and a music box."

"The music box works now," Simon muttered. "And Serena's clock never really chimed properly in the first place." Then his face brightened. "Look at this, Serena! It's a lens grinder, and he's going to let me help make the lens for a telescope! See, you cut the glass into blanks, only Mr. Clermont has already done that, and then you set them here in the holder, and use the screws to turn the gears to adjust the angle of the grinding plate, and when the angle is right, you lock it with this lever—"

He was pointing to five different places on the machine, and she was already thoroughly confused. She could see a disk of glass in a sort of vise at one end of the machine, and a series of plates and rods converging on it. Simon was turning the handle slowly, still talking, and she could barely even tell which way each section was rotating; she had never been good with machines. The one thing she did grasp was that this was a precise and complicated piece of equipment. Not the sort of thing idle young gentlemen carried around in their portmanteaux. Who exactly was Julien Clermont? Were his parents in trade, after all? But then why had Mrs. Childe and her aunt treated him like a duke?

She gestured towards the machine, hoping she looked as if she had followed Simon's explanation. "How do you come to be an expert at lens grinding, Mr. Clermont?" she asked.

"Hardly an expert," he said. His face had grown guarded again, as though he somehow sensed her suspicion. "But I am good enough to make lenses for myself; the one I use for the specimens, for example. My grandfather insisted that I learn."

"Was he a craftsman himself?"

For a moment he looked startled, then he shook his head and smiled wryly. "No. Call it a peculiar form of snobbery, if you will. The Hapsburg emperors required their children to learn a craft. Therefore, my grandfather required us to do so. My aunt learned weaving, my cousin studied engraving, and I took up optics." He was not looking at Simon, who was still grinding slowly, but now he said over his shoulder, "Best stop and rotate the blank, Simon, or you may go too far on that side."

"But I shall have to go off to lessons again in a few minutes, and I wanted to finish this bit," the boy protested.

"It takes hours—days—to grind a lens properly. I told you that."

Simon's face fell. "May I come back after lessons, then? Or must I wait until tomorrow?"

"Simon!" said Serena in her rarely used mind-your-manners tone.

Clermont ignored her. "You may come back," he said firmly, "after you have spoken with your father. That was the bargain."

Grumbling, Simon relinquished the handle and left, with a last dark look at Clermont.

"What bargain?" asked Serena warily. Bargains with her cousin were rarely a good idea.

"Simon tells his father that he took his pistol last week; I help him make a telescope."

"But that is an absurd imposition on you! You should not let him plague you; I will speak to Mr. Royce about it."

"Miss Allen," he said. "I am at present confined to my room, on a diet of jellies and broth. I find the viscount's company a pleasant distraction. Far more pleasant than the distraction of worrying that some poor tenant of your uncle's who happens to own a frieze coat might be charged with firing that gun at me."

"You don't really imagine he will go to my uncle and confess, do you?"

"Yes, I do." His face was almost stern. "He gave me his word. Very reluctantly, and with a ferocious scowl."

"But—"

"The scowl guarantees the pledge. Trust me; I am a very good judge of these matters."

"Would you care to place a wager on it?" she retorted. His calm assumption that he had Simon's measure was, for some reason, profoundly irritating, even though she herself had practically begged him to take the boy in hand.

"Certainly. A guinea against a chicken that he comes through by this time tomorrow."

"You want me to stake a *chicken*?" she said incredulously.

"Roast chicken. With dressing." A dreamy smile softened his face. "And mushrooms. I am very partial to mushrooms."

"Done." She put out her hand and he clasped it. "You know," she said, as she turned to go, "Dr. Wall and I had already decided that you could have solid food again tomorrow."

"Yes, but if Simon goes to his father this afternoon, I shall have my chicken tonight."

"I think it far more likely that you will lose a guinea," she warned him.

That was how she found herself, that evening, eating dinner in Clermont's chambers. In her concern to discourage Clermont as a potential suitor she had perhaps interpreted Dr. Wall's orders about diet a bit too zealously—something she had realized, with a stab of guilt, when her patient had proposed such unusual stakes for their wager. Still, after a head injury, a fever, and several days of near fasting, he would likely regret it if he ate an entire bird. She waylaid Vernon outside the sickroom and suborned him. At half past six (the early hour a concession to Clermont's invalid status) she arrived, dressed with great propriety in a gown of pale blue sarsenet and accompanied by Mrs. Digby in the role of chaperone.

Vernon had been as good as his word. Clermont was also formally attired, and the small table in the anteroom had been set for two with the best china and crystal. A tea tray next to the fireplace had been thoughtfully provided for Mrs. Digby, who had worn her Sunday best for the occasion and consequently looked something like a large crow perched on her chair.

"I am informed that I won the wager," Clermont said as Serena came over to the table.

"You did. Within ten minutes of the time Simon left the room."

He rose and held her chair for her. "Was your uncle very angry?"

"You mustn't get up," she said automatically, although he looked startlingly healthy now that he was fully dressed. Then, in a voice too low to carry over to the nurse: "No, and that is fortunate, since he can be terrifying when he is in a fury. Evidently he was more pleased than dismayed, counting it greatly in Simon's favor that he had come forward on his own. Or apparently on his own," she amended. "But he did punish him—a few strokes with a switch—and my aunt has collapsed in hysterics after calling my uncle an unfeeling brute."

Two footmen came in with the chicken, a dish of sautéed mushrooms, serving utensils, and a carafe of wine. While they were in the room Simon's ordeal was not mentioned. Once they had been dismissed, however, and Vernon had begun serving, Clermont started to say, "Have you seen Simon since—" He broke off. The valet had removed the cover from the platter, and it was now clear that there was only one chicken.

"White meat or dark, Miss Allen?" asked Vernon politely.

"There is only—I see there is but one bird," said Clermont, rapidly modulating his tone from outrage to polite surprise. He eyed it balefully and Serena knew what he was thinking: *And it is none too large, either.*

It had been the smallest one she could find. "It was very short notice," she said coolly. "And since it is indirectly thanks to you that my aunt has retired to bed with her smelling salts and my uncle to his study, I thought you owed me your company for dinner."

He glanced longingly at the tiny chicken but said nothing while Vernon divided the portions and doled out a few mushrooms on each plate. Nothing, that is, until he tasted his wine, at which point he choked and demanded, "What have you done to your uncle's hock?"

"Watered it." White wine would not have been her choice, in fact, but it did not reveal dilution to the eye as clearly as red. "Pritchett assured me that this bottle could be spared; it was past its prime." She added in her most helpful nurse-voice, "Perhaps you would prefer tea? I could ring for one of the maids."

He looked, if possible, even more horrified than he had after tasting the wine. Then his eyes narrowed. He leaned back and surveyed her. "You're enjoying this," he said thoughtfully.

"Well, yes," she admitted, "I am."

Amusement and indignation battled; amusement won. A reluctant smile appeared. "And what have I done to deserve this torment, Miss Allen?"

She smiled back, feeling oddly light and happy and sure of herself. So sure of herself that she answered honestly, "I don't know. But I intend to find out."

10

"The house," Serena explained, "was remodeled forty years ago. It was originally brick, a single long block, and it was refaced with stone and expanded to a U shape, with two wings extending towards the gardens in back of the house. This wing is fully occupied by the conservatory, as you see."

He nodded politely and tried to conceal his limp as he followed her around some potted orange trees. In spite of the headache, which still attacked him every time he stood up, it felt wonderful to be on his feet, dressed, and out of the room where he had been imprisoned for three and a half days. Her offer to escort him on a gentle stroll through the house had surprised him; he had thought he would be confined to his bedroom, or perhaps his bedroom and the library, for another day.

"The rarer plant specimens are in a special greenhouse better adapted for tropical species; perhaps tomorrow Dr. Wall will allow you a short walk on the grounds and I could take you there."

"That would be very kind of you." He hadn't done much research on the plants; would that reinforce her suspicions? Perhaps he should spend this afternoon in the library refreshing his memory of the late earl's botanical preferences. Someone who professed interest in butterflies would have at least some knowledge of the plants they fed upon.

"The other wing"—she gestured towards the opposite side of the house, clearly visible through the glass which formed one wall of the conservatory— "houses the library and collections on the upper floor and my uncle's study and receiving rooms on the lower floor. The two wings are connected on this level by a series of public rooms at the front of the house and by this gallery at the back of the house—there is a step up; mind your head in the doorway."

He followed her from the bright warmth of the conservatory into a long, narrow room with an elaborate parquet floor. The outer wall was set with a series of tall windows; the inner wall was studded with pictures. More precisely, with portraits. Men and women in a bewildering variety of costumes and poses jostled against one another or set their feet on the top of another picture. "Ancestors?" he asked, surveying the two-dimensional company in their frames.

"Yes," she said. "Not mine. Simon's. I am from Aunt Clara's side of the family."

He knew that, of course, but remembered to look as though he was hearing it for the first time.

"This gentleman is the founder of the line." She indicated a Cavalier whose dashing peruke and feathered hat contrasted oddly with his square, stolid face. "Henry Piers. A wealthy farmer who supported the king during the civil war and was rewarded with an earldom by Charles II. That is his wife; she was the orphaned daughter of a less fortunate royalist and brought only her looks and her noble ancestors as her dowry."

He studied the adjacent portrait, which showed a stunningly beautiful young woman with fair hair and wide eyes. "The first earl may have thought it an ample jointure, under the circumstances."

"He was apparently besotted with her," said Serena dryly. "He was originally from Lincolnshire and was granted a very large holding there adjoining his own lands, but when she begged him to settle near her former home in the Cotswolds he went back to the king and exchanged half a shire's worth of rich land for a few dozen hilly acres of rocks and trees."

He was still studying the portrait. "She looks familiar," he said slowly. "Is this portrait well known?"

"Come over here, and you will see why you recognize her." She led him down to the far end of the room and pointed to a small oval painting of a child.

"Simon," he said immediately. The resemblance to his ancestress was subtle but unmistakable: something about the set of the eyes and their shape.

"Yes, and look at this." She indicated a large picture on the adjacent wall. It showed two women seated on a lawn surrounded by trees. Their elaborately dressed hair and wide skirts suggested a date well back into the last century, and after a moment he recognized the small building in the distance as Boulton Park in its earlier, brick incarnation. Two small boys stood between the women, one leaning lightly on his mother's shoulder, the other petting a dog.

"Who are they?" He could see at once that both boys, although different enough in coloring, had the same wide stare as Simon.

"My uncle and his cousin."

He stiffened and glanced again at the picture. The dark eyes of the taller boy smiled at him mockingly from beneath a shock of hair so blond it was nearly white. He forced himself to look away, to ask the question his role demanded, "And the man of science, the fourth earl?"

"Here."

An ugly man, especially compared to Simon and the demon-eyed young Bassington, but his expression was kindly and thoughtful. After a moment Clermont realized that the ugliness might not be original: the nose,

whose bulbous asymmetry disfigured the face, looked
to have been broken.

"Did the late earl have a taste for boxing?" he asked,
turning to Serena.

She laughed. "You noticed his nose? I'm afraid he
was rather wild as a young man; there are a number of
stories about how his nose was broken and all of them
involve women and climbing into other men's houses at
night."

"So Simon has inherited more than his face from his
grandfather," he commented lightly.

"A misspent youth is apparently a Piers trait, yes," she
said. "You wouldn't think it now, but my uncle was also
quite an adventurer in his younger days. As for his
cousin Charles, his escapades were so shocking that he
was eventually forced to go abroad. He died recently on
the continent, and evidently it was an ugly affair. Even
Simon has not been able to discover what happened, and
a stack of old diaries was whisked away and locked up
somewhere."

"I know where they are." It was Simon's voice, coming from behind the wall. Both Serena and Julien
looked round, startled. A moment later a thin line in the
paneling grew wider, and Simon slipped through a narrow doorway set into the inner wall. The painting
hanging on the door swung tremulously as the door
opened and shut and at last subsided, slightly crooked.

"Simon, it is very rude to eavesdrop," hissed Serena.

"I wasn't eavesdropping," the boy said indignantly. "I
was just coming along the corridor and heard you talking about Cousin Charles's diaries. You use these
corridors yourself, Serena."

"Not nearly so often as you do," she said tartly. Surveying his clothing, she added, "Nor, it appears, have
you confined yourself to the corridors. You must have
come down the chimney stair from your bedroom; you
have soot on the back of your jacket."

"Bother," muttered Simon, twisting his head and trying to look over his shoulder.

"Let me guess. You have pleaded a headache to be excused from afternoon lessons and are meant to be in bed right now with a cloth over your eyes."

"Wrong!" said her cousin triumphantly. "Royce was called away; there's a new butterfly-man here. A real one."

Julien was about to deny the implied accusation, but his hostess anticipated him.

"Simon, do you have the remotest notion of proper conduct?" she demanded in an exasperated tone. "Eavesdropping—yes, you were, don't bother to argue; bursting out of the servants' corridor and interrupting us; and now insulting a guest. What next? Hiding under the desk in your father's study?" Clermont noticed that she did not correct the assumption behind the insulting slip, only the insult itself.

Simon flushed. "He isn't a butterfly-man; you know it as well as I do."

"Why do you say that?" Clermont asked, before Serena could intervene. He expected a sullen mutter, but instead the boy frowned, bit his lip, and thought for a minute.

"You dress too well," he said slowly. "And you have a very fine gun. And you were able to ride Tempest."

"Damning evidence," agreed Clermont, smiling.

Simon's eyes flashed. "Come with me, and I'll show you what I mean," he said imperiously. He darted to the end of the gallery, opened the door, and held it for the adults. "Quiet," he cautioned as he beckoned them through. "He's just down at the far end of the next room. You can see him from here if you edge over a bit."

The gallery had admitted them into a small reception room; it connected to a larger hall through double doors. At the far end of this second hall Clermont saw an older man standing, apparently absorbed in an Italian landscape on the wall adjacent to the door of Bassington's study. He carried a shabby leather bag, and his jacket pockets bulged with odd lumps. At that moment, the door to the study opened, and Royce came out to escort the visitor in. They were too far away to hear his name, but they saw him bob nervously as he followed the secretary through the door.

"That," said Simon in a vehement whisper, "is a real butterfly-man. You are nothing of the sort."

Clermont looked at Serena. The gray eyes measured him silently, and this time she did not bother to rebuke her cousin. Why should she? thought Clermont. She agrees with him. He saw her glance significantly at the now-closed study door and then at him; her infuriating half smile appeared. She was no fool. She knew that the last person he would want to meet here at Boulton Park was a genuine scholar.

Bassington had been looking forward to a leisurely afternoon in his sitting room reading the latest batch of newspapers from London. Instead he was here, elbows planted resentfully on his desk, contemplating a letter that was as unwelcome as the man who had delivered it.

The Right Honourable, The Earl of Bassington

Boulton Park

My Lord:

I commend to your kind attention the bearer of this letter, a learned and respected citizen of Frankfurt formerly attached to the Hessian court and now engaged in scientific researches upon the lepidoptera of the Americas. Mr. Meyer has engaged my good offices in securing for himself your assistance in furthering his studies. As you may recall, you spoke of this matter some days since when our mutual friend Sir Chas. Barrett was visiting, at which time you mentioned to him your concerns about the preservation and cataloguing of your father's collections. Any aid which you and your household can render him will be gratefully acknowledged not only by Mr. Meyer but also by

Your lordship's very obedient servant,
C. P. White

The earl looked up from this testimonial at the figure who stood quietly on the other side of the earl's writing table. This was a man of middle years, tall but slightly built, rather angular and stiff in his posture. Scalloped indentations on the bridge of his aquiline nose suggested that he habitually wore spectacles, and in fact a gold-rimmed pair were, at the moment, neatly tucked into a small pocket in his waistcoat. Everything about him advertised the scholar—the stoop of the shoulders, the neatly queued gray hair, the loose and old-fashioned cut of his well-worn jacket, the vague dreaminess of his expression. The visitor's attention at the moment seemed to be more on the bookshelves behind his host than on the earl himself. But when the earl, exasperated, set the letter down by his inkstand with a derisive snort, Meyer withdrew his gaze from the bookshelves and waited politely.

"This is preposterous," said the earl, glaring. "Barrett did not say anything of this when we met last week."

"At that time, the affair was not so urgent." Meyer studied his host, the abstracted air suddenly gone. His English had lost its faintly Germanic accent as well. "For example, you were not, at that time, embroiled in a case of attempted murder."

"I do not wish to offend you, Mr. Meyer," said the earl

coldly, "but if I had had any notion that Barrett was planning to involve you and White's courier service I would have refused his offer of assistance. And, I might add, I am still inclined to do so, in spite of my present difficulties, and in spite of the trouble you have obviously taken to arrange your visit. I cannot believe that your presence here will be at all useful. Quite the reverse, I should think. How could you possibly maintain such a charade? What if it were to become known that you were a visitor in my home?"

"Your father received Emmanuel Mendes daCosta in this very study, I believe," the other observed mildly. "And the name Meyer is not unknown in zoological circles. One of my cousins has published a monograph on Baltic eels. In Latin."

"That is nothing to the purpose," growled the earl. "I had assumed Barrett and White had in mind some sort of gentleman scientist, someone who would not be out of place as a houseguest."

Meyer raised his brows slightly, but made no remark. Scowling, the earl looked away—first across at the windows, curtained now against the late afternoon darkness, then into the fire, and finally down again to the surface of the desk. He studied White's letter. It had been dropped partially unfolded against the side of the inkwell, with the result that it resembled a paper model of one of the butterflies which filled the mahogany cabinets in the closet upstairs.

"You are telling yourself," said Meyer, reading his thoughts, "that if I had any notions of genteel behavior, I would take a hint and bow myself out. That my inability to understand the insult you have just put upon me is proof of the truth of that insult. That I know nothing about the charge of the Special Commission, about your present dilemma, or, for that matter, about butterflies."

Taken aback, Bassington looked up. But Meyer was

no longer standing by the desk. Moving with a speed and silence that seemed at odds with his initial, awkward bearing, he had vanished into a door at the back of the room, which led to a servants' staircase. A few moments later he reappeared, carrying a long, shallow wooden drawer with a glass cover and brass handles.

"You seem very familiar with the layout of my home, Mr. Meyer," said the earl angrily.

"It is my job to know such things." Meyer set the tray down on the desk with a small thud. "Top left," he said, indicating the first of the neatly pinned insects in the tray. There were no labels. "*Siproeta epaphus*. Notable for the orange-brown markings on the edge of the wings. Extremely rare; this is one of the prizes of your father's collection. Next to the right: a male *Colobura dirce*. Found also in the West Indies, although this particular specimen was taken in Venezuela. To the right of that: a female *Menander*. Remarkable for its attraction to agrimony; natives will follow it to attempt to locate the plant, which is sought after for the medicinal properties of its leaves. Top right—" He broke off, with an impatient gesture. "I assure you that I know far more about this collection than anyone in this house, than anyone in the entire county. I have been studying the Aurelian Club's inventory of your father's collection for the last four days. And I have been studying the art of swallowing insults for far longer than that." He gave the earl a hard stare. "In other words, I have no intention of leaving. If you insist, then I rather suspect you will be asked to resign your post as chair of the commission."

There was stunned silence for a moment, and then the earl turned bright red. "This is extortion," he hissed furiously.

"This is war," corrected Meyer. "You asked to head the commission. You believe in Castlereagh's scheme for a separate alliance with the Russians. You want to

make the strongest case you can to the Minister, do you
not? How can you make that case if you yourself are
under investigation for mishandling documents? If you
are harboring, in your own house, a French exile who
may well be a spy?"

"What French exile?" Bassington was bewildered.

Meyer gestured impatiently. "This Mr. Clermont."

The earl frowned. "He is French?"

"Not only French—suspicious enough in itself, given
your current activities—but someone who speaks perfect, unaccented English and who has not revealed his
nationality."

Bassington tried to remember if Philip Derring had
made any mention of Clermont's French birth in his letter of introduction. Probably not; he would certainly
have noted it.

"He is an old friend of our neighbors' son, and he
came with a personal recommendation," he said stiffly.

"Is that so? You will stake the success of England's negotiations—now at a very delicate stage, I will remind
you—on your belief that his visit has no connection to the
other recent events: the missing memoranda, the intruder
in the park"—Bassington started to interrupt, but thought
better of it—"the man-trap? You asked Barrett to help you
handle these other matters discreetly. He came to me and
expressed grave concerns about Mr. Clermont's presence
here. I assure you that I am no more eager to be here than
you are to have me. I have made arrangements to stay
elsewhere; it is not unusual for foreign scholars working
in private libraries to lodge in the neighborhood and visit
only during the day."

At this the earl looked slightly relieved, and then, embarrassed at his own reaction, he coughed and lowered
his eyes. There was an awkward silence. "It might be
more convenient if you were here in the house," he said
grudgingly at last.

"For the moment I believe I will be quite comfortable

where I am, but I thank your lordship for the kind offer," said Meyer in a hesitant voice very different from the cold, precise tones he had used a moment before. Only then did the earl became aware that a footman had appeared at the door. The man bowed apologetically.

"My lord, her ladyship has been expecting you in the small drawing room."

"Yes, yes, I have been engaged with this gentleman," said the earl, flustered. "Hubert, show Mr. Meyer out. Did you travel post?" he asked, turning back to Meyer.

"I did, but I was conveyed to my lodgings, and procured a gig there."

"Excellent," said the earl, attempting a genial expression. "I look forward to receiving you tomorrow, Mr. Meyer. Shall we say ten o'clock? I will arrange for a tour of the house and grounds; I understand that your primary interest is in my father's collection, but there are various curiosities from his travels scattered all through the place, and you must take advantage of your visit here. It would not do to spend all your time peering at insects."

A dry smile flickered at the corners of Meyer's mouth. "No, indeed." He bowed and followed the manservant, who was holding the study door ostentatiously open. One last glance at his host— part challenge, part acknowledgment—and he was gone.

As the door closed, the earl realized that he had been holding his breath. It whistled out between his teeth, accompanied by a muttered oath. Then he took the letter, meticulously smoothed out the wing-like folds, and tucked it under the blotter with one edge peeking out. If he left it there, Clara would certainly read it, and the entire household would know all about Mr. Meyer and his researches within hours. That would spare him at least some of the awkward introductions and explanations he was dreading. With a grimace, he tugged his waistcoat down over his bulky midsection and lumbered off towards the front of the house. His wife would accept the letter at face value. Simon was unlikely to have much interest in a shabby, graying scientist. And his sharp-witted niece Serena would be too busy to notice any oddities in Meyer's behavior. She was wholly occupied with their other unwanted guest. The earl was not sure what worried him more: the possibility that Clermont was not, as he claimed, a naturalist friend of the Derrings, or the possibility that the attack which had nearly killed him had in fact been intended for the earl himself.

There was a furtive tap at Serena's door later that afternoon, and before she could respond or drag herself out of her very comfortable seat by the fire, Simon peered around the edge of the door. He came in, turned the key in the lock, and said theatrically, "Are we alone?"

"I believe so," said Serena, setting down her book. "Unless you have a secret confederate hiding in the wall of my room. Which, I might add, I believe to be impossible, since the fireplace here is of recent date and not equipped with one of those little iron doors."

"Well, I did try once to squeeze through from the room next door, but the space is too narrow," Simon admitted. Then he remembered why he had come. "Serena, you won't believe what I've learned! I tried to find you right away, but Royce spotted me first and hauled me off to make up the lesson I missed earlier. I was wrong! The old man we saw isn't a butterfly-man at all!" He paused impressively, and Serena obligingly took her cue.

"What is he, then?"

"Some sort of military *policeman*," he said with horrified fascination. "Sent down from London to investigate Mr. Clermont! Don't you think I ought to warn him? Of all the shabby tricks, to pretend to be a scientist in order to spy on someone! That man, that Mr. Meyer, isn't really old and stooped; he straightened up when he thought they were alone. And when he was angry with my father he even used a different voice than his scientist voice, all cold and stiff."

She suddenly felt very cold and stiff herself. "And why is he investigating Mr. Clermont?" she managed to ask.

"Sir Charles thinks he is a French spy. Although I'm not quite certain of that bit, because I couldn't hear all of it. It depended on whether they were facing the fireplace when they spoke. But Clermont is French, I did hear that, and Sir Charles and my father are writing to the Russians, and the French want to stop it, and Sir Charles is worried because Clermont speaks perfect English and hasn't told us where he is from."

Only now did it occur to her to wonder how Simon had obtained this alarming piece of news. Or not to wonder.

"You unspeakable little monster!" said Serena, standing up and advancing on him. "When I asked if you were planning to hide under your father's desk that was a rhetorical question! How *could* you?"

"Well, no one saw me," Simon pointed out, defiantly holding his ground. "And I wasn't under his desk. That would be a ridiculous place to hide; I was behind the fireplace. You haven't answered my question: ought I to tell Mr. Clermont what I heard?"

Serena groaned. "I wish you hadn't told *me* what you heard. If I were a patriotic Englishwoman, I would go to my uncle right now and inform him that you should be shipped off immediately to the first school he can persuade to take you. Preferably one located in the Antipodes."

"But don't you see? Oh, I don't know how to say it!" He brooded for a moment. "It's not *sporting*," he pronounced at last. "Clermont doesn't *know* he's being spied on."

"Clermont may be a spy himself, if what you heard is correct," she pointed out. Simon's news was an entirely plausible confirmation of her own suspicions, and yet her reaction was a violent impulse to deny the report entirely.

Evidently that was Simon's reaction as well. "He isn't!" he insisted. "I know he isn't!"

"Just as you knew Mr. Meyer was a genuine butterfly-man?"

"That's different." His jaw set stubbornly. "I had never even spoken with him, and I've spent hours with Mr. Clermont."

"Why didn't he tell us he was French?"

"Did you ask him?" he retorted, with a child's letter-of-the-law view of justice.

She glanced at the clock. "I have to dress for dinner. Swear to me you will say nothing of this to anyone, especially Mr. Clermont, until I come upstairs later tonight." He was silent, and she touched his shoulder. "Simon, this is a very serious matter. I must have your promise."

"I promise," he said grudgingly. But there was a fevered light in his eyes, which was disquieting. Simon throve on illicit excitement. She rang for her maid with a gloomy sense that it could be a very long evening. Clermont was to dine downstairs tonight for the first time since his accident, and she was not sure she would be able to conceal her new knowledge from him. If she survived dinner, she then had the unenviable task of persuading Simon to keep quiet about one of the juiciest secrets he had ever discovered. And on top of it all, she was beginning to realize that Simon was not the only one who wanted to warn Clermont.

11

Insomnia is a frequent complaint among females, for nature demands this penalty in return for our greater sensibility. n.b. Tincture of Valerian is an effective remedy for this complaint.
—Miss Cowell's Moral Reflections
for Young Ladies

Meyer was hunched over the table in the parlor room he had hired at the Burford Arms. It was late; he had been reading for many hours now. The fire was nearly out, and the two tapers at his elbow had only an inch or so left. A puddle of candle drips was slowly collecting at the edge of the volume he was studying. With a preoccupied frown he took a knife from a half-eaten plate of cheese and pushed the liquid wax away from the buckram binding of the book. The title page read, *Papers presented to the fourth Earl of Bassington upon the occasion of his sixty-fifth birthday by divers Gentlemen. At the Aurelian Society. London, March MDCCCI.*

Satisfied that the book was safe, he resumed his scrutiny, leafing through pages and occasionally jotting notes on a small tablet. When the door opened behind him a moment later, he did not turn his head, but only asked quietly in Spanish, "Did anyone see you?"

"No, señor. I don't think so." A thin, dark-haired man with a weather-beaten face had slipped into the room and was peeling off a damp overcoat. With a suppressed sigh, the newcomer sat down on the other side of the table and began to tug at his boots, which were covered with mud.

At the sigh, Meyer turned and considered his servant's appearance with a frown. "You're wet," he said, surprised. "I thought it had stopped raining. Shall I ring for someone to make up the fire again?"

The Spaniard shook his head and smiled briefly. "After all my pains to climb that path unseen, you want to bring some servant in to stare at my wet things and ask where I have been this evening? I can make up the fire myself. And come to think of it, I had better clean my boots myself as well." He surveyed them with disgust. "Anyone who knows the area will recognize this loathsome yellow mud from the hill behind Boulton Park."

Meyer was already out of his chair, bending over the fire and blowing it back to life. He tossed on a fat piece of wood and sat back on his haunches, apparently intent on the blue flickers underneath the logs. "Take yourself a glass of wine," he said, poking at the flames with a stick. He had learned from long experience that it was unwise to badger Rodrigo for a report until he was ready to deliver it. In an emergency his valet could move like lightning. But normally he was a deliberate and taciturn man whose silences might be considered provoking by a less tolerant master.

Keeping a weather eye on the fire, Meyer settled back into his chair. "Cheese?" he asked, pushing the plate across to where his servant was sitting, sipping wine.

"I ate in the taproom." Rodrigo took a larger gulp. "The food was quite tolerable."

"Yes, my supper was excellent," said Meyer absently. He pulled the notebook over and began to read again. There was silence for several minutes, save for the scratching of the pen and occasional gusty swallows from Rodrigo. At last Meyer looked up and saw a grin on the leathery face.

"Your son would have throttled me by now," commented his servant.

"James is not known for his patience," observed Meyer placidly. "I take it you have brought me something significant? That is what these very long silences usually mean."

In response, Rodrigo reached into the outside pocket of the overcoat and pulled out a small coil of thin brown rope.

"Where did you find that?" demanded Meyer, abandoning the notebook and reaching for the bedraggled mass.

"At the top of that infernal hill. I found the place where the trap was set easily enough—the path was not difficult to follow, and one tree still has the line knotted around the trunk. And then I wandered about for a little with the lantern, looking for anything which might prove helpful, and spotted a place further down the path where a horse had relieved itself some days ago. That"—he gestured at the rope—"was lying under a shrub a few feet away. It matches the bit on the tree."

"Odd place to leave it," observed Meyer, frowning at the evidence. "I suppose one of the men who went up the hill to investigate afterwards might have cut some away from the tree and dropped it. Anything else?"

"Taproom gossip confirms our earlier report that the trap was set by someone on horseback. There were apparently hoofprints beneath both trees. The locals believe the culprit to be a tenant of Bassington. Evidently he has been feuding with the earl's gamekeeper. But the knots in the rope were not the work of an amateur, and the rope is rather unusual—expensive stuff, I would guess. Probably from a ship chandler's stock.

Now that we have our own sample, I shall make some inquiries."

Meyer studied it, then got up and put it away in a small leather case lying open on a sideboard. Returning to the table, he asked, "Did you learn anything about the Frenchman? I gather he was staying here until the accident; do the servants remember him?"

Rodrigo snorted. "Remember him? Señor, I would swear two of the barmaids are in love with him. So friendly, so charming"—Rodrigo imitated the voice and expression of a besotted tavern girl—"so handsome, so generous with his *pourboires*." He dropped his pose and added, "The ostler, for his part, was quite shocked at the initial report that he had taken a fall. The boy claims Clermont can ride anything on four legs. Evidently he mastered the most difficult horse in the county within a few hours, and hired it for the rest of his stay."

"How long did he stay here?" asked Meyer, leaning forward intently.

"A week, at least."

"Then he was here when the first memorandum went astray," muttered Meyer. "What did he claim he was doing here?"

"Butterflies," said Rodrigo. "He obtained permission to examine the collection at Boulton Park."

"So Barrett said." Meyer looked skeptical. "Any evidence that his interests extended beyond lepidoptera?"

"Well," said Rodrigo, "his servant asked a lot of questions about the earl's household." Meyer grunted; no surprise there. "As did Clermont. He seemed particularly interested in the niece—a Miss Allen. Our hostess, Mrs. Budge, thinks he is her lover. She swore me to strictest secrecy and then told me that it was the most romantic thing she'd ever seen, how he would ride out in the morning just when Miss Allen was accustomed to take her daily walk."

"She did not believe he was studying butterflies, then."

"No," said Rodrigo.

"Neither do I," said Meyer grimly.

"I cannot believe I am doing this," Serena muttered as she made her way through the darkened house. Dinner had been a nightmare. Every syllable Clermont had uttered—and he had been in a talkative, convivial mood—had set alarm bells ringing. Was that the trace of a French accent? Was it significant that he spoke of Austria, Prussia, and Spain but *not* of Russia or France? When he asked her, laughing, if he was indeed to be permitted a walk to the greenhouse tomorrow, was that a veiled hint that he knew she was now tempted to confine him to a dungeon? Her aunt was still treating Clermont with exaggerated deference, and Serena wanted to stand up and shake her and scream that her guest was a fraud, an assassin, a thief.

The quarter-hour in the drawing room waiting for the men to reappear had seemed an eternity. Could her uncle even now be confronting Clermont? Would it end in violence? Were soldiers already on their way from the garrison in Wallingford? When the earl and his guest came in, chatting quite amicably, she was so tense that she sprang up out of her chair, drawing a startled look from her uncle. Fortunately her aunt had recalled, belatedly, that Clermont was still convalescing, and at her insistence the tea tray had been brought in almost at once.

As soon as the other three had gone off to their bedchambers, Serena went in search of Simon, determined to ask him to repeat every word of the conversation he had overheard. He was nowhere to be found. Nurse Digby had come down to the drawing room earlier to tell the countess that Simon had been feeling poorly and had gone to sleep right after supper. That was a familiar tale, and sure enough, when Serena came up after the nurse had retired for the evening and quietly tested the door of his room, it was locked from the inside. She knocked softly in the pattern which told him she was alone, but there was no answer. Cursing under her breath, she retreated to her own chamber and paced up and down until the household grew quiet and she thought it safe to venture out again. Back to Simon's room: still locked, still no answer to her coded taps. That was when she had decided to go and confront Clermont.

At least this time I'm still dressed, she told herself as she went down the back stairs and into the servant's corridor, which led to the outer room of his suite. *I shall say I am looking for Simon—it is not precisely a lie.* But when she knocked softly and opened the door, the first person she saw was, in fact, Simon, standing in the doorway between the anteroom and the bedroom. His back was to her, and he was talking in a low voice, very earnestly, to Clermont, who was propped up on one elbow in bed.

"Simon!"

He whirled around, startled.

"You promised," she reminded him sadly, wishing that she felt outraged instead of relieved.

"I didn't tell him," he said fiercely. "I was just—just—"

"Didn't tell me what?" Clermont sat up. With a sudden lurch of her stomach she realized that although she was dressed, he was not. Not even in a nightshirt. The discarded garment was lying off to one side of the bed, and as the quilts slid down she saw the gleam of smooth skin, the line of his collarbone—she looked hastily at the floor. "Yes, forgive me for not getting up," he said, sounding amused. "It seemed the lesser of two etiquette evils. To what do I owe the pleasure of this visit? Is it a delegation?"

"No," said Serena.

"Yes," said Simon, at the same moment.

"I see." Clermont pulled the covers up higher. "Well, my experience with delegations is that the members often disagree amongst themselves. So, for the moment, I shall accept the viscount's response. Lord Ogbourne, could I trouble you for my dressing gown? On the chair right behind you."

After a minute Serena raised her eyes again. Clermont, swathed in deep red silk, was looking at her quizzically. "Who is the head of the delegation?" he asked.

"Serena," said Simon at once.

"There is no delegation. I was merely looking for Simon," she said stiffly. "I am very sorry to find that he is disturbing you again."

"He wasn't disturbing me; I was not asleep." It was true that the lamp by his bed was still burning and a book lay open beside him. She squinted, but she couldn't see from this distance what it was. "Fabricius on the habitats of tropical moths," he said helpfully. "From your uncle's library. No, I was reading, and the viscount came—arrived very conventionally, knocked at the door, etcetera—and told me he had an apology to make."

"An apology?" Serena swung round to look at Simon. He nodded.

"He apologized for comparing me unfavorably to the gentlemen we observed attending your uncle this afternoon."

"I told him that I was sorry," confirmed Simon, "*and that he was just as much a real butterfly-man as Mr. Meyer.*" He emphasized the second half of the sentence strongly, enunciating each word, and giving Clermont a hard stare.

Oh, Simon, thought Serena, feeling affection well up inside her. *I misjudged you.* His solution was crude, but he had kept his word, and, unless Clermont was an idiot, the oddly phrased apology should have put him on his guard.

Perhaps too much on his guard. "And what was it that you promised not to tell me?" he asked Simon.

He blinked, momentarily panicked. "That—that we know you are French!" he blurted out in a desperate rush.

Clermont was puzzled. "You didn't know I was French? Philip didn't tell your father? In his letter?"

He looked genuinely taken aback, thought Serena. Perhaps he was not a spy after all.

"He didn't," said Simon. "And you don't have any accent. And you call yourself CLAIR-mont, not Clehr-MOHN." His attempt at the French pronunciation of the name was only partially successful.

"I've been living in England since I was six," Clermont said absently. "I was sent out of France when they started chopping off heads." He frowned at Simon. "Why does it matter? Why would you not wish to tell me you knew I was French?"

Now it would all come spilling out, she thought, resigned. But she had reckoned without Simon's years of experience as a liar. Good liars steer their fictions as quickly as possible back to the *terra firma* of truth.

"Because Serena hates Frenchmen," explained Simon, relaxing.

She closed her eyes, hoping she had not heard him correctly.

"You see—"

"Simon." She put every ounce of authority she had into that one word.

He froze, opened his mouth, took one deep breath, and closed it again.

"Your cousin is not very fond of me in any case,"

Clermont reassured him, breaking the awkward silence. "I don't think one more black mark will make much difference."

In her most dignified manner, she turned and walked to the door. "Good night, *gentlemen*," she said scathingly. Then she slammed it behind her. If it woke her aunt and she caught Simon in Clermont's room it would serve them both right.

Clermont winced slightly as the door crashed shut. "Why does your cousin dislike Frenchmen?" he asked.

Simon shook his head. "I daren't tell you. Not now."

He thought for a moment. "Suppose," he suggested tentatively, "I wished to have a conversation with someone. Not your mother, but someone else who knew Miss Allen, knew her family. Who might that someone be?"

"Mrs. Childe," said Simon promptly. "Or my nurse. Mrs. Childe can be a bit starchy, though. Especially about anything involving what she calls 'lapses.'"

Clermont was reminded uncomfortably of his aunt, who would have approved and encouraged the revolting obeisance Mrs. Childe had inflicted on him at the dinner party.

"Perhaps Nurse is safer," Simon decided. "And she does love to gossip. But she is likely on her way to my bedchamber now, after that racket Serena just made. I must go." He headed for the door.

"Simon?"

The boy turned.

"Thank you for the—apology."

Simon nodded stiffly. "You're wrong, by the way. Serena *is* fond of you," was his parting shot.

"As the hawk is fond of the rabbit," muttered Clermont. He picked up Fabricius, extracted the diary he had tucked down inside it, and settled back to consider the very interesting entry he had discovered for

March of 1793. After a long list of scientific books, with prices, there was a short note: *n.b. funds returned from Lausanne.* It would have meant nothing to anyone else. Julien had been searching for it since his first day at Boulton Park.

12

A gentleman is well-informed upon a variety of subjects, but eschews pedantry and displays of erudition.

—Precepts of Mlle. de Condé

Serena returned from her postbreakfast walk in a foul mood. This excursion was usually the highlight of her day—a chance to be alone, to walk as briskly as she pleased, to think without interruption, to escape the well-meant but irksome restrictions her aunt and uncle placed on her. She knew every path on the grounds and loved them all, even on wet mornings like this one, when her shoes and skirt hem quickly caked over with mud. But today the misty landscape spread out beneath the hill had not even registered. She had stepped mechanically over stiles without seeing them. Her feet had carried her, inexorably, towards the fateful iron gate where Clermont had entered the park—illicitly, she now suspected.

Someone else evidently suspected the same thing. When she reached the spot on the path where the gate came into view, she saw Meyer, his gig abandoned in the middle of the road, examining the lock with great attention. Hastily she retreated, hoping he had not seen her and furious with Meyer for doing exactly what she had intended to do herself.

"Nasty, officious, meddler," she said under her

breath as she crested the hill again. The sight of the greenhouse by the garden gate irritated her further. She had been planning to take Clermont there once he was on his feet again. She was much more knowledgeable about plants than about insects; in the greenhouse, she had decided, she could form a clearer picture of Clermont's scientific credentials. But over the past two days she had become more and more certain he was a fraud. He had revealed himself when he had shown Simon the lens grinder. His rapt expression and unselfconscious delight were unmistakable; she had seen them many times on the faces of the Aurelians who came to venerate the butterflies. In the cabinet-room Clermont had been courteous, interested, well-informed—but not absorbed, as he had been with his machine. He could recite entire catalogues of tropical plant names and it would not change her mind. Whatever he sought at Boulton Park, it was not butterflies.

Then there was the problem of Simon. Royce had evidently gone off to London first thing this morning with dispatches; her uncle had decided that even the government couriers were insufficient protection for this particular batch of papers. That left her mischief-minded cousin free for the day. He had visited her to announce this fact at half past seven, an hour which normally would not even see him awake, let alone dressed.

"I'm to spend the morning in the library with Mr. Clermont," he said, looking so smug that she wanted to throttle him. "So you needn't miss your visit with Fanny Orset after all. I can help him find anything he needs." She pictured Clermont and Meyer in the library, circling each other like wolves. Worse, she pictured Simon confronting Meyer and informing him that his investigation was "not sporting." She had written a hasty note to Fanny putting off their engagement until another day, and ordered the lens grinder moved up to the library in the hope that its noise would make conversation impossible.

By the time she had changed into dry clothing, Meyer's gig was standing in the stable yard, and she was not surprised to receive a summons from her uncle: his apologies, but Royce was away; would it be too much trouble to go up to the library and show a new visitor the cabinet-room?

"What of Mr. Clermont? Where is he at the moment?" she asked the servant who had come to fetch her.

"Also in the library, miss. As is Master Simon, who evidently has permission to use the optical equipment." It was Coughlin, who knew Simon well, and he added pregnantly, "Mrs. Fletcher reports that a paring knife went missing from the pantry shortly after Master Simon visited the kitchen."

She hurried up the stairs, wondering what she would find when she opened the double doors. Meyer and Clermont hurling butterfly species' names at ten paces? Simon holding Meyer at knifepoint? Clermont being led off in manacles?

What she did find was the last thing she expected: four males, ranging in age from eleven to fifty-five, amicably huddled over the lens grinder. Clermont and Simon, with great enthusiasm, were explaining to Bassington and his guest the different possible adjustments and demonstrating the action of the polishing disks.

"May I?" asked Meyer, indicating the handle.

"It is Simon's lens, for a telescope," Clermont said. "Nearly finished, I believe. What do you say, Simon? Shall we let Mr. Meyer and your father take a quick turn at your lens, or would you prefer to put in a new blank?"

Torn between courtesy and a natural reluctance to risk his precious handiwork, Simon hesitated. Bassington suddenly recalled his responsibilities as host and cleared his throat. But Meyer spoke first.

"If it is not too much trouble," he said timidly, "I would be most interested in seeing the process from the very beginning."

Simon brightened, and the other two men looked relieved. Simon's lens was removed and duly admired; a new blank was inserted and the various brackets adjusted, with eager questions from her uncle and Meyer, who both insisted on taking several turns once the apparatus was ready. Serena retreated unobtrusively to a chair and watched—not the machine, which held little interest for her, but its operators. Meyer, whose performance as the reclusive scholar was so convincing she began to doubt Simon's report. Her uncle, looking more relaxed and cheerful than she had seen him in weeks. And above all, Clermont and Simon, who seemed like the older and younger halves of a single person. They hovered, watching and correcting, with the same expression of possessive enjoyment when the disks were turning, the same narrowed, intent gaze when some adjustment was required. Two left eyebrows flew up when her uncle asked a question which apparently revealed his ignorance of gear mechanisms. Two simultaneous nods answered another query by Meyer.

Absorbed in the pantomime (when the grinder was operating she could not hear any of their conversation), she did not realize her aunt had come in until she saw her go up to Bassington and literally shake him.

"George!" shouted her aunt.

He was bent over, turning the handle, but now straightened up and looked at her in surprise. He took in her folded arms and compressed lips. "Is something the matter, my dear?"

She pointed to the lens grinder. "Who put this machine here?"

Belatedly, Serena realized that the apparatus had been moved from the marble-topped bureau she had designated as its new home earlier that morning and was now resting on a large pier table. A large rosewood pier table, to be more precise, featuring an elaborate marquetry panel depicting the triumph of Neptune. It was a family heirloom; her own mother had spoken of it, envying her sister its possession.

"This," said the countess, indicating the table, "is an original Adam design. In rosewood, gilt, ebony, and ivory. It is worth thousands of pounds. It is also of great sentimental value to me, having been given to my mother by the Duke of Somerset on the occasion of her betrothal."

"The apparatus has felt on the bottom, Mama," Simon assured her. "We looked before we moved it."

"The apparatus," she said with exaggerated patience, "grinds glass. Which means that small, sharp pieces of glass are rubbed away from this round thing"—she gestured at the blank, sitting forlornly in its brass clamps—"and are deposited *on my table.*" Her finger stabbed towards the layer of translucent grit which now covered one side of the surface.

"I gave Simon permission to move it, my dear," Bassington confessed. "Four of us could not fit around the bureau where it had been set up by the servants. I'm afraid I did not think about the inevitable consequences of the grinding. Perhaps Mrs. Fletcher can contrive some means of removing the fragments without damaging your table."

"I will clean it myself," said the countess in a thin voice. "I would not put Mrs. Fletcher, or any of my staff, in such a difficult position."

All three men were looking sheepish.

"Ah, Serena!" Her uncle had finally noticed her. He coughed nervously. "I had promised Mr. Meyer a tour of the house. Perhaps now would be a good time?"

Simon and Clermont were looking as though they, too, would have liked an excuse to escape the library.

Serena half expected them to volunteer to accompany her, but Clermont was, quite properly, apologizing to her aunt and offering to move his equipment back to the bureau immediately.

She found Meyer courteous, attentive, and far more convincing as a scholar than Clermont. He ignored notable treasures of the house, such as the Lely portraits and the astronomical clock, and lingered instead over obscure engravings of rare plants. A small cabinet of fossils fascinated him. He made no attempt to impress her with his knowledge, but asked questions, very humbly, and accepted her replies with gratifying interest. She found herself dreading the inevitable confrontation of the two pseudoscientists.

It was not long in coming. Towards the end of their circuit through the main rooms, her sixth sense, which sometimes warned her Simon was on the prowl, came to full alert. They were in a small salon behind the main entrance hall, and Meyer was over by the window admiring a set of framed watercolors depicting English butterflies. Sure enough, there was the faint but unmistakable sound of footsteps on the other side of the paneling.

"Serena? Are you in here? Are you alone?" It was Simon's voice.

Sighing, she stepped over to the concealed door and pushed it open. "Must you always use the servants' corridor? It is very disconcerting to hear voices coming from behind the wall." And as he started to say something else, she stepped aside to let him see that Meyer was within earshot, adding pointedly, "I am still engaged with Mr. Meyer; we are just finishing our visit of the public rooms."

Meyer, startled, had turned around and was blinking

in surprise at the sight of his host's son emerging from the middle of a wall.

Her cousin made an instant recovery. His blue eyes widened ingenuously. "That's not a corridor; it's my secret passage," he said, in hurt tones. "I was showing it to Mr. Clermont." Sure enough, a tall figure was ducking through the low narrow door in Simon's wake. The dark eyes met hers, amused.

Simon had marched up to Meyer. "Our house has dozens of secret passages," he said in the confiding voice of a much younger child. "Would you like me to show you some of them?"

It was a masterful strategy, Serena decided. Meyer would now dismiss any rumors he heard of hidden recesses and tunnels—and there were indeed dozens, although most could barely accommodate Simon. More importantly, he would dismiss Simon as an over-imaginative child.

"There is a hidden treasure," he was assuring Meyer. "I'm the only one who knows where it is."

"Simon, you know better than to plague your father's guests." Her voice carried a warning, whose real message was: *don't overplay your hand*.

Clermont had wandered over to one of the watercolors. "You didn't bring me to this room," he said accusingly. "These are by Harris, are they not?"

She decided not to remind him that his own tour had been abbreviated because he was still convalescing. That might in turn remind the inquisitive Mr. Meyer of the suspicious accident on Clark's Hill. "Yes. They are the originals of some of the plates in his book."

"To the Right Honourable the Earl of Bassington, This Plate is most humbly Dedicated," Clermont read off. He sighed. "Beautiful work. Pleasing to the eye and remarkably accurate. Seems hardly fair that a single individual should have both talents."

Meyer had joined him. "Do you by chance have the

honor of the artist's acquaintance?" he asked, in reverent tones.

Clermont coughed. "Is there a younger Mr. Harris? The author of *The Aurelian* died when I was a small boy, I believe."

First service returned by Mr. Clermont for fifteen, thought Serena.

Meyer peered shortsightedly at the signature. "Ah, yes, my mistake," he said. He fished for his spectacles and put them on. "Vanity." He gave a self-deprecatory smile and shook his head. "I did not wish Miss Allen to think me an old man."

Miss Allen was in fact thinking that she did not like liars. That even the polite fictions necessary to maintain life in a well-bred household irked her ("Miss Allen is not at home," when she was standing right behind the drawing-room door as Pritchett sent the caller away). And yet here she was in a small room with three people who were all lying through their teeth. She wondered what would happen if she were to step between Clermont and Meyer and shout "Stop playacting!" at the top of her lungs.

Clermont counterattacked. "What I like best about Harris," he said, "is the way he creates an elegant composition while still depicting males, females, and larvae of each species. As with the Painted Ladies in this example."

"Yes, and note the broken china cup on the ground," Meyer riposted. "Delicately suggesting the traditional habitat of the Painted Lady, to whit, rubbish heaps."

Fifteen all.

"And the thistle—is that not the preferred food of the Marmoress, here?" Clermont was overdoing it, she thought.

"Is that so? The Marmoress? Ah, *Melanargia galathea.* I do not know all your English names for the insects. It is not as familiar to me as the Painted Lady." Meyer gave his embarrassed smile again. "I am the veriest amateur," he confessed. "I hope to profit from the coincidence of our visits, Mr. Clermont."

Game to Mr. Meyer, she decided gloomily.

Simon must have decided the same, because he suddenly intervened. Tugging on Clermont's sleeve, he said in an exaggerated, petulant whisper, "What of our shooting lesson? You promised! And I've brought you to ask Serena, just as you said I must."

Clermont looked at her, eyebrows raised.

Anything to get both of them away from the nefarious Meyer. "Half an hour, no more," she said grudgingly. The time limit was for Clermont's sake, but Meyer would not know that. And she had to admit that Clermont seemed nearly well this morning. No trace of a limp, and he carried his injured wrist easily, the bindings scarcely visible under his cuff.

"Is the viscount not somewhat young for firearms?" Meyer asked as Simon and Clermont disappeared.

"He is eleven," she informed him, adding, ambiguously, "He was very sickly as a child and as a consequence does not always behave like other boys his age." If Meyer took that to mean that her cousin was a bit simple she would not go out of her way to enlighten him. After lunch she would take Simon aside and order him to avoid Meyer for the rest of his visit. As for Clermont, she would devise some scheme or other to keep him out of the library. Better still, out of the house altogether.

The greenhouse was warm and had a wet, earthy smell, which reminded her of the first days of spring. Clermont was already walking down the center aisle, fingering the occasional plant and looking at the labels on the seedlings. Unobtrusively, Serena took a long-unused key out of her pocket—Mrs. Fletcher had located it, with some difficulty, tucked into the head gardener's planting book—and locked the door behind her. For added security, she took off her pelisse and hung it across two trellis hooks by the door so that it obscured the view through that wall. The whole building was glass, of course, but along the sides exotic plants like bamboo and papyrus grew tall enough to provide some degree of privacy.

Clermont's voice came from right behind her, making her jump. "Is this a tryst, Miss Allen? Dare I flatter myself that you were not seeking your cousin in my room last night?"

She whirled and saw him looking down at her with an ironic smile. "I wished to speak with you in private," she said stiffly. How had he moved so quickly without making any noise?

"Very well. May I suggest the bamboo grove, then, as an appropriately secluded spot?" He bowed and waved her on, following behind her down the narrow aisle. There was no place to sit, so she stood, hands clasped, and faced him. Framed in narrow-edged green leaves, he looked suddenly remote, unpredictable, even dangerous. It was hard to remember that he had been bedridden less than a week ago.

A frond brushed his neck, and he held it up between thumb and finger, examining it with care.

Her temper, already frayed, snapped. She ripped the leaf out of his hand and flung it away. "Do not tell me what type of bamboo plant that is," she said fiercely. "Do not point out the rare orchids. Do not ask to see the *Dionaea muscipula*—yes, we have one; Simon feeds it flies. I am sure you have conned your lessons very well, but I am not interested. I did not bring you to the greenhouse to see how well you knew your tropical plants. I have something to say to you, and I did not want to risk any eavesdroppers or interruptions."

"I see." He gave her that grave stare which had

haunted her from the first time she had seen it in her uncle's study. Not defensive, not anxious. Watchful. Patient.

Her heart was beating in her throat. He was the trespasser; she belonged here. Why did he seem so calm, when she, who had done nothing wrong, could feel her hands trembling?

"I am at your service, Miss Allen. What did you wish to tell me?"

She took a deep breath. "I know you are a fraud."

He winced. "An ugly word."

"Let us phrase it more politely, then. Your interest in butterflies does not appear genuine to me."

"You have said so before. But I do have some interest in butterflies," he said cautiously.

She shook her head. "No more than I do."

He was surprised, and momentarily distracted. "You don't care for them?"

"I think them repulsive," she confessed. "At first they look beautiful, but when you examine them closely you realize they are simply worms with giant wings." Then she forced herself back to the main point. "My feelings are not to the purpose. Once I saw you with something which did genuinely interest you—your lenses—it was painfully obvious that the butterflies were not your real object in coming to Boulton Park." He started to object, but she held up her hand. "Wait. Here is what I wish to say: I don't know why you are here, or why you decided to pass yourself off as an Aurelian. Until yesterday, your pretense seemed harmless enough. Perhaps my aunt had persuaded you to—to come and make my acquaintance; perhaps you wished to ingratiate yourself with my uncle. In either case, you made a poor choice of strategies: my uncle and I, although not related by blood, share a distaste for liars."

His jaw tightened, but he said nothing.

She swallowed. "I find that circumstances have

changed. You once offered to leave if I requested you to do so. I am asking you now to honor that pledge."

"You want me to leave?"

"Yes." Her voice was very low.

There was an expression on his face she could not read. Disappointment? Relief?

"Even if one of your surmises about my reason for coming to Boulton Park is correct?"

"Especially if one of them is correct." She could barely breathe.

He stepped closer. "Half French, and a liar. Two counts against me." The ironic smile was suddenly back. "What do you say? Shall we make it three?"

"What do you mean?" Now her voice was so faint it was almost inaudible.

He moved closer still, bent his head, and kissed her.

It had been a long, long time since she had been kissed. She had forgotten what it felt like. The taste of another mouth, the firm press of a hand against her back, the delightful, alien touch of shaved skin against her face. For a moment, recollection blended with sensation, and a sweet surge of nostalgia rose in her. Then everything changed, and she crossed into foreign territory. He moved his hand up to her neck, turning her slightly, pressing her closer. His mouth grew fiercer. She found herself flattened against him, felt his heart thud above her breast. And if he had only one usable hand, he was certainly making the most of it. It traced imperative circles, caressing her hair, now her neck again, now moving down along her shoulder—

She tore herself away. "No," she managed to say. "No."

He wasn't smiling now. He looked as though he had taken another blow on the head. "Miss Allen—"

"No!" She almost shouted it.

He didn't move, didn't attempt to stop her as she unlocked the door with shaking hands, not looking at him, swallowing something which felt suspiciously like a sob in her throat. She tore her pelisse off the hooks—literally tore it—and fled across the garden, ignoring the paths, headed straight for the sanctuary of the house.

Clermont watched her running through the bare flower beds, the unfastened pelisse billowing behind her. She paused once at the terrace door, turned to look straight at him, and then vanished into the house.

That was a mistake, Julien, he thought. *A very, very serious mistake.*

13

*Gentlemen may wear one or two pieces of jewelry.
Plain gold is preferable, but rubies and sapphires are
permissible if care is taken to avoid large, ostenta-
tious stones. Diamonds are effeminate, and emeralds
vulgar.*

—Precepts of Mlle. de Condé

"Mr. Meyer! Do come in." Bassington set down his
newspaper, which Meyer had already seen. It predicted,
for the tenth day in a row, that Napoleon would accept
terms of peace within twenty-four hours. The earl's
hearty greeting, however, was as false as the newspaper.
The moment Pritchett had bowed himself out, Bassington stood up and set his hands aggressively on the
desk, fists clenched. "Well?"

"Mr. Clermont is a cool customer," said Meyer.
"There is no point in continuing this charade. I've no
desire to discuss the habitats of tropical moths with a
slight German accent for the next three days. Mr. Clermont has done his homework; I have done mine; we
could circle each for days in a scientific stalemate. I
have concluded that a change of tactics is in order."

"Indeed. And what would that be? Drag him off to the
cellars and beat a confession out of him? Try to bribe
his servant? Search his room?"

Meyer grimaced. "No to the first option. I decided the

second was too risky. And my man has just returned from pursuing the third."

Shocked, the earl sank back into his chair. "You searched the luggage of a guest *in my house*?"

Without waiting for an invitation, Meyer sat down opposite Bassington. He had no intention of letting the earl get the upper hand in this conversation by keeping him standing. "Yes. Although that servant of Clermont's is like a guard dog. You would think the man had the crown jewels in the bottom of his trunk. Rodrigo had to wait for two hours to have a clear shot at the room, and dared not remain there long. Still, he found some very interesting items."

"Oh?" The earl's tone was scornful.

"Take a look at this." Meyer held out a lump of grayish wax.

Bassington turned it over, frowning, and studied the design stamped into the wax. His eyebrows shot up. "Where did you get it?"

"An impression from an engraved silver hairbrush, in his trunk. One of a matched pair. It seems Mr. Clermont is certainly French."

"It could have been purchased," the earl objected, "from the legitimate owner. Many French noblemen found themselves in financial difficulties after fleeing the republic."

"Perhaps." Meyer leaned forward. "But recall, my lord, that according to Mrs. Digby, Clermont wears a signet on a chain around his neck. Lady Bassington and the butler are the only ones who saw it on his hand—" He paused significantly.

"—and my wife treats him like royalty," Bassington finished. "Very well. I take your point." He stared down at the crest incised into the wax. "This certainly explains her interest in the young man. I suppose I should have asked her straight out who he was, but she enjoys having secrets occasionally, and I have been preoccupied with other matters."

"Those other matters, my lord, are of far more significance than Mr. Clermont's possible connections to an exiled royal house. The man is very likely a French spy."

"A spy? From that family? Don't be absurd!"

Meyer suppressed the urge to give Bassington a half dozen names of nobly born émigrés who had been caught working for Napoleon in London.

"Did you find anything else? Something which might provide at least a shred of evidence for your suspicions? Papers? Letters? Political pamphlets?"

Meyer shook his head. "Nothing my servant could find easily, at any rate. There were more than a dozen books in the room, though, and he could not examine all of them."

"What sort of books? Histories? Anything about Russia, or Austria?"

Meyer coughed.

"Let me guess. Proceedings of the Aurelian Society. From my library. As would be natural for a man here to study the collection."

"Precisely. Six calf-bound folios. Also, several volumes of your father's journals. And various other scientific tomes."

"May I ask, then, Mr. Meyer, why you wish to continue this inquiry? You have apparently found nothing, except possibly a hint that Mr. Clermont is connected to the last house in France I would ever suspect of assisting Napoleon Bonaparte."

"There could be any number of explanations for his change of allegiance," Meyer pointed out. "Money. A woman. A family quarrel—Barrett told me Derring had mentioned something of the sort, followed by three years of self-imposed exile in Canada. Or simple pragmatism. He would not be the only French aristocrat to decide his best interests lay with the empire."

"He would be the only one to do so after Napoleon executed his kinsman simply for bearing the family name," snapped Bassington. "And it is one thing for a nobleman of the *ancien regime* to accept a command in the imperial army; quite another to descend to rummaging through desks in a private home and stealing papers. To make such an accusation without firm proof is unthinkable."

Meyer sighed. "I do have firm proof—of fraud, at least, if not of anything more serious. I have not yet shown you the other item my servant discovered."

"What sort of fraud?"

"Mr. Clermont has insinuated himself into your household by manufacturing the accident on Clark's Hill," said Meyer.

"Nonsense! The man was nearly killed!"

"A miscalculation, I believe. Nor were we meant to find the trap. He intended it to look like a simple riding accident." Meyer took out of his satchel a length of rope. Clean, new rope. Its color was a warm gold, like beeswax, rather than the dusty brown of the samples taken by Googe, but there was no mistaking it. It was identical to the rope discovered on the trees. "From Mr. Clermont's saddlebags." Meyer's tone was almost apologetic. He laid it on the desk. "Only my concern for her ladyship prevented me from arresting Mr. Clermont immediately."

The earl was frowning at the rope. "This does not necessarily mean anything," he said.

"It seems quite straightforward to me: he hears, somehow, of your involvement with the negotiations and conceives of a plan to exploit his friendship with Philip Derring and gain entry to your house as a gentleman naturalist. When that limited visit proves unsatisfactory for his purposes, he arranges an 'accident' on your land and is then given lodging and complete freedom to search the premises."

The earl's expression told him he was getting nowhere.

Meyer tried another tack. "My lord, I am not asking you to risk the embarrassment of an open accusation. As I told you, I considered arresting the man but decided against it for the moment. There is a very simple solution to this dilemma. If you will return to London and place the correspondence in Sir Charles's hands, the question of Mr. Clermont's intentions will become moot."

"You will, however, report what you have found to your colonel."

"Of course."

"And therefore, Mr. Clermont, without his knowledge and without any chance to defend himself, will be suspected of an infamous crime and, most likely, placed under surveillance."

"That is true," Meyer admitted, "but you and the countess will escape becoming embroiled in a sensational scandal."

"You are suggesting that I sacrifice the reputation of a man who is potentially innocent of any wrongdoing to preserve my own comfort?"

Meyer held up the rope. "I find the potential for Mr. Clermont's innocence very small at the moment. Surely you see how damning this is?"

"Very well," said the earl, exasperated. "I will go up to London, although it is a wretched place to be at this time of year. I will take the confounded letters with me, carrying them on my person, and deliver them to Barrett. On one condition."

"Which is?" Meyer asked, wary.

"We settle this business with Clermont right now. I'll not have him hounded by you and your fellow couriers." He stood up, muttering, "Bloody spies. See plots and thievery everywhere." He did not bother to lower his voice much.

"I beg your pardon, my lord, but how do you propose to 'settle this business,' as you put it?"

"Ask the man to his face who he is, of course. And why he has rope in his saddlebags." The earl stamped over to the double doors which gave onto the gallery and wrenched them open. "Pritchett!" he bellowed.

A startled footman scurried off in search of the butler.

"Where is Mr. Clermont?" Bassington demanded when Pritchett appeared a minute later.

"In the library, my lord. With Master Simon."

"Tell him I would like a word with him." Bassington paused and looked at Meyer. "No, wait. I'll go up myself. Catch him off guard. You would prefer that, wouldn't you, Mr. Meyer?" His tone was contemptuous.

"I think such an interview very ill-advised."

"But you will nevertheless wish to hear what is said." The earl did not wait for an answer, but jerked open the concealed door in the paneling and started up the tiny staircase.

Meyer, perforce, followed, bitterly regretting his decision to confide in the earl. It was tempting to storm back to London and ask White why someone as irritable and stiff-necked as Bassington should be playing such a prominent role in the delicate negotiations with Russia. Still, he himself was at fault. Had he not antagonized the earl at their first meeting Bassington might consider him an ally rather than an adversary. The purpose of this confrontation in the library was, he thought, as much to humiliate Nathan Meyer as it was to exonerate Julien Clermont.

The earl turned at the top of the narrow stairwell and gestured to his right. "There is a doorway about ten yards farther along which will let you into one of the side rooms," he said in a near-whisper. "Go out—carefully—and you can enter the library as though coming from the upper hall. I'll join you in a few minutes."

Easing himself into the deserted anteroom, Meyer crossed silently to the far end, turned, and returned to the library doors on the near side using his shuffling old-man walk. They were closed, but not quite latched. He could hear the boy's voice, excited, asking a question, and Clermont's deeper voice answering. Then a young woman, sounding amused. Miss Allen was here as well, then; as he pushed the right-hand door open, he saw her dark head between the two fair ones. They were all bending over the lens grinder, which was partly disassembled.

The low murmur of voices stopped. Automatically he fell into the slight stoop he affected as Meyer the scholar, and blinked nearsightedly. But he was not, in fact, nearsighted, and as he saw the three faces turn towards him at the sound of his footsteps, he could read each expression clearly. The boy: a flash of defiance masked at once by an exaggerated look of innocent puzzlement. Clermont: polite interest. Meyer's hopes for a revealing slip during the coming interview died. This was not a man whose face or gestures would betray him. As for Serena Allen, she gave him a burning glance so full of knowledge and purpose that he felt it almost as a physical blow. *I know who you are,* her look said. *I know why you are here. And I will do everything I can to hinder you.*

"Must you go?" Simon was asking.

"I'm afraid so." Clermont unscrewed another clamp from the end of the machine and set it into a compartment in the big wooden case.

"What about my telescope?"

"Simon!" Serena said, laughing. "Have you no manners at all, you wretched boy?" She was buoyant with relief. Clermont was leaving, and the oppressive tangle of suspicion and tension and excitement which had enmeshed her for the past week would vanish with him.

"Your lens is finished; I'll send you a case and refractor from London," said Clermont absently.

She heard the noise at the door first; the other two were busy unfastening the next clamp. But as the door swung inward, they looked up as well.

It was her enemy. Meyer's mild air and apologetic smile didn't deceive her. She glared at him.

"Good morning, Miss Allen, my lord, Mr. Clermont," he said, bowing awkwardly to each in turn. He took in the open case and the half-dismantled equipment. "You are packing the machine?" He sounded disappointed, and Serena wondered if that was part of the scholarly mask or if he had let his real feelings show—his frustration at seeing his prize getting away.

"Yes, he's *leaving*," said Simon, with an aggrieved air. "Without finishing my telescope."

Meyer expressed regrets for the loss of the company of a fellow scientist and pulled up a chair when his offer to help pack the lens grinder was accepted.

There was a knock at the door, and a footman came in. "His lordship is not in his study, sir," he said to Clermont. "I am sure he will return shortly, however. Shall I wait for him there and see if he will be able to receive you?"

"I suppose so." Clermont was struggling with a recalcitrant screw. "And the countess?"

"Her ladyship sends word that she will be downstairs in three-quarters of an hour." The servant bowed and withdrew.

"She'll try to persuade you to stay," Simon predicted, "or invite you to come back after you've visited your grandfather. But you won't come back, will you?"

"Perhaps I shall see you in London," Clermont said, not looking up. He gestured for Meyer to hold the clamp in place so that he could get a better purchase on the bolt.

"Serena and I don't go to London these days."

Now he looked up. At her, then at Simon. "Why not?"

"I don't care for the city," she said quickly, before Simon could give a more complete (and more revealing) answer. "And Simon—" She paused, searching for a suitably ambiguous phrase. "Simon found that London did not agree with him."

Clermont wasn't fooled. "Got yourself into a mess of some sort?" he asked the boy.

"I broke into the vault underneath St. Paul's with my friends Ned and Jamie," Simon said, with some pride. "The verger screamed when he found us."

"Dear me," murmured Meyer, one eyebrow raised. He glanced at Serena and she knew what he was thinking: *that boy should be at school.* She was almost beginning to agree with him.

The footman reappeared, holding the door open for Bassington.

Clermont jumped up, perturbed. "Sir!" he exclaimed. "Your man must have misunderstood me; I proposed to come down and say my farewells when you had a moment to spare. I never meant you to interrupt your work to come up here."

The earl frowned. "You sent a servant to find me? You are leaving?"

"Yes, my regrets, but my grandfather sent down an urgent summons which reached me only this morning."

"Ah, your grandfather," said Bassington. "Indeed." His tone was thoughtful.

Serena saw Clermont raise his head slightly, like an animal scenting danger.

The earl walked over to the table. He had to look up at the taller man. "I understand that you sometimes wear a signet ring," he said. "Might I see it?"

His face suddenly expressionless, Clermont untied his

neckcloth, reached under his shirt, and pulled out a chain. The heavy gold ring swung at the end and made a small thunk, audible in the now-silent room, as it dropped into the earl's hand.

Bassington turned the ring over and examined the seal carefully. Serena caught a glimpse of three fleurs-de-lis encircling a diagonal bar. The raised elements were in yellow gold; the field of the signet was in white gold. The device meant nothing to her, but it clearly meant something to her uncle. He was frowning, tracing the design with his finger, nodding to himself.

Serena looked back and forth between the two men. Meyer was making no pretense of continuing work on the lens grinder; he, too, was staring at Clermont.

"You are a Condé, then," Bassington announced, after a long silence.

"Of a sort."

His shrug, at least, was French, thought Serena. The name Condé was vaguely familiar to her. Familiar and terrifying. Why did she know that name?

"I had assumed, between one thing and another, that the younger generation of the Condés was now extinct," her uncle said in his usual blunt manner.

"Oh, there are still a few left. They only arrested the genuine ones," Clermont said. His mouth had a bitter twist. "And most of my kinsmen had sense enough to leave France with their families before the slaughter began in earnest."

The earl handed back the signet and stood silently for a moment. "You have not returned since you were sent away as a child?"

Clermont shook his head.

"Probably a wise decision," said the earl, his face grim. "Considering what happened to your—second cousin? In spite of the precautions of your kinsmen."

"First cousin," was the response.

"Then your grandfather is Louis-Joseph de Bourbon-Condé? The prince?"

"Yes." Clermont stood braced as if expecting an attack.

"That explains why I thought I recognized you," her uncle muttered.

A prince. His grandfather was a prince. Now she knew why the name sounded familiar. The Condés were a branch of the French royal family. Their claim to the throne was thought by many to be stronger than that of the current king-in-waiting, Louis Bourbon. The man she had snubbed and lectured and accused of lying was a descendant of Louis XIV.

"Then of course you will honor his request and go to London at once." The earl sighed. "I'm afraid the countess will be very disappointed. She had hoped you might make a longer stay."

Clermont bowed and murmured that he planned to present himself to the countess shortly to apologize and thank her for her gracious hospitality.

Instead of the equally meaningless polite murmur she expected, her uncle beckoned to the footman by the door.

"I have an apology to make as well," he said. He took something from the footman and dismissed him. It took Serena a moment to see what it was: a piece of rope. It took her another moment to understand its significance.

"I am sorry to say that an underling in my household has been guilty of an appalling breach of courtesy," the earl said stiffly. "This person visited your chambers and searched your possessions. When he found this rope, recognizing it as possibly connected to that used on Clark's Hill, he cut off a sample and brought it to me." Horrified, Serena glanced instinctively at Meyer. The pseudoscholar looked appropriately bewildered as he glanced from one man to the other, but she was certain he had engineered this little drama. He, presumably, had searched Clermont's rooms; her uncle would never have done so.

"Yes, my manservant has been visiting chandlers to see if he could find some clue as to who might have set the trap," Clermont said. He did not look guilty or nervous. "I believe that particular sample comes from Maidenhead, but I can ask him, if you like. Does it match the rope tied to the trees, as my servant claims?"

"It seems so."

"Would you like the rest of the coil, then? And the name of the supplier? I had thought Constable Googe was the correct person to receive the information, but I beg your pardon if I should have come to you instead."

"No, no, my boy." Her uncle was looking embarrassed. "It is I who must beg your pardon. To search through a guest's saddlebags! Unthinkable! Needless to say the fellow will be leaving my household at once. Without a reference." He clapped the younger man on the shoulder. "I should have remembered your promise to send your servant out to make inquiries." He turned to go, then swung back. "By the by, I will be removing to London myself within a few days. If I can persuade my wife and my niece to accompany me, is there any chance we might see you in town?"

Clermont inclined his head. "I should be delighted."

The earl's conference with Meyer shortly afterwards was less friendly. Bassington was furious. "You made a fool of me," he told Meyer, nearly spitting the words. "In front of my niece and my son, to boot! A guest in my home was embarrassed, was accused, by implication, of the lowest sort of trickery—and not just any guest! A descendant of the noblest house in France!"

"That interview, I will remind you, was your idea, my lord. I was content with your promise to take the documents up to Sir Charles in London. A promise I trust you still mean to honor."

"Certainly. Although I presume you will not object if I receive the young man at my home in London, now that these absurd suspicions of yours have been put to rest."

Meyer raised his eyebrows. "My suspicions are not put to rest. Not at all. Mr. Clermont's composure and prompt answers prove nothing. Indeed, an innocent man would likely have been more outraged by the search of his baggage. But you are welcome to entertain him—if the documents are not in your house."

"Bah!" The earl stomped over to his cabinet, pulled out an old tin snuffbox from behind a pile of books, and took two enormous pinches. The violent sneezes which followed did seem to calm him somewhat. "I suppose there is some sense in giving the letters to Barrett," he said grudgingly. "After all, he has the notebooks. What's more, with both of us in town there will be no need to send drafts back and forth."

Meyer wisely said nothing.

"The weather is improving." The earl glanced out the window at the leaden sky and corrected himself. "Or will be improving shortly. And if London is thin of company, that makes it all the more likely I can persuade my niece to accompany us. Unless, of course, you and Colonel White have some objection to Mr. Clermont's apparent interest in my niece? Do you have proof that that, too, is a fraud?"

It was a rhetorical question, and Meyer did not bother to answer. His own observations, which were not always confined to political and military matters, suggested that Clermont was indeed intrigued by Miss Allen and she by him—however reluctant they were to acknowledge the attraction. But he did not think their romance was likely to have a happy ending.

14

"The man has not even been gone for two hours," Serena said, scowling, "and my aunt is already trying to persuade me to go up to London with my uncle. I should have told her straight out that the prospect of seeing Mr. Clermont again makes an already undesirable location even less desirable. We are well rid of Mr. Clermont and Mr. Meyer both. I am looking forward to a nice, peaceful fortnight with no visitors and no constables and no missing government papers. If any butterfly-men come I shall tell Pritchett to send them away."

She and Simon were in one of his favorite retreats, a small, windowless room accessible only from the servants' corridors. The countess had given Simon permission to fix it up as a secret hideout on condition that he always leave the door to the corridor open when he was there. She had read somewhere that children with weak lungs could become ill from breathing stale air in enclosed spaces. Simon ignored this requirement; as he pointed out to Serena, what was the point of a secret hideout if one could not close the door? The room contained three items of furniture: a lamp stand, an old armchair—granted by custom to Simon—and an even older trunk sporting an impressive series of straps and padlocks to keep prying eyes away from Simon's collection of interesting objects. Serena was sitting on the trunk. She had never, in any of her numerous visits to the hideout, seen the trunk opened.

Once she had asked what was in it.

"Things," Simon had said darkly. "Things people don't want me to have."

She had taken the hint, and treated the chest from then on only as a bench.

They sat in silence for a while. Simon was halfheart-edly fitting together the mortise and tenon of two panels from a dismantled wooden box. Serena's eyes were clos-ing; she felt very tired. When Simon spoke, she jumped.

"Serena, who are the Condés? Why is it dangerous for Mr. Clermont in France?"

"The Condés are a branch of the French Royal fam-ily," she said. Her tongue formed the words, but she did not yet believe them herself.

"But why can't he go back? Your count did. He was an officer under Napoleon, even though he was a no-bleman. The French are not killing aristocrats now."

Serena barely noticed this reference to a man she had forbidden Simon, on pain of a hideous and painful death, ever to mention again. "The Condés who survived the Terror remain in exile because Napoleon considers them a threat to his power—a greater threat perhaps even than the Bourbon king." Fat Louis, as most Englishmen dubbed him, was not a very regal figure. Serena had seen him several times in the days when she still went to Lon-don. He resembled nothing so much as a giant frog, and the newspapers took great pleasure in printing unflatter-ing cartoons of Louis in coronation robes held up by a simpering Lord Liverpool. Across the channel it was much the same: the Bourbons were heartily despised in France. The Condés, on the other hand, were much ad-mired, and had a claim to the throne nearly as strong as that of Louis Bourbon.

"Well, what would happen if he did go back?"

"Most likely, Napoleon would shut him up in the dungeon at Vincennes and then shoot him."

"He would not," Simon said scornfully. "This is 1814. No one can put people in dungeons and shoot them."

"Tell that to Mr. Clermont's cousin."

There was another silence.

"What happened to the cousin?" he asked after a minute, conceding defeat.

"Napoleon kidnapped him from another country, smuggled him back into France, put him in the dungeon at Vincennes, and shot him in a ditch in the middle of the night."

"You're making that up. I would have heard about it. My father would have had one of his shouting sessions where he stomps through the hall cursing Napoleon."

"You have heard about it, although it happened years ago. Mr. Clermont's cousin was the Duke of Enghien."

Simon's mouth opened, then closed. "The one with the dog? The one in the picture?"

"The one with the dog, yes."

The duke had been shot when Simon was a toddler, but English boys still repeated, with ghoulish fascination, the story of the duke's dog, who had howled at the site of his master's death for a full day, exposing the murder to the world. And ladies of a certain age still sighed mournfully over portraits of the fair-haired victim. Even the most flattering renditions of Napoleon could not match the delicate features and gilt hair of the boy duke, so tragically cut off in the flower of youth. The picture Simon referred to had now disappeared—it had been cut out from *The Ladies' Mercury* and pinned up in Mrs. Fletcher's office—but it had shown the duke, his pale lips gasping out his last breath, slumped against a stone wall, with the dog gazing mournfully at his face.

"Then Mr. Clermont cannot go back to France."

"Not at the moment."

"That's good."

"Why?" she said, caught off guard.

"I like him," he said, shooting a quick glance at her to catch her reaction. "In fact, I think we *should* go to London. He could help me assemble my telescope."

"You're forbidden to go to town," she reminded him. "Your mother said her nerves could not endure another episode like St. Paul's."

"I could make her change her mind," he said.

She raised her eyebrows. "Oh?"

"All I need do," he pointed out, with a malicious smile, "is tell her that if I am allowed to go, *you* will agree to come."

"And what makes you think I will agree?"

"Because," he said, with an angelic expression, "you don't wish to deprive your beloved young cousin of a treat."

"Try again," she advised.

He abandoned the halo. "Because you want to go. Or at least you don't want *not* to go."

"I do not. That is, I do. Oh, for heaven's sake! Stop trying to confuse me. I do not wish to go to London. Is that clear?"

He gave her a contemptuous look, pushed himself out of the chair, lit a candle at the lamp, and went to the door. "I am going to find my mother," he announced. "Now is the time to stop me." He stood, arms folded, for a long, insolent moment.

She glowered at him, but didn't move.

"Put out the lamp when you leave," he said. She heard him humming cheerfully as he darted off down the corridor.

"Damn you, Simon," she muttered.

Whenever she felt in need of advice or support, Mrs. Digby sought out Mrs. Fletcher, her most faithful ally in the war against certain undesirable elements in the earl's household. Thus Mrs. Digby found herself at eleven in the morning sitting in a stiff-backed walnut chair in the housekeeper's office and sipping a glass of cordial, which Mrs. Fletcher had offered in spite of the early hour.

"And so your Mr. Clermont is leaving us?" said the housekeeper, pouring herself a small glass of her own. "This is very sudden! You don't suppose he and Miss Serena have quarreled, do you?" Mrs. Fletcher, like most of the female servants, had fastened on Clermont as an ideal husband for Serena. He was suitably tall, he had (as Lucy put it) "such an air about him," and, most importantly, he seemed unintimidated by his potential bride's sharp tongue.

The nurse set her glass down. "No, indeed. Let me finish, do. He calls me to his room, as I was saying, and the luggage piled every which way, and his man running in and out, and he sits me down, very polite, and tells me how grateful he is for my care of him. And he presses something into my hand, as I've already mentioned, and a very tidy sum it was, I don't mind telling you, not that I took it right away, for, as I told him, it was only my Christian duty, but he insisted and I'm sure I'm very much obliged to him, for it's not every young gentleman would be so gracious to an old woman who had seen him make a cake of himself cursing and thrashing about in the middle of the night."

She ran out of breath, and the housekeeper prompted her: "What then?"

"Then I thank him and start to get up, and he stops me, and what do you think he does?"

"What?" said Mrs. Fletcher, on cue.

"He asks me about Miss Serena! He did it well, began by talking about young Simon, but he didn't fool me one bit, and sure enough a moment later he mentions her, as if by accident, talking about how fond she is of her cousin and next he wants to know does she ever go up to Town, and has she any young men come calling. Not in so many words, of course, but it was clear what he was after."

Mrs. Fletcher's round eyes grew rounder. "And what did you tell him?"

"Nothing I oughtn't, never fear. No need to let every gentleman who visits hear about that rascally French count, if he was a count, or even an officer, as we've all wondered many times since. These days every Frenchman seems to be the viscount of this or marquis of that, and how is anyone here in England to know? Poor girl, she was so happy, and her bride-clothes all made up, and the banns about to be read, which was a thing I couldn't quite approve of, since he was a Papist, but the vicar would do anything to oblige her ladyship. And then one day in walks Lucy to make up his fire in the morning and he was clean gone, just vanished, and a very fine gold clock and two candlesticks with him, as well you remember."

"*I* think his lordship should have given the alarm at once, sent word to the garrison that a French prisoner had escaped, but her ladyship was so overset he let it be. Mind you, that was before I found the candlesticks missing!" Mrs. Fletcher gave an instinctive glance at the locked cupboard full of plates on the far wall of her office.

"Well, then, of course I didn't say anything about it, merely mentioned in passing that Miss Serena had suffered an Undeserved Sorrow in her life. I didn't wish him to think her unmarried by choice, after all! But what I *did* say was that there's no call for her to spend her days playing nursemaid to her cousin and companion to her aunt. She ought to have a home of her own, that's what I told him. What does the earl pay Jasper Royce for, if Miss Serena spends more time with Master Simon than his own tutor? A more useless young man I have never seen—losing his lordship's important letters, letting Simon run

wild one minute and lecturing him the next. I know her
ladyship had hopes he and Miss Serena would make a
match of it, but he seems a mighty poor prospect to me.
As for Mrs. Childe, with her fancy gowns and her suite
on the second floor, which is twice the size of Miss Serena's rooms, where is she when her ladyship needs help
with welcoming visitors, or looking over the linens, or
writing invitations? She was a penniless widow when the
earl took her in, but you wouldn't think it to look at her,
would you?"

The two women were silent for a moment in the happy
contemplation of their undying hatred for the aforesaid
widow.

"If you ask me, Bertha Childe likely had something
to do with that Frenchie running off," said Mrs. Fletcher
darkly. "Thick as thieves, they were. And her twice his
age or more. Disgraceful." She turned her thoughts back
to the subject at hand. "Inquiring after rival suitors, was
he? So that's the way the wind blows! A pity he's been
called away to town, then."

"You haven't heard all of it, Eliza. Just as I get up to
go at last—and I was there a good quarter hour, at least,
and nearly all of it talking about Miss Serena—Master
Simon comes bursting in saying, 'I did it!' Those were
his very words. 'I did it, sir! I've persuaded her to
come!' Now what do you think of that? No need to ask
who 'her' is, is there? And then not five minutes later
her ladyship calls me in and tells me we are all to go
up to London at the end of the week! *All* of us. Including Miss Serena."

The housekeeper's mouth thinned. In her mind the
first person who ought to receive word of major up-
heavals in the earl's household was herself. But she was
able to satisfy her pride a moment later, when Pritchett
knocked on the door and informed her that the countess
would be down to consult her in a few minutes on a very
important matter.

"Thank you, Mr. Pritchett," she said, with a gracious smile. "In case you have not yet heard the news, you should know that his lordship and the entire family will be removing to the house in London at the end of the week. I think we should keep this to ourselves for today— no use getting all the upstairs maids into a twitter—but if you could spare two footmen to go up to the box room tomorrow to begin bringing down the trunks, I should be very much obliged."

So, thought Julien as the chaise pulled out onto the London Road, Miss Allen had—as his aunt would say—"made herself a reputation." Mrs. Digby, under the impression that she was being wonderfully circumspect, had proceeded to give hints a child of five could have untangled. Some French officer captured in Portugal had grown bored waiting at Boulton Park to be exchanged. He had amused himself by toying with a much younger Serena and had then broken both his parole and her heart by escaping. It had evidently been quite a scandal. He wondered cynically how much of that scandal had been fueled by Mrs. Digby's notions of discretion and loyalty. In the course of asserting that Serena had nothing to apologize for, the nurse had revealed nearly the entire story of the aborted marriage; worse, to bolster her claim that it had been a perfectly respectable match, she had felt obliged to deny (and therefore relate, in detail) a very salacious story about a gamekeeper discovering the couple together in the woods at dawn. No wonder Serena Allen didn't care for London anymore. Someone with her pride would be certain that every whisper, every averted glance, held condemnation. Or worse, ridicule. He knew, because he had lived his entire adult life with the same poisoned fog hanging over every social occasion.

The nurse's revelation wasn't at all what he had expected to hear. In his years in exile, he had become more

and more English in manner and speech while losses in
the war against Napoleon had mounted higher and higher.
The result was that he had become the unwilling auditor
of innumerable curses, execrations, and maledictions directed at his countrymen. The remarks were made, of
course, without any understanding that Julien himself was
French. Often they were the by-products of desperate, raw
grief, which was far more painful than the unintended insult. Oddly, soldiers were the least likely to indulge in this
sort of venom, even those who had been badly injured.
Women were the most likely. When Simon had announced that his cousin hated Frenchmen, Julien had
therefore assumed that she had lost someone in the war,
and in a way, of course, she had.

His reflections were interrupted by Vernon. "Sir, is it
permitted to ask whether your quest was successful?"

"It is not," said Julien, in a tone calculated to discourage further conversation. It had been successful, or
at least partially so. Very painfully, working by infer-
ence, he had pieced together from the fourth earl's
diaries a rough picture of when his son had been out of
the country. And of course, there was the reference to
the money.

"Have you spoken with his lordship?" Vernon persisted.

Julien gave him a quelling stare.

"That means 'no,' I take it." The servant gave a little
cough. "Sir, if I might venture—"

"Venture, and you're dismissed," Julien snapped.
Then he relented. Vernon had been suffering from a
combination of anxiety and righteous disapproval ever
since their arrival in Oxfordshire two weeks ago. He deserved to know that the end was in sight. "If it will ease
your mind, I will tell you that I expect to settle this business within a week or two, once we are in London."

All he needed now was the name of the earl's banker.

15

It was very late when the post chaise pulled up to Julien's lodgings in Brook Street, and he was surprised to see a light burning in the front parlor. He had traveled so quickly that he had not bothered to send a message ahead warning his small London staff that he would be returning.

Vernon had noticed the light as well, and frowned as he took the key from Julien and opened the door. The frown deepened when the very distinctive sound of clinking glass was heard from the illuminated room, whose double doors were only partially closed. The two men looked at each other, alarmed and puzzled. Then they heard a startled grunt and a set of quick footsteps. The doors flew open with a crash. A disheveled young man with several days' growth of beard stood staring at the two travelers, a wine glass in one hand and a pistol in the other. Julien recognized it as one of his own. He recognized the young man, as well.

"Derry!" he said, relieved. "What are you doing here? Were you told I was returning tonight?"

"No, I was not." Philip Derring's normally pleasant face was scowling. "And I know you've only the three rooms, but you'll have to put me up for the time being. I'm in hiding; that's what I'm doing here—thanks to you. The Foreign Office sent the dragoons after me because of your little jaunt down to Boulton

Park. I thought perhaps they had hunted me down when I heard the door open at this hour."

"The dragoons? After you? The devil you say!"

"Not the devil. Worse. Sir Charles Barrett."

With an effort, Julien recalled the nondescript gentleman who had made one of the luncheon party his first day at Boulton Park. He could not imagine how Sir Charles, Philip, and dragoons could be connected, let alone his own part in it.

"I'll just take your things upstairs, sir," said Vernon, after a glare in his direction from Derring.

"Yes, and find me something to eat," said Julien. "I'm ravenous. We came straight through from Henley with only one change of horses," he explained to Derring as the valet disappeared.

"How jolly for you," was the bitter reply. "I haven't dared show my face outside for nearly a week."

Julien stared at him. "Come back in and sit down," he said, leading the way into the little parlor. Signs of a lengthy and reluctant occupation were everywhere. On the sideboard were empty bottles of claret and hock, the remains of several cold plates, and an open tin of wafers with a few broken pieces left in the bottom. Five days' worth of newspapers were scattered across the floor. Next to the sofa, on a battered end table, a pair of dice sat atop a piece of foolscap with a long list of tally marks. "Right against left?" asked Julien, inspecting the tallies.

Derring nodded glumly.

"Who won?"

"Left. I'll be sure to throw with that hand if I ever dare venture out to my club again."

"It looks a bit . . . untidy in here. Did the servants take themselves off in my absence?"

"They began pestering me to write you if I wished to stay longer," Derring said. "Which seemed to me, under the circumstances, a remarkably foolish idea. So I told them if I saw either one of them in this room without a plate of food in their hands I would shoot them, and if they told anyone I was here, I would shoot them *and* their mothers."

"*What* circumstances?" said Julien. He sank into an upholstered armchair, promptly sprang up, extracted a small paring knife and an apple core from the back of the seat cushion, and tossed them onto a pile of newspapers. Then, cautiously, he sat down again. "I had forgotten what a slovenly fellow you are, Philip," he said. "Bologna was a long time ago. Now try to explain, in chronological order, what has happened. Slowly. It's one in the morning, and I've been on the road since before noon."

Derring took a long swallow of the wine in his glass. "It started ten days ago. There I was, minding my own business, walking down Piccadilly, and Sir Charles Barrett hailed me—didn't think the man even knew my name—and invited me in to White's for a little chat."

Ten days ago. Julien counted back. That would have been the day after Sir Charles had stopped in at Boulton Park. "Go on."

"He was very straightforward: he wanted information about you. Who were you, what were you like, how long had I known you, were you in fact a naturalist or were you pursuing Serena. . . ."

"And what did you tell him?" Julien asked sharply.

Derring threw up his hands in exasperation. "Who knows? I don't recall telling him anything out of the way. He seemed to be interested in your marriage prospects, so I told him you had no plans to marry, and why, but that is no great secret."

Vernon appeared at this point with a small tray of food, took in the state of the room in one horrified glance, and left again.

"Did you mention my title? Name my grandfather?"

"No! I swear, Julien, I never mentioned your family by name. I did suggest that they were highly placed, but that is all. And any fool could deduce as much from one look at you."

For a moment he had thought that perhaps Philip had been the one who had told the countess who he was. His friend had a guilty expression on his face, one Julien recognized from their school days. But no, it was his own cursed fault, for wearing the ring that morning. And in any case, his precautions had proved unnecessary. Bassington hadn't reacted at all to the news that Julien was a Condé. Either he was a master dissembler (which, given Julien's encounters with the earl, seemed unlikely) or his own long-standing theory was correct: Bassington had never even known the name of his victim.

Philip was still talking. "So LeSueur—a friend of mine, do you know him? Sandy hair, thin as a stick? Military chap? No? He's assigned to a crusty old martinet named White who runs a special courier service for Wellington. Surveying, messages behind enemy lines, counterintelligence, that sort of thing. He came to find me at my club a few days after I had spoken with Barrett. Apparently Bassington is involved in some critical diplomatic maneuvers and Barrett didn't care for the idea that a Frenchman was in residence at Boulton Park. Barrett asked White to look into things and LeSueur was detailed to haul me in for an 'unofficial interview.' I told him I'd be free the next afternoon and he should send a note round to my lodgings and then I slipped out of the club and went to ground here. I've heard of White's gang, and I didn't fancy sitting in one of their detention cells while they grilled me about your Bonapartist acquaintances in Bologna."

Derring rattled on, but Julien didn't hear him. Events in Oxfordshire were beginning to make much more sense. At the time, Simon's warning about "real butterfly-men" had merely made him resolve to watch his step around Meyer. Its precise significance was now all too clear.

Meyer was some kind of military Bow Street runner. *He* was the one who had searched Julien's effects—and engineered the confrontation in the library. Julien's fists clenched unconsciously around the knife he was holding.

"What is it?" asked Derring, breaking off in mid-sentence.

"Barrett thinks I'm a spy." He could barely choke out the words. "He believes I would worm my way into a man's house, look through his papers, and sell what I find to some greasy stooge of Napoleon's. Damn him!" He sprang out of the chair and began pacing up and down, kicking savagely at the litter on the floor.

"Be reasonable, Julien," said Derring. "He doesn't know you; I do. Everyone at Whitehall involved in the negotiations with the allies jumps at the drop of a pin these days. They're nervous as cats over there; things are going our way at last and they are afraid if they breathe the wrong way it will all collapse."

"Be reasonable? You're a fine one to talk! Why didn't you just go off to Whitehall with your friend LeSueur and answer their questions? Don't you realize your disappearance suggests you believe me guilty? What did you think they were going to do? Pull your toenails out until you told them I had a mistress in Italy who happened to be Corsican? This is *England*, for god's sake!"

Derring looked uncomfortable. "I'll find LeSueur tomorrow evening," he muttered. "Catch him at the club."

"Dammit, no. That's too late and too chancy. You're going to find him first thing in the morning. I'll wake you. I have a few calls of my own to make, it appears." Julien sat back down and tried to eat a slice of ham. His hands were trembling.

"By the by," asked Derring, reaching over to snag a pickled onion from the plate, "what *were* you doing for so long at Boulton Park? I can't imagine the butterflies were all that engrossing. Are you courting

Serena? Have you finally abandoned your nonsensical scruples about marriage?"

It suddenly struck Julien that what he had been doing at Boulton Park was exactly what Barrett had suspected: worming his way into Bassington's house and looking through his papers. His indignation seemed a bit hypocritical in that light. Was he going to compound his sin by lying to Philip Derring? The answer, apparently, was yes.

"I am not indifferent to Miss Allen," he said after a long pause. That was, he acknowledged, true. "But there are some impediments to the success of my courtship." Also true. Amazing how two half-truths added up to an enormous falsehood.

Derring's face lit. "Good man!" Then he cleared his throat and said, "There was a—a little incident when Serena was younger. You might have heard some rumors. I hope that is not what you meant by impediments."

"I know about it, yes. Mrs. Digby was kind enough to enlighten me. A 'little incident' in Miss Allen's past can hardly trouble a man who is the result of a very large incident in his mother's past."

"Then what is the problem?"

Julien grimaced. "She is not indifferent to me, either. At the moment I would have to say she despises me, but with hard work I may reach the point where she merely dislikes me." He rose, leaving his food unfinished. "Where have you been sleeping?"

Derring indicated the couch.

"Come upstairs. Vernon will make up the spare bed for you and attempt to get your clothing presentable by"—he glanced at the clock on the wall—"six hours from now."

"But that's eight in the morning!" Derring said, horrified. "No one gets up at eight! The *servants* are barely up at eight!"

"You need to be at Whitehall by nine," Julien said,

"and I estimate it will take at least an hour to get you shaved and cleaned up."

Derring ran a hand over his nascent beard and sighed. "Very well. But LeSueur isn't at Whitehall. His unit is housed in some armory building over at the Tower."

Julien thought for a minute. "In that case, Vernon will wake you at seven."

"*Seven?*"

"How did we ever manage to share rooms in Bologna?" Julien asked, half amused, half disgusted.

"You weren't such a paragon of virtue then," was the bitter reply, "as you may perhaps recall."

"I'm not a paragon of virtue now, either. I'm a bastard. A tidy, punctual bastard."

"I don't think this is a good idea," muttered Derring as they followed the subaltern through a narrow, twisting corridor. "If you want to call on someone and protest your innocence, call on Barrett."

"He wasn't at home." Julien dodged a dusty packing-case, which was blocking half the passage.

"Well, it was barely light out! I wouldn't have been at home to you either. Why couldn't you wait until this afternoon and try again?"

"I want this settled."

"How do you even know your Mr. Meyer is back in London? He was still in Oxfordshire when you left, was he not?"

"I'll wager anything you like he followed me as fast as he could."

"And what if he is, after all, a naturalist, and I have traded on my acquaintance with LeSueur for nothing? You will look like a fool, and so shall I."

"He's no naturalist. I am certain of it. A—a reliable source in the household warned me the man had been sent down to inspect me." Most adults would not consider an eleven-year-old boy a reliable source, but Julien had developed a healthy respect for Simon's eavesdropping abilities.

Derring looked at Julien's set, slightly flushed face and gave up. "You know," he commented as they turned yet another corner, "I may be untidy, but *you* are stubborn. My vice creates a small nuisance—"

"Hah!" interrupted Julien. "Tell that to what used to be my parlor."

"A small nuisance," Derring repeated more firmly, "which well-trained servants can easily remedy. Your vice, on the other hand, has far more serious consequences and I fail to see how you can hire anyone to assist you."

"Not hire. Marry. A wife. A gentle, loving wife who will advise me and persuade me to mend my ways. You see, all your arguments about the benefits of marriage have at last won me over."

It was Derring's turn to say "Hah!"

Julien wasn't sure whether the exclamation was directed at the picture of a reformed Julien or at the picture of Serena Allen—his presumed bride-to-be—as gentle and loving. Probably both.

The subaltern, who had maintained an even stride and an expressionless face through the entire journey, held open the door of a small room furnished with two plain wooden chairs and a deal table. "If you gentlemen will wait here, I shall inform you when the captain arrives." He gestured stiffly towards the chairs and then closed the door.

Derring sat down. "Told you this was too early even for the military," he grumbled.

Julien did not reply. He paced back and forth, hands behind his back, rehearsing every word of the speech he planned to make.

Five minutes went by. Ten. Ten more. At last he heard booted footsteps in the corridor.

"In here?"

"Yes, sir."

The door opened and a young man who was clearly LeSueur came in. He matched Philip's description perfectly, although Philip had unaccountably left out the captain's most distinguishing feature, a deep scar running down one side of his face.

"Hallo, old fellow," Derring said uneasily.

"Where have you been? You were meant to come see me—at Whitehall, not here, I might add—four days ago," said LeSueur, looking irritated. "And who is this? Civilians are not normally allowed onto this floor."

Derring started to introduce him, but Julien forestalled him. "I am a friend of Mr. Derring," he said coldly. "And I asked him to bring me here. I am looking for a man named Meyer."

LeSueur gaped. "You are?"

"There is someone who goes by that name associated with your—enterprise, is there not?"

The captain frowned, clearly uncertain about the proper response to this question. He shot a helpless glance back into the hall, but it was empty.

"He has insulted me grossly," Julien clarified.

Oddly, that phrase seemed to work some sort of magic. LeSueur's face cleared. He looked resigned, perhaps even amused. He stepped back into the hall.

"James!" he shouted. "Someone to see you. Affair of honor." He turned back to Julien. "What did you say your name was?"

"Clermont."

"A Mr. Clermont," he called loudly out the door. Then he stiffened and whirled around. "Out! Out!" he shouted, turning red. The scar, oddly, stayed white. "Norris!" The subaltern reappeared. "Escort this gentleman out at once. Down the *front* staircase."

"Not without seeing Mr. Meyer," said Julien, folding his arms.

Another officer had arrived, a dark-haired young man. His uniform and insignia marked him as a captain of rifles. The small room was getting very crowded. "Who wants me?" he asked LeSueur, glancing with no sign of recognition from Philip to Julien and back.

"Nothing. My apologies. False alarm," said LeSueur hastily. "This gentleman was just leaving." He jerked his chin at the subaltern, who stepped forward and laid a tentative hand on Julien's arm. "Not you," LeSueur said to Derring, who had stepped forward. "You have a few questions to answer, remember? In fact, you now have more than a few."

"I'm afraid you'll need to come with me, sir," the subaltern said. He no longer looked impassive. He looked nervous.

"You can't pretend Meyer isn't here," said Julien to LeSueur, furious. "I heard you call to him. I want to see him. I demand it. Doesn't British law say that a man is entitled to confront his accuser?"

The new captain pushed the other two officers aside. He was frowning. "What have I accused you of? Who are you?"

"Who are you?" Julien shot back. "And why are you protecting this Meyer fellow? What harm can it do to let me ask him a few questions?"

"I *am* Meyer," the officer said. "James Roth Meyer. Although in this uniform, I go by James Nathanson."

Julien stared.

LeSueur cleared his throat. "This is the, er, person in question," he said in a low voice. "The Russian affair. And he therefore needs to be escorted out. At once. Before any interesting visitors arrive."

"*This* is Mr. Clermont?"

"Yes, sir."

Julien found himself being scanned from head to toe. He raised his eyebrows and did his own inspection. The aquiline face was vaguely familiar.

"I'll take him down." A faint smile was beginning to appear on the officer's face. "I believe he must be looking for my father." He turned to Julien.

"Older man? Looks a bit like me? Very polite, and next thing you know it feels as though a steel trap has sprung around you?"

Still stunned, Julien nodded slowly.

"Are you planning to call him out? If so, I insist on being present." The officer held open a door on the other side of the waiting room and gestured Julien through to the landing of an open stairwell. "I've been waiting years for this moment. He has been very tiresome on the subject of my own early morning engagements."

"I couldn't possibly meet him," said Julien, shocked. "He's old enough to be my grandfather." Something made him pause, in the middle of the staircase, and look at his escort. "Isn't he?"

"He is forty-four."

"He—seemed older."

"Mmm," agreed the younger Meyer. And that was all he would say, nor did he respond in any way to Julien's indirect queries about his father's credentials as a scientist. At the Tower gate, however, he walked with Julien for a few yards until they were beyond earshot of the guards and said abruptly, "I'm going to give you some advice."

Surprised, Julien stopped.

"I don't like giving advice," Meyer—or Nathanson— said. "And I detest receiving it. I suspect you do as well. But for some reason I cannot help myself."

"What is it?"

"Stay away from the Earl of Bassington. At least for the next few weeks."

Julien felt himself stiffening. "Can you give me a reason?"

"No."

"Then I am unlikely to follow your recommendation." He bowed. "Good day, Captain."

James Meyer watched the tall figure walk away towards Lower Thames Street. Something about the set of the shoulders told him that Clermont now considered himself to have been insulted by both Meyers. He thought of the conversation he had had with his father last night. Nathan Meyer wasn't often wrong. But it did happen, occasionally.

16

Rowley, the London butler, was not as fond of his dignity as Pritchett. He had given Serena an enormous smile when the earl's party had arrived the evening before and had even whispered, "Welcome back, miss!" At breakfast this morning he had informed her that she was looking "prime"—a word which would never have crossed Pritchett's lips. And a few minutes ago, when he had carried in a tray with two cards on it, Serena had seen at once from the flying eyebrow he pointed at her that the callers were, in his opinion, for her, although he took the tray quite properly over to her aunt. Mrs. Digby had no doubt filled Rowley in on every detail of the latest events at Boulton Park, and the slanting eyebrow boded ill.

Her fears were confirmed by her aunt's expression once she had glanced at the cards, an expression which could only be described as smug.

"Show them up, Rowley," she said. He bowed and withdrew, but not without another eyebrow wiggle in her direction.

"Let me guess." Serena was feeling cross and tired.

She had hoped her aunt would not receive callers on their first morning here, but she should have known better. Aunt Clara was never too weary for social intrigue. "It is Mr. Clermont."

"And Philip."

Well, that was something, at least. She hadn't seen Philip in nearly a year.

"I think you have made a conquest at last, my dear Serena," Mrs. Childe said archly from her seat by the fire. "Our first morning here! He wastes no time, I see."

Serena had trained herself long ago to ignore the widow's remarks. Mrs. Childe's cloying sympathy after André Moreau's escape had been almost unendurable until she had woken up one morning to the blinding realization that it was completely false and designed to stir up her grief and distress rather than assuage it. Now she bent her head down lower over her embroidery. She had taken up embroidery two years ago. It was dull, it was ladylike, and it was very, very useful when you lived with Mrs. Childe. Simon now had a matched set of seat covers depicting various large insects, which her aunt had so far refused to allow on any of the chairs, even the ones in the nursery.

"Mr. Clermont. Mr. Derring," announced Rowley, trilling the *r*'s in Derring.

There was Philip, looking somewhat haggard, although the quick smile he shot her was the same as ever. And Clermont was the same as ever, too: revoltingly elegant. His bright hair seemed to glow at the corner of her vision as he greeted her aunt and inquired about their journey up to town.

Serena heard a rustle of skirts behind her. Mrs. Childe had risen and was sinking into a dramatic curtsey, just as she had on the night of the dinner party. Philip, who had been politely listening as her aunt described muddy roads and overcrowded inns, blinked in astonishment. Clermont's reaction was immediate. He leveled the coldest stare Serena had ever seen at the half-descended widow. It was only for a fraction of a second, but she halted in midplunge, wobbled, tripped slightly over her front foot, then collapsed awkwardly back into her chair, looking flustered. Serena was tempted to pass over her embroidery frame so that the older woman would have an excuse to keep her eyes lowered.

Derring was crossing the room. He murmured a greeting to her cousin, who gave the barest nod in return, and then came over to Serena.

"Philip," she said. On impulse, she stood up and kissed him on the cheek, which made him blush furiously. "How are you?"

"Very well. And you? I was delighted to hear you had come up to town with your uncle."

"Any news of Maria?"

He shook his head.

"First babies are always late," said her aunt, overhearing. "You mustn't worry, Philip, I'm sure we shall have comfortable tidings any day. Do sit down, both of you. I'll ring for refreshments."

"Well, I suppose—" said Philip.

"I'm afraid we cannot stay very long," Clermont said at the same moment. "But I had hoped that Miss Allen and Lord Ogbourne might accompany me this afternoon to an exhibition of zoological specimens at Somerset House. If you are not too tired from your journey, that is," he said to Serena, addressing her directly for the first time.

"Not at all," she said, with her best demure-maiden smile. "I should be delighted. And I believe I can vouch for Simon's interest." An understatement. He would be in seventh heaven. He had spent the entire coach ride discussing his plans for "lessons" with Royce while in town, and while he had mentioned traditional favorites such as Astley's Amphitheater and the lions at the

Tower, he had also listed the Royal Society, the Observatory, and the British Museum.

"You are inviting Serena to go see dead animals?" said Philip in distaste. "On her first day in town in years?"

"Specimens, my dear fellow. Not at all the same thing. A rabbit which has been caught by a fox is a dead animal. An *oryctolagus cuniculus*, stuffed and mounted, is a specimen."

"Quite right." Mrs. Childe had apparently recovered. She nodded. "Rare animals are so very interesting, don't you agree, Mr. Clermont?" There was a fractional pause before the word *mister*.

"Certainly." He bowed affably in her direction.

So, Mrs. Childe was forgiven.

The older woman smiled her odd, closed-lipped smile. "And what is an *oryctolagus cuniculus*?"

He gave Serena a quick glance and she suddenly knew Mrs. Childe had not been forgiven at all.

"A rabbit," he said gently.

That was almost enough to make her change her mind. But not quite.

Ten minutes later, with Clermont and Philip safely out of the house, she went up to her desk and wrote Clermont a note. Alas, she had now developed a headache and must beg to be excused from this afternoon's expedition. She actually wrote the word *alas*, enjoying herself very much. After some thought she added that she feared Simon would not be permitted to go without her. She *would* get a headache wondering what mischief her cousin might get up to with Clermont in her absence. "Take that, Mr. Courtly Clermont," she said aloud as she sealed up the note. "You thought you had me, inviting me in front of my aunt. But two can play the social graces game."

* * *

Somerset House, on raw days in March, seemed to exude a damp chill more appropriate for a prison than the stately home of three royal societies and several important government agencies. Especially when filled with stuffed carcasses of dead birds and animals. Rooms and rooms of them, it seemed, and Simon wanted to see every single corpse. She moved mechanically to the next case. "*Sterna paradisaea*," read the label. "Arctic Tern. Provenance: Cape Breton. Specimen donated by P.A.K." Inside was a gray and white bird, its lifeless eyes surveying her haughtily over a blood-red beak. Behind the bird a painted backdrop depicted snow-covered cliffs and a bay filled with chunks of floating ice. She shivered.

Her cousin—the same boy who had demanded extra hot bricks and wraps both mornings in the coach—seemed impervious to the temperature in the exhibition gallery, which was, in Serena's estimate, close to freezing. Of course, perhaps she was not suffering merely from physical cold. Perhaps she was suffering from nerves, because she and Simon between them were currently juggling (here she paused to count) seven complete falsehoods. For Simon, that was nothing, but she was already exhausted trying to remember what she had said to whom.

Serena had been prepared to pay a penalty for outmaneuvering Clermont. And she had known—or thought she had known—what that penalty would be: lying in a darkened bedchamber all afternoon on her first full day in London. Not too steep a price to pay, she had decided, for her victory.

She had reckoned without Simon. Twenty minutes after her note had been sent off, he had burst into her room without knocking. Emily, who had just helped the newly ill Serena into her dressing gown, opened her mouth to scold.

"Out," Simon said to the maid in a tone eerily reminiscent of his father's more autocratic moments.

Emily fled.

Simon closed the door behind her with a deceptively gentle click. "You *traitor*," he said to Serena. His blue eyes were like flint. "You weren't even going to tell me about Mr. Clermont's invitation, were you?"

She thought of denying everything, or of trying to convince Simon that she truly was ill. But in the face of his righteous anger—and it was righteous, she had to acknowledge that—she merely sat down on the edge of the bed and sighed. "How did you find out?" Eavesdropping was not as easy in the London house, although Simon had his methods.

"My mother. Who descended on Royce to warn him that his frail little charge was going out later today." He added, pointedly, "She looked very pleased with herself and nearly forgot to tell me to wear my muffler."

She should have realized Aunt Clara would go to Simon at once, so that he could be fortified with tonics before venturing out of doors.

"And then," he said, eyes flashing, "I came running to find you to see when we were leaving and what precisely this exhibition was, and I met Mrs. Digby. Who told me you were laid down on your bed."

Her conscience smote her. "We'll go tomorrow," she promised, and then instantly regretted it. It was never wise to show weakness in front of Simon.

"We'll go today," he said.

"I've already cried off. I'm ill." She swept her arm out to indicate the turned-down bed, the drawn curtains, and the cloth pad, soaked in lavender water, lying on the floor where the flustered Emily had dropped it.

"We'll go today. At two. Or I will tell my mother how you deliberately humiliated Mr. Clermont."

"You wouldn't!" He would, she saw. He was furious.

Her penalty, therefore, was much worse than four hours in a dark room. It was two hours in a frigid exhibition hall and more lies than she had ever told in one day in her life. To Emily and Mrs. Digby, the tale of the miraculous recovery, followed by a plea not to distress the countess with any talk of illness. To Rowley, an elaborate itinerary which precluded their using the carriage. The last thing she wanted was for Hoop, the Bassington coachman, to insist on waiting until their fictitious escort appeared to take charge of them. And to her aunt, a whole series of lies: she had promised Simon to take him first to Hatchard's for a book which accompanied the exhibition and had therefore sent a note asking Mr. Clermont to call for her at the bookstore. Yes, she was taking a maid. Yes, Mr. Clermont would bring them back in a carriage so that Simon did not have to walk both ways.

She stared at the tern without really seeing it. At another time she might have found the exhibit interesting. There was a whole family of beavers, for example, posed beside one of their dams, which some devoted amateur naturalist had reinforced with plaster of Paris, cut apart into numbered pieces for shipping back to England, and reassembled. There was an enormous, shaggy sort of deer, called a Caribou, and a short-quilled porcupine which apparently lived in trees instead of underneath hedges. But in any case her interest could never have matched Simon's blazing, concentrated enthusiasm. He had long since abandoned her, darting from case to case and from room to room. She gave up and settled down on a marble bench to see how long it would take him to exhaust himself.

Twenty minutes later she was beginning to wish she had brought a maid with her. The crowd was largely male, and she had drawn several rude stares. A lively family group went by, and she was tempted for a moment to get up and drift over until she stood in the protection of their little circle, where she would look like a maiden aunt or perhaps a governess. Another lie; she rejected it. Instead, she looked at her hands, neatly folded in her lap.

Some of the predatory males grew bolder, walking by her repeatedly and slowing as they did so. One even approached and inquired, with oily solicitude, if she needed assistance. She scorched him with her best glare—what Simon called her snake eyes—and then resumed contemplating her glove buttons. His smooth voice faltered, then died, and she heard his footsteps moving away.

"Well, well." A new voice, a very familiar voice. "What an unexpected pleasure. *Very* unexpected."

She forced herself to look up. Dark eyes, dark brows, gold hair, fine-carved mouth. All looking amused. Even his hair seemed to be chortling.

"I am delighted to see that you have recovered from your—indisposition."

She would *kill* Simon. In all the contriving and prevaricating which had gone into undoing her false headache, it had never, ever occurred to her that Clermont would, in fact, come to this exhibit. That the liar would tell the truth while she, the honest one, left a trail of slimy falsehoods all over London.

"What are you doing here?" she said. It came out as an accusation.

He sat down next to her. "Isn't that my line?"

"Simon forced my hand, if you must know. I had no intention of coming."

"So I gathered." He took a folded piece of paper from his pocket, and held it up between thumb and finger.

It was her note. The "alas" no longer seemed funny. None of it seemed funny. When had she turned into the sort of female who enjoyed humiliating people?

"Would you like this back?" he asked, in an oddly

gentle voice. His eyes no longer laughed. They held a mixture of sympathy and regret.

She shook her head. There was a lump in her throat. "Keep it," she managed to say. "Or better yet, give it to Simon. He can use it for his next round of extortion."

"Simon doesn't need any more weapons than he already has," he said, handing her the note. "Where is he, by the way?"

"Last I saw, in the room with the bears." She started tearing the note into tiny pieces, very neatly and methodically. A delicate rain of square paper flakes descended onto her lap. When she had finished she carefully scooped the fragments into her reticule and then inspected her skirts for stray bits of paper.

Clermont was showing remarkable restraint in his moment of triumph. He sat idly scanning the crowds coming through the doorway opposite, as though young ladies tore letters to shreds next to him every day of the week.

"I owe you an apology," she said, very quietly, to his profile.

He turned to face her. "No," he said. "I owe you one."

Startled, she blurted out, "You do? Why?"

He studied her for a long moment, his face curiously intent. But then his normal, slightly ironic expression returned, and he echoed lightly, "Why? Because it was quite unfair of me to use your aunt to trap you this morning. Come, I'll answer your question." He rose and offered her his hand.

"What question?" she said, standing and tucking her arm into his.

He smiled down at her. She forgot, she always forgot, how tall he was, until he was right next to her. "What I am doing here." He led her into the next room, to a case filled with birds. "Look."

At first she didn't understand. Some of the birds were beautiful, it was true—especially one goose with silver and blue feathering on its neck—but most seemed quite ordinary to her. It wasn't until she had read the labels carefully several times that she noticed what they all had in common: *Specimen donated by L.F.J.B.C.*

She reached out and touched the corner of the nearest label. "These are yours?"

He nodded.

"L.F.?"

He grimaced. "Family names. I don't use them."

"Then you *are* a naturalist," she said slowly. "My suspicions were unjustified, it appears."

"Another apology?" He raised his eyebrows. "Don't be too hasty, Miss Allen. To quote the estimable Mr. Sheridan, 'there is no trusting appearances.'"

For a Frenchman he had certainly read a good deal of English verse.

17

The conquest of the Bassingtons, Julien reflected, was a delicate balancing act, a house of cards constructed from layer upon layer of social innuendo. The Viscount was his pretext—an easy one; he found Simon rather appealing and could include the boy in genuine interests of his own without much difficulty. The lens grinder, in particular, had been a godsend. Julien had called twice now to confer with Simon about the construction of the telescope, and a further visit would be required to present the finished instrument. The layer above Simon, of course, was Serena Allen—the answer to any skeptics who wondered why a wealthy bachelor would act as an unpaid tutor to an eleven-year-old boy. Miss Allen's reluctance to encourage his attentions was another godsend. Not only could Julien assure his conscience (at least most of the time) that she would be delighted when he eventually disappeared, but her resistance only made her aunt and uncle more eager to welcome him. The countess was constantly inviting him to join her (and her niece) for various engagements and outings. He and Philip were to dine there tonight, in fact, and then escort the countess, Mrs. Childe, and Miss Allen to a concert in Hanover Square.

"More diplomatic maneuvering," said Philip from behind his newspaper. "Napoleon should have accepted the terms offered him a few weeks ago. Listen to this: 'We can now confirm that a treaty has been signed at

Chaumont, binding the allies to continue their campaign against Bonaparte. The agreement, drafted by Lord Castlereagh, promises to restore sovereignty to Holland and Italy. Spain will be governed by a Bourbon king. It remains only to settle the Austrian and Russian claims to the eastern territories.' "

Julien looked up from an essay in *Bulletin of the Royal Institution*, which was attempting to persuade him that wolves had a form of language. "Oh, is that all that remains? The merest trifle, to be sure."

They were at the Alfred, a club Julien strongly preferred to the more fashionable establishments on St. James Street. It was quiet, it had an excellent library, and its membership was more diverse than the dandified precincts of White's and Boodle's. More intelligent, too. An older man sitting nearby looked up at Julien's sarcastic comment and snorted in agreement.

"You are a pessimist," said Derring.

"No, a realist. Austria and Russia are more afraid of each other at this point than they are of Napoleon. If he offers one of them help against the other, Castlereagh's treaty won't be worth the paper it's written on." Julien went back to his magazine, but a low cough interrupted him again. It was one of the Alfred's waiters, holding a tray with an engraved card face up in the center. Three steps behind the servant, not bothering to wait for a response to the card, an elderly man with a hooked nose and piercing light-blue eyes was leaning on a gold-headed walking stick. He was wearing silk, although it was barely noon. He always wore silk. As the others in the room gradually became aware of his presence, those who knew him rose, and others, taking their cue from their fellows, scrambled out of their chairs and listened, awed, to the whispered name.

Julien, too, had risen.

"Monsieur," he said, bowing stiffly. He was trying not to look as astounded as he felt. Having used his grandfather as an excuse to leave Boulton Park, Julien had made a point of calling in Gloucester Place on his second day back in London. As usual, he had been denied. And as usual, he had left a note professing himself his grandfather's devoted servant to command. He had not seen his grandfather in a very long time—and the prince, on the few occasions when he was willing to speak to his bastard grandson, normally summoned the aforesaid grandson to him.

"A moment of your time, if you would be so good," said his grandfather in French.

"Certainly." Julien signaled to the club's butler, who was gawking in the doorway of the library, and they were shown to a small side chamber furnished with a globe and writing table.

The prince walked over to the globe and rotated it so that France was facing up before turning to Julien. "I overheard your remark to the young man with the newspaper just now. Had you any particular reason to make that remark? Any special knowledge of the current tensions between Austria and Russia?"

"I beg your pardon, monsieur, but I do not understand your question."

"You are, I have recently been informed, an acquaintance of the Earl of Bassington? You have been a guest at his home?"

"Yes, monsieur."

"And you are courting his niece?"

Julien hesitated. "The countess and Miss Allen have been very amiable," he said, temporizing. At least, the countess has, he added silently.

"She is not for you." His grandfather disposed of Serena with a wave of his lace-cuffed wrist. "I have been remiss, however. It is time you were married. When my affairs are not so pressing, I will consider the question."

"We have discussed this before, *grandpère*. My views have not changed."

The wrist waved again, dismissing the topic. "Let us return to the man Bassington. It happens that he is of some importance to us—to our family and their prospects after the return to France—in regard to this very question of a treaty with Russia. I came to find you here in the hope that you would agree to contrive a meeting between myself and the earl. As if by accident, you understand, so that no great importance would attach to any discussion we might have. But now it occurs to me that I could not rely completely on anything Bassington might tell me, even at such an informal, chance encounter. Information obtained more discreetly, by someone who was welcome in the household, would be far more useful." He paused, significantly.

With a detached portion of his brain—the portion that was not stunned by the proposal—Julien noted that the grandson of Louis XIV had just asked his own (admittedly tainted) flesh and blood to spy on an ally while he was a guest in the man's house. He stopped to consider whether that request was in any way more despicable than his own mission and concluded that it was.

"I am desolated, monsieur," he said. Sometimes he missed speaking French. Only in French could you abase yourself extravagantly and say no at the same time.

"You are an ungrateful, arrogant young man," snapped the prince, "unworthy of the recognition we have given you."

Every meeting with his grandfather seemed to end with that phrase. Usually Julien apologized. The man was his grandfather, after all. Had raised him, however grudgingly; had endowed him with a title and lands. Had even wept once in his presence, a mark of trust which Julien considered the closest thing to a gesture of affection the fierce old man had ever made. It was the day that the news of the murder of the Duke of Enghien had reached England.

He didn't apologize today. He didn't bow. On his way out the door, he removed his signet, set it down on the writing table, and walked away without looking back.

It was returned to him by a liveried messenger within the hour. On the Alfred Club's ivory-colored notepaper his grandfather had written:

You cannot change who you are, just as I cannot change your mother's lack of a marriage certificate. I am not ashamed of what I asked you to do. The fate of nations is more important than your pride, and, in the expectation that you will come to this understanding in time, I remain eager to receive any news you may have on the subject of our discussion.

The Concerts of Ancient Music were governed by a very rigid protocol. The musicians, garbed in frock coats and wigs, were formally introduced. Only the most elevated works, sanctified by the passage of time, were presented. A director who had defied the rules twenty years ago by selecting a then-new work of Haydn had been fined an enormous sum. No conversation or applause was permitted until the end of each piece. Ushers had been known to ask patrons to leave if they spoke—even in whispers—during the performance.

Julien had been grateful for that promise of enforced silence. It could have been the opera, he had told himself, where he would have been trapped for an entire evening in a box visible to hundreds of spectators while he conversed with Miss Allen in front of her aunt—or worse, in front of Mrs. Childe. Ten minutes in the concert rooms at Hanover Square had revealed his mistake. Conversation, in the campaign he was conducting, was a shield. It permitted deflections, sidesteps, counterattacks. It was amusing. It was distracting. And now, sitting next to Serena Allen, there were no distractions.

He was achingly aware of her, of the tension in her shoulders and her fierce grip on the program in her lap. She was pretending to read it, and beneath her swept-up hair the back of her neck curved downwards, delicate and vulnerable. Even when he forced himself to look straight ahead he could see the pale, graceful arc out of the corner of his eye. Looking at his own program was no better; then he saw her gloved hand curling around the paper. He could not stop thinking about the last time he had sat next to her, on the bench in Somerset House, watching her shred another piece of paper into unimaginably tiny squares. The music was no help. There was a certain wistful quality to Corelli which echoed through his head like an accusation: *coward, coward, you have delayed too long.*

He could excuse his own thoughtlessness, at least in part. It was understandable that someone who had grown up alone, with no family, no plans for marriage, would fail to see that most people were not like him. They were not alien, drifting hollows. They had parents, brothers, sisters, wives—people who were bound to them, who would bleed with them, hurt with them. Nor would the damage be confined to the earl's family. Mrs. Digby, Bates, even the bumbling Royce were all entangled in his deception. It struck him suddenly that the only member of Bassington's household who would not suffer was the enigmatic Mrs. Childe. Because she was like him: solitary and coldhearted. It was not a pleasant thought.

Another few days, he thought. He only needed another few days. His appointment at the bank was on Friday. He would enlist Derry, drop some hints about what was coming, to soften the blow. Derry would never forgive him, of course. Neither would the boy. Or the countess, who was sitting across the aisle right now glancing over at her niece every two minutes or so. She caught his eye and smiled. He felt sick.

It was a cold, wet night. In spite of the weather, the hall was very crowded, and he had no chance to speak with Derring during the interval. It was as much as he could do to bring back his share of the refreshments to the women without being trampled. He managed to sit next to Derring during the second half of the concert, but his two attempts to whisper brought frowns from both Serena and the usher. There was chaos afterwards, as well. All the coaches were crowding into the square, gentlemen were darting out into the rain to find vehicles for their party, and the entryway was mobbed with patrons collecting their coats and hats. It was not until he had handed the three women into the carriage that he was finally able to grab Derring and haul him under the shelter of a porte cochère on the other side of Prince's Street.

"Derry, listen," he said. He had to nearly shout to be heard over the rain and the noise of the coaches. "I have a favor to ask of you."

"Name it, dear fellow." Derring was in a very good mood, Julien saw. "Or better yet, come back to my rooms; have a glass or two of port, and *then* name it."

He shook his head. The fewer questions Derry could ask, the better. "I would be grateful if you could—" How was he going to put this? He paused, stymied, and started over. "Something has happened which may require me to leave the country very shortly."

His friend's easy grin disappeared. "Your grandfather?"

"In part." That unsettling encounter at the Alfred this afternoon could prove useful, he realized. "I cannot say anything more at the moment. Here is my dilemma: Miss Allen and the countess have been very kind, and I am not sure how to tell them of my departure without seeming presumptuous."

Derring was quiet for a moment. A coach rattled by,

splashing both of them with cold water. "So you want me to find out whether any expectations have been raised?"

"Yes, that's it exactly," Julien said, relieved.

"I know Serena quite well." There was an edge in his voice. "Perhaps I should approach her, caution her that your very public, very determined pursuit of her will abruptly cease? That she will once again be humiliated, the center of a delicious scandal? Can I give her a date? The fifteenth?"

"Oh, God." Julien slumped against the stones of the archway. "Is it that bad? I didn't suppose anyone would take our—our flirtation very seriously. She's given me very little encouragement."

Derring glared at him. "You told me your courtship had been unsuccessful. You told me she detested you."

"I thought she did," he said, almost plaintively. Had he really believed that? He remembered her mouth, warm and breathless, in the greenhouse. He remembered her eyes, glittering with unshed tears, lifting to his as they sat on the marble bench.

"You idiot! You numskull! Are you blind? Do you think Serena Allen normally sits through an entire evening staring at her lap? I could feel her willing herself not to look at you from two seats away! I could feel *you* not looking at her from three seats away! Do you know how long it has been since she came to London? Since she appeared in public at concerts? Accepted invitations to dances, like the one Lady Barrett is hosting two days from now?"

Mutely, Julien shook his head.

"Five years. She has been hiding down at Boulton Park, scaring off every suitor her aunt manages to get down there on one pretext or another, for *five years*. Ever since that damned count abandoned her a month before their wedding. No one in that household has any doubts at all about why she suddenly decided to rejoin the world. There are probably wagers among the footmen about when the engagement will be announced. And now you want me to give her a gentle warning that you, too, are about to disappear?" He pointed a shaking finger at Julien's chest. "Don't you dare walk away and leave her unprotected. I don't care what your grandfather told you. I don't care if the royalists have promised you the bloody throne of France. I don't care if White's couriers are about to assassinate you. If you go without offering her a respectable excuse for rejecting your suit, I'll kill you."

"Well, that shouldn't be too difficult," Julien said, folding his arms. "I'll just tell her I'm a bastard."

Derring frowned. "She doesn't know?"

"I don't even think Bassington knows. I have hinted at it, but it isn't the sort of thing one just announces. 'Good morning, my lord, have I mentioned that my mother never married my father?'"

"Well, you are not just *any* by-blow," Derring said, looking uncomfortable. "Royalty has its privileges."

"Do you want me to provide Miss Allen with a pretext for sending me away or not?" he demanded.

His friend didn't answer for a moment. Then he said, slowly, "What do *you* want, Julien?"

I want this to be over, he thought.

In a cramped room at the back of his house on Harland Place, Sir Charles Barrett and a guest were standing by a window. It was a small, barred window, and even during the day it offered little in the way of light. Outside was a passageway only a few feet wide, which ran between the Barrett house and the house next door. Although the walkway provided a quick route from the square to the kitchens, the Barrett servants almost never used it, preferring to wend their way through the mews. For one thing, the passage was so narrow that even handcarts could not come through. For another, it was unlit, and secluded enough to frighten any prudent resident of London. The lower floors of both houses had no other windows or doors opening onto the passage.

"Do you suppose there is something wrong?" said the guest, an officer with a large white mustache. "He is normally very punctual."

Barrett, listening intently, lifted a hand. Over the noise of the rain outside, both men heard quick footsteps and then a soft tap on the outer wall.

"Ah," said the officer, looking suddenly much more relaxed. "Excellent. I'm right here; I'll get it." He pressed down on one side of the paneling below the embrasure. With a loud click, the window and the entire section of wall it was set into swung open. A dark-coated figure hoisted himself through the opening and stood dripping for a moment in silence. Then he pulled his hat off, scattering water everywhere, and pulled the panel behind him back into place.

"Good evening, Colonel," said Nathan Meyer. He nodded towards Sir Charles. "Evening, Barrett." His hair was no longer gray, and he no longer stooped. If Clermont had seen him now he would have had no trouble recognizing him as James Meyer's father. "I'm afraid I'm soaked. Have you any notion of how much water collects in that passageway when it rains?"

"Come into the study," said his host. "There's a fire in there, and I've left word that White and I are not to be disturbed."

"A fire sounds wonderful." Meyer shrugged out of his coat and hung it up beside the window. Stains on the wood beneath the hook suggested that this was not the first time a wet coat had hung there.

The three men passed through a doorway into a larger room lined with bookcases and cabinets. Piles of papers were on one table; a map was unrolled across another. The massive desk, at the far side of the room, was incongruously clean; it held only three neatly stacked books. They were bound in dark red leather and a small monogram was stamped on the spines.

Sir Charles waved the two other men to a pair of armchairs by the fire and pulled a third chair over for himself. "I haven't seen in you in some days, Meyer," he said.

"I've been keeping a low profile." He stretched out his legs and let his damp boots rest at the edge of the hearth.

"Avoiding the outraged Mr. Clermont?" Barrett's tone was amused.

"You and James may find the episode entertaining," said Meyer. "I do not. The man is either very innocent or very dangerous. Have you heard what happened this afternoon?"

White shook his head, as did Barrett.

"His grandfather came to find him. At the Alfred."

"The prince?" Barrett looked startled. "Supposedly they haven't spoken in years."

"They are speaking now," Meyer said grimly. "Bassington, I know, refuses to believe that a Condé would spy for Napoleon. Has it occurred to you that the Condés might find our negotiations with the Tsar useful on their own account?"

"The Condés are our allies," said White uneasily. "After Napoleon surrenders, the prince is to escort the king into Paris at the head of an émigré regiment."

"The Austrians are our allies as well," Barrett said. He was no longer smiling. "And for the last two months, through Bassington's contacts in the Tsar's entourage, we have been maneuvering to shut them out of the eventual peace treaty. England is committed to returning Louis Bourbon to his throne, flawed though he might be. What do you imagine Austria would do, should she learn of our secret communications with the Tsar? Might she not throw her weight behind a much more respected figure, one with the same royal blood in his veins—the Prince of Condé?" He turned to Meyer. "Is that what you are suggesting?"

Meyer sighed. "I am not sure what I am suggesting. One moment, I am convinced Mr. Clermont is a quixotic fool, and the next moment I think he is a cold-blooded plotter. I tell myself a real spy would not storm over to Whitehall demanding to see me. Nor would he arrange to meet his grandfather in front of a dozen of the shrewdest men in London. And then I remember how he contrived a riding accident to gain access to Boulton Park. How he feigned interest in the butterfly collection. Continues to feign interest in Miss Allen."

Barrett stirred. "My wife," he said, "believes the last item to be genuine. She and the countess have formed an alliance to promote the match. And I should warn you that in their own way they are as formidable as the Austrians."

"Does that explain the invitation I received this morning?" asked White.

"Yes." Barrett grimaced. "I, er, added you to the invitation list as a precaution. After I discovered that, without consulting me, my wife and Lady Bassington had decided to host a supper party with dancing. Here, in this house. And Mr. Clermont is to be the guest of honor. Needless to say, this room will be locked and I will post a servant in the hallway." He rose. "Shall we compare notes, gentlemen?" He gestured towards the pile of leather-bound journals on the desk.

"Nothing." White produced two matching volumes and handed them across.

"Nor in the ones I looked through," said Meyer. "Just a moment, let me give them back before I forget." He went into the other room, extracted three notebooks from his coat pocket, and set them on the desk.

"Nothing in my three, either," said Barrett. "Personally, I find it maddening. Here we are with the most vicious, most detailed account imaginable of every secret, illicit action at the Tsar's court for the past ten years, and we still cannot identify Austria's agent in St. Petersburg." He collected all six volumes and set them on the table. "I'll keep these here for the moment and take one more look before I give them back. If I do, in fact, give them back. So far Bassington has been reluctant to read them, and I cannot say I blame him. Who would want to face the evidence that a kinsman had made his living ferreting out the Russian aristocracy's nastiest secrets and then demanding money to keep them quiet?"

"Piers died well, at least," White said after a moment.

"Yes," Barrett sighed, "he did. Unfortunately, his noble end is not recorded in these diaries. Instead, the last entry describes an evening with two respectable matrons—respectable if this diary is never published, at any rate. Bassington would have nightmares for a week if he saw it. Perhaps I should burn them."

18

"I think it is monstrously unfair." Simon scowled at the froth of gauze and satin draped over Serena's bed. She had just had her last fitting, and the gown needed only a few tucks in the bodice before she wore it tonight. Even she had been impressed with her reflection in the mirror, although not as impressed as her aunt.

"Simon," she said wearily, "eleven-year-old boys are not invited to supper parties."

"But I'll have my telescope! Mr. Clermont is bringing it by this afternoon. And the Barretts' roof is flat." He changed his tone to the "veiled threat" mode. "Do you *want* me to break my neck climbing out on our roof?" The Bassington town house, like the other two residences on the east side of Manchester Square, had a steep slate roof.

Serena laughed. "Even you are not such a fool as to climb out on our roof at night in March, Simon! Besides, the moon will still be nearly full tonight, and the Barrett's house will be lit outside to welcome the guests. You won't be able to see much. Wait ten days or so. Ned and Jamie Barrett will be home for half-holidays then, and I'm sure will be only too happy to go up on their roof with you."

"Ten days!" She thought he would storm out of her room, as he often did, but after a tense pause he subsided into a chair and hunched over, looking at the floor. "Serena," he said, his voice muffled in his shirt collar, "haven't you ever looked forward to something, looked forward to it a great deal? And then you have it—it's in your hand—but you can't use it yet, can't enjoy it? And everyone tells you to wait for the right time, but you worry that something might happen, it might break or get lost before you even try it."

It was one of the most reasonable arguments she had ever heard her cousin make. Disturbingly reasonable, and applicable to more situations than new telescopes. "I'll go out with you this evening," she said, touching him lightly on the shoulder. "Before the supper party. It will be dark by half past six, and we are not invited until nine. We can go over to the park for a bit."

"You won't be able to go out," said her cousin bitterly. "You'll be primping."

"For *two hours*?"

"I heard my mother. She's engaged a hairdresser, and a seamstress, and all manner of other people to twitter over you."

Serena's hand went instinctively to her chignon. "A hairdresser?"

"Your hair," he said with cruel precision, "is 'too severe and spinsterish.' At least according to Miss Robbins."

Robbins was her aunt's dresser. She had impeccable taste—had helped select Serena's gown, in fact. Serena peered into the cheval glass, which had been set up in the middle of the room for her fitting. It was true, her hairstyle was old-fashioned, pulled straight back off her face. Everyone else these days had little curls dangling. Even her aunt. Even Mrs. Childe. She wondered how she would look with just a few tendrils loose.

"We'll go out earlier, then," she said. "Somewhere high, where we can see the city, since it will still be light."

His face lit; he jumped up. "You will? Serena, you are a trump!"

Half laughing, she pushed him away as he tried to embrace her. "Go on, get out. You've twisted me round your little finger, as usual; now get back to your lessons."

At the door, he turned, and said impulsively, "You're not severe, you know. Not when you smile."

After Simon left she went and stood in front of the mirror. She pulled out a strand of hair from her chignon and draped it across the side of her forehead. Then another, on the other side. She tried a smile. It looked ghastly. When she held up the gown and tried again it looked even worse. She hated Robbins. She hated Clermont, with his gold hair and his dark, unreadable eyes. She hated herself. Perhaps she could arrange to break her ankle this afternoon on her expedition with Simon.

There was a Mr. Hewitt at Hewitt's Bank, Julien discovered, but he himself did not usually meet with clients these days. His firm had prospered in the past ten years—war was not always a bad thing, for an astute financier—and there were bank officers now, men with soothing, well-bred voices, who handled most visitors. Hewitt made an exception for high-ranking peers, of course, and for ministers, and for one or two very lovely actresses. He was making an exception today, as well. Clermont had gone to Royce and obtained a letter of introduction. He had planned to make the request of the earl personally, but his nerve had failed him at the last minute. It was just as well, he decided. A letter from Bassington himself might alarm Hewitt, make him more cautious.

He arrived precisely on time, at ten, and the elderly banker looked up from his desk in astonishment when an assistant ushered him into the room. Four ledgers were open in front of him, and he hastily closed them and piled them to one side.

"Mr. Clermont?"

Julien inclined his head. "Mr. Hewitt. Thank you for

agreeing to see me. I understand it is a rare honor, and I am to convey to you Lord Bassington's appreciation for your courtesy to him." In fact, when Bassington found out, he would be furious. But by then it would be too late.

The assistant withdrew, closing the door behind him.

"Please, have a seat," Hewitt said, gesturing to a leather chair by his desk. "My apologies; I was not expecting you just yet. Most young men of your class are not very punctual, especially for morning appointments."

Julien smiled dryly. "Even those who come to borrow?"

"Even those." Julien sat down, and the banker studied him for a moment. "What can I do for you, sir? I understand the matter is confidential."

"Yes." He paused. "Lord Bassington has informed me that you are a man who can keep his own counsel. And that of his clients." With a little prompting, he had managed to get Royce to word the letter perfectly. "Could you suggest that the matter requires discretion?" he had asked, leaning over Royce's desk. "Perhaps the earl has employed Mr. Hewitt for confidential transactions in the past?" And so the note had gone off, with Royce's compliments, and many expressions of thanks for Mr. Hewitt's past services to the Piers family. Could Mr. Hewitt receive Mr. Clermont and assist him in a transaction of some delicacy?

Julien took a small, folded piece of paper from an inner pocket. He had guarded that paper with fanatical devotion since it had come into his possession six months ago. Had shown it to no one, had concealed it even from Vernon. It normally resided in a hidden compartment in one of his silver hairbrushes, but he had been unwilling to leave it when he went riding off to Clark's Hill, and had sewn it into the cuff of his shirt, where it had fortunately survived a vicious assault by the earl's laundress after his accident.

Now he passed the document across to the banker. "Do you recognize this?"

Hewitt looked at the paper, at Julien, back at the paper. "It is a draft on this bank," he said. "Signed by me, and addressed to a Mademoiselle DeLis, at the Convent of the Sacred Heart, in Lausanne. It is not a forgery, if that is what you wish to know."

Julien cleared his throat. "The earl has been very kind to me. He has refused, however, to allow me to repay the monies sent abroad to Miss DeLis. I am a wealthy man, Mr. Hewitt. Even were I not, this touches my honor. Nor, I think, is it truly Lord Bassington's right to deny me. The payments were authorized by the late earl, were they not?"

The older man said nothing, but he shifted slightly in his seat.

His guess had been correct, Julien saw. "I am asking you, as a personal favor, to provide me with the total amount disbursed. I know that this was only one of several such payments."

Hewitt read the paper once more. "This is all very irregular, Mr. Clermont," he said, frowning. "I understand that the earl has taken you into his confidence, but I am still reluctant to provide you with information about an account which belongs to another client."

"My alternative," said Julien, "is to arbitrarily suppose ten payments, all equal to this one. And to deposit that sum in this bank under Lord Bassington's name." It was a staggering amount of money, and Julien knew that any banker would be horrified at the waste. He leaned forward. "Do you not believe, Mr. Hewitt, that a debtor has a right to know the extent of his debt?"

"And do you regard it as a debt?" Hewitt looked up and met his eyes. "Those who have been wronged normally regard such payments as justice, not charity."

So, he knew.

"I do."

"Very well." Hewitt rang a small bell on his desk and sent his assistant off to fetch a file. Julien wondered how long it would take to find highly confidential documents nearly thirty years old.

It took half an hour, during which time Julien was invited to wait in a sitting room around the corner from Hewitt's office. At the end of the half hour, Hewitt himself came in and handed him a small slip of paper. "This is the total," he said.

Two thousand pounds, thought Julien. *Two thousand pounds for a human life.* It was slowly sinking in that after weeks—months—of work he finally had his proof, could be certain that Bassington was indeed his man. He took a blank draft on his own bank out of his pocket, filled in the amount, signed it. His hands were shaking slightly. It was sheer pride, that gesture. He could easily have promised to send the draft next week, by which time he would be gone. But when he had devised this plan—the only plan he could think of, short of simply asking Bassington for the truth—he had decided that the price for tricking Hewitt into betraying a client was to consider his pledge to the banker binding.

"I will arrange to deposit the funds into the earl's account today, sir," said the banker, tucking the draft into one of the ledgers on his desk. "Would you like me to send a copy of the transaction to his lordship?"

"That won't be necessary," said Julien. "I'll tell him myself. I'm calling at his house this afternoon, in fact."

Bassington rang for the fourth time. He knew the bell was working; his study was on the ground floor, and he could hear the chime faintly in the basement hallway below. Where the hell was the blasted footman? Or Rowley? He didn't want to leave his office and go in search of anyone. He couldn't leave the letters un-guarded in his office—there was enough there to blow Castlereagh's treaty sky-high—and he had promised Barrett that if he could have the file today he would not let anyone so much as glimpse the wrappers. He didn't much fancy going down to the kitchens with a dispatch case full of diplomatic bombshells under his arm, which seemed the only option at this point. Be-sides, this was his house, damn it. He was entitled to expect someone to appear when he rang the bell. He stomped up and down, fuming, for at least a minute be-fore reluctantly going over to his desk and extracting yet another pinch of snuff from a container he had rigged out of an old ink bottle. Clara was a ruthless extermi-nator of snuffboxes; he had learned to be clever.

At the footman's knock on the door he whirled and yanked the door open, roaring, "Where the devil have you been?"

Only it wasn't the footman. It was Simon, holding a long wooden tube—presumably the promised telescope. Behind him stood Royce, his niece, and Julien Cler-mont, with expressions ranging from terrified (Royce) to amused (Serena) to polite surprise (Clermont).

"Papa—I—we—" stammered Simon, backing up into Royce.

"Sorry, sir," interjected the tutor, red-faced. "We didn't mean to disturb you."

"No, no," said Bassington, trying to unobtrusively slip the pinch of snuff into his waistcoat pocket. "My apologies. I thought you were Hubert. I've been ringing for ten minutes and no one has answered the bell." He looked at his son. "Is that your new instrument?"

"Yes, sir." Simon handed it to him, and, warned by his possessive grip, the earl took it very carefully. He turned towards the window, eased the yard-long cylinder care-fully up to eye level, and sighted. "Very good," he said absently, and then, a moment later, as the magnified image came into focus, he added, surprised, "By Jove! It really is good!"

Simon hovered next to him. "It has two lenses," he explained, breathless. "The smaller one, the magnifying one, is mine. The refracting lens is on the bottom. Mr. Clermont contributed that one. There's a carrying case and a tripod as well, but I left those upstairs. Serena and Mr. Clermont and I are going to go try it out now. And Jasper, if you can spare him."

"Are you? Where?" The earl gave the telescope back, somewhat reluctantly. It was really quite impressive, for a homemade instrument.

Royce said, somewhat apologetically, "Miss Allen and I agreed St. Paul's would be best, sir, but we thought it might be wise to have your permission first. Given, the, er, unfortunate incident last year."

"Hmmmph. Yes, I can see why." He eyed his son and heir sternly.

"I'll behave, Papa. Word of honor," Simon said hastily. "And that verger might not be there today."

The earl took some coins out of his purse and handed them to Royce. "I profoundly hope the man has retired. But in case anyone recognizes the viscount, you may need this."

"Can Jasper go, then?" Simon asked.

"Certainly." Bassington looked at his secretary-cum-tutor. "I'm working with the Russian correspondence this afternoon, in fact. You won't even be allowed into my office." He shot a hasty look at his desk to make sure the dispatch case was closed up. One blue sheet of paper was sticking out. Fortunately, that side was blank. He stepped into the outer room, closing the door behind himself, and turned back to his son. "Has your mother been consulted about this expedition?"

"We couldn't find her," said Royce. "We couldn't find anyone, in fact."

Bassington heard footsteps. The footman, after a mere twenty minutes, had finally arrived.

"Could you give permission, sir? *Please*?" His son's voice was urgent.

"I suppose so," said the earl, just as his wife's voice behind him said, "Permission for what?"

"To climb the dome at St. Paul's with Serena and Jasper and Mr. Clermont so that I can try my telescope." Simon opened his blue eyes wide. "We'll be very careful."

His wife was looking horrified.

Bassington stepped over to her side. "I already gave Simon permission, my dear," he said in a low voice.

"Oh, Simon may go, of course," she said. "Mr. Royce will be there, will he not? And perhaps Mr. Clermont, although he has been far too generous already. But Serena cannot possibly go."

He saw his niece and Clermont exchange a quick glance.

"I would be back in plenty of time to get dressed, Aunt Clara," Serena said.

"That might be so," she said, "although your ideas about how much time is required may not coincide with mine. But no young woman in my charge is going to climb five hundred steps a few hours before a dance. Your uncle took me up to the Stone Gallery when we were courting, and I couldn't walk for three days afterwards."

The earl prepared himself for a battle royal between aunt and niece. He had seen many of them over the years. But, to his surprise, Serena turned to Clermont. "Are there really five hundred steps?"

He nodded. "Five hundred thirty-four, to be precise."

"Then I'm afraid my aunt is right. I'm sorry, Simon. Do you mind?"

Simon looked at Clermont. "Will you still come, sir?"

Another of those silent, almost instinctive exchanges between Serena and the young Frenchman.

"Of course," said Clermont. "If Mr. Royce will not be bored to death listening to us talk about focal length and eyepiece rims."

"Not at all." Royce gave a thin smile. "It will certainly be useful to have another pair of hands to carry the instrument and tripod. And there don't appear to be any footmen available."

That reminded Bassington of his grievance. He turned to his wife. "Yes, where are the servants, Clara? I rang the confounded bell four times, and no one has responded yet!"

"You'll simply have to make do, all of you," she said. "I've lent all the maids and footmen to Sara Barrett for the afternoon and evening; her staff here in town is not sufficient for an event of this size."

"I thought this was a small, informal supper with some dancing afterwards," he said.

"It—grew a bit. Now there will be dancing first and then a supper."

Suddenly suspicious, he demanded, "How many guests will there be?"

She waved her hand airily. "Oh, perhaps a hundred. It seems there were more of our friends in town than I had originally thought."

A hundred people. He had thought there would be two dozen; mostly people he knew well. He had planned to excuse himself after supper, get some more work done. Instead, he and Barrett were apparently cohosting a preseason ball.

"Well then," he said, trying to sound genial. "I will look forward to seeing all of you this evening. Mr. Clermont, many thanks for your kindness to Simon." He stepped back into the study and sat back down with a sigh. His evening was ruined now, and the deadline was fast approaching on the reply to the Tsar. He was hoping for some uninterrupted time to write. But he wasn't really surprised, after those telling glances back and forth between Clermont and his niece, to answer a knock at his door a few minutes later and find the Frenchman there.

"I beg your pardon, sir," said Clermont. "I meant to write you and request an appointment tomorrow evening, but it occurred to me that my note might not reach you today if the servants are all at Sir Charles's home."

"Quite right." He started to add, "Do come in," but a hasty glance revealed telltale blue pages all over his desk. Once again he found himself in the anteroom leaning against a closed door. "So, you wish to speak with me tomorrow? A personal matter?"

Clermont nodded.

"Would you care to dine with us first?"

Clermont swallowed. "That is very kind, but I—believe I am engaged tomorrow until eight or so."

Bassington remembered how nervous he had been just before he approached Lord Bell to request Clara's hand. "No matter. Shall we say half past eight, then?"

The younger man bowed. He looked pale.

Bassington went back into his office smiling a bit. He hadn't thought much could shake Clermont's poise, but obviously his niece had managed to do so. Clara would be overjoyed. Should he tell her? His hand was on the bellrope when he remembered that no one would answer. That if he wanted to find her he would have to pack everything up and march through the house with the dispatch case. No, better to have his own secrets for a change.

19

The first steps down the path of Ruin are often taken on the dance floor.
>—Miss Cowell's Moral Reflections
>for Young Ladies

Serena stood waiting for the other couples to take their places in the set with a sense that some evil destiny had brought her to this moment. A series of small, seemingly insignificant decisions had taken on a life of their own and propelled her into a scene from her worst London nightmares. If she looked back now, of course, she could identify all the wrong turns, but retrospection could not alter the color of her dress, or change her partner, or remove one hundred people from the Barrett's ballroom.

Her first mistake had been yielding to Simon's plea and coming to London. Or rather, to be honest, yielding to her own fascination with the enigmatic Mr. Clermont, which her cousin had ruthlessly exploited. Then her aunt had asked if Serena would be willing to attend a small dinner. That was her second mistake. She had watched with horror as the "small dinner" became, in the space of ten days, something quite different. Perhaps a dance or two, after the dinner, the countess had next proposed, if someone could be induced to play for the young people. Before they had even left for London, it had become a slightly larger dinner with a trio of musicians engaged afterwards.

Finally it had blossomed into a full-fledged ball, with an orchestra and midnight supper, and, as a result, the event had been moved to the Barrett's house, which possessed an actual ballroom instead of merely two large drawing rooms with connecting doors. Her aunt bombarded her with well-meant suggestions. Did Serena not think she needed new gloves? New slippers? Could Robbins and the hairdresser try something a bit different with her hair? Would she not like a new gown?

Like a dutiful niece, she had said yes and yes and yes. She had even admired her ball dress, had flushed slightly with pleasure at her appearance in the mirror as she saw how the silver threaded through her new curls echoed the silver trim of the gauze as it floated over a blue silk slip. The gown, of course, was her third mistake. Because here she was, at the top of the set in the Barrett's very large and very crowded ballroom, with Clermont opposite her. Julien Clermont, the plague of her existence, the most beautiful man in the room. Who was wearing, in addition to his very correct black knee breeches and coat, a blue waistcoat trimmed with silver, which matched her gown nearly exactly.

She had tried to avoid standing anywhere near him. When he had approached to request this dance, she had manufactured an excuse to move away after agreeing. Now, however, she would be standing with him for at least fifteen minutes—more, if the line of couples grew any longer. And everyone in the room could see for themselves the blazing declaration, in blue trimmed with silver: Mr. Julien Clermont and Miss Serena Allen were a pair.

Clermont, damn him, was amused. He had recognized the sartorial gauntlet thrown down by her aunt the minute he arrived and had raised those dark eyebrows in acknowledgment. Now he said, in the most courteous, bland tones imaginable, "I have been admiring your gown, Miss Allen. Is it new?"

"Of the same vintage as your waistcoat, I imagine," she snapped, refusing to look at him.

"Oh, so I am to blame?"

She hissed fiercely, "You don't suppose I had anything to say about it, do you? If you must know, I am absolutely mortified."

"Softly, sweet. Everyone is looking at you. And if you keep glaring at my waistcoat and then at your flounce, they will take more interest in those two items than they might otherwise."

"It doesn't matter what I do, or where I look," she said bitterly. "Every female in the room can see at once that we are wearing matching clothing."

The orchestra, after a pause to retune an errant cello, struck up the first bars of the dance. He bowed; she curtseyed; and they began to weave down the floor, separating to perform the first figure.

"If you must glare," he said in a low voice as they came together again, "be sure to glare at Philip Derring and Jasper Royce as well."

"I haven't seen them yet. And why should I glare at them?" Another partner whirled her away.

"Philip just got here; he is leaning against the wall, far end of the room," he informed her as he reclaimed her. "I don't see Royce. Ah, no, there he is, talking to Countess Lieven's escort. A few yards away from Philip." She twisted her neck, but she was facing the wrong way. Not until they had reached the bottom of the line did she catch sight of Derring. He was indeed leaning against the wall. He was looking very unhappy, but she didn't pay much attention to his expression, because her eye was drawn at once to his waistcoat. It was silver, trimmed with blue. Royce was moving towards the dance floor, chatting easily with the young Russian attaché. His waistcoat was white and silver, with blue piping at the edges.

"You see," he said mildly, "I became suspicious when

a garment I had never purchased appeared in my wardrobe a few days before this dance. A garment obviously meant for formal evening wear. And when I asked my valet about it he told me three different, contradictory stories about what it was doing there. He is normally a very honest man, but I believe dreams of romance may have triumphed where bribery would have failed. In any case, once I forced a confession out of him he promised to do his best to limit the damage."

"But then I ruined your good work by glaring." She sighed. "I believe I owe you another apology."

Another couple arrived and claimed the bottom position in the set. As they moved up towards the front of the room, he said lightly, "No need to apologize. But I would be very grateful if you could contrive to dance with one or both of them and scowl at their chests with equal intensity. Or—"

The figure of the dance separated them for a moment. "Or what?"

"You could smile at me," he suggested, "although I must confess you have one of the most glorious scowls I have ever seen."

She favored him with a particularly ferocious example.

They did not speak as the next couple went by, but then she said abruptly as they moved up once again, "Why did you wear it? If you knew?"

He shrugged. "I'm not certain."

She didn't believe him. He didn't have the look of an uncertain man.

He maintained a flow of polite trivialities for the remainder of the dance, but as the last couple twirled down towards the far end of the room he said, "I must speak with you later tonight. Would you have another dance free? One where we may talk without so many interruptions?"

"That would be a waltz," she informed him. "I am al-

ready engaged for the waltz." In point of fact she was
not, but if Julien Clermont thought she would waltz
with him, he was dreaming. The idea made her dizzy
right now.

"May I take you in to supper, then?"

She glanced over to the doorway, where her aunt was
watching the result of her plotting with unmistakable
delight. "I suppose if I tried to go in with someone else
my aunt would poison them in any case. Very well."

"Go scowl at Derring," was his parting shot as the
dance finally ended.

Philip, had, in fact, worked his way through the room
so that he could approach her once the music stopped.
He still looked unhappy.

She went over and linked her arm through his. "Why
the long face?"

He attempted a smile. It was a poor attempt. "It's
nothing." They walked in silence towards the edge of
the room, where the crowd was thinner.

"Your waistcoat seems to be all the crack," she said
lightly, trying to tease him out of his bad mood. "I've
seen at least two others very like it."

His expression did not change; if anything, he seemed
even more upset. He drew her over beneath a large
painting of a hunting scene. Just at her eye level—and
Philip's—was a dying stag, an arrow fixed in its bloody
flank. "Are you in love with Julien Clermont?" he said
in a low voice.

"What?" She drew away, instinctively, and stared at
him. She wondered if she had misheard him. But then he
repeated it. Fortunately the room was noisy, and there was
no one nearby.

"Are you in love with Julien Clermont?"

"Certainly not!" She followed Clermont's advice and
scowled at Philip. "And what concern is it of yours? You
have been a good friend to me, but that gives you no
right—"

He interrupted. "Has he made you an offer of marriage? Hinted at one?"

More and more bewildered, she said, "No. But what—"

"Listen to me," he said urgently. "I know Julien is my friend, but I felt I had to warn you. Don't trust him. There's something—he's—" He bit his lip. "Don't make too much of his attentions towards you. That's all I am at liberty to say."

"Philip, are you *jealous*?"

He flushed. "Of course not. Merely concerned. For both of you. Will you remember my warning?"

She looked at his tense, guilty, expression and wondered whether his "of course not" had been a lie. "I have never trusted Mr. Clermont," she said, "from the first moment I met him. Does that relieve your mind?"

"Yes," he said. "Yes, it does."

He had danced with four young women whose names he could not remember three seconds after he was introduced. He had conversed—or, more accurately, fenced—with Countess Lieven, who was holding court on a gold settee in an anteroom. Her arch comments about blue and silver butterflies gave him a good idea of the sort of gossip that was already circulating in the overheated ballroom. He had made sure to visit briefly with both of his hostesses and even with Mrs. Childe, who was playing whist with three fantastically turbaned dowagers in the card room. He had fulfilled all his obligations, in other words, and now, as the musicians set down their instruments and the dancers began drifting out to go downstairs for supper, he could turn his attention to his meeting with Serena Allen.

It was not hard to spot her. She was taller than most women in the room. She was talking with Royce, and although her head was turned away, he recognized the silver band in her hair. He made his way over to her just as Royce, clearly angry about something, made a stiff bow and stalked away.

"Oh, dear," said Serena, following the tutor's departing figure with her eyes. She was smiling in amusement, though. The little curls around her face were actually very attractive, he decided. They made her look softer, less remote. "Does it count if Jasper scowls at me? Because he just did. And scolded me, as well."

He made a very educated guess. "Simon?"

"He has disappeared, apparently. Probably to the attics; he likes the ones in the London house because you have to go up ladders to get into them. At any rate, for some reason Nurse Digby fretted herself into a state, as though this doesn't happen every third night, and Rowley sent a message over here to Jasper. Why on earth he should leave the party to chase after Simon I cannot imagine, but he decided it was his duty, and when I disagreed he informed me that Simon is shockingly spoilt, largely thanks to me."

"Well, he is shockingly spoilt," he said, drawing her arm through his and leading her towards the stairway. "But I think your aunt and Mrs. Digby and Mr. Royce himself must take most of the blame. You, in fact, are the only one of all of them who does not have any official responsibility for the boy."

"But I am also the only one he listens to," she pointed out.

"The two facts are not unconnected." He paused in dismay as they came out into the stairwell and he saw the throngs milling around the tables in the hallway below.

"What is it?" she asked. Then she saw the clusters of people crowding the hall. "Are you hungry?" she asked, looking up at him. "Would you mind missing supper? I don't think we will be able to talk there."

"I do not need supper, no. Where would you suggest?"

She turned and led him back into the now-empty ball-room, down to the far end, and then into a little side room where footmen had been stationed earlier, loading trays of drinks. "Here," she said.

There was no one in there now; the servants were all downstairs serving supper. She pushed open a door he had not even noticed, set into the back wall. It was completely dark on the other side. "More secret passages?" he asked.

"It's just a servant's corridor; Simon knows all of them in every house he's ever been in. It will only be dark for a minute. Mind your head; the ceiling is a bit low." She ducked into the corridor, and he followed, keeping his distance lest he tread on her skirts accidentally. He could hear them rustling in front of him. Suddenly there was light—not lamplight or candlelight, but moonlight, accompanied by a rush of cold air. He stepped out through the door she was holding open and emerged onto a tiny balcony.

They were at the back of the house, looking out over the small terrace and garden to the right and the mews and kitchen courtyard to the left. A few other couples had obviously decided not to wait in line for supper either; there were figures on the terrace below and even a few hardy souls in the garden. It was chilly out; he tugged off his jacket and draped it around Serena's shoulders.

"What an odd place for a balcony," he said.

"It isn't a balcony. It's the top of a stair."

Looking more closely, he saw that the railing on the left side was in fact a gate. Narrow iron steps descended along the wall of the house; there was another small landing on the floor below, with, presumably, another door.

"It's for the servants, to carry food back and forth to the kitchen when there are large parties," she explained. As she spoke he saw someone come out onto the landing below with a tray and start down the lower flight of steps.

They remained silent until the figure disappeared into the bright doorway at the bottom.

"Well then, Mr. Clermont," she said briskly. "What did you wish to say to me? I trust it will not take long. My aunt will notice our absence even in this crush if we stay out here for more than a few minutes."

He had come to the ball with one purpose: to fulfill his promise to Philip. The minute he had heard Vernon's confession about the waistcoat he knew he had his means. Nothing could be more calculated to goad Serena Allen into snubbing him than that crude stratagem on the part of her aunt. He had worn the hideous thing; he had persuaded Philip and the tutor to wear theirs. The result (as predicted) was an entire country dance's worth of glowering indignation from Miss Allen. Everyone had seen her snap at him, and she hadn't smiled once during the entire set. Surely that would be enough to shield her from pity after tomorrow night. Surely everyone would believe that he and Philip and Jasper Royce were all courting her, equally unsuccessfully. Surely tonight would inspire other young men to try their luck.

What *did* he wish to say to her? Daydreams of warning her, of explaining, of begging for forgiveness were revealed as impossible fantasies now that they were alone together. There was no reason, no reason at all to ask to speak with her privately. In fact, it was potentially disastrous. If anyone saw them, everyone would remember the tale of the brazen girl who had emerged from the woods at dawn with her French lover. Only this time it would not be the garbled story of an elderly gamekeeper; it would be Countess Lieven, or Mrs. Childe, or some other well-bred scandalmonger.

"Well?" she repeated impatiently.

He shook his head, helpless. Her face was in the moonlight, and he could see the moment when she realized he had no answer. No good answer, at any rate. He reached out with one hand and touched her cheek.

She started to step back, but the landing was very small. There was no place for her to go. Her eyes were enormous. "You're going to kiss me, aren't you," she whispered.

Apparently that had been his plan all along. "Not if you don't want me to," he said. It didn't sound like his voice. He brushed one of the little curls back from her temple.

"We—we should go back inside." It didn't sound like her voice either.

He decided speaking again would be a mistake, so he nodded. Turning around, he reached for the door handle. It wasn't there. No handle, no knob, no latch bar. Nothing but a flat iron plate with a keyhole at one side. A small tendril of anxiety unfurled in his lower stomach. He felt along the edge of the door, trying to tug it open. It didn't move. "We're locked out," he said flatly.

"We can't be!" She stepped past him and tried the door; tried it several different times, tugging at both the bottom and the top. "We can't be," she repeated, leaning against the obstinate door. She wrapped her arms around her chest. She looked utterly miserable. "What are we going to do?"

The obvious answer was to go down the stairs, walk up to the people who would be staring at them by the time they reached the bottom, and announce an engagement. After tomorrow night, however, that option would be closed. So he chose the next most obvious answer. "Would you be willing to reconsider your decision on that kiss?" he said.

Simon had enjoyed a very pleasant evening so far. His complaints about being excluded from the festivities had found an even more sympathetic audience in Mrs. Digby than in Serena. As a result, he had been taken over to the Barrett's kitchen to sample the treats being prepared for the party. Then he had been sent to bed, but had been allowed to sit up reading with a generous allowance of lamp oil. At ten, he had dimmed the lamp, gradually, over a five-minute period. When Mrs. Digby came to check on him he was lying artistically draped across the pillows with the book tumbled open beside him and the lamp burning low.

"Poor lamb," he heard her murmur as she tucked him in.

Fifteen minutes later he was on the Barretts' roof. He had gone up the back outside staircase to the first landing and slipped in the door, which was propped open for the servants carrying up plates for supper. From there he had only to wait for a clear moment on the inner stair and he was in the attic and then out onto the roof, unstrapping the telescope case and fitting the two halves of the cylinder together.

It was a beautiful night, although a bit cold. He studied the moon for a long time, watching smudges bloom into craters and lava beds as the lens swept over them. Then he went to the front of the house, where he could look down on the cul-de-sac which led to the Barretts' house. There were a few late arrivals, and he enjoyed testing his power: could he see the buckles on a man's shoes? the shading of feathers in a lady's headdress? He could, and more. The telescope made his field glass seem like an old man's spectacles. By this time the ballroom had grown warm; windows were opened, and the music floated out below him. Eventually he headed back to the attic trapdoor at the other end of the roof. From here he had a good view of the back of his own house, and he was struck by an unusual number of lights on the upper floors. Weren't most of the servants—and all the adult members of the family—here at the Barretts', in the rooms beneath him? He raised the telescope carefully and sighted.

His own room was illuminated, and he could see torches moving outside the servants' entrance to the house.

That was very bad news. He had promised that there were would be no more episodes like the one at St. Paul's. And while he had convinced both his mother and Nurse that he sometimes walked in his sleep, no one was going to believe that he had dressed himself and carried a telescope up to the roof of a neighboring house while sleepwalking. He lowered the instrument and stood there, calculating his chances of getting back home without being seen. He hadn't planned on coming down off the roof this early; there would be far too many servants using the outside stair right now. Sitting down by the trap door, he quickly disassembled the telescope and packed it away. Then he went very quietly over to the edge of the roof and peered over the raised parapet.

He noticed the servants first, carrying supper dishes down to the kitchen. There were lanterns at the lower landing and at the kitchen door. It took him another minute to see that on the dark platform immediately below him two people were standing. Standing very close together. In fact, they were embracing. In fact—

He leaned over the edge. "Serena!" he hissed.

She jumped away from the man—it was Mr. Clermont, which didn't surprise him one bit—and looked up. He expected a scolding, but instead she looked almost relieved. "Simon! Thank God! Can you help us? We're locked out."

Clermont's face tilted up as well. He looked tense.

"Knock," Simon suggested. "Someone will hear you eventually. Or just go down to the bottom and go back in through the kitchen."

Clermont cleared his throat. "It's a bit more complicated than that."

"Oh." He was, in fact, dimly aware that adulthood

was not the paradise of freedom he had imagined as a six-year-old confined to bed for weeks at a time. That Serena was not supposed to be out on a dark staircase kissing Mr. Clermont, even if she was going to marry him. "I'll come open it, if I can."

He couldn't. When he came down from the attic, he could hear guests talking as they made their way back to the ballroom. He beat a hasty retreat back to the attic and found the window above the staircase. By dragging a crate over, he managed to open it and get his head and shoulders out. Serena and Clermont were facing the door, looking apprehensive. Clermont had his arm around her, and she was leaning on him slightly. At the noise of the window opening, they both looked up.

"Can't get there unseen," he said, breathless. "Too many people now. You'll have to take your chances going down from here; the footmen will be coming in a minute to open the door."

"Will you fit through that window?" Clermont asked.

He nodded.

"Do you have your telescope with you?"

Another nod.

"Lower it down, and then wriggle through. I'll catch you."

He obeyed, more nervous about the telescope than about his own descent. It was only a five foot drop to Clermont's arms, though. He was set on his feet quickly enough, and reached out to repossess the telescope.

"Not so fast," said Clermont. Something in his tone made Simon nervous. "Tell me, have you ever dreamed of being a hero? Of rescuing a damsel in distress?"

He had a notion of what was coming and started to shake his head.

But Clermont didn't give him time to reply. "Good," he said cheerfully, as though it were all settled. "Now is your chance."

20

In the end, they had gone along with Julien's proposal. Simon was understandably reluctant to be a human sacrifice, but when Serena had explained, very patiently (for her), that she would truly rather be dead than discovered alone with Julien, the boy had agreed. He had even offered some improvements to the scheme. He and Serena had crept down to the lower landing, taken the lantern from its hook outside the door, and produced a dramatic chase scene. Serena, armed with the lantern, went running down the stairs after the fleeing Simon, scolding and threatening him loudly. Everyone—servants, guests on the terrace, link-boys chatting at the kitchen door—had turned to look. And behind them, in the dark, Julien had followed, holding the telescope case as though it were a tray, balanced between his two hands. Nobody would look at yet another servant on the darkened staircase when they had a virago in a ball gown chasing a runaway boy as an alternative. That had been their plan, and it had worked. At least so far.

He was around the corner now, in the narrow passageway Simon had described. It was utterly dark and deserted. He had no idea where it led, or what he would do if Simon didn't manage to elude his pursuers, who by now surely included people truly intent on catching him. After several minutes had gone by, he began to feel nervous. He even took a few steps further down the passage, but there was a figure lurking a bit farther on, and light and voices at the other end, and he retreated.

Quick footsteps came up behind him. "Sorry," Simon whispered, panting. "Had to go around through the garden next door. Tore my jacket on the fence; mother will be furious."

"Your jacket will be the least of your worries," he whispered back. "Where are we going? There are people at the other end of this alley."

"Of course there are, that's the front of the house. Some of the coachmen are pulled up there already."

"Don't you think I will be a bit conspicuous if I emerge from a hole in the wall into Harland Place? How will I explain myself?"

"I already told you, I'm letting you into the house so that you can make your way to the library. Just be patient a minute; my knife is sticking."

In the dark Julien couldn't see very clearly what Simon was doing. He appeared to be running a small knife blade along the join between a window frame and the wall of the house. Since there were stout iron bars on the outside of the window, prying it open didn't seem very useful to Julien, but when Simon told him to crouch down, he obeyed.

"Ah!" Simon sounded relieved. "Got it."

To Julien's astonishment, the window swung out suddenly at chest height, along with a section of the wall below it. It missed his head by inches.

"Climb in." Simon's voice was tense. "This is a small room adjoining Sir Charles's study. The door into the study is opposite this window. No one will be anywhere near it tonight, I'm sure. When you come out of the study, turn left, go around a corner, and the narrow wooden door ahead of you is the rear entrance to the library. Hurry, I have to go let Serena catch me."

Julien started to pull himself into the black opening.

"Wait!" Simon whispered urgently. "Where's my telescope?"

"At your feet." He added, very low, but not in a whisper, "Thank you, Simon."

"Just don't tell anyone I know about this door. Even Serena. Ned Barrett swore me to secrecy."

"I won't," promised Julien. He heard the light footsteps running back towards the kitchen entrance, and after a minute, a great shout. The reprobate had been captured, and it was time for Mr. Julien Clermont to establish his presence elsewhere.

Out in the passageway the band of sky overhead had at least offered a dim glow. Inside, once he had pulled the panel closed, it was pitch black; he would have to rely on Simon's description. He stood and moved forward in a slow, shuffling step, his hands outstretched, until he ran into a wall. Then he crouched and ran his hands along the baseboard until the molding abruptly stopped. This was the door, then. There was no light underneath. Very, very slowly he reached up, found the handle and eased it open.

In the adjacent room there was a faint source of illumination from under the double doors on the opposite side. To Julien's deprived eyes it was a feast. He could make out furniture shapes—a desk, bookcases—even the dim outline of a fireplace. He strode confidently across this larger room, put his ear to the door frame, and listened. Satisfied with the silence outside, he tried to open the door. It was locked.

He swore silently in three languages. The god of locks apparently had it in for him tonight. After a minute, he swore again, realizing that he was now irretrievably trapped. He had no idea how to trigger the catch of the concealed door from inside the house. Desperate, he looked around in the near-darkness. There was a window in this room as well. He pulled aside the curtains and at once let them fall back. That window looked directly out onto the space behind the kitchen, where some amused servants who had come out to see the hunt for Simon were still lingering. And it was, like the other window, barred.

Julien forced himself to stay calm. He tugged the draperies aside again cautiously, just enough to let some moonlight filter into the room. His gaze traveled over the desk, the bins full of papers, the stacks of books on the table, the cabinets and shelves against the wall. There must be some other exit, or some way to open the door. Perhaps he could pick the lock with a letter opener. He wished he had thought to borrow Simon's penknife. Then he heard footsteps and voices. The light under the door grew stronger. By the time the key turned he was behind the curtains, pressing as close to the corner of the embrasure as he dared and praying that the maid emptying a kettle on the paving stones five yards away would not look too closely at the window she was facing. His damned hair had a tendency to reflect even small amounts of light.

Through the narrow gap between the curtains he saw the room brighten and smelled candle wax. Several people—he could not tell how many—had come in. There was a rustling of paper.

"Here it is. Odd, I thought I had left it folded." The voice was vaguely familiar. Sir Charles, presumably.

A pause, then another voice, gravelly and curt. "Yes, we'll need this Monday morning, you were right. In the meantime I would prefer it kept in the safe with the others, even though it says nothing revealing."

"The door to this room is now locked at all times."

"Even so," said the gravelly voice.

"Very well," said an invisible Barrett. "What about Piers's diaries? Put them away as well?"

"No need. They are of no obvious value to anyone save ourselves—unlike the letters."

The light was receding, along with several sets of

footsteps—and not in the direction of the outer doors. When he heard a muffled clang, the sound of keys rattling, and sotto-voce imprecations from the direction of the smaller room, Julien realized that the safe must be in there. And so, perforce, were the two men, with their candle. The god of locks had finally taken pity on him. He pulled off his pumps and slithered as quickly and quietly as he could towards the half-open doors and freedom.

"Blast it, the mechanism has never been the same since Bassington's son had a go at it," he heard Barrett complain as he gained the hallway.

He was so relieved, so eager to get out to the front of the house and be seen, that he was careless. Coming round the corner, he nearly ran into the footman who was stationed there. Both men froze. The man's eyes, dropped, incredulous, to the shoes Julien was holding in his hands.

"Er—may I help you, sir?" His tone told Julien clearly that no guests were meant to be anywhere near this place.

He tried to look wild-eyed and slightly tipsy. Wild-eyed, at least, was not difficult, after the last twenty minutes. "Have you seen a woman?" he asked in an affected drawl. "A tall woman—" Oh, God, he was describing Serena! He improvised quickly. "A tall woman, wearing green. A blonde," he added for good measure. He produced a leer. "She has *her* shoes off, as well. I lost sight of her on the back staircase."

The footman was looking horrified, as well he might. This was not that sort of party. Julien reflected that at least it didn't matter if his reputation was in shreds after tonight. It would only advance by one day the shredding which would begin tomorrow. The important thing was to protect Serena. He produced two silver coins. "One of these, my fine fellow, if you say nothing of this," he announced pompously. "And another if you can tell me where the lady went." Another leer.

"I couldn't say, sir, I'm sorry." The man looked as though he was about to choke.

Julien gave him both coins anyway, and made his way as much by accident as anything else to the back of the library, which adjoined the entrance hall. It was empty, as Serena had hoped—too public for an illicit rendezvous, too far from the ballroom to serve as an auxiliary sitting room. He had barely gotten his breath back, barely regained some of his lost composure, when two men he knew walked by, arguing about a speech delivered in the House of Lords earlier that week. He hailed them, invited them in, joined as naturally as he could in their conversation, and eventually went out with them to the central staircase. It had been a narrow escape, but all was now well. Three gentlemen, emerging from the library after supper together—would not everyone assume they had been together for some time? And the library was, after all, in the front part of the house, on the ground floor, quite a distance from the site where Serena had apprehended her cousin.

He was feeling almost jaunty as he made his way up the stairs and returned to the ballroom. He would be a model guest for the remainder of the evening, he promised himself. He would bring ratafia to the dowagers in the card room. He would dance with wallflowers. There was his hostess, in fact, smiling at him in that way that all hostesses smile when they spy a potential partner for a lonely guest. His hostess, Lady Barrett. His tall, blond hostess. She was, of course, wearing green.

No wonder the poor footman had been on the verge of apoplexy.

"I think that went off rather well," the earl said. "Don't you, my dear?" He sank down with a sigh into a large, old-fashioned chair which would have been banished from the countess's dressing room long ago had it not been his favorite seat.

"No, I do not." She knew she sounded cross, but after hours of smiling and chatting and rapping men on the knuckles with her fan and laughing—laughing!—about the frustration of her hopes, she was too tired to pretend.

"Well, I suppose there was that little incident with Simon," he conceded.

"You may cane him with my blessing this time," she said, stalking over to her dressing table and sitting down with her back to her husband. "Imagine! Chased across the back courtyard in front of half the Barretts' staff, and a dozen guests besides! Poor Mr. Royce has offered to resign his post as tutor, as though it was his fault. He spent more than an hour searching the house and grounds, you know, and came in quite cold and miserable."

"Clara, I am not blaming Royce for tonight. But it did remind me, once again, that he is not a very good tutor. Perhaps it is time to consider some other arrangement."

"Dismiss Jasper?" she turned around. She had come to like the awkward, stiff young man, even though it had become increasingly clear that he would never make a husband for Serena.

"No, no," he reassured her. "I would retain him as my secretary, of course. There is certainly more and more work of that sort for him these days. No, I was thinking that it might be time to send Simon to school."

Her husband had made this suggestion before. For the first time ever, she did not reject it out of hand but sat silent, thinking.

He misinterpreted her silence. "I know you are concerned about his health, my dear, but I cannot recall any truly serious illnesses in recent years. And just now, when we returned, you found him sleeping soundly, with no trace of fever or cough, whereas young Royce was sweating and trembling after only an hour outside."

She was still thinking. She was thinking of Serena, of how lovely she had looked tonight, even when frowning at her partner. Of how her body had contradicted that frown, leaning towards Clermont every time the movement separated them. Of how Clermont's eyes had followed her when she walked off with Philip Derring. Clermont had been amused by the waistcoat, as she had suspected he would be. But *someone* had to give the two young people a push, or they would circle around each other like fencers for months. And she was thinking of how Simon had ruined all of it by popping out of some alcove off the ballroom and giving Serena an excuse to do what she wanted to do anyway: leave.

"Where would you send him?" she asked finally.

He gave the little cough he always produced when surprised. "Winchester, of course."

"Do you think that wise?"

"Why not? The Piers family has always sent its sons to Winchester."

"The Barrett boys are at Winchester," she reminded him, "which means he would be even more likely to get into mischief than he is already. Do you want him to be the first Piers to be expelled from the school?"

"My cousin Charles has already claimed that honor, as you may remember."

She had not remembered; given the flamboyant nature of Charles Piers's later misdemeanors, expulsion from school shrank to insignificance. "By all means, then, send him to Winchester. Perhaps he could even begin this Easter term." She was conscious that her casual tone was a bit forced, and evidently her husband noticed it as well.

He got up and came over to her. "Clara, are you so very angry at Simon? Surely you don't think his escapade tonight ruined the dance? If anything, it offered an amusing topic of conversation."

Her pent-up frustration exploded. "Yes, I am angry!

The boy monopolizes Serena! He positively *clings* to her, like a—a limpet! And she to him! Well, tonight she had a chance to spend time with people her own age—to flirt and dance and have someone fetch her shawl and all those other little diversions a young woman of her birth and looks should enjoy. And our wretched son managed to make a spectacle of himself *and* my niece, with the result that she left after supper—and you know perfectly well that it will be another five years before I can persuade her to emerge in public again!" She added, despairing, "I am the worst mother in the world! I cannot make Serena and Simon behave, try as I might. I don't understand either one of them, and I never will."

He sat down next to her, which made the little uphol-stered bench very crowded. Taking her hand, he said gently, "Would it make you feel better to learn that Julien Clermont has made an appointment to speak with me tomorrow evening about a private matter?"

She turned toward him, incredulous.

"And that I received a confidential message from Mr. Hewitt late this afternoon that Clermont has deposited a large sum at the bank to be held in my name?"

"Settlements," she breathed. "He means to make an offer. Oh, George." Her eyes filled with tears, and she blinked them back. An odd, half-selfish happiness filled her—happiness for Serena, happiness for herself, that she had not bungled so badly after all. "Yes, it would make me feel better."

"Not a word to anyone, mind you! Not to Robbins, not to Mrs. Digby, and especially not to Serena."

"Of course not," she said automatically. "Of course not."

By noon of the following day, every single person in the Bassington household had learned that Julien Cler-mont was coming that evening to ask the earl for Miss

Serena's hand. Every single person except Serena, that is. When she got up and came downstairs, she did notice that the servants were giving her peculiar glances, but she assumed those sideways looks were the result of her involvement with Simon's disgrace. Her aunt was nowhere to be seen; that, too, was a bit odd. Probably the countess had come home very late last night and was still abed.

Feeling restless and oddly discontented, she went off to the sitting room she and her aunt shared on the second floor and sat down at her desk to catch up on her letter writing. Her principal correspondents were her mother's cousins, the same ones who had foisted Mrs. Childe on her aunt. She had never enjoyed writing to them, or reading their slightly condescending replies, but she considered it a duty. This morning, however, she found the task impossible instead of merely distasteful. After ten minutes, she sighed, threw all her attempts in the grate, and went in search of Simon.

He was not in his room, not in the nursery/schoolroom on the fourth floor, not in the library, not in the kitchen, where the servants all melted away as soon as Serena entered. She heard a breathless giggle from one of the scullery maids as the girl scampered away. The cook, who was too large to scamper, made a great pretense of stirring something on the stove. He was an Austrian, the earl feeling it unpatriotic to employ a Frenchman at this particular moment.

"Dietrich, have you seen Simon this morning?" she asked.

He shook his head, still stirring.

Puzzled, and beginning to be annoyed, she went up to her room and rang. A maid answered the bell—not Emily, but one of the new upstairs maids. Serena didn't even know her name. "Where is Emily?" she demanded.

"Begging your pardon, miss, but the countess summoned her earlier this morning and left word that I was to answer your bell."

"I would like to see Rowley, then," she said. "At once."

When the elderly butler appeared, he evaded her questions masterfully. The servants? Why, they were exhausted from their labors last night. Or they were helping clean over at the Barretts'. Or they had been given a half-holiday. Yes, he believed Emily was assisting the countess with something. He had no idea what it was. Where was her ladyship? He was not certain. Would Miss Serena like him to inquire? Only when she asked about Simon did she get an answer. The viscount was with his lordship, in the bookroom. They had been closeted together for quite some time, Rowley believed.

Why hadn't she remembered that Simon would be called to account this morning for his misdeeds? No wonder the servants were avoiding her. In their eyes, she was the traitor who had turned in her own cousin. Little did they know that it was far worse than that. She was the traitor who had sacrificed her cousin to protect herself. Feeling lower than a worm, she dismissed Rowley and walked slowly back downstairs to the bookroom. The doors were still closed. She could hear her uncle's voice. He wasn't shouting. And she didn't hear the sound of a cane. Her guilt eased slightly. But when the earl was still talking, in the same low, serious voice, ten minutes later, it began to creep back. When Simon was caned—a relatively rare event, but not unknown—it was all over in a few minutes. Was there something worse than caning? Some punishment males never even mentioned in front of delicately nurtured females? She began to pace back and forth in front of the door.

After an interminable interval, her uncle's voice stopped. There was a brief exchange; she heard Simon answering a question. Then the door opened. Her cousin, very pale, came out first. His lips were pressed together and he walked stiffly. Perhaps he had been caned, before she arrived. Her uncle emerged behind him, looking stern. When he saw Serena, he brightened.

"Serena, my dear!" he said. "I thought I heard someone pacing out here." He kissed her cheek. She tried to remember the last time he had kissed her, and failed. "Are you recovered from last night's revelries? I trust Simon's misbehavior did not spoil your evening entirely."

"I am fine, Uncle. Merely worried about Simon. I hope you were not too hard on him." She was battling an overwhelming urge to confess everything.

"Hard on him? I don't believe so. We have had a long-overdue discussion, that is all. Eh, my boy?"

Simon nodded, eyes lowered.

"Well, I must get back to my desk. Barrett and I have a meeting this afternoon, and I've a great deal to do beforehand." With a genial nod, he went back into the bookroom, which also served as an antechamber to his office.

She walked with Simon all the way up to his room in silence. He didn't seem to be limping, she noted. But he wasn't talking, either, which was very unlike him.

"May I come in?" she asked when they reached the door.

"If you like."

Only after they were both inside, with the door closed, did his expression change. He looked furious.

"Oh, Simon," she said, feeling wretched. "I am so sorry. This is all my fault. Did he beat you very badly?"

He sat down on the edge of the bed and said between his teeth. "He didn't touch me."

"He didn't?"

"No." He brooded darkly over the injustice of this departure from tradition. "I'm to be sent away. To school.

But that wasn't the bad part. I don't think I shall mind school so much after all."

"Then what is it? What else?" A very logical punishment suddenly occurred to her. "Simon, he isn't confiscating your telescope, is he?"

"No, nothing like that. No punishment at all. I wish he *had* caned me. He simply talked to me. It was horrible. He told me I was his heir, and that I had responsibilities, and that Mr. Clermont had opened his eyes to what I was capable of—capable of in a good way—and that he was ashamed to find his son malingering and teasing his own mother with feigned illnesses. And he told me things about Cousin Charles—awful things, Serena, things I wouldn't repeat to you even if he hadn't sworn me to secrecy. And he said I reminded him of Charles, and he was afraid for me."

"Well, it's true you look like Charles, Simon—at least like the portrait of him as a boy—but physical resemblance doesn't mean anything."

"He wasn't talking about my appearance," he said, scowling. "He was talking about my character."

"I think you have a wonderful character," she said gently. "Look what you did for me last night. The rest is just mischief, Simon, mischief and boredom and the knowledge that you are more intelligent than your tutor and your nurse."

"He said that as well. I was too clever for my own good, he said. That was why I needed to be in school." He clenched his fists and burst out, "I hate him! How dare he compare me to—to some rascally *cheat*! It would serve him right if I ran away and became just like Charles!"

She sat down next to him and put her arm around his shoulders. She could feel him trying very hard not to cry.

He looked up at her. "When you are married may I come and live with you? During school holidays, that is?"

"I am not likely to be married any time soon, silly.

That's no solution. Go and apologize to your mother; you'll feel better."

His jaw dropped. "You're not getting married? To Mr. Clermont?"

"No! Why would you—" Then she remembered what Simon had seen last night and blushed furiously. After a constrained pause, she said carefully, "Men and women do not always marry after they kiss each other, Simon. Although they are often expected to do so if someone has seen them alone together. That is why I am so grateful to you for helping me."

"Don't you want to marry him? Don't you love him?"

That was the second time in less than twenty-four hours that someone had asked her if she loved Julien Clermont, and her response to Philip was beginning to seem a bit disingenuous, in retrospect. She hedged. "That is beside the point. Mr. Clermont has made it very clear that he has no interest in marrying me. He has merely been trying to be an agreeable companion. That is a far cry from making me an offer."

He stood up. "Is that so?" His blue eyes flashed. "Well, Miss Know-It-All Allen, if he doesn't want to make you an offer, then why is he coming this evening to ask my father for your hand?"

21

At a little after half past eight, Julien was shown into the very same bookroom which had witnessed Simon's downfall earlier. Had he known that fact, it would not have made him any more nervous than he was already. For a man who had hidden under floorboards during the Terror, fought a hired assassin in a duel, and shot a bear at point-blank range, he was remarkably apprehensive about this interview. It was no use telling himself that the die was cast, that his visit to the bank had committed him beyond retreat. The candlelit chamber, with its fine old rugs and cheerful fire, seemed unaccountably sinister. He could feel himself fraying, had to force himself to breathe slowly, to take the earl's hand in a grip that did not tremble, to lower himself into the offered seat instead of collapsing.

"Well, Mr. Clermont," said Bassington, very genial, "I won't pretend to be ignorant of your purpose in coming here tonight, and I shall say at the outset that I shall be delighted to welcome you to the family. The countess, of course, feels the same."

He was stunned. In all his rehearsals of this scene, it had never occurred to him that the earl would react in this fashion. "You know why I am here?"

"Mr. Hewitt was kind enough to inform me of your visit to the bank." Bassington smiled. "I must say, I think your gesture was unnecessary, but I understand that young men have their pride."

He swallowed. "You don't believe there will be a scandal?"

"Scandal? Why?"

"Because I'm illegitimate," he said bluntly.

The earl snorted. "There are as many Condés on the wrong side of the blanket as on the right, from what I can tell. The great-grandson of Louis XIV need not blush for his parentage. Even in staid Protestant England we are aware that kings and princes are exempt from the restrictions which bind lesser men."

His head was spinning. Bassington had discovered who he was, was prepared to acknowledge him. A dream he had relinquished by the age of ten was suddenly unfolding as reality in a small, softly lit room in London.

"You will have been raised Catholic, of course," the earl mused. "That is why you were at school with Philip. I do not think that an insurmountable problem."

Julien was not particularly devout, but he would have said that nothing could make him consider converting. He would have been wrong. In this new, unexpected world opening out before him, everything had changed. If Bassington wanted him to join the Church of England, surely the fifth commandment would require his compliance. He ventured a grave smile, to show his willingness to compromise.

"Something to drink?" the earl asked. "I keep some very fine brandy in here, no need to summon the servants."

"Thank you, no." He wanted to be sober, he wanted to survey his unexpected treasure with a clear head.

Bassington rose and took a decanter and matching glass from a tray on an adjacent table. He spoke as he poured the drink, so that he wasn't even looking at Julien when it happened. "By the way," he asked casually, "who is your father? The Duc de Bourbon? Or is the prince, in fact, not your grandfather but your sire?"

The dream exploded into thousands of tiny, cruelly sharp pieces. It was all the more painful because it had been so plausible, so vivid. At the back of his mind the nagging question intruded: why, if the earl did not know the truth, had he welcomed Julien so effusively, stated that he understood why Julien was here? But he had no room for anything at the back of his mind right now. He had to answer the earl's question. At least now he could go back to his original script.

"You are," he said. "You are my father. That is what I came to tell you."

Bassington turned, slowly, and set the glass down on the table. He looked stupefied. "I am your father?"

Julien nodded.

"But—you are a Condé!"

"My mother was Louise-Aline de Bourbon-Condé. You knew her perhaps as Aline DeLis."

The earl shook his head. "I cannot recall anyone by that name."

The old bitterness rose up in Julien, the familiar, grim will to hurt as he had been hurt. This was better, much better than the cheerful welcome he had received, through some peculiar misunderstanding, a few minutes ago. This was what had driven him through all the lies and manipulations. His father might have grown into someone Julien respected now, but thirty years ago he had been the kind of man who didn't even remember the name of a gently born girl he had seduced and abandoned. It was unpleasant, perhaps, but not unjust that the good man of today should pay for the sins of the bad man of yesterday. Indeed, part of the neatness of his chosen means of revenge lay precisely in the knowledge of how the upright Bassington of 1814 would squirm contemplating both his younger self and the son that younger self had spawned.

He stood. He couldn't remain seated any longer. "Let me remind you, then," he said. "My mother was a blonde, with green eyes. She was by far the youngest in her family, and very willful, or so I was told. When she was seventeen, she was sent to a finishing school at a convent near Beauvais. She hated it. A few months after arriving, she ran away with the help of a servant she had bribed. The man had promised to escort her to Amiens, to a married cousin. He abandoned her at the first inn they came to, a rough, noisy place catering to wagoneers on the Paris road. Within minutes she knew she had made a terrible mistake; she swallowed her pride and asked the innkeeper to send her back to the convent. The inn's customers, however, had other ideas. More frightened than she had ever been in her life, with one of the filthy louts actually holding her by the arm—or perhaps worse than the arm, I don't know—she suddenly sees a young man in the doorway of the inn. A handsome young man, well dressed. He is a foreigner, but someone accustomed to command. He rescues her from the lout, takes her to a private parlor, orders food and drink, comforts her, promises to take her back to the convent. By the end of dinner she is desperately in love with him. He is an English lord; not an ineligible husband, even for a Condé. A mile before his coach reaches the convent gates he asks her to marry him, and she says yes. She has given him a false name and, fearful that her family will try to prevent the match, she does not enlighten him even after the betrothal."

The earl was frowning, looking puzzled.

"He did not marry her," Julien said coldly. "In case you do not remember the end of the story. He persuaded her to stay with him in a small village near the coast while he sent for funds from his estate in England, and then one day he simply vanished. I, however, did not vanish. I grew larger and larger, in fact, and my mother, after using up nearly all the money her would-be husband had left with her, finally made her way back to the convent. I was born there. My mother was immediately sent away to another convent. My aunt took me home to my grandfather's house and gave me to a wet nurse. When I was old enough to understand, she told me that my mother was dead, that I had killed her, and that I was a walking incarnation of the sin of lust. My mother was not, in fact, dead—not yet. By the time I learned where she had gone, she was. I never met her."

He paused, staring at nothing. A small gesture by the earl—of pity? of bewilderment?—went unacknowledged.

"In '90, when I was five, the new National Assembly did something to make my grandfather even angrier and more outraged with the republicans than usual. As a reply, a sign of his contempt for the weakness of the king and his fellow nobles, he recognized me as his grandson and endowed me with one of his titles. He conferred a number of estates on me, most of which were confiscated after the revolution, but he also gave me a large sum which would have been my mother's dowry. That money, and that money alone, I have been willing to use. I was fortunate enough to make some very good investments after leaving school. You need not think this evening's visit is a request for money. In fact, I have deposited in your account at the bank every penny of the payments which were eventually made to my mother in Switzerland."

"What payments?" The earl had finally found his voice.

"The payments Mr. Hewitt confirmed for me when I visited the bank yesterday. Six payments, totaling just under two thousand pounds, sent to my mother under the name DeLis at her convent in Lausanne. Come, sir, surely you will not bother to deny it?"

Bassington took an unsteady step forward. "I have never heard of the woman in my life."

Julien drew the draft from his pocket and laid it on the table next to the untouched brandy. "Authorized by your father," he said. "Hewitt told me as much."

The earl looked down at the creased paper in bewilderment. He sank back down into his chair. "I assure you—I was no saint in my youth, God knows, but I have never, to my knowledge, sired any child but Simon. And I would certainly remember any episode such as the one you describe. Even if the tale is distorted, as it may well be, with your mother shut away and unable to speak for herself, I would not confuse a gently bred maiden with the tavern wenches I favored in my time in France." Something struck him. "When were you born?"

"In the summer of '85."

Bassington gave a sigh of relief. "It is all a dreadful misunderstanding, then. I cannot possibly be your father. For that entire year, and most of the preceding one, I was in the West Indies."

Julien sneered. "I am to believe this?" He was angry now, and secure in his anger.

"Do you dare suggest I am lying?"

"This from the man who ruined my mother? Yes, I do suggest it! Or do you fancy I will believe my mother's deathbed letter a lie? She told me her lover was the son of the Earl of Bassington. Had your father two sons? I saw a portrait of you as a boy at Boulton Park; it could be me at the same age, save for the clothing. How do you explain that? What of Hewitt? Do you accuse your own banker of deceit? Why, if you were not my father, did *your* father send payments to my mother?"

"I have no idea!" roared the earl, as angry as Julien. "How dare you come in here and make these nonsensical accusations? Damme, it seems a rather odd coincidence now that you should have come hunting butterflies at Boulton Park! What is your game, you scoundrel? What do you want with me? I've half a mind to call the constable!"

"What do I want with you?" Julien's voice was cold. "I want you to understand what kind of son you bred. What living as a bastard, 'an incarnation of the sin of lust,' has made me. My aunt had more grandiose ideas of revenge. When we discovered your name after my mother died she proposed that I should seek you out and kill you. I pointed out that parricide was usually regarded as an even graver sin than fornication. Her next thought was that I should seduce Miss Allen. Since she was your ward, not your daughter, I did not even risk the taint of incest.

"It seemed to me that it would be punishment enough to know that your son was the sort who would cheat his way into your house. At first I intended only to visit for a few days, on the pretense of studying the collection. But I was curious—I admit it. And I was looking for proof, indisputable proof that you were my father. So I rigged the trap on Clark's Hill and rode my horse straight into it. And then I was living in your home, the perfect situation to investigate my own past. I read your father's diaries. I spoke with the servants, with your son, your niece. Despicable, no? But not, perhaps, as despicable as what was done to my mother." He paused. "Would you like to know the richest part of the jest? I came to admire you. I liked you. I liked your family— my family. I started to soften. When I came in just now, and you told me you would welcome me, I was almost ready to forgive you."

"Out," said Bassington, breathing hard. "Get out." He staggered to the wall and rang the bell.

Julien picked up the bank draft, pale but composed. "Your great-great-grandfather was a wealthy yeoman ennobled by a money-hungry Stewart. Mine was one of the greatest kings of Europe. And yet I would have been willing to claim you as my father—in spite of your

treatment of my mother. If you choose not to acknowledge me, even here in private, that is your right. But I
would not have thought it of you."

"Out," repeated Bassington implacably. He pulled the
bellrope again, harder. "Serena is well rid of you. I shall
tell her so myself."

With her name the nagging thought which had disturbed him earlier slithered back out from its hiding
place. *I shall be delighted. I shall be delighted to welcome you to the family.*

"Where are those blasted footmen when you need
them?" muttered Bassington, staring at the door.

"Wait—I hadn't realized—it must have seemed—"
He broke off, swallowed. "Why *did* you greet me so
warmly just now? What did you think I was here for?"
But the answer was emerging, the cruel, ironic answer,
as he spoke.

"I believed you had come to make an offer for my
niece." The earl gave him a scathing look. "Don't pretend ignorance. To someone of your warped nature, I
am certain that the chance to wound her only added
extra spice to the affair. I have no idea why you should
have fastened upon me and my family as the victims of
your malice, but you may count yourself lucky that my
reluctance to upset my wife inclines me not to prosecute
you."

Julien had not heard a word since the phrase "offer
for my niece." "Oh, Christ," he said. "Christ." An aching
void was opening up inside him. He felt very cold.
"Does Serena—does Miss Allen also believe I am here
on her account?"

"She does," said the earl grimly.

"May I see her? Briefly? To—explain, apologize?"

"You may not." A breathless footman had appeared in
the doorway, and Bassington raised his voice to make
certain the servant would hear. "I forbid you to set foot
in my house. I forbid you to see my niece, or write her,

or send her any sort of message. All contact between you and any member of my household is at an end from this moment on. Do I make myself clear?"

Clermont bowed, tight-lipped.

"Show Mr. Clermont out. And tell Rowley to instruct the staff that this gentleman is not to be admitted, here or at Boulton Park, under any circumstances."

"Yes, sir," said the footman in a voice carefully devoid of expression. It was Hubert, Clermont realized. He avoided Clermont's eye as he escorted him to the front entrance and handed him his coat and hat.

The door closed with a solid thud, and Clermont stood at the top of the stone steps clutching his gloves in one hand, staring blindly at the massive black shapes of the surrounding houses, which rose silently against the cloudy sky. Here and there a lighted window broke up the darkness.

"Christ," he said for the third time, his voice raw. And then, hurling his gloves against the wall of the nearest house, "You idiot!"

Late in the afternoon, the countess had finally informed the bride-to-be of Clermont's proposed visit and its purpose. Serena had been warned by Simon that she was not meant to know anything and she managed to feign surprise very creditably. She *was* still surprised, in fact. And annoyed. It was impossible. It was outrageous. After all their joint efforts last night to prevent this, why would he ask her to marry him? And how dared he go to her uncle without speaking first to her? She had been pacing around her room ever since Simon's warning, veering between wonder and fury, with stops along the way for humiliation and bewilderment. From her aunt she did learn that Clermont had requested the appointment hours before the ball had even begun. This did not solve the puzzle; far from it, although at least it reassured her that he had not felt himself compelled to offer because of what had happened on the staircase.

Dinner was served early, and the courses were removed at a speed which astounded her. They were done in just over an hour, and instead of proceeding to the drawing room, the countess took Serena upstairs, where Robbins and the missing Emily were waiting. Her maid, it transpired, had spent the entire day supervising the construction of a suitable garment for the occasion. Serena submitted to being gowned in rose crepe and having her hair dressed. At just after half past eight, there was knock at the dressing-room door. It was Rowley.

"My lady, he is here," he said, his eyes sparkling with delight in a very unprofessional manner. He gave Serena a warm smile, bowed, and withdrew.

Her aunt turned to her, her voice quivering with emotion. "Dear, dear Serena! Let me be the first to wish you happy. This is beyond anything I could have hoped. A most amiable, learned young man, and from one of the first families of Europe!"

Serena had been clipping loose threads off the hem of the new gown while Emily reattached a ribbon to her sandal. At Rowley's announcement her hand suddenly began shaking, and she put down the scissors so quickly she nearly dropped them.

Her aunt mistook terror for impatience and patted her on the shoulder. "It will not be long now! As soon as your sandal is mended, we shall go down to the drawing room together. I don't imagine your uncle will keep him more than a few minutes."

Like a mannequin, Serena allowed herself to be fitted into the repaired sandal and led downstairs. She sat obediently on the chair where she was placed, her hands folded in her lap, her heart pounding, her throat tight. What would she say, when he came in and her aunt coyly excused herself? What would she say when the man who had kissed her for ten solid minutes last night—kissed her until she was drunk on him and the moon and her own ragged breathing—asked her to marry him? Would she tell him she had deliberately taken him to the most deserted, lonely spot she could think of in the Barrett house? That she knew of half a dozen anterooms where they could have talked during supper last night—if talk was what either of them had had in mind? That she had felt a curious, hollow hurt when he had honored her request to go back inside? Did he expect her to *agree* when he asked to kiss her? At least after they were locked out he hadn't waited for an answer to his rhetorical question. He had simply reached out and pulled her right up against him, as though it were the easiest thing in the world to draw her out of her sphere and into his.

She had no notion of the passage of time, but she did gradually see that her aunt was fretting, glancing at the clock. She went back to twisting her hands in her lap. Her thoughts went around and around, and never came to any conclusion. Did she want to marry him? She kept hearing Philip's voice, asking her if she was in love, and her own immediate, decisive, reply: *Certainly not!* Not *certainly*, and perhaps not even *not*, she acknowledged. What if he asked her to be his wife, and her mouth opened and said "Certainly not!" without really thinking about it?

The next time she looked up, the countess gave her a nervous attempt at a reassuring smile. "It would be just like George to start talking about politics or investments at a time like this."

That was when they heard the roar. The bookroom was one floor below them, but the sound was unmistakable. Startled, Serena glanced at her aunt. The countess had turned white. Both women sat in complete silence for five more minutes. They heard no more shouting, but they did hear the front door open and close. Finally they heard footsteps—slow footsteps—and a knock. The countess started up.

It was Rowley. "His lordship requests a private word, my lady." He looked haggard, and he avoided Serena's eye.

She rose. "I'll be in my room, Aunt Clara." She walked out the door, past the stricken butler, past two gaping footmen, up the stairs, into her bedchamber. Emily was there. She made the briefest motion possible with her hand, and the maid withdrew. Then she sat down to wait for someone to come and explain. Her hands were folded in her lap, just as they had been downstairs. When her uncle came, she did not get up. She listened very carefully and nodded when he asked if she would be all right and shook her head when he asked if she wanted her aunt or Emily. After he left, she did get up. She locked the door. She took off her sandals, and her new dress, tearing the shoulder slightly in the process, brushed her hair, put on her nightgown, and climbed into bed. When her aunt tapped on the door a bit later and called her name softly, she did not answer. She lay curled on her side like a wounded animal, thinking about what her uncle had told her and wondering why someone who had never trusted Julien Clermont should be so heartsick when she turned out to be right.

22

A lady wearing a high-necked flannel nightdress is more immodest than one clothed in the most daring French gown, for the latter garment is proper to any public entertainment whilst the former is restricted to those private chambers where only a husband may enter.

—Miss Cowell's Moral Examples
for Young Ladies.

He reasoned to himself as follows. If the earl was in fact his father, his lies to Julien negated any filial obligation. If the earl was not his father, the obligation had never existed. In either case, then, Julien was not bound to observe Bassington's command to stay away from Serena Allen. This specious excuse for logic made a serviceable screen to conceal a deeper imperative: he would be damned if he was going to leave London without seeing her. He needed to tell her he was sorry. He needed to explain how he had come to be such a thoughtless, selfish fool. This, too, was a screen, but he refused to look at what lay behind it.

Unfortunately, logic and remorse were insufficient for his purpose. He also needed a way into the house. When he returned to Manchester Square six hours after leaving the earl, he was discouraged but not surprised to see a guard stationed in front of Bassington's front door. Simon's adventures last night provided a solution to that problem, at least. He turned around, made his way over to the Barrett house on Harland Place, and went through the passageway by Barrett's study to the kitchen yard. From there it was an easy scramble over a stone wall into the garden facing the rear of the earl's home. He broke in by climbing onto the roof of a porch and forcing open a window on the first floor. Then, again thanks to his visits with Simon, he found his way to the back stair and went up to the third floor. Only now, as he stared down the dark corridor, did he realize he had no idea which room was Serena's.

He crept down the hall, looking for light under the doors, listening for noises. Nothing. He tried to guess the dimensions of the rooms from the spacing between doors, and then estimate which size might be appropriate for an earl's niece. It was hopeless. Time to turn to Simon again. At least he knew where the boy's room was; he had been there twice. He made his way back to the servants' stair, climbed up to the fourth floor, and stole quietly into the bedchamber.

Simon was asleep, a lamp burning low beside him. Given what he knew about the viscount's nocturnal habits, this was something of a miracle. He had been afraid the bed would be empty. Placing his hand gently over the boy's mouth, he leaned down and whispered, "Simon!"

It took a minute. Then the blue eyes opened, widened in surprise, and immediately narrowed again in anger. Behind his hand, Julien felt the boy deliberately spit.

"I need your help. I must see Serena," he said, speaking very low. Then he took away his hand.

"You pig! You scum! You toad! I'd like to kill you! When I grow up I *will* kill you!" Simon was whispering. Fiercely, and with venom, but he was whispering. That was a hopeful sign.

"In ten years, if you still feel that way, send word, and

I will meet you. You have every right to be angry. What I did was contemptible."

Evidently Simon had expected Julien to defend himself. He was silent. Then he whispered again. "Are you really a spy?"

"Is that what your father said?"

Simon nodded.

"No. I'm not a spy. I had a private quarrel with your father, and chose a very bad method of pursuing it." *

This time Simon didn't whisper, although he did speak quietly. "Is that why you gave me my telescope? So that you could come to our house?"

He winced. If it felt like he was being kicked in the stomach when the boy asked that question, what was it going to feel like when Serena asked him why he had flirted with her? "It isn't, not completely at any rate, but I don't see why you should believe me."

"I don't." But he looked a little less angry. "Why do you want to see Serena?" he said, after a minute.

"To apologize. To try to take away at least some of the hurt I've caused." He could see the boy was weakening. "I need to know which room is hers. Otherwise I'll go downstairs and knock on the first door I see."

"That would be Mrs. Childe's."

"The second door, then."

Simon stuck his lower lip out, then said grudgingly, "Fourth door. On the left. It's probably locked. She shuts herself in when she's upset." He dove suddenly down the side of his bed, startling Julien considerably. He could hear the boy groping for something on the floor. After a few seconds he pulled himself back up, red-faced. He was holding a wooden puzzle box, which he cracked apart in four expert twists. Inside was a roll of felt wadding, and folded into the roll were at least a dozen keys. Simon held them up to the light one by one. "This one," he said at last, handing it to Julien.

Julien blinked. "You know," he said, "your talents are wasted here. You should be at school."

Simon grinned, a boy-grin, a real one. "I'm going next term. To Winchester."

"I shall remember the worthy masters of Winchester in my prayers." Julien stood up.

"She'll want to kill you, too," warned Simon. "And she's already past her twenty-first birthday."

"That had occurred to me." He held up the key. "Thank you for this. I don't deserve it, but thank you anyway." Then he took a deep breath and marched off to face his doom.

Serena had not been able to sleep. For that matter, she hadn't been able to cry. She suspected one might be a prerequisite to the other, but as she had no particular desire to do either at the moment she eventually got out of bed, wrapped herself in a shawl, and sat down by the window. The curtains had been drawn; she tugged them open enough to look out at the moonlit facades of the houses on the opposite sides of the square.

Then she steeled herself and began to prod the various mental bruises inflicted during the evening. First: Clermont had lied to her about the butterflies. Well, what of that? She had been convinced from the first he was no naturalist. Second: he had misled her, had raised expectations of marriage. But had she ever thought, before Simon's announcement this morning, that his interest in her was anything more than an amusing diversion? No; her aunt's misperception of the purpose of his visit tonight was at fault here, not Clermont. Third: he had deceived her aunt and uncle. This, the heaviest charge, and the one she could not answer in any way, ought to have perturbed her the most. She loved her aunt and uncle—especially her aunt, in spite of or perhaps because of the countess's misguided attempts to make Serena happy. In her current confused, unbalanced state, however, the thought of their distress seemed remote.

If she was being honest, she had to admit to herself that the aching sense of loss she felt was not the result of anything Julien Clermont had done, tonight or last night or last week. It was the result of her own stupidity. A few kisses, a few stares from those grave, dark eyes, and she had lowered her shield and thrown down her weapons. She was almost sorry she would never see him again; she would have liked to explain to him, very patiently, that she was not angry with him, however justified that anger might seem, but rather with herself.

That was when she heard the key turn in the lock. *Simon*, she thought as she turned around. He often came down late at night. The door opened and closed with the room still in darkness. There was no sound, no movement for a moment. She knew suddenly that it wasn't her cousin. Then the intruder took four slow steps until he came within the small block of moonlight near the window.

"You're not asleep," he said.

"You're not dead," she retorted. "If I were a man, you would be."

"Simon said the same thing." He knelt by her chair. She wasn't sure if this was an act of contrition or a prudent attempt to keep their conversation quiet. Then she saw what he was holding out to her. It was his pistol. "It's loaded," he said.

Her vision of herself calmly telling Clermont that she was not angry at him died a quick and painless death. She took the pistol, held it firmly in both hands, and pointed it straight between the level black brows.

He didn't move.

"I suppose you think I won't shoot," she said scathingly.

"No. I think if you are angry enough to shoot, I deserve it. I've wronged you more than anyone, and that I did so partly in ignorance only makes it worse."

"You've wronged me more than anyone? Do you mean what happened tonight?"

He sighed. "I suppose it won't do any good to apologize? To tell you that I was so engrossed in my own affairs that it never, never occurred to me what everyone would think—what you would think—of my request to see your uncle?"

"Just a moment. Let us have a complete confession, so long as I have the pistol. You cheated your way into my uncle's house."

"Yes."

"You read through his private papers."

"Yes."

"You contrived the accident on Clark's Hill."

"Yes."

"You imbecile," she said in disgust. "You nearly killed yourself." Then she returned to her list. "You cultivated Simon, and me, as an excuse to maintain contact with the household here in London."

"Yes. No. Yes, at least at first."

"Then why would you ask me to forgive you for one embarrassing misunderstanding when you have just confessed to four much more serious crimes?"

"Because those crimes, at least, had some justification, inadequate though it might be. The humiliation you suffered tonight was the result of my self-absorbed carelessness."

Nettled, she said, "Humiliation? You are assuming I was going to say yes to this phantom proposal of marriage." She still held the pistol pointed right at him.

He gave a wry smile. "No, I'm not that fanciful. When I left here earlier, full of remorse, I pictured you sitting in your *chambre de fille*, blushing and eager, waiting for the summons to appear in the drawing room.

Dreaming of the moment when our eyes would meet, and you would drift across the room to my embrace. Then I decided it was far more likely that you had been stamping up and down, fuming about my audacity in seeking out your uncle without first consulting you."

This was so nearly an exact description of her behavior that afternoon that she bit her lip.

"Even if you meant to refuse me, Serena, tonight's debacle must have been a blow. Looking back, I cannot believe my folly. I called on you or Simon every day. I met you at concerts, at exhibitions. I danced with you. Philip warned me you would suffer when I disappeared, and I ignored him. I wanted to believe that my task here would not harm you. I deceived myself, and in so doing I wronged you, I wronged Simon—I compounded fraud upon fraud, mischief upon mischief. You have every right to pull that trigger."

"If I were a man, I would pull it." She waited for nearly a minute before lowering the gun. "I'm not a man," she said.

"I know." He took a long breath. "God, I certainly know that."

Somehow it seemed wrong to be in the chair when he was on the floor. She slid down next to him, her nightgown spreading out like a soft white nest around her on the floor. The gun dropped into her lap. It didn't make any noise, but it startled her. She had forgotten its existence. Her hand reached out, touched his hip, moved up to his chest, his shoulder, the side of his neck. Her fingers skated over the soft, bright hair. He had closed his eyes.

"Shooting me would be faster," he said in a harsh whisper.

She kissed him, softly and quickly, and pulled his jacket off.

His hand groped, found the gun, set it carefully aside. He still hadn't opened his eyes. He was moving his lips

in some soundless incantation, pulling her closer and
closer until she was pinned up against his chest and he
was looming over her in the colorless band of light beneath the window.

Then he opened his eyes, and she knew there could
never be any shield, any protection, any hope at all, once
that dark gaze had found her out. It was his turn to run
his hand slowly up her body, to lift her hair, turn it in the
moonlight. It was his turn to kiss her—not softly, and
not quickly. They sank to the floor tangled together,
sliding down the wall beneath the window until she was
lying nearly on top of him. He was pushing her nightgown up the backs of her legs, stroking her calves and
thighs, layering kisses down her neck and tearing impatiently at her collar until the buttons came away in his
hand and the kisses went lower still. They said nothing;
in the silent house their breathing rasped loudly and the
soft touch of lip on skin seemed to leave an echo behind. He was fierce and urgent beneath her; her own
body was a stranger to her, wild and purposeful in a way
that made a mockery of what she had felt with André.

If only, she would tell herself later. If only you had let
well enough alone. But she didn't. Her skin felt smothered in flannel; she wanted his hands on her breasts, on
her back; she wanted to move without being caught in
folds of cloth. She stood up suddenly, looked down at
the beautiful, intent face of the man who was about to
be her lover, and pulled her nightgown off over her
head.

"Serena," he whispered, "do you have any idea how
exquisite you are?"

She sank back down beside him, her hair falling onto
his chest. She reached for his neckcloth, tugged at it—
and stopped.

He had seized her hand. "Serena," he said, this time
in a very different voice, "we cannot do this. I cannot do
this. I will not ruin you."

She laughed bitterly. "I'm already ruined. Or didn't you know?"

He struggled up to a sitting position. His lips were a hard, straight line. "You are not ruined. That was a girl's mistake. This is different. And even if you were far less innocent than you are, I would not wish for a son of mine the life I have led, as a fatherless boy. I won't risk it, for you or myself or the child."

So, he was a bastard. She should have guessed that. Otherwise he would have been a duke, like his uncle and cousin. He was a bastard, and he had planned to ask the ward of an earl to marry him. Or rather, he hadn't planned to marry her. Which was more insulting? She wanted to be angry again, but instead she felt light-headed, frail, empty.

He tugged the nightgown out from under her leg and put it gently back on, pushing her arms through the sleeves as though she were a sick child.

She started to cry then, silently, huddled on her knees, her face in her hands.

"Serena," he said a third time, sounding lost and help-less. He lifted her in his arms, carried her over to the bed, and held her while she wept, stroking her hair until the sobs died away and she lay, half-dozing, and then dozing, and then asleep, her head in the hollow of his shoulder and her hand lying lightly over his wrist in case he might try to slip away without saying good-bye.

He felt her stir against him as the sky was turning faintly gray around the edges.

"Are you awake?" he asked softly after a minute, pulling his arms away from her.

"Yes." She shivered a little.

"I must go. The servants will be coming in soon to make up the fires."

She sighed. "I suppose if they find you here my uncle

will have you shot." She sat up and looked at him, her face still soft with sleep, her hair tousled, and he gritted his teeth to keep himself from grabbing her and retracting his earlier decision. "Are you truly a spy? Trying to steal government secrets?"

"Dammit, no!"

"Then why did you trick your way into my uncle's house?"

He was silent for a minute. "He didn't tell you what I said?"

She shook her head. "He said you had made up some absurd story, but that it was clear what, in fact, you were after."

"He's my father." He saw her stiffen. "He denies it, but I have proof. That's why I came to Boulton Hall. To be certain. And then to make him writhe for what he did to my mother. The Condés locked her in a convent for the rest of her life as punishment for producing me, you know."

She was struggling to take all this in. "What proof?" she said at last.

"My mother wrote me, when she was dying. She said her seducer was heir to an English title called 'Bassington'—this at a time when the fourth earl was still alive. I have bank drafts of payments sent to my mother's convent, authorized by the fourth earl. I have a miniature done of me at the age of eight which is the spitting image of the portrait of your uncle as a boy at Boulton Park." He made a sound of disgust and frustration. "Your uncle claims he was in the West Indies and couldn't possibly have sired a child in France in 1784."

She reached out and touched his arm. "But he was in the West Indies," she said. "He was. I know it. Everyone knows it. Coughlin, one of our servants at Boulton Park, was indentured there. He was transported for stealing a fish. My uncle rescued him from the most dreadful master and brought him back to England. It will be thirty years next spring; Coughlin talks about it all the time."

"I think my evidence is a bit more concrete than some old servant's grateful recollections. But it makes no difference now." He stood up, picked up his jacket, which was lying crumpled on the floor, and put it on. Then he looked down at the woman he could have married had he not been so focused on the man his mother should have married.

"I am sorry," he said. "I am sorry for everything. I know that is rather inadequate, under the circumstances, but it is all I have to offer. You deserve happiness, Serena, and I have faith that you will find it." He tucked her shawl around her so that it hid the tear in her nightgown. "Good-bye," he said softly. "I shall think of you every time I see a butterfly. And I will not be picturing worms with wings, either."

She smiled a little at that.

He went out through the dark house and the dark garden and the dark passageway by Barrett's house, seeing that half smile and wondering bitterly if anyone else in the world would have been stupid enough to continue with a sour, spiteful plan for petty revenge when they had stumbled onto Serena Allen.

"Light, guvner?" called a sleepy link-boy in Harland Place.

It was nearly dawn, and his lodgings were not far away, but at the moment, any forlorn-looking child had his sympathy. He paid the boy double and followed the bobbing torch down Duke Street.

Half an hour later, on the verge of falling back to sleep, Serena was hazily considering for the tenth time the odd contradictions between her uncle's story and Clermont's. She had been puzzling over it since his departure, torn between his vehemence and his undoubted resemblance to Simon on the one hand and her belief that her uncle had been nowhere near France twenty-nine years ago on the other. Who was lying? Her uncle? Julien's mother? Hewitt? Coughlin? A collage of bank drafts, letters, miniatures, portraits, and indentures drifted by beneath her closed eyes. She wondered sleepily what her uncle had looked like at Julien's age. There were no portraits of him as a young man.

Portraits.

She opened her eyes.

Simon, at the age of eight. Simon with dark eyes and dark eyebrows at the age of eight. Julien's hair. Simon's hair.

She sat up, suddenly wide awake.

23

Vernon should have been gloating. Julien had expected little sidelong glances, perhaps even a few more quotations from the Bible. "Pride goeth before destruction, and a haughty spirit before a fall." That would be a good one. Or, "One thing I know, that whereas I was blind, now I see." Instead his servant was dutifully packing, folding shirts and neckcloths and jackets as though each item was made of spun glass and demanded his entire concentration. That way, he didn't have to look at his master and feel sorry for him.

Julien hadn't slept at all. When he had arrived back in Brook Street it was nearly six, and all he wanted to do was run and hide. He had woken Vernon—a rare turnabout, that—and informed him, in the most neutral tone he could command, that they would be leaving as soon as possible. It must not have been a very neutral tone; Vernon had actually patted him briefly on the shoulder as he climbed stiffly out of bed. Julien had washed, though, and shaved, and put on clean clothing. At the inn tonight he would have a bath, he decided. A long bath. Maybe he would just sink under and never come up. Terminal baptism. It was one way to make a fresh start.

When the bell rang downstairs he assumed it was one of the porters, come to make arrangements to take the larger trunks away. Instead of the gruff accents of East London, however, he heard a very familiar voice. The owner of that voice was supposed to be in her bed in Manchester Square, where he had, with considerable nobility (in his opinion) left her, alone.

He tore down the stairs, furious at her for being so reckless. The wild notion that she had come to ask him to take her away with him suddenly took hold of him, and he wondered if he would be able to say no. The thought only redoubled his anger.

What the hell are you doing here? he started to say as he reached the entry hall. He stopped just in time. It was Serena, of course. In sharp contrast to one of his more recent and more memorable views of her she had virtually no skin or hair visible at all. A very proper bonnet covered all but a few curls; her pelisse was buttoned up to just below her chin; her slender fingers were encased in gloves. She wasn't alone, however. Next to her was a maid. He emended the question slightly. "What are you doing here?" he said harshly.

The maid seemed to be asking the same question. She looked terrified. Vernon wasn't happy, either.

"I came to return this." Serena drew his pistol out of her reticule. A few tiny square flakes of paper came with it. She looked at the maid. "Emily, wait here for a moment. I need a word with Mr. Clermont in private."

He took her into the parlor, leaving the doors conspicuously open.

"For God's sake, Serena," he hissed. "Do you want to be forced into a convent like my mother? Are you mad?"

"Emily won't say anything. I told her my uncle would sack her if he found out I had been here, and he probably would." Her tone was calm and utterly ruthless.

"What of the pistol? Did anyone see it in your room?" If someone knowledgeable—the earl, for example—had found the very distinctive weapon in his niece's bedroom, he might have to elope with her after all.

She shook her head. "I found it shortly after you left.

I told Emily Simon had stolen it from you and I had to get it back to you."

"You could have sent it round with a footman."

"No," she said, still calm. "No, I couldn't. Because I wasn't willing to write down what I'm about to tell you. I thought you should hear it in person."

"What is it?" He was impatient, nervous. She needed to leave. Her maid could be bribed. Someone might see her coming out of the house. He wasn't expecting her to say anything very important. She had used the pistol as an excuse; she wanted to see him, perhaps; it was only natural. For his part, he had been sternly suppressing fantasies of climbing into her room every night for the rest of his life since leaving at dawn. But one last romantic farewell wasn't worth the risk she was taking.

He was wrong, though. She did have something important to say. She led him into the farthest corner of the room, away from the maid and Vernon and the open door, and said, very quietly, "My uncle isn't your father. He wasn't lying to you."

He gave her a cold, disbelieving stare.

"Wait; hear me out. You were right as well: you are a Piers. But not my uncle's son. Your father is his cousin, Charles Piers. The boy in the portrait—with the fair hair and dark eyes—you thought it was my uncle, didn't you?"

He had, of course.

"My uncle is the smaller one. His hair was brown when he was a child, and it stayed brown until it began to turn gray. You were looking for the older boy, and you saw two boys, one of whom was taller, the one with fair hair and dark eyes, and you assumed it was my uncle. But Charles was always taller, apparently, even though he was a bit younger. And Charles Piers *was* in France in 1784. He was forced to leave England as a young man and spent most of his life on the continent. When he died recently his diaries were sent to my uncle; supposedly they are very shocking. I was never allowed to see them. He often told people he was the heir to the Bassington earldom. I think he even believed it sometimes; he was sure my uncle was going to die childless. The late earl was constantly paying his debts for him and bribing foreign officials to keep him from going to prison."

It all made perfect sense. The payments to France that Bassington had never heard of were just another debt taken care of by the exasperated head of the Piers family.

"I'm sorry," she added gently, "but from what I hear he was not a particularly pleasant person."

"Like father, like son," he muttered.

"I tried to see my uncle this morning, to explain that you had, in a sense, been right. You do have a claim on him. You were not inventing something out of whole cloth. But the minute I mentioned your name, he refused to hear me." She looked down, biting her lip. "You must leave right away. He told me he means to have you arrested."

He gestured at the piles of luggage in the hallway. "Behold, I hear and obey."

She held out her hand. "Good-bye, then."

"Good-bye." He didn't kiss it. He just held it.

Then she drew it away and a minute later he heard the gentle, implacable sound of the front door closing behind her.

"It's gone." Barrett shook his head in disbelief. "I take full responsibility, of course. It was entrusted to me."

Bassington was thumbing through the papers in the dossier lying on Barrett's desk, examining each one carefully.

"I already went though them," said a third man. This was Nathan Meyer. "But I suppose it doesn't hurt to have someone else make certain Barrett and I haven't overlooked it somehow."

"You're certain it was in here?" Bassington asked, still turning sheets over.

"Certain." Barrett ran his hands through his thinning hair. "I put every single letter, and all the drafts of the replies, into that packet and locked it in the safe. That was about midnight. Then I locked the door of the study and went up to bed. The door was still locked when I came down this morning, and there was no sign anything had been disturbed, until I opened the safe and found the letter missing from the top of the pile in the dossier."

Meyer got up, crossed over to the door, and knelt by the handle. He stayed there for a moment, pressing and releasing the catch, and then vanished into the side room. "No sign of tampering with either lock," he said, returning. "Who else in your house has the keys, Barrett?"

"No one! And since the arrival of these letters, both keys have been on my person at all times."

"I have a key," Bassington interjected. "But only to the safe, not the room."

"Where is it?" Meyer said.

The earl patted his waistcoat pocket. "Here." Then he went back to the papers.

"Quite the little mystery." Meyer sat down next to Barrett and grimaced. "A very inopportune time for a puzzle of this sort."

Barrett sighed. "I'll resign, of course. But that isn't the real question. The real question is, who has the letter?"

"I already told you who has it," muttered Bassington. "That damned French trickster Clermont. I should have had him arrested last night as soon as he confessed his lies."

"Colonel White has sent someone to keep him under observation," Barrett said. "It's true one of my footmen saw him near this room on the night of the ball. Suppose he doesn't have it, though. Suppose the thief is someone else. What is he likely to do with it?"

"Sell it," said Meyer promptly. "That letter would be worth a fortune to either Metternich or Napoleon. Whoever has it can name his price. It's clear proof the Tsar is planning to double-cross Austria once Napoleon formally cedes his eastern territories."

"No, it isn't clear proof," said Bassington, looking up from the folder. "It isn't signed."

Barrett made an impatient gesture. "What of that? We have other letters in the same handwriting on the same subject with the signature appended."

"Correct," said the earl. "*We* have them. I've gone through and counted. They're all here. Clermont is missing a crucial piece of evidence. Everyone suspects the Tsar is negotiating with us; an unsigned letter cannot do much more damage than rumor has already. What will Clermont's employers do? Compare the letter with samples from every man in the Russian court they suspect might be acting as the go-between? And, I might add, our man is one of the more unlikely candidates. So far as we know, only my cousin discovered his identity, and he died ensuring that it remain secret."

Meyer said slowly, "Does anyone know that the letter is missing, Barrett? Besides White and the three of us?"

Barrett thought for a minute. "I asked Crosswell to ascertain if anyone had been seen lurking near the house last night, but I didn't tell him why. What are you thinking?"

"I am thinking that the thief has not read the entire letter carefully. He may not even realize it is not signed. He saw the first paragraph, which admittedly is damning, and grabbed the letter and ran, thinking he had his prize."

"And?" Bassington said impatiently.

"And, if he has no notion we have discovered the loss, he may come back for more."

The luggage was all packed; indeed, everything except a small cloak bag was already in the dispatcher's office at the White Horse Inn, ready to be loaded into a post chaise early tomorrow. Julien should have been in the White Horse Inn as well, sleeping in the very expensive room he had hired for the night. Instead he was halfway across London, his coat collar turned up against the rain, staring at the narrow passageway which ran between Sir Charles Barrett's house and the adjacent one in Harland Place.

This morning, racked with guilt at the wounds he had inflicted on Serena and Simon, he had thought himself cured of the obsession which had ruled his life. He had looked back at his misguided quest to find and confront Bassington and had sworn to forget about the past. Then Serena had appeared and presented him with a new and rather unappetizing candidate for the role of father, and within an hour he was wondering what the man had really been like. By midafternoon he was trying to recall every scrap of information about the mysterious Charles that he could. By dinnertime he was dwelling on the thought of those tantalizing diaries. He even knew where they were, as it happened: they were in Barrett's study. Was it not at least worth attempting to open the window-door with his knife, as Simon had? What if the diaries described his mother? What if this Charles, blackguard though he was, had really loved her? He had spent every night since learning Bassington's name in the belief that his father was an honest, respectable man who had done one bad deed. What if the reverse were true? What if his father was a villain who had briefly dreamed of marrying a good woman? Wasn't that some-

thing he ought to know, for his own sake and the sake of
the dead man?

He looked around the little cul-de-sac. It was deserted. Moving slowly, he sauntered past the front of
Barrett's house. There was still no one in sight. He hesitated one more moment, and then turned into the black
gap between the houses.

It was much darker than it had been the other night,
and the passage was full of puddles. Rain dripped off
the eaves and windowsills on both sides and somehow
managed to find the back of his neck. He almost walked
past the little window, it was so hard to see anything, but
his eye caught the shimmer of glass and he stopped.

He looked up. There were no lights in the upper windows on either side. No lights that he could see at the
back of the house, by the kitchen. It was past midnight,
after all, on a Sunday night. He felt for the join between
the window and the wall and after a few false starts
managed to insert his knife into the space. He slid it
along, slowly. Nothing happened. Again, in the opposite
direction. Still nothing. He tried poking the knife farther
in at various intervals. No good. Instead of frustration
or disappointment, he realized that what he was feeling
was relief. That made him angry. All very well to pursue a father who was a respected statesman, a scholar, a
sire to boast of. But now, when it appeared his father
was in fact a criminal, he was happy to abandon the
search? That was cowardice. Gritting his teeth, he stuck
the knife in as far as it would go and dragged it across,
scraping his thumb on the stone until it bled.

When the door came open, he was so startled he
nearly shut it again as he flinched. The muted click of
the spring releasing had been inaudible in the noise of
the rain. As before, the side room was dark and silent.
He hoisted himself in, this time leaving the outer door
open; he didn't want to be locked in again. Quietly, he
crept across and opened the door into the study. There

were no lights in the hallway outside tonight. He would have to use his small lantern. It took him a minute to get it lit; the wick was a bit damp. Then he swung the light up in a circle, looking around the empty room.

He saw the books immediately. They were piled on a table just to the left of the outer door, unmistakable in their red leather bindings, stamped with a crest he knew all too well. They were virtually identical, in fact, to the journals of the late earl. Holding his breath, he crossed to the stack of books and picked up the first one. It was for the spring of 1807. The next one was for the winter of 1810. He opened another, and another. The oldest was from 1799. Cursing, he looked around for more volumes. There were none in sight. There was, however, a crate beneath the table. He knelt, and opened it. It was full of red leather books.

And then he heard, too late, a soft footfall behind him and felt the barrel of a gun pressed into the side of his neck. "Don't move," said a stern voice. "Barrett! LeSueur! I have him."

The door to the hall opened; suddenly there was light, lots of light, two unshielded dark lanterns shining straight at him. The gun left his neck, and its owner stepped over towards his companions from the hallway. Julien blinked, and raised his own lantern. Facing him, looking very grim, were Barrett, LeSueur, and Nathan Meyer. LeSueur was in uniform.

The young officer straightened and cleared his throat. "Mr. Clermont," he announced, "You are under arrest."

Of course he was under arrest. He wished Meyer had just shot him. He got to his feet and looked at Barrett. "Will it—will my name be released? Is this public?"

"What *is* your name?" asked Meyer. "Your full name. And title."

"Louis-François Julien de Bourbon-Condé, Marquis de Clermont," he said wearily. He looked again at Barrett. Damn it, did he have to beg?

Barrett understood. "Is there a name you would prefer that we use for the records?"

He shuffled mentally through his estates until he found an obscure one. "Savignac. Louis de Savignac—no, just Louis Savignac. That will do. If this can possibly be kept from my grandfather, I would be very grateful."

Meyer gave him an odd look.

"Well, Mr. Savignac," said LeSueur. "We don't take parole from scum like you, even if you are a marquis. If you would condescend to stretch out your hands in front of you, I can fasten these manacles and we can be on our way."

"Where are you taking me?"

"The Tower."

"The Tower?" Was this some sort of nightmare, nurtured by too many evenings with Shakespeare's history plays? "I thought it wasn't used as a prison any longer."

"It isn't, for ordinary criminals." LeSueur snapped the locks closed on the bracelets. "But in any case you will not be held with the other prisoners there. For situations like this, we find it convenient to use our own cells. If you are truly concerned about your privacy, you should be very happy with your situation there. No one will ever know where you are, or what has happened to you, unless we choose to tell them."

24

Scions of a noble house, especially one of great prominence and antiquity, must always be conscious that they represent not only themselves, but all the men bearing their name, whether long dead or yet to be born.

—Precepts of Mlle. de Condé

The human mind is a complex and devious entity. Even intelligent, well-educated people are often capable of holding two contradictory sets of beliefs simultaneously. They merely store them in different areas of their brain. For example, if someone had asked Julien Clermont the following morning what crime he would be charged with, he would have answered "trespassing." Or perhaps, "trespassing and attempted burglary," although in his own mind he had more right to those diaries than anyone else now living. If that same person had then asked him which official normally arrests persons charged with such crimes, and where the accused man might be incarcerated, he would have answered "the watch" and "Newgate." He had been living in England nearly his entire life, after all. He was not unfamiliar with English law, or with London's ramshackle system of policing its streets. And yet it didn't occur to him to wonder why he had been taken into custody by a military officer, why he had been subjected to a humiliating and very thorough search of his person, why his cell was not a cell but a small windowless room which had clearly been recently used as an office—it still had a desk and chair in it—and then hastily furnished with a pallet and latrine bucket.

Admittedly, he had only had five hours of sleep in the last two days. He was unwashed, unshaven, and hungry. But when two sentries unlocked the door of his room at nine o'clock and escorted him downstairs, he still expected to be taken before a magistrate. He expected to be fined, possibly deported—although the real penalty, to his way of thinking, would be the eternal contempt of everyone he had ever cared about, from his grandfather all the way to Serena Allen.

The first clue that his expectations were wrong came when the sentries opened the doors of what he had thought would be some sort of courtroom. Instead he was shoved into what looked like a small council chamber. There was a long table, with chairs on both sides. On the left side were three officers: LeSueur, the younger Meyer, and an older man with a large mustache he vaguely recalled seeing at the ball. On the right side were Sir Charles Barrett, Nathan Meyer, and a smooth-faced man he did not recognize. At a clerk's desk in the far corner another man, perched on a stool, was laying out pens and a blotter next to a large notebook. There was no judge. There was also no chair for Julien.

The sentries withdrew and closed the doors behind them; in his corner, the clerk held his pen poised over the blank page of his notebook. Julien stood, weary and heartsick, looking down the table at the faces of the six men.

Barrett raised one eyebrow at the man with the mustache. "Colonel White?"

"I'll let you do the honors," the older man said. "You caught him in your house, after all."

Barrett nodded. "Well, Mr. Clermont," he said, in a calm, pleasant voice which Julien found unaccountably terrifying, "I see no reason to beat about the bush. You are an intelligent man, and I'm sure you are aware that the game is up. The letter wasn't on your person, and when we searched your luggage early this morning at the White Horse we did not find it there, either. The matter is too important to me to worry about justice in its pure form. If you will assist us in recovering it I will guarantee your safety."

"Letter?" Julien looked at LeSueur, who was regarding him as if he were a poisonous reptile, at the older Meyer, and then back at Barrett. "What letter?"

"Don't waste our time, Clermont," said the colonel. Julien recognized the voice now; it was the man he had overheard in Barrett's study the night of the ball. "We could just execute you out of hand, you know. We have enough evidence to hang you five times over."

"For *trespassing*?" Then even his tired brain began to function at last. Colonels did not convene tribunals in the Tower to interrogate trespassers. He should have known what was happening the minute he saw Nathan Meyer pointing the gun at him last night. Resignation and despair suddenly gave way to rage. Julien swung to face his tormentor. "This is your doing, isn't it? You've persuaded them I'm some sort of spy." He pointed an accusing finger. "You turned Bassington against me; that's why he wouldn't listen to me the other night. I would have called you out after your visit to Boulton Park, but I thought it beneath me to kill a vulgar old catchpoll for being overzealous at his job. I let it go. I let it go, but you didn't. You kept after me, had me followed. And now you've somehow arranged this farce of a tribunal."

Out of the corner of his eye, Julien saw LeSueur forcibly restraining the younger Meyer, who had risen halfway out of his chair.

Barrett said, still in that same calm voice, "Mr. Clermont, you can hardly accuse Mr. Meyer of overzealousness at this point. Bassington has told us about your stratagems to gain access to Boulton Park. You were seen lurking near my study on Friday night during the ball. Saturday night you were seen in the vicinity of my house again, both by Bassington's guard and by a link-boy. Sunday morning I find an important letter missing from my safe. Sunday evening you reappear in my study—demonstrating, I might add, an intimate knowledge of that room and its special features. It is useless to protest your innocence."

He retorted hotly, "It may be useless, but what else am I to do? I *am* innocent." Then, recalling his activities of the past month, he added, "Innocent of stealing papers, at least. I do not deny forcing my way into the earl's household. I regret it now deeply, but I believed I was justified at the time."

"Do you deny that three of us here found you in my study last night?"

"No."

"How did you know of the hidden entrance?"

He tried to keep his face from shouting "Simon." "I accidentally witnessed someone using it and deduced where it led."

"What were you looking for there?"

"It is—a personal matter. A family matter. Related to my purpose in visiting Boulton Park."

"A family matter? In my study?" He sat back. "Very well, what *was* your purpose at Boulton Park?"

"I am not at liberty to say. I confided my reasons to Lord Bassington."

White leaned across the table and said in a low tone to Barrett, "Did you invite Bassington this morning?"

"Yes, but he refused to come," Barrett said in the same low voice. "He is very distressed, as is the countess. He gave me a statement, however, which does not support Mr. Clermont's version of the facts." He turned back to Clermont and raised his voice again. "Do you deny that you were also in my study late Saturday night?"

"I do."

"You were observed in Manchester Place at three in the morning. A link-boy then saw you emerge from the private walkway by my house, a walkway which leads to the concealed entrance to my study, two hours later. Mr. Meyer saw you approach by that same route last night and gain entrance to my house. Do you still deny you took that letter?"

"I know nothing of any letter. Yes, I deny it."

"Where were you, then, during those two hours?"

With Serena Allen. Coming just one step short of duplicating his father's crime against his mother. He couldn't think of a plausible answer, and he certainly wasn't going to tell the truth. He settled for the simplest lie. "I went for a walk."

"In the middle of the night? A two-hour stroll which miraculously wound up one street away from where it had started? Nowhere near your own lodgings, or any neighborhood where late-night entertainment is available?"

"Yes." He prayed that Barrett would not ask him to describe his route.

"Did anyone see you while you were walking? Anyone save the guard and the link-boy?"

"No."

White made an exasperated gesture. "Mr. Clermont, do you think we are children? Do you understand the consequences to yourself of this absurd pretense? You are accused of a capital crime. You have been offered a very generous inducement to cooperate."

Pride goeth before destruction. "I went for a walk," he said, setting his jaw.

Barrett sighed and looked at LeSueur. The young officer stood and opened the door, beckoning to the two sentries. Julien found himself seized, not gently, and marched down three more flights of stairs to a small basement room. It looked more like the Tower he had pictured: stone walls, stone floor, small barred window. LeSueur kept him there for what seemed an eternity, still on his feet, hungry and thirsty and dizzy with fatigue, asking the same questions over and over again. By the end he had condensed all his answers down to two phrases: "I am not at liberty to say" and "I went for a walk."

At last there was a knock on the door. It was the younger Meyer. "I'll take him back up," he said. LeSueur had lost his crisp military bearing some time ago. His hair was tousled, and he had loosened his neck-cloth. He merely nodded.

Meyer glared at Julien all the way back up the four flights of stairs to his makeshift cell. "If you get out of this tangle alive," he said as he unlocked the door, "I should kill you myself, for insulting my father."

"I don't think I'm getting out of this." Julien leaned against the door.

"I don't either." Meyer pushed the door open, and Julien hauled himself upright again. "Although I don't believe you took that letter."

"I didn't. But your opinion seems to be a minority view."

"Where did you go between three and five the other night, though?"

Julien just looked at him.

"Ah, yes. You went for a walk." The younger man wasn't glaring any more. "I'll have them bring you something to eat," he said abruptly.

"Could I have some water, as well? For shaving?"

Meyer shook his head. "They won't let you have a razor." But an hour later, just as Julien was finishing his long-delayed breakfast, the two sentries reappeared, escorting a nervous middle-aged corporal with a basin and shaving gear. He only cut Julien once.

Fed and reasonably clean, Julien sat down cross-legged on his pallet and considered his options. He could ask to have Serena summoned to testify on his behalf. He rejected that option instantly. He could write to Bassington and beg him to tell the full story of their interview. He rejected that option almost as quickly. The chances of such an appeal succeeding were slim, and he found himself reluctant to parade the Piers's dirty laundry in front of strangers. He could ask his grandfather for help. That was out, as well. The phrase "I would rather die" suggested itself as apt. Finally, he could wait and hope for a miracle. He could wait, and hope for a miracle, and catch up on his sleep. He stretched out, covered his shoulders with the tiny blanket lying on the pallet, and closed his eyes.

After two more unsuccessful attempts to see her uncle by fair means, Serena resorted to foul: she way-laid him in the front hall as he was returning from his club late that evening.

"Not now, Serena," he said curtly, handing his coat and hat to Rowley. He started to brush past her.

"I am sorry, but I must insist. It is very important."

"If it is about Mr. Clermont, I have already told you, the subject is closed."

Rowley was hurriedly backing through the nearest door, out of the line of fire.

She moved so that she was between her uncle and the staircase. His face grim, he lifted her off her feet, set her to one side, and started up the stairs. Shocked, she stood frozen for a moment. Then she called after him, not caring if the servants heard her or not, "Uncle, I have never known you to be unjust."

He didn't turn around, but he stopped, one hand on the banister.

"Please?" She could hear her voice tremble.

Slowly he came back down and led her into an anteroom which opened off the hall. She thought he would be annoyed, but instead he looked sad. "Believe me, Serena, Mr. Clermont isn't worth your concern. He is a very dangerous, unscrupulous young man. I do not wish to be unreasonable, however. I will hear you out, if you can be brief."

She took a deep breath. "I called on him yesterday morning." She added hastily, seeing him start to get angry again, "I took a maid. And he would not allow me to stay. He told me I should not be there."

"Well, at least he has that much sense," her uncle muttered.

"I am perfectly well aware that I should not visit gentlemen at their lodgings," she said, stung. "But you had forbidden him your house, and I needed to see him."

"And he had as little success evading you as I did just now," he commented dryly. "Very well. Why did you feel this imperative need to speak with a man who had just insulted you grossly?"

"That's just it," she said. "He didn't insult me, not intentionally. He told me why he had requested an appointment with you."

Now he was angry. "A damned lie! I beg your pardon, Serena, but that he could bring himself to repeat that scandalous drivel in front of you is past bearing."

She put her hand on his arm, afraid he would try to leave again. "Uncle, wait. Wait, and let me finish. I told him you were not his father. He didn't believe me at first. Consider the evidence from his point of view: his mother mentions the name Bassington. He discovers that he bears a strong resemblance to your son, and to certain family portraits. Your own banker tells him that your father ordered payments made to his mother."

"Lies. Coincidence," he said impatiently. "Once he had met Simon he noticed a slight similarity, yes, and determined to take advantage of it, perhaps to extort money from me."

"A 'slight similarity'?" She folded her arms. "Uncle George, haven't you realized the truth yet? Who else, as a young man, sometimes claimed to be your father's heir? Who was in France the year before Mr. Clermont was born?"

"My cousin," he said slowly. "My cousin Charles."

"And what did your cousin Charles look like when he was Mr. Clermont's age? Didn't he have very fair hair, and wide-set dark eyes?"

He cleared his throat. "Difficult to compare the two men. We wore wigs in those days, you know." But he was frowning. "It is possible," he admitted after a minute. "I must admit, it is entirely possible. I had never thought of it."

"Go see Mr. Hewitt," she urged. "That is all I ask. If Mr. Clermont proves to be Charles's son, then he is a Piers. And in that case he had some justification for what he did."

He was shaking his head. "No, best to leave it, my dear. I am sorry, but even if your surmise is correct, the family would no more wish to claim him than they did his father. He seems to have inherited more than his coloring from my cousin."

She felt the blood leave her face. "What do you mean?"

He touched her shoulder awkwardly. "Forget him, Serena."

25

Julien tried to keep track of time, but it was difficult. Sometimes when they came to get him and take him down to the basement it was light outside, sometimes it wasn't. Sometimes he was able to sleep as long as he liked; at other times they were shaking him awake from a groggy trance. His treatment on the way to and from the basement grew rougher and rougher, but the questioning itself was always coldly, meticulously precise and courteous. "May we ask who is employing you, Mr. Clermont?" "Could you tell us the whereabouts of the letter, Mr. Clermont?" "Could you describe your activities during the two hours before dawn on Sunday, Mr. Clermont?" Usually it was LeSueur asking the questions; occasionally it was another, older officer he did not know.

On what he thought was his third morning in the Tower, one of the sentries deliberately pushed him down half a flight of stairs. He landed at the bottom, slightly stunned, and looked up to see the sentry staring down at him with no expression on his face whatsoever. He was wise enough not to say anything about it to LeSueur, nor did he react in any way when the same sentry came to collect him at the end of the session. But when he had regained the relative safety of his cell he sat down at the empty desk and thought hard.

He had always prided himself on his independence

from his mother's family. They had treated her brutally; they had made her son feel guilty for his own existence; they had admitted him to their ranks only as an insulting last resort, when the guillotine was claiming other, more legitimate aristocrats. He had resolved long ago to take from the Condés only the minimum he felt was owed to him.

Being pushed down the stairs by a pockmarked enlisted man who stank of onions made it suddenly clear that he had unconsciously accepted much, much more from his grandfather than he had ever realized. He had accepted a set of beliefs about who he was and how he would be treated. For example, he had simply assumed that there would be no serious consequences of this arrest until they had decided he was guilty. No beatings, no rotten food, no freezing rooms without bedding or blankets. In fact, now that he was being honest with himself, he was not certain whether he had fully believed there would be serious consequences if he *were* judged guilty. Would they, in truth, execute Julien de Bourbon-Condé, the grandson of the most respected and influential member of the French royal family? When he had nobly resolved to lie about his visit to Serena, had he actually thought the choice was between his death and her dishonor?

Too late to change his story now, though. After three days of stubborn denials, no one would believe him if he recanted. An innocent man with a reasonable explanation would have produced it in the first five minutes. Since there was nothing to be done at this point, he tried to persuade himself to forget about it. He washed his face, which was throbbing slightly on one side, and sat back down with his only reading material—a copy of the *Observer* from several months ago. The servant had sold it to him this morning for the outrageous sum of twelve shillings. It proved difficult, however, to find a story which didn't mention anything unsettling—letters, for example. Or France. Or fathers.

He was still feeling shaken, physically and mentally, when the same sentry opened the door an hour later. "You have a visitor," the man said sullenly. He stepped aside, and Bassington came into the room.

What was he supposed to say to a first cousin once removed whom he had accused of debauching his mother? Julien settled for getting up out of the chair and nodding stiffly.

The earl took off his hat and set it on the desk. "Might I have a few minutes alone with him?" he asked the sentry. The man muttered something under his breath, but he withdrew and closed the door behind him.

"You are bruised," said Bassington abruptly, moving closer. "Have you been mistreated?"

Julien put his hand up to his cheek and touched the tender spot in front of his right ear. "I fell."

There was a long silence. The earl wandered around the room, examining dark squares on the wall where maps or pictures had been hanging. He sat down at last in the chair behind the desk and looked at Julien.

"I was perhaps too hasty in dismissing the evidence you presented to me the other night," he said slowly. "My niece tells me that she spoke with you on Sunday about this matter. At her urging, I have been to see Hewitt, and it seems almost certain that she is right. You are the son of my cousin Charles."

So it was true. An aching sense of loss filled him. He didn't want some dissolute black sheep for a father. He wanted George Piers—irascible, stubborn, snuff-addicted, honorable, intelligent George Piers.

"Charles was a great trial to my father," the earl said, after another pause. "I am afraid I was not very sympathetic to my father's complaints; I always had a secret fondness for my cousin. In those days he seemed quite dashing and glamorous to me. As a result my father stopped confiding in me. Will you believe me when I tell you that I had no idea there was a child in France?"

Apparently Julien was expected to respond to this. He cleared his throat. "Yes," he said, "I believe you."

"Now that I know you are a kinsman, I feel some responsibility towards you. I thought it my duty to come and inquire after you here. Although I fear I cannot help you much in your present circumstances."

Maybe he didn't want Bassington for a father after all. The last thing he needed was another disapproving relative passing judgment on his mistakes. "Thank you, sir," he said stiffly.

There was another silence, then the earl asked cautiously. "Did you steal that letter?"

"No." It was his turn to say: "Do you believe me?"

"I don't know. Nor, to be honest, would it make much difference if I did. It's in White's hands now." The earl tapped his fingers nervously on the desk. "Is there anything I can do for you?" he asked abruptly. "Clothing, books, that sort of thing?"

"If you could get word to my servant—tell him—well, not the truth. Tell him I have gone out of town unexpectedly. He will be very anxious."

Bassington looked uncomfortable. "He has already called at my house; I'm afraid he was sent away. I will have Rowley locate him and pass on your message."

"And perhaps you could convey my apologies again to the countess? And Miss Allen?"

The earl looked even more uncomfortable. "If there is a suitable opportunity, yes."

Julien wondered what a suitable opportunity would be. His funeral, probably.

Bassington rose. "Anything else?" He walked over to the door and rapped on it sharply. Julien heard the key turning in the lock from the outside.

"Wait—there is one more thing." He thought the answer would be no, but it didn't hurt to ask. "My father's diaries. Is there any chance I would be permitted to have the volumes from the year he met my mother?"

"The 1780's, wasn't it?"

"1784."

Bassington thought for a minute. "I don't see why not. He didn't settle in Russia until 1805. I will ask Barrett."

"Thank you," said Julien. "Thank you very much. I have quite a bit of leisure time for reading at the moment."

"Are you certain you want them?" Bassington asked in an unexpectedly gentle tone. "I haven't looked at them myself, you know. I had heard so many ugly stories about Charles already, and now that he is dead it seemed almost cruel to go in search of more. You are welcome to borrow anything in my library, if you want something to read."

"I need to know," he said. He raised his eyes to meet the earl's. "When I thought it was you, I wanted to learn everything about you. I read your speeches in the newspaper; I dug out old volumes of the *Royal Society Bulletin* to look at your essays; I walked by your house in London. And eventually, as you saw, that wasn't enough. I can't take revenge on a dead man. The idea of avenging my mother was wrong in any case; I admit that. But I still want to understand who he was."

"Well, don't judge him too harshly," said Bassington. "He will likely paint himself as black as pitch in the diaries; he always relished the thought of being a devil. But no one is ever all bad. I choose not to read the diaries, and to remember instead that Charles was willing to risk his life on behalf of his adopted country. In fact, he died protecting the author of that missing letter. Which means that I, at least, hope you are telling the truth when you say you did not steal it."

* * *

Sir Charles Barrett looked at the hat resting on the stand in the front hall. "We have a visitor?" he asked his butler. "At this hour?"

"It's Major Drayton, sir. Apparently he came in last night from Portsmouth and took the liberty of stopping by this morning to see her ladyship."

"Drayton," said Barrett thoughtfully. "I see. Where are they, Staples?"

"The library, sir." At a nod from Barrett he stepped over and held open the door.

Sara Barrett looked up as her husband came into the room. "Charles, look who is here!" she said, beaming. "Richard!"

The dark-haired young officer next to her rose.

"So I heard." Barrett crossed the room and shook hands with his brother-in-law. "Good to see you back in England. Is there any news yet?"

The younger man grimaced. "Not yet. The doctor tells me it will be another few weeks. I don't know how Rachel can stand it."

Barrett laughed. "Patience, my boy. Be glad you will have some time with your wife before the new arrival claims all her attention. In fact, you should count yourself lucky to be given leave at all."

"Oh, nothing much was happening in Gibraltar. The action has all moved up north. My colonel said he could spare me." Drayton sat back down. "How are things here? I thought I might call down at the Tower, see how White and the others are doing."

Barrett eyed him speculatively. "Curious you should say that."

His wife glared at him. "Charles, he's on *leave*. His wife is about to be confined, for heaven's sake. I don't know what sort of crisis you're involved in at the moment, but I'm not blind. There is something going on. And I do not see why you should drag Richard into it."

"I'm not dragging him into anything, Sara. I would merely like to consult him."

She took the hint and rose. "If you *dare* to leave this house without coming to find me, I shall never speak to you again," she told her brother. "As for you," turning to her husband, "if White and his couriers send Richard off to France again I shall never speak to you, either."

"Well," said Drayton, after the door had slammed behind her. "Sara seems a trifle . . . on edge."

Barrett sighed. "It's been a difficult week. Sara and Lady Bassington were matchmaking, and the hero of their romance is now under arrest for stealing confidential diplomatic correspondence. From my safe."

Drayton whistled softly. "How very awkward."

"Indeed. It gets worse. The same man turns out to be a by-blow of Bassington's cousin."

"Of Charles Piers? The scandal-monger?"

"So you've heard of Piers?"

"White mentioned him, yes. We purchased some information from him last year, I believe. That is an unfortunate connection."

"Very unfortunate. Bassington is the chief author of the initiative discussed in the aforementioned correspondence. And there's more: the alleged thief is also the grandson of the Prince de Condé on his mother's side. Formally recognized by the family, complete with the title of marquis."

"Well, why don't you make him the secret husband of Metternich's daughter, while you're at it?" said Drayton sarcastically.

"Don't laugh, Richard. I'm not making this up."

"You're telling me that a Condé, who is also related to Bassington, is stealing government documents?"

"We caught him breaking into my study at midnight," Barrett said flatly.

"Oh." The younger man brooded for a moment.

"Well, what did you want to consult me about?" he asked.

"This thief. This young man, Julien Clermont. That's what he calls himself; he doesn't use the Condé name."

"What about him?"

Barrett frowned. "We've reached something of an impasse. Clermont denies everything, we can't find the letter, and now some people, including Bassington, are starting to say that perhaps Clermont *did* have a reason to break into my house—that he was after Piers's diaries, which were also in my study."

"Who would break into a man's house at midnight to read his father's diaries? Why didn't he just ask you for the bloody things?"

"It's complicated." Barrett gave a précis of the events of the past month. When he had finished, his brother-in-law ran his fingers through his hair.

"Let me get this straight. The man sneaks into Bassington's house, trifles with his niece, accuses Bassington of seducing his mother, and is caught red-handed in your study at midnight, but he may be innocent?"

"Correct. I think the chances are very slim, but if he is innocent, the real criminal is still at large. We need to know, and that is where you come in."

Drayton looked at him, puzzled. Then he sucked in his breath. "Oh, no," he said, shaking his head. "No. Wrong man. You want Nathanson. Or his father. Not me."

"What we want," said Barrett, "is a fresh face. Someone new in town, as it were."

"Hell and damnation," muttered Drayton.

"The cursing has to go," Barrett reminded him.

Drayton's answer was unprintable.

* * *

"Miss, please. Please don't get me in trouble again," begged Emily. "Let's go home before anyone sees us."

"You didn't get in trouble," Serena said. "I explained everything to my uncle, and he said no one could attach any blame to you."

"Tell that to her ladyship," muttered the beleaguered maid. "She threatened to turn me off without a reference."

"Yes, but then she apologized." Serena strode quickly along, and poor Emily trotted after her. "I am not going to call on any gentlemen this morning."

The maid stopped dead. "We just did!"

"And he wasn't home." She grabbed the maid's arm and started walking again. "We are not doing anything wrong. The White Horse is a perfectly respectable inn."

"Miss Serena! You can't go into a public inn looking for a young man!"

"I know that," said Serena impatiently. "That's why you are with me. Can't you walk any faster?"

"The porter didn't say he was staying at the inn," Emily pointed out. "He merely said the trunks had been sent there. Your young man is likely long gone."

"Then there is nothing to worry about, is there?"

They had arrived at the bottom of Fetter Lane, where large gates led into the yard of the inn. Even Serena was momentarily taken aback by the size of the place. She was used to genteel establishments along the Bath road, not four-story monstrosities which stretched along an entire block. The courtyard was full of coaches and horses and shouting ostlers and piles of corded trunks; the noise was overwhelming. But a liveried attendant greeted them civilly enough and conducted them along a covered walkway to the main entrance of the inn.

"Go up and ask," hissed Serena, pointing to the clerk at the desk.

"Miss!"

"Just go! You will make me very conspicuous if you

argue." An older woman wearing an elaborately fringed pelisse had already turned and was surveying the two of them through a lorgnette.

Sullenly, Emily went up to the desk while Serena pretended to be absorbed in the decorations on a case clock against the near wall. Her hands were clenched so tightly around her reticule that they hurt.

"He's not here," said Emily's voice behind her. "They have no forwarding address."

Not here. As she expected. And what would she have done if there had been an address? Written to him? Followed him? She gave herself a shake.

Emily was tugging at her sleeve. "May we go now?"

"Why do you suppose anyone would put Egyptian beetles on a clock?" Serena said to no one in particular. She adjusted her bonnet and turned to follow the maid.

"Miss Allen! Miss Allen!" A slight, middle-aged man came hurrying across the room. "Miss Allen, if I might have a word with you?"

Emily was looking absolutely terrified; she clutched Serena and whimpered. "Someone's seen us! Miss Serena, I'll be sacked for sure!"

"Don't be a goose," Serena whispered. "It's Mr. Clermont's servant." She couldn't remember his name; her brain didn't seem to be working.

"Begging your pardon, Miss Allen," the man said, breathless. "If it isn't too great an impertinence—"

Vernon. That was his name. He looked dreadful; pale and haggard. "Not at all, Mr. Vernon." She wondered what she would say if he asked why she was here. He was a servant, she reminded herself. A valet. They were noted for their discretion, weren't they? He wouldn't ask. And surely he would know where Clermont had gone. She could send a message. A verbal message. That would not be as forward as writing.

"Miss Allen, I hope you will forgive me for asking, I don't want to presume—that is, I would not under ordinary circumstances venture such a question—" He was hopelessly tangled. He stopped and started again. "Do you have any news of Mr. Clermont?"

Shocked, she stared at him. "You don't know where he is?"

He shook his head. "I—I haven't seen him since Sunday evening. We were to leave for Portsmouth early Monday. This morning I received word from him through your uncle; the message said he had been called away unexpectedly, but then why didn't he at least take his cloak bag? And why were his trunks searched? And why didn't he send me money? Miss Allen, he *always* makes sure I have money before he goes out of town. I've been going back and forth between here and Brook Street, not knowing what to do. I've even been to your uncle's house, and to the Prince."

Serena became aware that the lorgnette was trained on her again. She drew Vernon over towards the clock and lowered her voice. "All his bags are still here? All his clothing? Everything?"

"What's left of it," he said bitterly. "The dragoons ripped his jackets to pieces. I don't know what they were looking for, but they didn't find it, and the longer they went without results the more damage they did. They pulled his new trunk apart; they punched out the tops of his hats; they cut open the bindings on all his books. They searched *me*, if you can believe it. When he returns I shall advise him to file an action."

How absurd, she thought. You couldn't file an action against dragoons. Didn't Vernon know that? Dragoons were sent on government business, to apprehend state prisoners—fugitives, or traitors, or spies.

That was when she remembered her uncle's threat to have Clermont arrested.

She said something to Vernon; she had no idea what. Her face felt numb; looking over at Emily she saw that the maid was white as a sheet. Serena suspected that she herself probably looked worse. Without another word she turned and went out the door.

It had taken nearly half an hour to walk from Brook Street to Fetter Lane. She made it back to Manchester Square in less than twenty minutes. She had no idea if Emily had managed to follow her. The minute Rowley opened the door she ran past him and burst into her uncle's study without knocking.

"Uncle, where is he?" she asked. "What's happened to him? Why were his bags searched?"

He was frozen, his pen halfway to the inkwell.

"Don't lie to me," she said, half sobbing. "Please don't lie. Don't tell me he's been called away for a few days. I just spoke with his valet. He doesn't believe it either. Did you have him arrested?"

The earl laid the pen very, very carefully down on the blotter. "How did you happen to see Mr. Clermont's servant?"

She didn't care if he knew, if her aunt knew. "I went to his house, and they directed me to the inn where his luggage had been sent. Mr. Vernon noticed me in the lobby and came over to greet me."

"Serena," he said, sighing.

"I know it's unmaidenly and shameless and I'm a disgrace—" She was struggling against tears, and losing.

Visibly distressed, her uncle got up and led her to a chair. "Sit; sit down; you must compose yourself, my dear. I shall ring for Emily—"

She interrupted him. She was crying a little now. "She's not back yet. She was with me, and I walked too quickly for her. You mustn't let Aunt Clara dismiss her, Uncle. It's not her fault."

"Of course not," he said, patting her hand as though she were a child.

"Don't ring for anyone. I'll be fine in a moment." She took out her handkerchief and pressed it to her face.

Then she took a few deep breaths. She lowered the handkerchief and looked up at her uncle.

"I am sorry," he said. It was not so much an apology as an answer to her question. He wasn't going to tell her anything.

Something had happened; she knew it. Sir Charles had been coming and going at odd hours; two officers had been closeted with her uncle yesterday; this morning he had disappeared for several hours without telling anyone, even Royce, where he was going. She had assumed this was all connected to the government work he and Barrett were doing. Now she wasn't so sure. She nodded, dabbed at her face again, and stood up.

"Shall I walk you upstairs?" he asked, still hovering in concern.

"No. Thank you. I apologize for my outburst."

He patted her hand again. "You were overwrought," he said. "Understandable. It will pass. Do not dwell on these past weeks overmuch; you will meet other young men." He escorted her out into the hall and looked anxiously after her as she started up the stair.

She kept going until she heard the bookroom door close behind him. Then she came back down, went through the dining room to the back staircase, and climbed up to the fourth floor. Simon was in the old nursery, studying. Two days ago Royce had told him he would be quite a bit behind other boys his age at Winchester, and he had been frantically conning Latin ever since.

When he heard her come in, he put his thumb in the volume of Livy he was reading and looked up.

"Simon," she said, "I need you."

26

When they brought him a priest, Julien knew he was in trouble. He didn't think much of the young Spaniard. His English was good, but he was barely older than Julien, and he had a rather awkward manner that did not bode well for his ability to comfort his parishioners. Julien supposed it was not all that easy to find Catholic priests in London, though, and on the whole he was grateful.

"I am sorry to find you here, my son," the priest said after the guard had left them alone.

"I'm not very happy about it myself," said Julien. "Won't you please take a seat, Father?" He pulled the chair away from the desk.

"How long has it been since you heard mass?" the priest asked as he sat down.

Julien thought for a moment. "Eight years?" he guessed. Then, hearing the indrawn breath, "I know; I'm sorry, Father."

"And how long since you made confession?"

"The same."

Frowning, the priest leaned forward. Julien thought he was in for a lecture, but instead the priest asked, "Is that a bruise on your face?"

Julien instinctively backed away from the lamp. "It's nothing."

"Barbarians," the priest muttered in Spanish. He

reached into the fold of his cassock and took out a small book. "I brought this for you."

Julien wasn't sure what to expect—perhaps a book of meditations. He found himself holding a seventeenth-century translation of Athanasius' *Life of St. Antony.* He said, surprised, "But this must be very valuable! Are you certain you wish to leave it with me? A—a friend has already engaged to send me some books."

"If you derive some comfort from it, that is all that matters."

Julien wasn't sure how comforting it would be to read about Satan tempting the saint with beautiful women. Perhaps he could alternate Athanasius and Charles Piers, if the diaries ever materialized.

"Oh, and this, as well." The priest held out a rosary. The beads were amber and the pendants gold filigree. It was even more priceless than the book.

Suddenly suspicious, Julien demanded, "Did my grandfather send you? Does he know I am here?" That rosary looked just like the ones his aunt had given him for his birthday every year until he left France.

"No, no. One of the English officers here is acquainted with my employer, Don Isidro. Captain Nathanson. He sent for me. I was glad to come."

Very relieved, Julien accepted the rosary without further protest. He had met several exiled Spanish aristocrats here in London, and they were prone to extravagant gestures of this sort.

The priest sat there, not saying anything. He wasn't looking at Julien; he had taken out his breviary and was thumbing through it absently. The silence was surprisingly comfortable. After a few minutes, Julien sat down on his pallet. He debated for several more minutes. He thought about looking like a coward. He thought about his troubled relationship with the church. But he said at last, "Do you think I should make confession?"

The priest closed his breviary. "You mean, do I think you are in imminent danger?" he asked dryly. "We are all in peril of our immortal souls at every moment, my son. I will answer as I would to any other man: if it would ease your mind, I would be glad to hear it."

It would ease his mind, Julien decided. He wasn't sure whether he really believed this earnest young Spaniard could grant him absolution, but he longed to tell someone the whole sordid story—someone objective, someone who had heard many other stories from many other men. "It may take quite some time," he warned.

"After eight years, I would be surprised if it did not. Just one moment." The priest rose and went over to the door. There was a low-voiced conference with the sentry. "I have asked him to move away, out of earshot," the priest explained as he sat back down.

"Thank you." Awkwardly, Julien knelt. "*In nomine Patris et Filii et Spiritus Sancti,*" he began, "*Ignosce mihi, pater, quia peccavi.*"

It did take a long time. Julien told the whole story from the beginning: his mother's disgrace, his hatred and love for his grandfather, his boyhood vow to punish his missing father, his descent into malice and fraud at Boulton Park, his near-seduction of Serena, his horror at discovering that his father was in fact a scoundrel, his arrogant refusal to defend himself after his arrest.

When he had finished, the priest said, looking thoughtful, "What, in your own mind, do you repent of the most?"

"Miss Allen," said Julien slowly, surprising himself as he said it. "Not the carnal sin, but the pledge behind it, the pledge I made without words and which I cannot redeem." He asked, trying not to sound anxious, "Can you grant me absolution, Father? For that, and for the rest?"

"You have not made a complete confession."

"I confessed to every one of the seven deadly sins except sloth," retorted Julien. "Do I need that one, too?"

"Every one except two," the priest corrected. "Sloth and Despair. Of all the great sins, despair is the worst. It can conceal itself within any of the others. In your case, it masquerades as pride. You should have told your story, in confidence, to one of the officers the moment you were arrested. But now you are right, it is too late. We will have to pray that justice prevails in spite of your error." He made the sign of the cross. "*Ego te absolvo a peccatis tuis in nomine Patris et Filii et Spiritus Sancti. Amen.*"

"Amen," said Julien automatically. Then he frowned. "Don't you want to give me a penance, Father?"

The priest looked around the cell. "I think you already have a penance. Peace be with you, my son."

Serena had never been good at concealing her emotions, and those emotions were usually strong ones. Sometimes she thought the fates must have had a hearty laugh when her parents had chosen to christen her Serena. Dignified grief was not her forte; anguish and fury were. Nor were her joys revealed by the quiet, glowing radiance recommended in deportment books. Even if Jackson had never seen her coming out of the woods so many years ago with André, everyone in her uncle's household would have suspected they were lovers. She had been so happy she had nearly danced instead of walking; she had jumped up whenever he came into the room; she had spent entire meals staring at him in a delighted trance. But she was older now, and wiser. She had learned that if she could not hide what she was feeling, she could at least hide herself. For the second time in three days she had shut herself in her room.

She had told her aunt she was feeling unwell, and in this case, unlike the infamous day of the Somerset

House headache, it was the truth. She did feel ill. She was feverish, giddy, so agitated she could not sit still. Every knock at the door brought her up out of her chair, swallowing nervously. The first time it was her aunt. The second time it was Emily, with food she could not eat. The third time it was Mrs. Childe, who was persuaded to leave only after Serena climbed into bed and pulled the covers over her face.

The fourth time it was Simon.

She pulled him into the room and locked the door behind him. "Were you able to find out anything?" she asked. "Was he arrested? Who ordered his luggage searched? Where did your father go this morning?"

"I'm not sure."

"Not sure about what?"

"Any of it." He added, looking worried, "The servants don't seem to know anything. Rowley and the footmen don't, at least. But I went over to the Barretts' and chatted with the grooms. It seems Sir Charles has been over to the Tower quite a bit recently. He's there now."

"The Tower?" she said faintly.

"Yes, so then I went to talk to Hoop—"

The earl's coachman was a dour, close-mouthed man. Serena didn't expect Simon would have had much success there. "And he told you it was none of your affair where he had driven your father," she guessed.

"Don't interrupt," he said crossly. "I wasn't such a fool as to ask him point-blank. I complained a bit about how dull London was without Ned and Jamie and then I said could he take me along the next time my father went to the Tower, because I wanted to see the menagerie. And he gave me this nasty look"—Simon gave an exaggerated imitation of a suspicious glare—"and said I knew too much and I was a cockatrice in my mother's bosom, or some such thing. And *then* he said it was no business of mine where he took my father. But he didn't say it very loud. More like muttered it."

"Let's go," said Serena, pulling her half-boots out of
the wardrobe.

"Go? Where?"

"To the Tower." She stuffed her feet quickly into the
boots, grabbed her reticule and a shawl, and darted out
the door, with Simon, protesting, right behind her.

"Serena, it's nearly half-past five! They'll never let us
go out now."

"I shan't ask anyone." She was hurrying down the
back stair. Dietrich, emerging from the kitchen, looked
at her in amazement as she brushed by.

"You should take a maid, or a footman," Simon objected as she swept him out the servants' entrance towards
the mews. "Shouldn't you? Mother was angry when you
went to Somerset House without taking anyone."

She stopped to consider this. "No," she said, "I
haven't time. Emily would come if I told her to, but by
then Aunt Clara or Uncle George might see us leaving."
At the gate behind the stables she stopped again.
"Simon, you needn't come," she said, looking down at
him. "I'm going to do something very, very unladylike
and I don't want you to be punished again for helping
me."

He considered this for a moment. "It's less unladylike
if I'm with you, isn't it?" he asked.

"Yes, but only a little."

"I'll come." He grinned suddenly. "Going to see a
prisoner in the Tower is much more exciting than going
to see decrepit old lions in the menagerie."

They hurried out through the mews onto Duke Street.
Serena had no idea how to find a hackney coach, but
Simon did. "We have to go down to Oxford Street," he
said confidently. "Ned Barrett found us one there last
time."

"You mean when the three of you went to St. Paul's?"
He nodded.

"I hope that isn't a bad omen," she muttered.

It certainly did not prove to be a good omen. Simon found them a driver easily enough, although the man gave Serena a round-eyed stare when she stepped out behind her cousin and climbed into the carriage. But when they reached the Tower it was a different story. The ornately clad warders at the gate did not even want to let them in. "Menagerie is closed, young sir," said one of them to Simon. "Come back tomorrow."

"We're not here for the menagerie," Serena said impatiently. "We're here to inquire about a prisoner."

The guard looked even more incredulous than the hackney driver. His companion said in gruff tones, "Begging your pardon, miss, but the prisoners are not on display to the public. You should take your pupil home; the streets here in the City are not safe after dark."

"I am not a governess," said Serena in cold, precise tones. "I am the ward of the Earl of Bassington, and this is my cousin, Viscount Ogbourne. I have reason to believe that my betrothed has been arrested on false charges and is being held here. I demand to see the Constable immediately."

The two guards glanced at each other in consternation. They were rescued by the appearance of a sharp-faced young man in more normal military clothing. This proved to be an officer attached to the garrison, who after hearing Serena's explanation and receiving it with equal amazement, escorted them into an unfurnished anteroom in an adjacent building. "Wait here," he said brusquely.

He returned twenty minutes later. "Miss Allen, you must have been misinformed. No prisoner by that name is currently housed in the Tower."

Serena had not been sure what answer she wanted to hear. In spite of all his lies and treachery, she did not want Julien Clermont locked up in the Tower as a spy. And yet it did not relieve her anxiety at all to hear that Simon's investigations had led them down a false trail.

"Are you certain?" she asked. "Perhaps he is using a different name. He is tall, with very fair hair and dark eyes. He would have been brought here late Sunday or early Monday."

"I am afraid that is impossible, ma'am. The wardens told me no new prisoners have been brought here for over six months." He added, as he saw her stricken expression, "You might try Newgate. Or the Fleet. It is very unlikely your Mr. Clermont would be in the Tower. It is not used for debtors or young bucks who brawl with the watch."

"He is a spy," Simon informed the officer helpfully.

"No, he isn't!" snapped Serena, glaring at her cousin.

"Well, he is not here, at all events," the young man said in what were meant to be soothing tones.

Serena clenched her fists and willed herself to respond politely. "Yes, I understand. Thank you for your assistance."

The officer cleared his throat. "I, er, spoke with my commander as well. He sends his compliments, and requests that you permit me to escort you home."

"We would be very grateful, of course," said Serena stiffly. In fact all she wanted was to be alone and sort through what Simon had told her and what she had just learned now. She had a feeling that an important piece of the puzzle was missing, that if she didn't find it in time something dreadful would happen.

Simon was looking around at the dark stone walls with great interest. He seemed far more cheerful now that he had heard Clermont was not imprisoned here. "Serena, will you bring me here again?" he asked, as they walked back towards the west gate. "I'd like to see the menagerie after all. And the mint. And the guns. And the scaffold."

"The mint is not open to visitors," the sharp-faced man

said. "Nor are the armories. But you may see the Royal crown and scepter, if you like, in the Jewel Office."

"Where do they execute people?" Simon said eagerly. "Do they still behead them?"

The officer laughed. "I am afraid we have descended to more mundane methods. Usually criminals are hung, up on Tower Hill. The last execution here in the Tower itself was over two hundred years ago."

"Well?" Colonel White said impatiently. He was sitting in the anteroom of his office, one floor below Clermont's cell. Next to him on one side sat Barrett; on the other side was Nathan Meyer, whose son was pacing back and forth across the narrow width of the chamber.

Drayton peeled off his cassock and dropped it onto the floor. "You didn't tell me Clermont had attended some blasted seminary school for ten years!" he said angrily to Barrett. "My Spanish is good; my French is passable. And he speaks English like a native. But would you like to know what language he confessed in? Latin! Twenty minutes of Latin! I didn't even *know* some of those words!" He threw himself into the one remaining chair and added in disgust, "I had to ask him to repeat a few key items. He now has a very poor opinion of the priests of the parish of San Ignacio."

"We are not interested in the language of his confession," White said coldly, "merely in its substance. Or is your Latin so rusty you could not understand him?"

"No, I followed it. After my initial shock. He's innocent. James was right on both counts. Clermont was after the diaries on Sunday night, and he was with the girl during those two hours on Saturday night. He's protecting her. His grandfather seems to be a cold-hearted tyrant, by the way. No wonder he wanted to find his father."

"Congratulations," Meyer said to his son. He didn't sound very happy.

Drayton looked around the room. No one else appeared pleased by his news, either. "What's wrong? I should think you would be relieved."

"Well, for one thing," said Barrett, "if he isn't the thief, we need to know who is. And what that person will do with the letter. And whether he plans to come back for more evidence. I don't fancy living with armed guards in my study for the duration of these negotiations. We've now spent four days following a false lead." He sighed. "Thank you, though, Richard. It was very good of you to help us out."

Drayton ran a hand over the newly shaven spot on the crown of his head. "You realize I won't be able to go out in public for weeks?"

"It grows back in faster than you'd think," said James. "In the meantime you can stay home with my sister and contemplate the approaching blessed event. Shall I walk you home? I believe my wife is at your house in any case."

There was a thoughtful silence after the two younger men had left.

"Are you thinking what I am thinking?" Barrett asked White.

"That we will to have to shoot Clermont even though he is innocent? Yes." He sighed. "I hate this sort of thing. When I took this post I thought I would be working under Wellington, not Castlereagh."

Meyer muttered agreement under his breath.

"They are on the same side," Barrett reminded them.

"Yes, but Wellington has scruples," White retorted.

"You are a colonel," Barrett said. "Colonels are not entitled to scruples. Or at least, they are not entitled to act on them against explicit orders from the Foreign Office." He turned to Meyer. "Can you make sure the appropriate individuals are present as witnesses?"

Meyer nodded glumly. "When shall we perpetrate this travesty?" he asked White.

"Tomorrow at sunset?" White was looking at Barrett. "No point in delaying. If the Prince somehow gets word of his grandson's whereabouts, he will raise holy hell and we will no longer be able to deny we knew he was a Condé."

"When we tell my son about this he will raise unholy hell," said Meyer. "Perhaps we should do it at noon."

"Noon it is." Barrett rose. "Until tomorrow, gentlemen."

27

A gentleman does not appear in public in his shirt-sleeves. Indeed, such attire is inappropriate even for the lower classes when not actually engaged in manual labor.

—Precepts of Mlle. de Condé

Julien had spent the morning very pleasantly—at least in physical terms. The corporal had come and shaved him again and had brought him a clean neck-cloth. His breakfast had arrived hot, for once, and there had been coffee instead of ale. The tedious and somewhat frightening interrogation sessions had magically ceased.

Unfortunately, now that he was rested, well-fed, and relatively clean, he had been free to contemplate his behavior over the past month. It was an ugly picture. His victims rose up before him in an accusing pageant: the countess, smiling proudly as she watched him dancing with Serena; the earl, horrified at his duplicity; Simon sitting up in bed, saying, "Is that why you gave me my telescope? So that you could come to our house?" And Serena, of course. Serena, looking up at him on the staircase behind the Barretts' ballroom. Serena in her bedchamber, pointing the pistol at his head. Moving her hand awkwardly up his body. Huddled on the floor, crying silently.

That one had been too painful. He had taken refuge

in the sufferings of St. Antony. It hadn't worked for long. The saint's victories over temptation and deception contrasted all too starkly with Julien's own behavior. In fact, Julien thought, his actions bore a disturbing resemblance to those of the defeated Satan. Lies. Seduction. Vengeance. He was sitting at the desk with the last of the coffee, reflecting that his quest had been appropriately rewarded by the discovery that he was the son of Charles Piers, when the priest reappeared.

In his present mood, Julien was quite happy to see him. "Good morning, Father," he said as he rose. "Thank you for the book; as you see, I have been studying it."

"I am glad you like it." The young priest did not look glad. He looked harried. "But we have more pressing affairs now."

A logical and ominous explanation for the absence of LeSueur and his brutish intimidators suddenly presented itself. Justice had not prevailed. They had concluded that he was guilty; hence, no need for further questioning. "I see."

"The colonel has asked me to prepare you. They will come for you at noon."

Instinctively Julien looked around for a clock. There wasn't one, of course, and he had left his watch behind when he went out on that fatal Sunday night for what he thought would be a quick visit to Barrett's study.

"It is just after eleven," said the priest, understanding what he wanted to know. "We have nearly an hour."

Julien thought that on the whole it was better not to have too much time for further contemplation. He had spent the whole morning engaged in that activity, and he would have preferred being pushed down the stairs again. But he could not suppress a morbid curiosity about the details. "Will they hang me?" he asked.

"Certainly not!" The priest was shocked. "That would

be far too unreliable. It will be a firing squad. Very dignified."

There was a certain delicious irony here, Julien thought. The English had screamed the loudest and the longest when Napoleon had shot the Duke of Enghien. And now they were going to shoot Enghien's cousin. Against the wall of a medieval dungeon, just like Vincennes. All he needed was a dog to howl over his body.

"Might I—do I have time to write a letter or two?" he asked.

"If they are brief. You must be ready, you know, when the soldiers come, and there is a great deal at stake."

His immortal soul, of course. Julien wondered how many sins he could possibly have committed between yesterday afternoon and this morning while locked in a windowless cell, but he did not think his letters would take long. The sentry fetched pen and ink and paper, and Julien sat back down with the dregs of the coffee and composed four brief notes. The first was to his grandfather. He said merely that circumstances had arisen which made it unlikely they would meet again, and that he wished to convey his respect and admiration for the Prince. He could not bring himself to lie and thank the man for the grudging gift of his name. Instead he would have to hope that respect would be sufficient. He wrote a similar but warmer note to Derring, and asked him to help Vernon find a new position. The letter to Bassington took a bit longer. After some false starts, he produced the following:

> *My Lord:*
>   *When you receive this, the sentence will have been carried out—quite publicly, they tell me— and it will no longer be possible to conceal the fact of my arrest and trial. As a last favor I beg not only that I might express once again my regrets to you and your household, but also that I might*

*be permitted to address your niece by means of the
enclosed.*

*Your servant,
Julien de Clermont*

When it came to writing Serena, however, he could
not think of what to say. He sat staring at the blank piece
of paper until the priest, with very unclerical impatience, coughed suggestively. At last he wrote only two
lines, and signed it with his initials. Then, before he
could change his mind or add any postscripts, he sealed
it up, enclosed it in the letter to the earl, and looked at
the priest.

"That's the lot," he said.

The priest muttered something about people's odd notions of what was important and motioned him to his
feet.

Julien stood. He was remembering the priest's remarks about despair. "Would you advise me to protest?
Request a delay?"

The other man shook his head. "Not a good idea.
Trust me, the sooner the better with this sort of thing.
Your audience would be very unsympathetic, in any
case."

That was certainly true. Julien pictured himself explaining to Barrett or the earl that he could not
possibly be the thief because he had been breaking
into the earl's house—again—and spending time with
his niece. In her bedchamber. Watching her take off
her nightgown. Bassington would shoot him right then
and there.

"Very well," he said. Dignity. He would have dignity.
That was something. "I'm ready."

"Good. Take off your jacket."

* * *

Serena was still keeping to her room the following morning. To her surprise, there had been no scoldings as a result of her expedition with Simon. The countess seemed to feel that it was a miracle she had not gone into a decline and expired; eccentric behavior was to be expected after the shock of her suitor's perfidy. Her uncle was preoccupied with whatever affair was taking him to the Tower—perhaps Clermont's arrest, perhaps something else; he had not been seen at a meal in two days. Royce, too, was looking gaunt and anxious; he had been spending long hours copying drafts of the public portion of the earl's reports and ferrying sealed packets back and forth between Whitehall, the Barretts', and Manchester Square.

When there was a knock at her door, Serena assumed it was Simon. Now that Royce was so busy, her cousin had taken to bringing her his Latin when he could not work it out on his own. "Come in!" she called, hiding her book hastily under her skirt. Unable to resist the temptation to impress Simon, she had been reading an English translation of Livy.

It was Rowley, looking flustered. "There is a young man below with a message for you, Miss Serena," he said. "I have shown him into the small drawing room."

"A message?" Who would send her a message? Rowley clearly didn't know; he was giving her puzzled little glances as he led the way downstairs. Could it be from Clermont? But no, her uncle had expressly instructed all the servants to return unopened any communications from their disgraced former guest. An emissary from Julien would never have been admitted to the house. As for Philip, he had left town; his sister had at last produced his first nephew and he had been summoned to Lincolnshire.

The man in the drawing room was a complete stranger. He was wearing a green military uniform; he looked young, almost too young to be an officer. Mrs. Childe and her aunt were attempting to make polite conversation, but he was barely listening to them. The moment she came in, he swung around without even bothering to excuse himself.

"Miss Allen?" At her nod, he said, "I have an urgent message for you. May we speak apart for a moment?"

She drew him across the room to the embrasure by the window. "Who are you?" she demanded. "Who sent you?"

"Never mind that," he said impatiently. "I need to ask you something. You must excuse me; I have no time to spare your feelings. Was Julien Clermont with you just before dawn on Sunday morning?"

She stood frozen, hardly believing what she had heard.

"Miss Allen, please!" he said in low, urgent tones. "Was he?"

She had never been a good liar. "Yes."

"Are you willing to swear as much before a tribunal? I cannot guarantee that your testimony will not be made public, although I will do my best."

A tribunal. He had been arrested. "Yes," she said again, louder. "Mr. Clermont was with me at that time, in my bedchamber. For several hours. I will swear to it." Her aunt had risen and was staring at her, one hand pressed to her throat.

"Will you come with me now? He is in imminent danger of being executed, largely because he has been unable to account for his whereabouts during those hours."

The countess was shaking her head. Serena wasn't sure if she was telling her to say no, or denying that she had ever harbored such a depraved young woman in her household. "Serena," she said feebly. "Surely—there must be some mistake." She turned to the young man. "There is some mistake," she repeated.

He didn't even look at her. He had seized Serena's

hand and was hurrying down the stairs with her and out
the front door. Her aunt and Mrs. Childe followed, making little noises of distress and protest.

At the sight of several carriages blocking the south-
ern end of the square, the young officer swore under his
breath. He beckoned to the groom holding his horse. "I
will ride ahead and see what I can do," he said. "You
have until noon."

Royce came up, out of breath, clutching a dispatch
case. "What is this? Why was I called out here?" he
said, looking back and forth from Serena to the two
older women to the officer, who was now in the saddle.

"Are you acquainted with Miss Allen?" the officer
asked.

"Yes, although, if I may—"

The young man cut him off. "Get her to the Tower. At
once." He touched his hat and wheeled away.

"Serena, you cannot mean to go!" Her aunt was
clutching her arm. Then she saw Serena's face. "At least
let me come with you," she begged. "I will order the
carriage . . ."

"No time," said Serena mechanically. With a vague
notion of finding another hackney she began walking
towards Oxford Street, with Royce on her heels. Then
she broke into a run, but she was hampered by her
skirts, and her thin slippers skidded sideways on the un-
even paving. She stopped and looked at the vehicles
clustered at the lower end of the square.

"Whose carriage is that?" she asked Royce, pointing
to the closest one.

"I don't know."

"Lady Wallace's," said her aunt, who was hurrying
up behind her.

"Can you drive it?" Serena asked Royce.

"Yes, but why? What has happened?"

"If I don't reach the Tower by noon, they will kill
Mr. Clermont."

That silenced him. He turned gray.

She marched over to the coachman. "We need to borrow your mistress's carriage. It is a matter of life or death."

"I'm sorry, miss, but it would be much as my place is worth—" He stopped, gulped, and got down from the box. Royce had taken a very serviceable-looking pistol out of the dispatch case and was pointing it right at him.

"Thank you," Royce said. "Could you assist the ladies?"

Serena had already jerked open the door. She had decided it was faster to take her aunt and Mrs. Childe than to argue with them, and she came close to pushing her elderly kinswoman into the coach when she had trouble managing without steps. "Hurry," was all she said to Royce.

She hung out the window all the way down Oxford Street, which was jammed with wagons and pedestrians. Royce was screaming at other vehicles to get out of the way, lashing both drivers and horses with his whip. When they came into High Holborn the traffic eased somewhat and she sat down again briefly, but as they passed St. Paul's the clock began to chime, and she thought her heart would stop as the notes rang out.

La, fa, sol, do. Do, sol, la, fa. La, fa, sol, do.

Silence.

She clutched the doorstrap in relief. Not noon, not yet, only the third quarter hour. She put her head out the window again. They bumped down Cornhill, with Royce taking the carriage right over some boards piled in the street in front of a shop; the two older women screamed slightly as the wheels bounced back onto the paving. At the Custom House, Thames Street narrowed precipitously to accommodate the scaffolding for the construction and there was a line of vehicles waiting their turn to pass; Royce somehow managed to scrape around them.

When they pulled up at the Tower, Serena already had the door open. She jumped out before the coach stopped moving, tore past a trio of astonished guards through the inner gate, and then halted in dismay. She was here, but where was she to go? She turned frantically, seeing nothing but stone walls. Then, with a sob of relief, she spotted the man in the green uniform. He was running towards her, pointing towards a doorway in one of the circular keeps built into the inner wall. She dashed through it, and he caught up with her as she emerged into the vast central courtyard.

"Hurry," he said, leading her at a near trot towards the far end of the quadrangle. There were newer buildings there, red brick instead of stone, pleasant, homely buildings which seemed out of place amid the ancient blocks which rose around them. On one side of the nearest brick building a small crowd was gathered—mostly soldiers, a few civilians. She recognized her uncle, and Sir Charles. Out of a door in the building came two more soldiers, with a familiar figure walking between them. He was in his shirt. His hair shone in the pale March sun; he was tilting his head back, looking up at the sky, where a few birds were circling lazily. Next to him a priest was walking, moving closer occasionally to speak into his ear. She saw Clermont nod, then accept something from the priest. It looked like a rosary. He held it in one hand, clutched to his chest. With the other hand he pushed his hair back from his face. The crowd fell back; the milling soldiers suddenly formed a line. Clermont had disappeared. Then she saw him, still with the priest, his white shirt billowing slightly in the breeze against the windowless brick wall. The priest moved to one side.

"No," she said. She tried to scream. "No!" Her legs were trembling; she could barely walk, let alone run, but she forced herself to keep moving, to wave her hands and cry out.

Her companion was sprinting forward, shouting someone's name in a high, hard voice. The clock chimes began to ring. Four notes down. Four notes up. The soldiers raised their rifles. They hadn't blindfolded him, or tied his hands. It wasn't noon yet. Four more notes down.

Eight guns fired in near-unison, just before the last ascending peal of the carillon.

"It isn't noon yet," she said in a faint voice. Royce was beside her now, clutching her arm. "They didn't wait for noon," she told him, despairing. "I could have reached him if they had waited." The tall, fair-haired figure was slumped at the base of the wall. Before she turned away, shuddering, she saw the red stain spreading across the ruins of his shirt.

Then the bells began to toll.

28

LeSueur burst in through the door of White's office a few minutes after noon. Meyer looked up from the list of names he had been scanning. "How did it go?" he asked.

"It was ghastly." The scar was livid against the pallor of his face. "Count yourself lucky Barrett decided you should not be there."

"Did James manage to find Miss Allen? And the others?"

"Yes." The captain grimaced. "The secretary—Royce?—must have driven like a madman. They arrived a few minutes early; we had to bring Clermont out before the clock struck noon. Miss Allen was very shaken, of course, as was the countess, but we didn't need the smelling salts for either one of them. As for the older woman, you were right about her." Le Sueur shuddered. "She smiled—she actually *smiled* when they fired. Not a nervous smile, either."

"What of Royce?" Meyer leaned forward. "Did he see it?"

"Yes. He was the one who needed the smelling salts. He fainted."

Barrett came in, looking exhausted. "What a bloody mess," he said in disgust. "In all senses of the word. They've brought Clermont inside, but I can't stay here more than a minute. You'll have to go down and see to things without me. Miss Allen has gone off with her aunt, but not, apparently, before leaving word with the Constable that she intends to file a charge of false imprisonment and wrongful death. I must go and intercept that message at once. Meanwhile Bassington is demanding an immediate explanation of our 'rash and precipitate actions.' I've put him down the hall in Southey's old office. I hope to God we got some results, Meyer."

"We may have. I'll know more after I talk to Drayton."

Barrett looked around. "Is there anything to drink in here? Anything fortifying, that is?"

Meyer got up and took a small flask out of a coat hanging in back of the door.

After a quick swallow, Barrett set it down. "Right. I'm off to the Constable. Don't let Bassington talk to anyone before I get back. If he asks to see the body, put him off."

LeSueur looked at the two older men. "You didn't tell Bassington about this? Didn't warn him in advance?"

Meyer said wearily, "We haven't told him anything for quite some time. If Clermont was innocent, as we now believe, then someone else is guilty. Someone with a very detailed knowledge of the earl's household *and* Sir Charles's household."

"You cannot possibly think—"

"I don't know what to think." Barrett went to the door. "I'm not allowed to think. I'm not allowed to do anything until I find that damned letter and the damned spy who took it. I never thought I would see the day I would be praying that Napoleon would *not* surrender. At least not quite yet." He slammed the door behind him.

The captain looked at the still-quivering doorknob. "Sir Charles seems a bit upset," he said cautiously.

Meyer, who knew how rarely Barrett lost his temper, said only, "He is in a very delicate position." He passed the sheet he had been reading over to LeSueur. "Here you are. You will be posted down to Oxfordshire with a detachment of twelve men. All those on this list are to be kept under strict watch at all times."

LeSueur ran his eye down the column of names. "All of them? Even the women?"

"All of them." Meyer rose. "The colonel may have further instructions for you this evening, after we have spoken with Major Drayton." He handed LeSueur the flask. "Take this down to Lord Bassington. He'll need it."

"Where will you be, sir? When Sir Charles returns?"

"In the cellar. Assisting Major Drayton with his necromantic rites. Send James down as well, when he reappears."

Serena didn't remember much about what happened at the Tower after her last glimpse of Clermont. Someone fainted, perhaps more than one someone, and there was a great deal of confusion as the victim or victims were pulled off to the side and revived. Her aunt, however, did not faint. She did not succumb to hysterics or demand her vinaigrette. Instead, she had listened patiently to Serena's half-incoherent request. Within a few minutes she had found a clerk to take Serena's message to the Constable's office. Then she had herded Serena and Mrs. Childe back into the stolen carriage and had found a driver to take them home. Serena had no memory of that trip, no memory of being taken to her room, no memory of Emily helping her undress. She was vaguely aware that her aunt and Mrs. Digby and Mrs. Childe were hovering over her, pressing cups of tea on her. They whispered about "poor Serena"; they seemed to think that she was confused, or shocked, or grieving, that this was only a larger, more terrible version of the night Clermont had come to see her uncle.

She was not confused. She was not shocked, or grieving; that was for later. She was not poor Serena. She was encased in rage; saturated, stiff, choked with it. All she wanted was to confront her uncle. Until he appeared, nothing had any meaning; no one else existed.

Eventually they stopped hovering and left her alone. She didn't lock her door this time. Without noticing that she was wearing a nightgown and wrapper, she paced the upper landing, leaning over the balustrade to survey the entryway below. The servants sidled past her, whispering to each other.

Her uncle came home more than an hour later. She saw him listening to Rowley, who had met him at the door; saw Rowley gesture towards the staircase. The earl walked slowly over to the center of the hall and looked up at her. His face was drawn. As he climbed the steps towards her, leaning on the banister, he looked like an old man, weary and stiff.

When he stopped in front of her, silent, she did not know what to say. She had expected to see pity, or stern resolve, or defensive anger. Perhaps even guilt, although her uncle was normally a man too sure of himself to display remorse. He did not look sure of himself now, and the certainty of her own anger faltered as well. She had planned to accuse him, denounce him.

Instead she asked, her voice trembling slightly, "Did you—were you responsible for that? For what happened? Did you have him arrested?"

She could see in his face that the answer was no, and a terrifying void opened in front of her, a formless future with no purpose and no justice.

"I was very angry with him after I discovered he had been deceiving all of us," he said heavily. "I won't lie to you, Serena. When he was arrested I felt vindicated, and I accepted his guilt too quickly. But I had good evidence for doing so, at the time." He took her elbow and led her into the nearest room, which happened to be a small parlor attached to one of the spare bedchambers. "Come here," he said, sitting down and pulling a chair over for her. "Let me try to explain. You know that there had been some concern about the papers I was working on with Sir Charles. You know that it was decided to keep those papers in Sir Charles's safe here in London."

She nodded.

"Mr. Clermont was arrested in the act of breaking into the room where that safe is located. I had nothing to do with the arrest; he was apprehended by soldiers who were already watching for him. They were watching for him because on the previous night, someone had broken into that same room and abstracted part of a valuable document. It was hoped that the thief would return for the rest. And he did. Or so everyone thought."

He sighed. "Now we come to the part where I *am* to blame. Once you had proved to me that he was Charles's son, I realized that he was telling the truth about his motives for staying at Boulton Park. More importantly, I knew now that he did have a reason to break into Barrett's study. Now that he believed my cousin to be his father, he wanted his diaries. He could no longer approach me to ask for them, and somehow he had learned where they were."

"Simon," she whispered.

"But I only mentioned this in passing to Colonel White. I should have made sure the tribunal heard my story, but I hung back because I was still angry, angry at his treatment of you. And now I hear that the most damning evidence against him, from the night of the theft, was misleading as well. That he was with you just before he was seen near Sir Charles's house."

"He was."

"Where?"

"In my bedchamber."

"In that case I am not sure his death is to be regretted," he said with an expression of distaste.

She gripped the arms of her chair. "And am I so precious, Uncle? Am I worth a man's life? Are you so certain you know what happened in my room that night?"

"Isn't it enough that he was there?" But his scowl was fading.

"I will tell you what happened. He came to apologize. I tried to seduce him—" He snorted in disbelief, but she put out her hand. "No, listen to me. I have no reason to lie, not now. He was kneeling at my feet, begging my forgiveness, and I threw myself at him. I kissed him. I even started to take off my clothes. And he stopped me." She was silent for a moment, then went on: "Do you know what he said? He said, 'I will not ruin you the way my father ruined my mother.' He said he would never beget a bastard to live as he had. He said I deserved happiness. Do I look happy to you, Uncle? Do I?"

He didn't answer.

"I want him exonerated," she said fiercely. "I want his name cleared. That is all I ask of you, and I think, under the circumstances, that it is a very modest request. After all, he is a Piers. You should want justice done, however belatedly, for the family's sake."

He sighed. "I will see to it, once I am back in London. It should not be difficult; the Foreign Office decided that he was not a spy approximately an hour after they had him shot." He added, after a pause, "We will therefore be returning to Boulton Park immediately. I have been asked to resign my place on the treaty commission."

For the first time since noon, something besides the murder of Julien Clermont made an impression on her. The treaty commission had been the culmination of her uncle's dream of restoring order to a continent ravaged by twenty years of war. She said, horrified, "You have?"

"Since Mr. Clermont is not the thief," he said harshly, "someone else is. Most likely, according to Sir Charles, someone residing at Boulton Park. Me, for example. Or your aunt. Or Simon. Or even you. We are all under suspicion. The entire household will be under surveillance, at a safe distance from London."

"I thought Sir Charles was your friend," she said numbly.

"He is." He walked to the door. "I would do the same, in his place." Then he turned back. "Oh, I had nearly forgot. Mr. Clermont wrote me. He asked me to pass this on to you." He held out a folded square of cheap paper. "The seal has been broken, but not by me. I believe the warders read all letters written by prisoners in the Tower before they are sent on."

She unfolded it. "They must be very well-educated warders," she said, raising her eyebrows. "It is in Latin. A quote from St. Augustine, apparently." There was nothing else there; just the quotation and the source, above his initials. *sero te amavi. Augustinus.*

He hesitated. "Do you need Royce to translate it for you?"

She shook her head. "The Latin is not difficult. I can read it."

He left her alone, holding the note. It was very, very simple Latin. Even Simon would have no trouble with it. *sero te amavi.* Too late did I love you. Too late have I loved you. Too late did I come to love you.

St. Augustine had been talking to God. It was never too late to love God. Loving men was a chancier proposition.

29

"You could have told me a bit earlier that it was all a sham," Julien said acidly to the priest. He was still a bit dizzy; he had slammed his head against the brick wall as he fell and had been in a genuine stupor when the soldiers carted him back into the armory. It had been quite some time before he could sit up without losing his equilibrium. "Before I wrote those letters, for example."

"I thought you knew. The letters seemed a clever, authentic touch. My apologies." The priest was wiping the pig's blood off of Julien's hands and chest.

Julien jerked away. A disquieting thought had occurred to him. "You didn't actually deliver those letters, did you?"

"We did, of course. Why?"

He closed his eyes and groaned softly. "I thought I would never see Miss Allen again in this world. I told her I loved her."

"Is it true?"

"You heard my confession."

"So I did." He daubed at a stain on his own cassock. "You know, if you had told her that yourself, a bit earlier, you would have been spared a lot of misery. As would she." He surveyed Julien's torso critically and then handed him a clean shirt. "Still, this may prove to be the best thing for all concerned, in the end. You did quite well, especially considering we were only able to rehearse once before they came for you. Are you up to playing dragoon now?" He indicated a heap of military clothing on the table. "These should fit; Dauncy is quite tall. We must somehow smuggle you out of the Tower. The most dramatic and effective method, from our point of view, would be a coffin, but I fancy you would not be very comfortable. And Miss Allen might demand to see the body if she saw us hauling a casket through the water gate. She has already threatened to denounce the Constable for executing an innocent man."

"The devil! Serena is here? Where? Do you mean to say she witnessed that farce?" He was almost through the door before the other man could stop him. "Let me go," he panted, straining against the iron grip on his arm. "She'll think she's partly to blame, she'll be frantic—" He was slightly taller than his opponent and unencumbered by clerical skirts; though confinement had taken the edge off his strength, he was inexorably forcing his way towards the door until the other man, exasperated, hauled off and struck him, hard, across the face. Black waves danced across Julien's vision as he leaned against the wall.

"You can call me out, if you choose," the priest said, breathing hard, "but for your own sake—for Miss Allen's sake—stop and think for one minute. Why on earth do you suppose we put you through that ordeal? To have you pop out of this room like Punch in the puppet show an hour after your execution?"

"What do you mean?" Dazed, Julien sank back into the chair. It was beginning to sink in that instead of being rescued, as he had thought, he had been used. He stared at his companion, eyes narrowing. The Spanish accent had mysteriously vanished some time ago; now he saw the telltale raw edges of the tonsure.

"You're no priest." It was a statement, not a question.

"No."

"You sneaking piece of filth," choked Clermont, remembering with terrible clarity what he had confessed to the "priest," "I *will* call you out! Of all the low-down, despicable—"

"There's gratitude for you," retorted the other man. "Save a man's life, and what is your reward? Three members of that board of inquiry were quite ready to shoot you in earnest, you know. And you certainly were not contributing anything to your own defense. So my colonel persuaded me to come hear your confession. I did not pass on all the items you told me, if that relieves your mind. White and Barrett already had their doubts; once I gave them my word as an officer of the Crown that you were elsewhere on the night of the burglary they had no interest in your activities."

"Your colonel?" Clermont had some confused notion of a lay brother serving as chaplain until he remembered Catholics could not hold commissions in the British army.

"Permit me to introduce myself. Major Richard Drayton. Second-in-command of His Majesty's garrison force, Gibraltar. White is not, in fact, my colonel. I'm meant to be on leave at the moment. But I reported to him until I was sent to Gibraltar."

It took Julien a full minute to assimilate this revelation. "You are a major? Not even Catholic?" He stopped. "It's impossible. It's true your Latin was a bit rusty, but you knew the office; you rattled off the blessing perfectly—"

"I spent four hours being drilled by another officer in our service who has traveled through Spain disguised as a priest."

Julien gave up trying to follow this on his own. "I don't understand," he said. "Who are you? What concern am I of yours? Why did you pretend to shoot me? Who are you working for? Are you spies?"

Drayton winced. "Spy is such an ugly word. We prefer to call ourselves couriers. We are assisting the Foreign Office in a confidential investigation; that is all I can tell you."

"You mean that you thought I was purloining documents from Bassington," said Clermont bluntly.

"*He* did not. I did, at first. You must admit that there was good reason for me to do so." It was Meyer, standing in the doorway.

Julien looked back and forth, from false priest to false naturalist. "But then, once you knew I was not the thief, why the sham execution?"

"If you are not the thief, someone else is," was Meyer's enigmatic answer. "And that is why we cannot, as yet, reveal that you were not killed just now."

"Oh, come, you cannot expect me to be content with that!" Clermont got up again and headed for the door. "You have no legal cause to detain me, by your own admission. If you are going to talk in riddles I will take my leave. Miss Allen's peace of mind is of far greater concern to me than your underhanded machinations for finding this so-called thief."

Drayton blocked his way. "Don't you want to see him caught?" he demanded. "Don't you realize that the thief almost certainly took advantage of your presence in Bassington's household to frame you, to set you up as the culprit? You could help us trap him."

"My recent experiences have given me a profound distaste for the pursuit of vengeance, as you might realize if you called to mind some of the less salacious portions of my confession."

"Vengeance? What about justice?"

"I have no desire to turn catchpoll," said Julien with hauteur. "England has a perfectly adequate constabulary for those purposes."

Meyer stirred. "Do you know who the thief had chosen as his scapegoat before you appeared? The viscount. Who is now once again a suspect. Don't you believe you owe the boy something?"

Julien looked at him darkly. "Do I? What did you have in mind? Should I let your men use me for target practice again? Volunteer for another week in gaol? Publish a posthumous confession in the *Gazette*?"

"What we would like," said Meyer, "is to have you tell us everything you know about every person in the earl's household. You thought the man was your father, after all. You were so curious about him and his family that you went to a great deal of trouble to gain entry to Boulton Park. Surely you learned something during your stay which might help us identify the real thief."

Julien turned to Drayton. "Forgive me if my memory is playing me false—I have taken a few blows on the head lately. But did you or did you not, yesterday afternoon, grant me absolution for spying on the earl—after agreeing with me that it was one of the most loathsome schemes you had ever come across in your clerical career?"

"It was loathsome," said Drayton calmly. "Violating the seal of the confessional was loathsome as well, even though I am not a priest. But I did it. It seemed less loathsome than allowing them to shoot you with real bullets."

Julien digested this for a moment in silence. "And after I betray Bassington and his family yet again? Then what?"

"Then," said Meyer, "we send you down to Oxfordshire with eleven real dragoons and hope that your dramatic resurrection produces an equally dramatic revelation."

For two days Serena had been trying to find an opportunity to talk privately with Simon. During the hurried departure from London it had been impossible; during the journey itself even more impossible. Her aunt had been so solicitous and omnipresent that Serena had been forced to feign sleep for hours at a time in the carriage. But now they were finally back at Boulton Park, the servants were unpacking, and she had taken advantage of the confusion to grab Simon and drag him off to his secret room. After her conversation with her uncle the day before they left town, she was well aware that neither she nor Simon would be allowed to disappear at will from now on. She had seized what might be her only chance. For one thing, she wanted to tell him to watch his step. She was afraid he would do something foolish right in front of the soldiers. And for another thing, she had a very awkward question to ask him, and she wanted to ask him here, where no one could hear them or even see his face when she asked it. But Simon, of course, didn't want to listen to lectures. He wanted to talk about the soldiers and their search for the mysterious document thief.

"It is Mrs. Childe," he said, for the third time.

"She probably thinks it is you," Serena pointed out. "I know she isn't very agreeable, Simon, but why would you fasten on her as a suspect?" At least he hadn't decided it was his own father. She had edited her report of Clermont's fate and the earl's warning drastically for Simon's benefit.

He shrugged. "I don't know. She never looks anyone in the eye. And she has nearly as many jewels as mother, even though she is a poor widow."

"Perhaps they are paste." Then she said, suspicious, "How do you know how many jewels she has?"

"I got her jewelry case open a few months ago." He said, with a malicious smile, "I shortened the chain on her favorite clasp, as well, so that she would think she was growing stout. And it worked. Haven't you noticed she is drinking vinegar after breakfast now?"

"Simon!"

"She's horrid, Serena. You know she is. And if it isn't her, it will be someone I *like*."

She said, exasperated, "You do realize that pranks of that sort will be taken as more than boyish mischief? That the soldiers who are here will ask the servants who might know how to get into Sir Charles's safe, and all the servants will immediately name you?"

He scowled. "I don't care."

She took a deep breath and asked the question she had been postponing. "It wasn't you, was it, Simon? You didn't take those letters, did you?"

She couldn't read his expression. It might have been outrage, it might have been surprise and alarm.

"You can tell me," she said hastily. "But you must tell me right now. I can protect you, I promise. No one will shut you up in prison or shoot you."

"Mr. Clermont wasn't even the thief, and they shot him," he pointed out.

Black guilt swallowed her. He was right. How could she promise him safety when she hadn't even been able to exonerate someone who was innocent? She stared down at the cracked floorboards.

"Serena." He was shaking her. "Serena, stop looking like that! It wasn't me."

"Good," she said dully.

He shook her again. "Serena! It wasn't."

This was important. This was why she was here. She pulled herself together. "You swear it?"

"Word of honor."

"Let me see inside your trunk, then." She had already searched his room in London, as thoroughly as she knew how, on the pretext of helping Mrs. Digby pack.

He was shaking his head.

"Either I inspect this trunk, or I ask Hubert to carry it out for the dragoons to search. Which do you prefer?"

"Turn your back, then, so you cannot see how I open it," he ordered.

Obediently, she turned towards the wall. She heard rustling noises, and the clink of a buckle, and then Simon's voice. "You can look now."

It was empty. She ran her hand around the lining to

make sure there were no papers tucked inside and inspected the lid for good measure. Nothing.

"Simon." She couldn't help herself, she had to ask. "Why do you keep an empty trunk sealed up in your hidden room?"

"I knew you would say that," he said in disgust. "Because I might want to keep something in there sometime, that's why. Because it was funny to see the servants look at it and hear them talk about what might be in there." He sighed. "I suppose having secrets isn't a very good idea at the moment, is it?"

"No," she said sadly, "it isn't." She got to her feet and dusted off her skirts. "Let's go, before anyone misses us. Does anyone else know about this room and your trunk besides me and the servants?"

"My mother. Jasper. Mr. Clermont." He thought for a moment. "I offered to show this room to Mr. Meyer, but he never came."

"Well, I don't think anyone will tell the soldiers about it, but just in case, I would leave the trunk open for now." She was thinking of what Vernon had told her about the damage to Clermont's luggage and clothing. She wasn't sure how Simon would feel if he came back here and saw his trunk torn to pieces, and she didn't want to find out.

Julien was back at the Burford Arms. It felt very odd. No one looked at him, of course, one of a dozen faceless dragoons milling around the taproom, but he took care to keep well away from Budge and the barmaids, just in case. He spoke as little as possible to his fellow soldiers. He might speak English like a native, but he didn't speak it like an enlisted man.

"Dauncy!" It took him a minute to remember that that was his name and turn towards the speaker. One of the senior troopers had come in. "Colonel wants you," the man said, jerking his head towards the door to the hallway.

That was his cue. His mouth felt dry suddenly and he took a last gulp of ale. It didn't help. He climbed the narrow wooden staircase wishing that it could be a month ago, that he could be returning to Vernon to announce that he would not, after all, be calling on the Earl of Bassington. Or better, that he would be calling at Boulton Park, but for the purpose of courting the earl's niece, having discovered that he was not as ineligible a suitor as he had always supposed.

Instead he was on his way to a meeting which would likely result in someone else being shot. With real bullets. He concluded gloomily that there might be worse things than being executed for a crime you had not committed. Condemning someone else to be shot, for example, without being certain they were guilty.

He heard voices behind the door of his former room, but when he knocked they fell silent.

"Come in." It was Barrett.

They were all there—both Meyers, Barrett, LeSueur, and the colonel. He closed the door and leaned against it. "Surely you do not really wish to involve me," he said, making one last attempt to escape. "I am a duplicitous bastard who became involved by accident, remember? The son of the man who would be the most likely suspect were he not dead?"

"We must force the thief's hand," said White. "Our evidence at the moment is very thin. We have searched all the private rooms in the residence as thoroughly as we could without revealing our suspicions. The missing letter is not there. Our best hope is to trick the thief into incriminating himself—or herself. That is where you come in, Mr. Clermont."

"I may have been a bit underhanded in my dealings with Lord Bassington," said Julien angrily, "but I do not believe that episode entitles you to consider me an expert in deception. Use Mr. Meyer here, if you need a play-actor. Or that false priest, that Major Drayton fellow."

White growled something under his breath, but Barrett, ever the peacemaker, held up his hand. "Mr. Clermont, just a moment. We seem to be misunderstanding each other. We will not ask you to take part in any deception. You will not be there to conceal the truth, but to reveal it."

"What do you want of me, then? What am I to say? What am I to do?"

"All you need do is be present. The spy believes you to be dead. Even the most self-possessed criminal may falter momentarily when confronted by a man who has been executed in his place."

"And who is the criminal?"

Barrett sighed. "We are not certain. The plan is to assemble several individuals who seem likely suspects and then bring you out and observe their reactions."

"Haven't you attempted something of this sort before?" Julien folded his arms. "I thought that was the point of my mock execution."

"It was." White's tone was peremptory. "Our list of likely suspects derives in part from what we saw that day at the Tower. Our chief suspect fainted when you were shot. Our second candidate seemed extraordinarily pleased by the sight of your blood-stained corpse."

Julien had not known that. It made him feel slightly—very slightly—less dubious about the proposal to entrap the thief.

"Another purpose was to persuade the thief to take no action for a time, to tempt him to shelter himself under your alleged guilt. There, too, we have been successful. So far as we can tell, there have been no further attempts to tamper with the diplomatic correspondence. In effect, shooting you bought us some time to continue our investigation."

There was a knock at the door, and one of the dragoons came in and held a brief, low-voiced conference with LeSueur. He glanced sideways at Julien as he left.

"Come along," said the captain, rising from his chair. He led Julien back downstairs. "The rest of the dragoons are going off to relieve the troops from the garrison at Boulton Park. Keep out of sight for a few hours, until we can find a room to hide you in. Colonel White is taking no chances. Should the thief spot you, he might take alarm and flee." And then, after a look at Julien's face, he added in an almost sympathetic tone, "Try to get some sleep."

Enlisted men did not rate bedchambers. Julien went off to the stable and found an empty stall with reasonably clean straw. First he thought he would not lie down at all; he had too much to think about. Then he decided a short rest would do no harm and might even make the solution to his problems clearer. The next thing he knew, a rough hand was shaking him awake.

"You're wanted upstairs again," the man said, sounding suspicious.

"Damn," muttered Julien. He ran his fingers through his hair and got most of the straw out; then he stumbled across the yard to the pump. The water was like ice. Where was that corporal with the hot water and the razor when he needed him? He felt groggy and filthy, and the thought of what would happen the next day was making him sick to his stomach.

Barrett was still in the upper parlor, looking harried and anxious. The others were gone. "Mr. Clermont? This way, if you please." He led Julien down the hall and up half a flight of stairs to a small, steep-roofed room full of linen presses and drying racks. "I must ask you to remain here, with the door locked, and to open only to those who give my name. Now that the other soldiers are leaving, you should not be seen downstairs or in the inn yard. It is of the utmost importance that no one at Boulton Park hear of your presence."

Julien nodded, too tired to argue or ask questions.

"In the meantime," Barrett said, "you might wish to have this." He held out two sheets of note paper.

A letter, Julien saw as he took them. He did not recognize the writing. Only when he reached the signature and saw the name "Charles" did he understand what it was.

"This is your father's last letter," said the older man. "I am sure that you find the thought of our proceedings tomorrow afternoon extremely distasteful. I certainly do. I thought it might help to see that your father was willing to risk his life to maintain the confidentiality of the negotiations your kinsman and I are conducting."

Julien still found it odd to hear Barrett refer to the earl as his kinsman. Knowing he was half English had not meant much to him until an actual family had suddenly taken the place of the mythical, absent father. He acknowledged to himself that his relationship to Bassington was probably the principal reason he had agreed to assist his former persecutors in their quest.

Sir Charles now produced a familiar red-bound book. "I understand that you are also interested in seeing your father's diaries. This is the volume which describes his meeting with your mother. You may read it if you choose; some of it is very unpleasant. He did not take it well when your mother left him."

Startled, Julien drew his hand back from the book. "She left him? I thought it was the other way around."

"He did intend to marry her, at least according to his own record of events. He met her at an inn; she had run away from school. They were living together, and he was arranging for a Protestant minister to travel across from England to wed them—and to bring funds which he had begged from his uncle—when she went to mass one day at the village church and never returned. She sent him a message that she had sinned and would not demean her blood further by living with a seducer and a heretic."

That certainly sounded like a Condé, Julien thought bitterly.

"I am not sure how trustworthy his account is," cautioned Barrett. "Although I will say that in the rest of these diaries—and I have read several years' worth at this point—he has no compunction about painting himself in the ugliest colors. Indeed, this volume is mild compared to some of the later ones. He made his living trading in gossip, you know, and if none was to hand he would do his best to create it."

Julien took the book, but did not open it.

"Remember," said his host as he left, "stay concealed."

Abstractedly, Julien turned the key and locked the door. He was already absorbed in the letter. It was actually two different documents. The first page was a brief note in French, apparently written by one of Piers's servants, informing the earl that his cousin had been killed in a duel that morning and that, per his instructions, two boxes of his effects were being shipped immediately to England. It was unsigned, but there was a postscript, which initially made no sense to Julien: "I believe my master would have wished you to know that M. Ivanov was also killed in the engagement."

The letter itself was in English.

12th February, 1814

My dear George—

No doubt you will be very surprised to receive the two crates of books which accompany this letter. Call it superstition; call it prudence. The consequences, should these diaries fall into the wrong

*hands, are too grave to contemplate, and I am thus
compelled to err on the side of caution. It pains
me to think of the waste—this carefully cultivated
garden of scandalous blossoms, many of which
are still in full flower (so to speak), in the hands of
someone too righteous to make proper use of
them. But even I have my occasional moments
of virtue, and it appears Tuesday morning will be
one of them. In brief, Ivanov has begun to suspect
the identity of your correspondent, and once he is
certain he will sell both of you to Austria without
even blinking. Unfortunately, I had nothing in my
collection at the moment I could use to silence
him. I am therefore compelled to use cruder methods; to whit, ten paces at dawn. Madame Ivanov
was most cooperative in providing a pretext for the
engagement. I believe she is nearly as anxious to
be a widow as I am to make her one. At any rate,
although I have little doubt about my marksman-
ship—I have kept my hand in, as you know—it is
never wise to count one's chickens before they
hatch. I have therefore made arrangements to
have these sent to you at once if word comes to my
household that my villainy has met its just reward.
What affair is it of mine? Believe me, I have asked
myself that question. I may be fairly certain I will
kill Ivanov, but there is always some risk, and I do
not like taking risks. Still, while I have never
balked at extorting money from individuals, I believe I should draw the line at betraying an entire
country, especially one which has been rather hos-
pitable to me. And I most definitely draw the line
at allowing an amateur like Ivanov to do so.*

I remain, at least until dawn on Tuesday,

Your most affectionate,
Charles

Julien sat down and read it again. Then a third time.
The postscript made sense now. His father had silenced
the threatening Ivanov—but not without taking a mor-
tal wound in his turn. Barrett was wrong, though. The
letter did not make him feel better about cornering the
thief. The thief was beginning to look a lot like Julien's
father: an opportunistic man who made money selling
other people's secrets.

He turned to the diary. It was just as Barrett had described it, and not so different from his aunt's account:
the vision of a frightened girl at an inn. The self-inter-
ested rescue, intended at first as nothing more than a
pleasant diversion with a timid but very pretty village
maid. The gradual realization that she was of gentle
birth. The decision to wed her—all the more plausible
to Julien because his father also described Aline's un-
thinking revelations of her as-yet-unnamed family's
wealth. And then the frantic search when she did not return after mass. She had asked him to let the priest
marry them, and with an Englishman's typical horror of
popery he had refused, had told her their marriage
would not be lawful in England if it were not performed
by a proper clergyman.

Julien closed the book. It was all there: the pleas to
the fourth earl for help, the eventual discovery of a
Mademoiselle DeLis at a convent in Lausanne. His father had tried to see her and had been refused. He had
never known of Julien's existence. No one had; the
Condés had concealed him well. The payments were for
his mother's place at the convent, not, as he had supposed, for his own upkeep.

The seduction of his mother made painful reading;
the absence of any reference to himself was almost as
painful. But what haunted him most, long after he had

set the book down on the table, were the pages of self-recrimination his father had written in the days after Aline DeLis had disappeared. Why had he been so self-righteous? Why had he failed to see what would happen when she went to mass, and spoke to the priest? Why hadn't he married her when he had the chance?

Why, indeed? Julien got up, unlocked the door, and peered out into the dark upper hall. He had his own ghosts to confront tonight. He hadn't exactly promised Sir Charles to stay in this stuffy little room. Or even in the inn. Or even in the village, for that matter.

30

Even in this enlightened age, females remain un-accountably susceptible to the sight of a military man in uniform.

——Miss Cowell's Moral Examples for Young Ladies

Boulton Park was being guarded by the dragoons, which would have made it difficult for Julien to get into the house had he not been one of the aforementioned dragoons. As it was, he simply rode past the man on duty at the lodge, stabled his horse with the other mounts, and walked in a purposeful, military fashion over to the man who was stationed on the terrace.

"What now?" said the man in a peevish tone. Julien had supposed he would say something like "Who goes there?" but Julien was in uniform, after all, and had ridden next to the man for several hours on the way down from London.

"It's Dauncy. You're to go round the gardens now." He paced, sentry-like, until his fellow soldier had vanished into the mist beyond the inner hedges, and then he took off his hat and boots and began climbing up the wall of the house.

He knew where Serena's room was. They had sat down with him and shown him a floor plan of Boulton Park, the fools, and asked him where Simon's secret passages were, and who he had seen in which rooms at which times. He knew he could get up the wall, as well. It was exactly the same rusticated stone as the new pavilion at Chantilly, which he had climbed when he was six in one of his many attempts to escape his aunt. His feet didn't fit into the grooves as easily, but he was stronger now and his reach was longer. Her window took less than a minute to open. He was feeling very pleased with himself until he eased himself into the room and discovered that the bed was empty.

Panicking, he lit a candle and looked around. This was her room; this had to be her room. Her shawl hung over the back of a chair, and the fan she had carried at the ball was lying on the table next to the fireplace. He crossed to the door. It was locked from the inside. She was Simon's cousin, however, so that didn't necessarily mean anything. He set the candle down on the floor, turned the key, and was about to ease the door open when he heard a slight noise.

Instinct, more than anything else, saved him. Before he could really think he had whirled around just in time to catch the poker aimed at his head. She had swung hard; his palm was stinging. Grabbing the poker with both hands, she tried to tug it free. He jerked it away and clapped his hand over her mouth to prevent the scream she was about to give.

"Will you marry me?" he said into her ear once he had gotten his breath back.

She kicked him. "I'll report you to your captain," she said, her voice muffled behind his hand. "My uncle will kill you."

For the first time it occurred to him what she must have thought, seeing a soldier climbing into her room. The poker hadn't been aimed at him, but at someone she believed to be a stranger. At least, he hoped that was the explanation.

The candle had gone out. He staggered over to the window, half carrying, half dragging her, until they reached a faint pool of light. "Serena, look at me," he said.

She looked. He wasn't sure what he was expecting her reaction to be—relief, astonishment, joy? He got astonishment. Briefly. Then her eyes narrowed.

"You are dead." It sounded like an accusation.

He didn't have much time. "Will you marry me?" he said again. "I swore that when I saw you, those would be the first words out of my mouth." He hefted the poker. "I almost didn't get it said before you brained me."

"They shot you." She wasn't listening. When she spoke, it was as though she was talking to herself, as though he was not really there. "I saw them. I saw the blood. You are supposed to be dead."

That was what she had said the last time he had come to her room at night. He looked down at the poker and wondered briefly why he was determined to marry a woman who kept threatening to kill him. "I'm alive. The firing squad was a ruse. But until tomorrow afternoon, I am still officially deceased. You cannot let anyone know you have seen me." He set the poker down and glanced nervously out the window before turning back to her. "You haven't answered my question."

"What question?" she said. She sounded more like herself. Suspicious, edgy.

He said it again, slightly louder. He was starting to feel that this whole expedition had been very ill-advised. Only an idiot would go galloping off in the middle of the night because of a passage in a dead man's diary. Still, an oath was an oath. "Will you marry me?"

"Will I marry you?" She stepped back, so that her face was in shadow. He saw the white nightgown billow as she sketched a sardonic curtsey. "I am most sensible of the honor you do me, Mr. Clermont, but I must decline your flattering offer."

He amended ill-advised to disastrous. By now he had expected to be wrenching himself away from a poignant embrace. Another glance out the window. There was still no sign of the real sentry. "Is it my birth?" he said, feeling the old wound tear open, raw as ever.

She laughed bitterly. "Your birth? Say rather your death. Am I to marry a man who is such a fraud that even his execution is a sham? A man who let me watch that—that horror show? Who never attempted in any way to warn me, or to let me know, afterwards, that he was still alive?"

Out of the corner of his eye he saw movement in the garden. "Damn," he muttered. "I must go. There's a patrol outside, preventing secret meetings like this one. Serena, I will explain, but not now. I haven't time. All I can say is that I am sorry." He grimaced. "I seem to spend a great deal of time apologizing to you, don't I? Perhaps I was a fool to think that a proposal of marriage would be a welcome change in my conversational repertoire."

She was silent.

He stepped closer to her, and she did not move away. Heartened, he risked taking her hand. It was shaking. When he drew her back into the moonlight she did not resist. Against his cheek her eyelashes were damp, and when he kissed her he felt her tremble in a way which had nothing to do with fear or anger. Perhaps his cause was not so hopeless after all.

"I cannot stay," he said, after another, harried glance out the window. "Or I'll be seen climbing down. Si— someone asked me to remain concealed tonight. I broke out of a locked room to come and speak with you."

"You did?" He detected a distinct thaw in her tone. She hadn't moved out of his arms, either.

He thought about proposing again, now that she seemed a bit happier about his reappearance. But he didn't quite have the nerve. He compromised on another kiss. It was meant to be quick, but the thaw turned out to be more like a heat wave. It occurred to him, dimly, that if he were found here she would be forced to marry him. What would be so terrible about that?

It occurred to him that he was thinking like his father.

He unlaced her arms—reluctantly—and when he saw the tears in her eyes he almost changed his mind. Almost, but not quite. "Remember, you haven't seen me," he warned as he climbed out the window.

She nodded.

He barely made it back down to the ground and into his boots and hat before the other sentry loomed up out of the darkness. "Morrow says he's been posted to the garden, not me," he said. "And that you're not on duty at all tonight."

"My mistake," mumbled Julien. "Must have misheard the orders."

"Well, get back to the village," the other man said sourly. "And straighten your hat. It's on nearly backwards. Captain sees you, he'll fine you a week's pay."

He rode back to the inn, wondering what would happen tomorrow. Would the thief confess? Would Serena hate him all over again for his part in the ugly scene Barrett was engineering? Would he hate himself? He suspected that the answer to all three questions was yes.

He kept his face shadowed as he turned his horse over to an exhausted-looking Jem back at the Burford Arms, but he didn't even try to get back to his garret unobserved. Instead he went and knocked on the door of the little parlor. He didn't think any of the conspirators would be asleep yet, and sure enough, he heard movement in response to his knock, and then quick footsteps.

"Who is it?" The colonel's voice.

"Clermont."

The door swung open.

"What do you want?" White sounded just as irritable as the sentry from the terrace.

Behind the colonel Julien could see Barrett and Meyer. Neither of them looked surprised or angry. They had not noticed his absence, then. He could pretend he had a question, or wanted permission to check on his horse.

"I went to Boulton Park," he said, addressing Barrett. "I thought I should let you know. No one saw me, save for Miss Allen."

"As you predicted," Barrett said to Meyer, rising. He escorted Julien back down the hall. "Did you tell Miss Allen anything about our plans? Or give her any hints she might pass on to others?"

"Any hints beyond the obvious alarm a guilty party might feel seeing the house surrounded by dragoons? No."

"We have provided an explanation for the patrols. Death threats against Lord Bassington."

Julien snorted. "Who is going to believe that?"

"It happens to be true." Barrett opened the attic door and waved Julien in. "Some members of the French émigré community took the news of your assassination—as they term it—very hard. You cannot imagine how eager I am to resurrect you."

"I myself find being dead increasingly tiresome," Julien said.

"Will you give me your word to remain in this room until you are needed?"

"Yes." He could not help adding, "I would have been in a very difficult position had you asked for my promise earlier."

Barrett sighed. "I was reproaching myself for that omission when we found you gone, but Mr. Meyer was certain you had gone only to see Miss Allen, and luckily he proved to be right."

Julien was growing very tired of the knowledgeable Mr. Meyer.

"We have sent for your servant," Barrett added. "He

should be arriving in a few hours to help you restore your normal appearance."

Julien ran one hand over his chin. "I am usually a bit cleaner," he admitted.

Barrett paused, one hand on the door. "Was Miss Allen happy to see you? Or is that too personal a question?"

"Will she radiate joy, do you mean, and so advertise my presence to your quarry? You may rest easy on that score. She tried to crack my skull open with a poker. Then she accused me of failing to die properly and laughed at me when I proposed."

If Barrett had smiled, Julien would have throttled him. But all he said was, "I see."

Serena woke up in stages the following morning. First, there was the sense that a wonderful gift was waiting for her somewhere. The precise nature of this gift eluded her at first; she lay there for a while simply enjoying the absence of guilt and misery. Then she remembered what the gift was: Clermont was alive.

That got her out of bed. Terrified that it had all been a dream, she searched her room for some evidence that he had actually been there. It took her twenty minutes to find it: a smear of dirt on the not-quite-closed window. She drifted along in a daze for several hours, savoring her private happiness, trying not to reveal her change of mood when Emily came in to dress her or when her aunt stopped by for her now-routine visit of consolation.

The second awakening came later in the morning, and was more metaphorical in nature. In the middle of another daydream-cum-reminiscence centered on last night's visit, she became aware that her silver lining was surrounded by a very ugly cloud. Why had Clermont's execution been staged? And why, at this particular moment, had he been allowed to reappear? An obvious and very unpleasant answer suggested itself, and she went at once to find Simon and warn him. Now her concern was not so much that she might seem too happy, but that her agitation would be too obvious. She retreated to her room again. But at two o'clock she could not bear the waiting any longer. She decided to go in search of her uncle.

Her excuse was to be the rumors Emily had passed on to her earlier. The servants were all terrified, convinced a horde of rabid Frenchmen were planning to storm Boulton Park and kill every living soul in the place. She would ask him whether the wild rumors circulating in the kitchen had any foundation.

Pritchett did not know where his master was—unusual in itself. She tried her uncle's study and the library, and the sitting room attached to the earl's bedchamber, and the drawing room (this last a forlorn hope; he never set foot in the place if he could help it), and at last returned to the study. The first time she had obtained no response to her knock. Now she rapped more loudly, and called out, "Uncle, it's me."

"Serena?" It was her aunt, behind her.

Feeling guilty for some reason, she blushed as she turned around. "I was looking for Uncle George," she said.

"Oh, dear." Her aunt looked flustered. "I was hoping you might know where he is. The servants—"

"—are about to resign *en masse*," Serena finished for her. "Did he say anything to you about this business of the royalists?"

"He told me not to fret, and patted my hand in that absentminded way he does when he wants to get to work. I was sure he would be here."

A door in the paneling opened and Simon stepped out. "Papa is in the records room," he said.

His mother jumped slightly. "Simon! I do wish you

would *not* appear and disappear in that disconcerting manner."

Serena merely gave him a warning frown. She had told Simon not to use the servants' corridors while the soldiers were here.

"What would your father be doing in the records room?" the countess demanded. "He only goes in there on rent day, or when he and Mr. Cruik are going through so many accounts they cannot bring all the ledgers to his study."

"I don't know," said Simon. "But he is there; I heard him talking. And there are a lot of soldiers in there, as well. And two guarding the door."

Serena and her aunt looked at each other and set off at a near-run around the corner.

The records room was a sizable apartment used for estate accounts. It was in the same wing as her uncle's study. Royce used one part of it for his office, but the place was not suitable for a military council, if that was what this was. The room had no amenities at all—no windows, no carpet, no chairs save those at Royce's desk and the worktable.

The guards allowed the two women in without comment.

No one really noticed the new arrivals. The earl, looking stunned, was standing by the worktable, where a pile of jewels lay gleaming in the lamplight. Mrs. Childe was protesting furiously as a slender man Serena found vaguely familiar examined each piece and then set it aside.

"All genuine," the man said finally to Sir Charles. When he spoke, Serena recognized him. It was Meyer, looking years younger. The vague, scholarly dreaminess had vanished; he looked stern, almost menacing. "Most pieces quite recent, although the brooch there is older, likely French. I would estimate the total value at something over three thousand pounds."

Next to Serena, the countess gave a little gasp.

"May I ask how you obtained these jewels, Mrs. Childe?" said a tall man in a colonel's uniform who was standing to one side.

"You have no right!" she spluttered. "These are family pieces, gifts! Protection for my old age!" She caught sight of the countess. "Tell them, Clara," she demanded. "Men have no notion of how thrifty women are, how we save and plan for the future!"

The countess did not answer. She was staring at the glittering pile of gold. Serena, after a rapid calculation, discovered that the annual income from an investment of three thousand pounds was nearly as much as the entirety of her own (admittedly meager) dowry.

"I told you her jewels were real," Simon said. He spoke to Serena, but he did not bother to lower his voice. Serena hadn't realized he had followed them in, although she should have known he would never have missed an opportunity like this.

"There!" Mrs. Childe pointed at Simon. "If you are looking for a thief, there is your culprit! Nasty, sneaking little worm! He has been in my room often enough, and his father's study, as well! There's not a lock in the house can stop him!"

Royce, standing behind his desk on the other side of the room, was looking on in horror.

"Come now, Mrs. Childe," said the colonel crisply. "There is a great deal of difference between childish mischief and theft. The criminal we seek reads French and German, and possibly Russian as well. Surely you do not believe the viscount to be such a prodigy? For that reason we eliminated the servants as suspects. You must admit that it looks very odd for a supposedly penniless widow to amass a small fortune in jewels while residing in a kinswoman's household. If you have a reasonable explanation, by all means let us hear it."

"You have no proof, none at all," she said, glaring in

turn at the colonel, at Bassington, at Meyer, and at Royce. The secretary instinctively backed up a step and tripped slightly over the leg of his own chair. "You come storming in with your dragoons, Colonel White, and say that Mr. Clermont was not guilty after all, and the real thief is here in the house. Well, how is anyone to know, now Mr. Clermont is so conveniently dead? Will you arrest everyone in turn and shoot us as the fancy takes you?"

White gave a nod to one of the soldiers by the door. The man opened it, and Clermont stepped in.

It would have been more dramatic if he had been exactly as she had seen him that day at the Tower, hair tousled, in his shirt sleeves. Or if they had carried him in, limp, with the blood everywhere. But it was shocking enough as it was. He simply walked in, the dark eyes shadowed, and stood in the center of the room, looking gravely at each person in turn.

Mrs. Childe, for once, had nothing to say. She simply stared. The earl and the countess stood speechless, openmouthed.

Only Royce moved. Shuddering, he collapsed into his chair and put his head in his hands. "Thank God," he said weakly. "Thank God." He looked up again, as if to reassure himself that Clermont was really there.

Clermont walked over to the desk. He looked tired and unhappy. "It was you, wasn't it, that night at the ball?" he said to Royce. "I noticed you talking to one of the Russian attachés. And then you disappeared, ostensibly to hunt for Simon, and no one saw you for two hours." He turned to Barrett. "I have already told you that I was concealed in the passageway outside your study, Sir Charles, while Simon and Miss Allen made their appearance at the kitchen door. What I did not recall until just now is that there was someone else in the passageway with me."

"You did not see this person." It was Barrett.

"Naturally not, as my main concern was that they should not see me." He looked again at Royce. "You were hoping to get into the study while I was known to be in Sir Charles's house, were you not? But then you heard me and Simon in the passageway and realized that I was headed there myself. Did you learn later that I was seen by a footman as I left? Did that decide you to break in the following night and take the letter, now that I was sure to be blamed? A much more serviceable scapegoat than the viscount, don't you agree?"

The whole room was silent. No one moved.

Royce's face was flushed. "I suppose I could deny it," he said. "You have no proof, as Mrs. Childe was reminding everyone just now."

The earl gave an inarticulate cry. He was trembling, and had to put his hand on the back of a chair for support. "You—you—" he stuttered, then closed his eyes.

Royce was stacking papers on his desk, closing up the ink, stowing pens in the drawers. A pistol suddenly emerged in his hand from one of the drawers. It was not pointed at anyone in particular, but the expression on Royce's face left no doubt he was prepared to use it. He backed slowly towards the door behind the desk. Simon had moved closer to Serena and was clutching her sleeve like a much younger child.

Bassington looked up as his secretary reached the door. "What was it, then?" he whispered. "Money? A girl? Some family scandal?"

"No, I suspect I will be the family scandal," said Royce bitterly. His hand was on the key.

"Dammitall!" cried the earl, taking one step towards him. He contemptuously ignored the pistol. "I receive you into my home, I sponsor you, I trust you not only with my affairs, and the affairs of the nation, but with"—his voice began to shake—"with my son, and you throw it all away for money?"

"I didn't do it for the money!" flared Royce. "Acquit me at least of that, sir! I never spent a penny of it on myself." He gestured at Mrs. Childe. "You wanted to know where those jewels came from? I gave them to her, to buy her silence after she caught me copying one of your letters a few months ago. She asked for more and more, thinking she was squeezing a poor fool for all he was worth, not knowing I was overjoyed to pay, to get rid of the foul stuff."

"Then why?" The earl's voice cracked.

"Has it never occurred to you," said Royce passionately, "that some Englishmen might in fact *admire* Napoleon?" He gestured towards a stack of books on his desk. "I was a patriot until I came to work for you, my lord, and began reading about English law and English taxes and English land reform. Reform? Hah! Robbery, more like! And the taxes are worse! As for our laws—have you consulted our penal code lately? Do you know that it is still possible to hang a man for stealing five shillings' worth of meat? To transport a youth who throws mud at a soldier in a village? To own slaves? Do I regret the deception I was forced to practice? Yes, I do. But my honor seemed a small price to pay for improving the government of Europe. You, of all men, should understand. You share the same ambition. It simply happens that we have different views about the best means to that end."

Barrett interrupted. "And how does selling diplomatic correspondence to Austria help Napoleon?" he asked in a sharp tone.

"Napoleon is finished," said Royce. "I saw that months ago. The allies will carve him up like a trussed pig. I chose the state I believed most likely to carry on Bonaparte's program, the guardians of his heir, the Hapsburgs. The King of Rome will take up his father's legacy." He pulled a folded set of blue sheets out of a book on his desk and tossed them contemptuously on the floor. "You can have the letter back, if it will ease your mind. It was useless without a signature."

There was a stifled cry of dismay from Mrs. Childe. "Foolish boy! You should have kept it! Exchanged it for a pardon! Now you have nothing!"

"I have this," said Royce, hefting his pistol. He trained it once more on the earl. With his other hand he groped behind his back and opened the door, removing the key. A clumsy bow of acknowledgment to Bassington, a wider one to the room at large, and he had backed through the door. They all heard it close, and lock.

One of the soldiers started forward, but Bassington waved him back. "It's a storage closet," he said grimly. "Full of boxes of old tax receipts. This is the only door."

Serena held her breath, waiting for the sound of the gun. All around her she could see everyone in the room frozen, strained towards the closed door. After a minute, the men began to look at each other uncertainly. After two minutes, the colonel looked at Meyer.

"If he's still in there he could blow my head off when I try to pick the lock," Meyer said mildly.

"What do you mean, if?" snapped Bassington. "Where else would he be? It's a cupboard, not an anteroom!"

"Idiots," muttered Simon under his breath. Fortunately, no one but Serena heard him.

Meyer was kneeling by the door. After a minute he pushed something or pulled something, and the latch clicked.

Cautiously, two of the soldiers, pistols primed, pushed open the door.

The room was empty.

Cursing, White and the soldiers ran out into the anteroom. Bassington and Meyer were hard on their heels, along with Simon, who was offering loudly to show everyone where the passage came out. Serena saw Mrs. Childe scuttle furtively after them, with as much of her hoard scooped into her skirt as she could carry. No doubt she was hoping to escape in the confusion, but the countess seized her arm.

"I think we should wait for the gentlemen upstairs," said the countess in a hard voice.

Julien had come over to stand beside Serena. "I am sorry," he said in a low voice. "Another apology to add to your collection."

She shook her head. "No need," she said.

He looked taken aback. "You don't mind that I played the ghost in that vicious little version of Hamlet?"

"I did something worse. I broke my promise. I told Simon I had seen you. I went to him this morning and explained that you were alive and what I thought might happen today. And then I told him to come down and show Jasper that hidden door, just in case."

"You knew? You knew it was Royce?"

She hesitated. "I suspected. He was ill, physically ill, when he realized that they were going to execute you. He nearly killed us both trying to get us to White-hall in time to stop them. When he thought we had arrived too late he was so distraught he fainted. Ever since then he has been stumbling around as though he had died, instead of you."

"I am not sorry he escaped," he admitted. "I know I should be more outraged—he tried to frame Simon, he succeeded in framing me, with considerable assistance from my own stupidity, and he betrayed your uncle. But I think I am as relieved to see him get away as he was to see me alive."

"If he got away."

He smiled at her. "Didn't I just hear Simon offering to show the nice soldiers where the passage comes out?"

"True." She felt a bit of the dread which had enveloped her all morning fade. Perhaps Jasper would escape after all, and her uncle would be spared the ordeal of a trial.

He offered her his arm. "Shall we go upstairs and protect Mrs. Childe from your aunt?"

She shuddered, but laid her hand on his sleeve and moved towards the door. "I suppose I must. Aunt Clara looked ready to stab her."

"I have never seen your aunt angry before." He paused. "I hadn't thought you resembled her very much, until I saw her march over to Mrs. Childe just now."

"The women in my family are noted for their tempers. My mother and my aunt were nicknamed the Furies by their brother."

He raised his eyebrows. "What happened to your aunt, then?"

"She married my uncle and reformed."

Amused, he said, "If you marry me, are you planning to reform?"

"I am not marrying you."

"My question was phrased in the conditional mode," he pointed out. "Intellectual curiosity." His hand was covering hers, though, and it didn't feel like intellectual curiosity when his fingers curved in a possessive circle over her knuckles.

"Hypothetically speaking, then, if I were to marry you—or anyone else—I have no plans to reform."

"Good," he said. "Hypothetically speaking, that is."

31

This time he was going to get it right. He had his rooms at the Burford Arms again; after searching for Royce for twenty-four hours the soldiers had given up and gone back to London. He had Tempest—he had bought the mare outright from the amazed landlord of the Queen's Rest. But he had not ridden her tonight; no, he had deferred to Vernon for once (and to his own sartorial splendor) and had hired the inn's dilapidated coach. Overdressed in knee breeches and the ridiculous blue-and-silver waistcoat, he stood outside the earl's study and tried to compose himself.

The butler gave him an inquiring glance, and Julien nodded.

"The Marquis de Clermont, my lord," Pritchett announced as he opened the door.

The earl, Julien was relieved to see, looked just as nervous as he was. "Ah—do come in, Marquis," Bassington said. He rubbed his nose absently and gestured towards a chair. Julien suspected he had been fortifying himself from one of his illicit snuffboxes.

"You've come about my niece," said the earl.

Julien sat down. "Yes, sir."

Bassington shifted uncomfortably in his chair. "She hasn't much of a dowry, you know."

"I am aware of that. I would be prepared to make a very generous settlement on Miss Allen. I indicated as much in the note I sent you this afternoon."

"Have you spoken with her? Told her of your intentions?"

He sighed. "Once. Briefly. She refused me."

Restless, the earl tapped his fingers against the desk. "Why have you come to me, then? I have little say in the matter. She is fully of age. It is true that her dowry cannot be released without my consent, but if you are as wealthy as your letter suggests, that would make no difference to you."

Why had he come to Bassington? "I wanted to do the thing properly," he said slowly. "There is too much between us that cannot be forgotten or overlooked. I felt I should at least make certain you were willing to have me in the family, after everything that has happened."

"It seems to me you are part of my family whether I am willing or not," said the earl.

"No." Julien leaned forward. "There is a difference between the dry facts of kinship—who is descended from whom—and inclusion in the life of a family. My own childhood taught me that. I can disappear. I have done it before. I have estates in France which may well be restored to me soon. I own land in Canada—good timber land, miles of it. On foot, it takes days to cross from one side to the other. I have a house in Montreal and a farm southeast of the city. I need not trouble you or the countess further."

"And Serena?"

"As you say, it is her decision. I will ask her again to marry me, but if you have reservations about my suit, I will do so in writing rather than in person. I will not force you to endorse my offer by escorting me into her presence."

Outside the window an owl hooted softly. The earl sat, frowning, turning a letter opener over and over in his hand. At last he said, "I am not sure what I can say, what is right, what is fair to you and to me and to my niece. I distrusted you from the start, without knowing

why. And liked you, in spite of my suspicions. I must
have recognized, dimly, your resemblance to Charles.
Can I judge you, judge your fitness as a husband, when
every time I look at you now I see my cousin's face?
Can I judge anyone, when the man I chose to educate
my son and assist me in my work proved yesterday to be
a traitor? You taught Simon more in a month than Royce
taught him in two years."

"He has a natural aptitude for science," said Julien,
embarrassed. "Likely inherited from your father."

"I am not speaking of lens grinding. Who persuaded
my son to confess his theft of the dueling pistol? Who
persuaded him to shield Serena on the night of the ball?
Who persuaded him to stop playing invalid and agree to
go to school?"

Julien blinked. "You have been talking with Serena—
with Miss Allen?"

"No." The earl gave a sad smile. "With Simon. He
came to me this morning, and told me he had helped
Mr. Royce escape. He concealed him in some hidden
room yesterday afternoon, brought him clothing and
money, and led him out through a tunnel into the woods
once it grew dark."

"The secret forest," Julien said, half to himself.

"You see?" Bassington gestured helplessly. "I knew
nothing of any such place. You did. I asked Simon why
he had come to me, and he told me about your bargain
with him concerning his theft of the gun, and about the
incident at the Barretts', and about his nighttime visits
to your room. Simon, too, resembles my cousin. It has
worried me for years. But now—" He broke off and got
to his feet. "I am not being very clear, am I? We are talking of Serena, not Simon."

"I should not have come this evening," said Julien,
rising also. "It is too soon, after the events here yesterday. I beg your pardon."

"No." The earl laid a hand on his arm. "Let me try

again. What I mean to say is that you already are a part of the Piers family, not merely by the dry facts of kinship, as you call them, but also by the choices you made when you sought me out—both the wise choices and the foolish ones. Even if Serena does not accept you, I would hope to see you again."

"Thank you," said Julien in a low voice. "If I do go abroad again, I shall be sure to write and let you know where I am."

"I would appreciate it," said the earl. He moved towards the door. "I believe we should go up to the drawing room now, before the ladies grow too anxious."

Julien nodded. He doubted whether the ladies could possibly be as anxious as he was. He had known, of course, that the earl would tell Serena. That there would be a very public meeting with his intended bride, in front of her aunt and uncle. Then her guardians would withdraw, discreetly, and he would be left alone with her. But not for very long. And not at night, in a dark bedchamber, where her body could say yes while her reason was saying no. That was the price for doing things right.

All the way up the stairs he reminded himself to count his blessings. He was alive. He was not in prison. The earl had forgiven him. Royce had escaped. The loathsome Mrs. Childe would not be present to smirk when he walked into the drawing room in a moment. He did not know where she had gone, but apparently the countess had evicted her less than two hours after Royce's confession.

"My lord," said Pritchett, hurrying up to Bassington as the two men approached the drawing room. "My lord, you have—"

"In a moment, Pritchett," Bassington said curtly. He gestured towards the doors of the drawing room. "Announce the Marquis, if you would. Miss Allen will be waiting."

"But my lord—"

The earl walked over and reached for the door handle. Horrified, Pritchett hurried past him and threw it open. "The Marquis de Clermont," he announced, with considerably more pomp than he had used downstairs.

Julien stepped in.

"Very well, what is it that is so urgent?" he heard Bassington ask as the door closed behind him.

But Julien already knew the answer. It was sitting opposite him, in a gilt-armed chair, wearing lace and silk and looking, as usual, inimitably elegant and aristocratic.

"My dear Julien," said the prince in French. "I rejoice to find you alive. And using your proper title, for once." He did Julien the signal honor of rising to greet him.

Numbly, Julien crossed the room and kissed his grandfather's hand.

"Now," continued the prince, in quite a different tone, "What is this I hear of an offer of marriage?"

Her bedchamber was not a safe refuge any longer. Too many people were coming in uninvited (her aunt) or even opening the door when it was locked (Simon). She tried Simon's secret room, but evidently he had used it yesterday to hide Jasper, and the servants kept coming by to gape at the empty trunk and the battered chair. Rumors were already spreading that Simon had stashed away a fortune in gold and jewels in the trunk, which he had given to the villainous Royce as a bribe to leave the country quietly.

In the end she had gone out for a long walk, leaving word for her aunt that she needed some fresh air. Through the garden, where the crocuses were finally showing. Into the park, up the hill to the first fence. The great house lay cupped in its valley below her, its outline blurred in the fading light. It looked peaceful, inviting—not at all the sort of place to have witnessed yesterday's dramatic events.

She sat down on the top step of a stile and considered her options. Soon—very soon, judging from the rapidly falling darkness—Julien Clermont would be calling on her uncle. He had made it quite clear what his errand was. At this very moment she should be in her room, changing her gown.

Well, she had played by those rules once, and lost. She was not going back down to the house until she knew what answer she would give him. That was more important than which dress she wore.

After a while she saw torches in the garden and heard, faintly, voices calling her name. She still had no notion what she would say when he asked her to marry him. She couldn't think. Too much had happened too quickly. It was unfair of him to give her so little time. Two days ago she had thought he was dead, and now he was in her uncle's study discussing dowries and settlements.

A torch was climbing towards her. It was Bates. With a sigh she got up and brushed off her skirts.

"Miss Allen? Her ladyship sent me to find you and light your way back down the hill."

Perhaps she would never know the answer. Perhaps he would ask her to marry him, and she would simply stare at him until they both fainted from hunger. She followed the groom back to the house in silence.

"You're to go to the drawing room at once, miss," he said as they reached the side entrance.

"Thank you, Bates." There were two carriages in the stable yard, she saw. One had the Condé crest. Julien was here, then, in formal state. Her aunt had told her this afternoon that he was a marquis. She looked at the coach, with its gilded crest and polished brass rails, and then down at her muddy dress. It would never work. She would tell him no. With a small sigh she went into the house and started up the stairs.

Her uncle was standing outside the drawing room, talking to Pritchett. "Serena!" he exclaimed. "I thought you were with your aunt!"

"I went for a walk." She blushed, looking at her bedraggled hem in the merciless light of the wall sconces. "I lost track of the time," she said lamely.

"Come in, then, come in," he said. "Mr. Clermont—the marquis, that is—will be wondering where you are."

"But, Uncle—" she said, spreading out her skirt helplessly. She suddenly wanted to change her gown. She wanted to sweep in garbed in crepe and silk, dripping with jewels, head held high, and tell him—what?

Emily came hurrying out of the side room where she had been waiting. She took one look at Serena and gave a small shriek. But she hustled her mistress off and did the best she could with a clothes brush and a comb. The earl was tapping his foot impatiently when she reemerged.

Pritchett opened the doors and her uncle marched in, steering her by the elbow towards the center of the room.

She saw Julien at once. He was arguing with an old man, a stranger. They were talking rapidly and heatedly, and it took Serena a moment to realize that they were speaking French. Julien caught sight of her in turn. He stopped in midphrase and bowed to her.

Her heart seemed to lurch sideways as his eyes met hers.

Then her aunt hurried over. For once she seemed oblivious to Serena's untidy state. "George," she said in a low, agitated voice, "it is the prince!"

"So Pritchett said." Her uncle cleared his throat. "Monsieur de Condé, this is a great honor."

The older man whirled. He surveyed first her uncle and then Serena, giving each a long, cold stare.

"Is this the girl?" he said to Julien in French.

Julien stepped forward. "Grandfather," he said in English, "may I present the Earl of Bassington and his niece, Miss Allen? My lord, Miss Allen, the Prince de Condé."

Grudgingly the prince gave a small nod to the earl and an even smaller one to Serena. He did not bother switching to English. Instead he attacked her uncle at once in a stream of ornate French. It was outrageous, unthinkable. He would complain to the Foreign Office. He would complain to the king. Such an insult, on the eve of the triumphant return of the Bourbons to France! A Condé, arrested, abused, terrorized with threats of execution, used as bait for thieves, and now forcibly wed to some provincial nobody without a penny to her name!

"No one is forcing me, *grandpère*," Julien interrupted. He moved to stand by Serena. He was angry; she could see the rigid line of his jaw.

The prince snorted. "You are too young to know what is good for you. Have you not heard the news? Schwarzenberg has beaten the usurper thoroughly. Bonaparte retires in disgrace. France will be ours again within the month, and you will be able at last to assume your rightful position. To throw yourself away on this one?" He gestured at Serena. "Bah!"

"And what is wrong with the niece of an earl as a bride, pray?" snapped Bassington. He spoke English.

"Her dowry?" inquired Condé disdainfully in the same language.

The earl glared. "Six thousand pounds."

Serena gulped. Even removing a zero, the figure was too high.

"And who were her parents?"

"Her father," said Bassington, "was the British ambassador to the court of the Sultan. He was the grandson of a marquis and held numerous important posts under Mr. Pitt."

Serena's father had held numerous posts—including a temporary one as ambassador when the

real ambassador had dropped dead one sultry day—
but they had only been important to the Allens'
exasperated creditors.

"Her mother," continued the earl, "was a Beaufort,
and closely connected with the family of the Duke of
Somerset."

That part was true. She hoped that the prince had
never heard of the Beaufort women and their infamous
tempers.

"*I*," said Condé, "can offer him the daughter of a
count."

The earl laughed contemptuously. "A French count?
London is full of *Monsieur le Comte* and *Madame la
Comtesse* these days. Shabby creatures, living off the
charity of gullible English folk who believe anyone with
a Parisian accent is an exiled aristocrat."

Julien had bent over; her aunt was speaking very low
into his ear. He nodded.

"Come with me," he said to Serena, grabbing her
elbow.

This was certainly rather bold, especially seeing that
she had not yet agreed to marry him. She followed him,
however, not at all unhappy to leave the two older men
to discuss her lineage without her.

He stopped at the door. The earl and prince were still
arguing furiously. Julien said loudly, "You will excuse
us, I am sure." At that the two men turned, but he was
already bowing to the countess. "Lady Bassington, your
most obedient." And then they were out in the hall and
he was nearly running, pulling her along. "Where is the
nearest secret passage?" he said, his expression grim.

"They are not secret," she said automatically. "The
servants all—"

He had spotted one of the concealed doors, and
yanked it open. "Which way?" he demanded, as they
ducked into the corridor.

She was still recovering from the shock of being

dragged bodily from her uncle's drawing room. "Where do you want to go?"

"Your bedchamber." He added hastily as she stiffened, "Only for a moment, and your maid will be there. Everything very proper. You will need her to help you pack, in any case."

"Pack?" She pulled her hand away. "Where am I going?"

"Not you. We. Both of us. And your maid. We are eloping."

She stamped her foot. "You haven't even asked me to marry you!"

"Yes, I did," he reminded her.

"Not properly! I was half asleep! I thought you were an intruder!"

"You want me to grovel? I will grovel." He sank to his knees on the dusty floor. "Will you do me the honor of accepting my hand in marriage?" he said, eyes raised to her face.

She arched one eyebrow. "That is all? No professions of undying devotion?"

"Serena," he said, still on his knees. "We will have three days in a carriage for me to tell you how I feel about you. Right now we have ten minutes before my grandfather stops shouting at your uncle and realizes that I may have run off with you. He travels with armed retainers. I have spent a great deal of time this past month facing people who were pointing guns at me, and I would prefer to leave Boulton Park before my grandfather adds himself to the list."

There was very little light in the corridor, but there was enough to see that he was not joking. "You mean it," she said, incredulous. "You are truly intending to carry me off to Gretna Green."

"I am not carrying you off. I am asking you to marry me, and if you agree, we will depart immediately for Scotland."

"Why Scotland?" She was fencing now, avoiding the real question. "Sixteen-year-old heiresses run away to Gretna. Surely we are more respectable than that."

"It is the obvious solution," he pointed out. "We avoid the difficulties attendant upon the marriage of a Catholic and a Protestant. We escape the wrath of the Condés. We wait three days to get married instead of a month. Given the amount of time I have spent in your bedchamber lately, that last item alone would make it worth the journey." He got to his feet, brushing the dirt off his knees as best he could.

"But—there will be a terrible scandal."

He looked down at her. The grim look had faded; he was almost smiling. "Do you truly suppose anyone will be interested in our marriage when they have the delicious tale of Royce and Mrs. Childe to occupy them?"

"What of my aunt?" she said, clutching at one more pretext to postpone her decision. "She will be mortified. She will never speak to me again."

"She suggested it," he said. "My respect for her is growing by the hour." He held out his hand. "Are you coming?"

She had run out of excuses. And she had known what her answer would be the minute his eyes met hers in the drawing room. "The fastest way to my room is up the back staircase," she said. "That way."

He gave a sigh of relief as he took her hand and headed down the corridor. "Good. I was prepared for more groveling, but I can do it in the carriage."

EPILOGUE

She was married. It didn't take very long to get married in Gretna Green. A few questions from the "blacksmith," a signature, and it was done. Even Julien had been surprised at the spare nature of the ceremony.

"Doesn't she promise to honor me?" he had asked. "To obey me?"

Their witness, a wizened old soldier, shrugged. "Och, no. Not in Scotland."

"Just as well," Julien had muttered. "No use starting off with a perjured bride."

The wedding supper had been a hasty meal at an inn at Gretna. Then they had driven on to Canonbie, because, as Julien had said, he would be damned if he would spend his wedding night in a town where every carriage that clattered in, no matter what the hour, was greeted by a crowd of urchins screaming out the names of potential witnesses for a ceremony.

Canonbie was quiet, unless you counted the sleet rattling against the window. Or the gusts of wind. Or Emily's cheerful singing in her small room next door. She was on the third verse of "Sweet Lass of Richmond Hill." The first two verses had accompanied the task of clothing her mistress in a lace-trimmed confection that Emily had triumphantly unearthed from the chest where Serena's bride-clothes had been banished six years earlier.

"I hadn't realized your maid was so—musical,"

Julien said from the doorway. "She always seemed a timid, quiet sort of girl."

Serena jumped. She hadn't heard him come in. It was true, eloping had brought out a side of Emily Serena had never seen: the romantic. The resurrected night-gown was only the beginning. Emily enthused over everything: the Condé carriage, which Julien had high-handedly appropriated from the drive at Boulton Park; the knowing looks at the tollgates; the quaint inns along their route; even the ragged boys who had welcomed them to Gretna by shouting "Elliott! Only five guineas!" or "Locksley! Free dram of whiskey, and rings supplied upon request!"

"I could go down the hall and ask her to stop," she offered.

He shut the door and leaned against it, surveying her slowly, from her unbound hair to her slippered feet and back up again. "You are not exactly dressed to go out in public. Of course, that fact did not seem to restrain your nocturnal wanderings at Boulton Park."

"I hardly think you are in a position to criticize my behavior," she shot back. "Not only did you break into my bedchamber—my *locked* bedchamber—in both London and Oxfordshire, but you also came into my room at every inn on the way here."

"Only after your maid was asleep," he said piously. "And I was a perfect gentleman."

She didn't think a perfect gentleman would have driven her half-insane with protracted bouts of kissing, but Emily was a very sound sleeper, and even gentle-men sometimes found themselves unable to resist temptation. Ladies, too.

The singing died away at last, and there was a moment of awkward silence. Then Julien pushed himself off the door and walked over to a chair. "I believe there is a wedding present on the bed," he said in a very casual tone as he took off his jacket.

"Another one?" He had already given her a necklace of gold lilies set with sapphires—his mother's, apparently—with a note which read: *Herewith proof I had no need to steal the Bassington rubies.*

"It's on the pillow. At least, it should be, if Emily carried out my instructions." He was untying his neckcloth now and tossing it on top of the jacket.

Emily would throw herself under Tempest's hooves if Julien told her to. Serena wondered if she would be forced to hire only the oldest, ugliest maidservants from now on. Sure enough, there was a parcel up against the headboard.

"Open it," he said, coming up next to her. "Carefully. It's delicate."

She folded back the paper. Inside was her ruined nightgown. She had never had a chance to mend it; it was still torn halfway down the shoulder from that fateful night in London when she had nearly seduced him. "Hardly a very generous gift for your bride," she said, laughing.

"Greedy girl. It isn't for you." He smoothed the torn seam. "It's for me. I have been dreaming about watching you take off that nightgown again ever since my visit to your room two weeks ago. The next item after that will be my shirt, if memory serves me correctly."

"Oh." She felt herself blushing. "But"—she looked down at the cascades of lawn and lace—"I am already wearing a nightgown."

He gave her a wicked smile, reached out, and untied the ribbon at her neck. "In that case, I can watch you take off two," he said. "Even better."

Historical Note

The major political events described in this book are true. Early in 1814, as Napoleon's defeat began to seem inevitable, the British Foreign Office was indeed playing Russia off against Austria, looking ahead to the delicate dissection of Europe that would be performed at the Congress of Vienna later that same year. The Condé family is real as well—although Julien and his mother, as well as the other main characters, are entirely products of my imagination.

Readers who would like more information about the events in this story or the earlier books in this series are cordially invited to visit my Web site (www.nitaabrams.com) to see photographs of various places which figure in the books. I also provide links to other sites with information about the Napoleonic Wars, Anglo-Jewish history, spying, and, of course, country houses with secret passages. For special help with the last topic I would like to acknowledge the staff of Syon Park, a spectacular Georgian mansion which served as a partial model for the Bassington country home in this book.

Discover the Magic of
Romance With
Jo Goodman